THE FATAL FRONTIER

The Fatal Frontier

EDITED BY ED GORMAN AND MARTIN H. GREENBERG

Carroll & Graf Publishers, Inc.

New York

Collection and headnotes copyright © 1997
by Ed Gorman and Martin H. Greenberg

First Carroll & Graf edition 1997

Carroll & Graf Publishers, Inc.
260 Fifth Avenue
New York, NY 10001

Library of Congress Cataloguing-In-Publication Data

The Fatal Frontier / edited by Ed Gorman and Martin H. Greenberg.
    p.   cm.
  ISBN 0-7867-0350-4 (cloth)
    1. Detective and mystery stories, American—West (U.S.) 2. West
(U.S.)—Fiction. 3. Western stories. I. Gorman, Edward.
II. Greenberg, Martin Harry.
PS648.D4F37 1997
813'.087408—dc20   96-30929
                                               CIP

Manufactured in the United States of America

"The Boy Who Smiled" by Elmore Leonard. Copyright © 1953 by Flying
Eagle Publications. Reprinted by permission of the author.

"Vigilante" by H. A. DeRosso. Copyright © 1948 by Popular Publication,
Inc. Reprinted by permission of the agents for the author's estate,
the Scott Meredith Literary Agency, 845 Third Avenue, New York, NY
10022.

"The Time of the Wolves" by Marcia Muller. Copyright © 1988 by Marcia
Muller. Reprinted by permission of the author.

"The Woman at Apache Wells" by John Jakes. Copyright © 1952 by New
Publications, Inc., renewed © 1980 by John Jakes. First published in
Max Brand's Western Magazine under the title "Lobo Loot." Reprinted
by permission of the author.

"Not a Lick of Sense" by Bill Pronzini. Copyright © 1996 by Bill Pronzini.

"The Tarnished Star" by Jon L. Breen. Copyright © 1996 by Jon L. Breen.

"Hacendado" by James M. Reasoner. Copyright © 1988 by James M.
Reasoner. Reprinted by permission of the author.

"The Skinning Place" by John Harvey. Copyright © 1982 by John Harvey.
Reprinted by permission of the author and his agent, Blake
Friedmann.

"Winston's Wife" by Wendi Lee. Copyright © 1996 by Wendi Lee.

"Gunman in Town" by Joseph Gores. Copyright © 1969 by *Zane Grey
Western Magazine, Inc.* Reprinted by permission of the author.

CONTENTS

Contents

Bill Pronzini

INTRODUCTION

The modern American crime story and the traditional Western story are more closely allied than might be apparent at a glance. For one thing, there is a fundamental similarity in much of their subject matter: murder, murder for hire, bank and other types of robbery, kidnapping, extortion. Even such Western fiction staples as cattle rustling and range wars have present-day counterparts. For another thing, the heroic figures that are the centerpieces of both genres can be traced back to the early years of the republic, to the myth and reality of the American frontier.

The history of the United States abounds with larger-than-life figures whose accomplishments, whose very survival, depended on an uncompromising toughness and a willingness to enter into struggles against seemingly insurmountable odds: Daniel Boone, Kit Carson, Davy Crockett, Jim Bridger, Mike Fink, Jim Bowie. Such rugged individualists inspired the creation of mythical heroes—Paul Bunyan, for instance—and of fictional men of action. Both James Fenimore Cooper's Natty Bumppo and Herman Melville's Captain Ahab are hunters driven by forces outside themselves, and in that sense are perfect paradigms of the modern fictional detective. Similarly, the justice-seeking private eye, police officer, and other type of manhunter (both male and female) can be viewed as direct descendants of the frontier lawman, of the no-nonsense operatives of the U.S. Secret Service and such detective agencies as Allan Pinkerton's.

American history also abounds with scoundrels and outlaws; persons motivated by greed, lust, power; persons who hold values and human life in little regard: John Wilkes Booth, William Bonney, John Wesley Hardin, the corrupt Silver Kings, the ruthless Big Four—and all the little-known and long-forgotten grifters, gamblers, confidence swindlers, whores, thieves, and paid assassins who inhabited the towns and cities, followed the railroads westward, and flocked to the gold- and silver-mining camps. These individuals likewise inspired nineteenth- and early twentieth-century authors—literary figures such as Mark Twain, Bret Harte, and O. Henry, and the legion of dime novelists responsible for feeding the "common man's" hunger for sensational fiction. They, too, are antecedents of the villains and antiheroes who live in the pages of both the Western tale and the crime story.

The slender, cheaply printed booklets and story-paper weeklies known as dime novels (after the "Dime Novel Library" created by their founder, Erastus Beadle, in 1860) revolutionized mass-market publishing in the nineteenth century. Over its last four decades, thousands of one-shot and series titles were made available to readers for a nickel or a dime. Many had historical, sea, and city street-life settings, but the most popular from the beginning were wildly melodramatic action stories set on the ever-expanding Western frontier, especially those that featured such legendary figures as "Bruin" Adams, Kit Carson, Buffalo Bill, Big Foot Wallace, and Wild Bill Hickok. Later, commencing with the publication of "Old Sleuth, the Detective" in *Fireside Companion* in 1872, the mass-audience detective story enjoyed an equally widespread vogue. By the end of the 1870s there were dozens of professional and amateur investigators afoot in every major city from Boston to San Francisco. And not all were men; successful series starred such women sleuths as Round Kate and The Western Lady Detective.

A melding of these two popular story types, the frontier adventure and the detective story, was inevitable. Such intrepid manhunters as Old King Brady (and later Young King Brady), Old Cap Collier, and Nick Carter often ventured into Wild Western locales for their crime-solving feats. Conversely, Western heroes took their turn as detectives on numerous occasions. Deadwood Dick, the king of Beadle's Pocket Library in the 1880s, and his female counterpart, Calamity Jane, appeared in such yarns as "The Frontier Detective; or, Sierra Sam's Scheme." Even Frank and Jesse James, turned into romantic Robin Hood figures by the dime novelists, did their share of sleuthing in several New York Detective Library titles, among them "The James Boys and Pinkerton; or, Frank and Jesse as Detectives" and "The James Boys Afloat; or, the Wild Adventures of a Detective on the Mississippi."

In the early years of the twentieth century the dime novel was supplanted as the monarch of popular fiction by the better-produced, more attractive, and easier-to-read pulp-paper magazine. Pioneered by Frank A. Munsey, the pulps were seven by ten inches in size and sported vividly colored, enameled covers whose artwork usually depicted scenes of high melodrama. The first detective pulp was a 1915 conversion of Street & Smith's dime-novel thriller *Nick Carter,* which in its new incarnation featured the adventures of other investigators in addition to its eponymous hero. Street & Smith also established the first Western pulp in a similar fashion in 1919, revamping its *New Buffalo Bill Weekly* into the pulp format and retitling the new publication *Western Story Magazine.*

As was the case with dime novels, the most sought-after pulp titles were those that emphasized detective stories and Western yarns; and thus, again, numerous hybrids were born. Pete Rice, a contemporary Western sheriff who, with a brace of deputies, specialized in solving murders and other nefarious doings in Buzzard Gap, Arizona, had his own monthly forum, *Pete Rice Magazine,* in the 1930s. Many other Western heroes doubled as investigators of one type or another, among them Steve Reese and his two range-detective sidekicks whose exploits were regularly featured in the long-running *Range Riders Western.* Crime-fiction titles, particularly in the years prior to 1930, often offered selections with contemporary Western settings and characters. In the 1920s, most issues of *Black Mask* contained one or two frontier yarns, notably Erle Stanley Gardner's series about adventurer Bob Larkin. In the 1930s Gardner concocted an even more well-regarded Western mystery-adventure series—his "Whispering Sands" tales set in the deserts of the Southwest and featuring roving prospector Bob Zane. One of the finest of these is included here.

Given the ongoing popularity of both genres and their hybrid offspring, and the basic similarities in protagonists and central plot elements, it is not surprising that hundreds of magazine and book-length fiction writers have specialized in one genre and often or occasionally mined the rich veins of the other. In addition to Erle Stanley Gardner, one of the first historically important crime writers to pen Westerns was Carroll John Daly, whose *Two-Gun Gerta,* written in collaboration with C. C. Waddell, chronicles the Mexican border exploits of silent movie cowboy Red Conners. Among the other early crime-fiction "crossovers" are such major names as Frederic Brown,

Cornell Woolrich, John D. MacDonald, Frank Gruber, W. T. Ballard, and Norbert Davis. Significant Western writers who successfully worked in the mystery/detective genre include B. M. Bower, Frederick Faust (Max Brand), William MacLeod Raine, Luke Short, W. C. Tuttle (whose Hashknife Hartley series is a fine example of fair-play detection in a frontier milieu), and Louis L'Amour.

The list of modern crossover writers is even longer and more distinguished. No one has received more plaudits for his work in both genres than Elmore Leonard, whose urban crime thrillers such as *Fifty-Two Pickup, City Primeval,* and *Get Shorty* were preceded by such neoclassic Western novels as *Hombre, The Bounty Hunters,* and *Valdez Is Coming.* Best-selling historical novelist John Jakes and best-selling mainstream novelist Evan Hunter have each written first-rate crime fiction (Hunter, of course, as Ed McBain in his 87th Precinct series of police procedurals) and above-average Western stories.

The Fatal Frontier showcases some of the best frontier tales by these writers, and by such top-line crime-fiction specialists as Marcia Muller, Loren D. Estleman, Brian Garfield, Jeremiah Healy, Ed Gorman, and Robert J. Randisi. Some selections are purely Western in style and content; others are hybrids. All are prime examples of short fiction (not just Western short fiction) at its most evocative and entertaining, and amply demonstrate why both the Western story and the crime story are alive and flourishing as the twenty-first century approaches.

—Petaluma, California
April 1996

THE FATAL FRONTIER

Elmore Leonard

THE BOY WHO SMILED

While he's best known for his darkly comic suspense novels, Elmore Leonard began his career as a Western writer.

Even back then, Leonard was an original. While he used the trappings of the conventional Western, his tales were always character-driven and concerned with such matters as loyalty and honor. That's why the stories have held up so well, as you're about to find out in this most unique and powerful of Western pieces.

When Mickey Segundo was fourteen, he tracked a man almost two hundred miles—from the Jicarilla Subagency down into the malpais.

He caught up with him at a waterhole in late afternoon and stayed behind a rock outcropping watching the man drink. Mickey Segundo had not tasted water in three days, but he sat patiently behind the cover while the man quenched his thirst, watching him relax and make himself comfortable as the hot lava country cooled with the approach of evening.

Finally Mickey Segundo stirred. He broke open the .50-caliber Gallagher and inserted the paper cartridge and the cap. Then he eased the carbine between a niche in the rocks, sighting on the back of the man's head. He called in a low voice, "Tony Choddi . . ." and as the face with the wide-open eyes came around, he fired casually.

He lay on his stomach and slowly drank the water he needed, filling his canteen and the one that had belonged to Tony Choddi. Then he took his hunting knife and sawed both of the man's ears off, close to the head. These he put into his saddle pouch, leaving the rest for the buzzards.

A week later Mickey Segundo carried the pouch into the agency office and dropped the ears on my desk. He said very simply, "Tony Choddi is sorry he has caused trouble."

I remember asking him, "You're not thinking of going after McKay now, are you?"

"This man, Tony Choddi, stole stuff, a horse and clothes and a gun," he said with his pleasant smile. "So I thought I would do a good thing and fix it so Tony Choddi didn't steal no more."

With the smile there was a look of surprise, as if to say, "Why would I want to get Mr. McKay?"

A few days later I saw McKay and told him about it and mentioned that he might keep his eyes open. But he said that he didn't give a damn about any breed Jicarilla kid. If the kid felt like avenging his old man, he could try, but he'd probably cash in before his time. And as for getting Tony Choddi, he didn't give a damn about that either. He'd got the horse back and that's all he cared about.

After he had said his piece, I was sorry I had warned him. And I felt a little foolish telling one of the biggest men in the territory to look out for a half-breed Apache kid. I told myself, Maybe you're just rubbing up to him because he's important and could use his influence to help out the agency . . . and maybe he knows it.

Actually I had more respect for Mickey Segundo, as a human being, than I did for T. O. McKay. Maybe I felt I owed the warning to McKay because he was a white man. Like saying, "Mickey Segundo's a good boy, but hell, he's half Indian." Just one of those things you catch yourself doing. Like habit. You do something wrong the first time and you know it, but if you keep it up, it becomes habit and it's no longer wrong because it's something you've always been doing.

McKay and a lot of people said Apaches were no damn good. The only good one was a dead one. They never stopped to reason it out. They'd been saying it so long, they knew it was true. Certainly any such statement was unreasonable, but damned if I wouldn't sometimes nod my head in agreement, because at those times I'd be with white men and that's the way white men talked.

I might have thought I was foolish, but actually it was

McKay who was the fool. He underestimated Mickey Segundo.

That was five years ago. It had begun with a hanging.

★

Early in the morning, Tudishishn, sergeant of Apache police at the Jicarilla Agency, rode in to tell me that Tony Choddi had jumped the boundaries again and might be in my locale. Tudishishn stayed for half a dozen cups of coffee, though his information didn't last that long. When he had enough, he left as leisurely as he had arrived. Tracking renegades, reservation jumpers, was Tudishishn's job; still, it wasn't something to get excited about. Tomorrows were for work; todays were for thinking about it.

Up at the agency, they were used to Tony Choddi skipping off. Usually they'd find him later in some shaded barranca, full of tulapai.

It was quiet until late afternoon, but not unusually so. It wasn't often that anything out of the ordinary happened at the subagency. There were twenty-six families, one hundred eight Jicarillas all told, under my charge. We were located almost twenty miles below the reservation proper, and most of the people had been there long before the reservation had been marked off. They had been fairly peaceful then, and remained so now. It was one of the few instances where the bureau allowed the sleeping dog to lie; and because of that we had less trouble than they did up at the reservation.

There was a sign on the door of the adobe office that described it formally. It read: D. J. Merritt—Agent, Jicarilla Apache Subagency—Puerco, New Mexico Territory. It was a startling announcement to post on the door of a squat adobe sitting all alone in the shadow of the Nacimentos. My Apaches preferred higher ground and the closest jacales were two miles up into the foothills. The office had to remain on the mail run, even though the mail consisted chiefly of impossible-to-apply bureau memoranda.

Just before supper, Tudishishn returned. He came in at a run this time and swung off before his pony had come to a full stop. He was excited and spoke in a confusion of Apache, Spanish, and a word here and there of English.

Returning to the reservation, he had decided to stop off and see his friends of the Puerco Agency. There had been friends

he had not seen for some time, and the morning had length-
ened into afternoon with tulapai, good talking, and even coffee.
People had come from the more remote jacales, deeper in the
hills, when they learned Tudishishn was there, to hear news
of friends at the reservation. Soon there were many people and
what looked like the beginning of a good time. Then Señor
McKay had come.

McKay had men with him, many men, and they were looking
for Mickey Solner—the squaw man, as the Americans called
him.

Most of the details I learned later on, but briefly this is what
had happened: McKay and some of his men were out on a
hunting trip. When they got up that morning, McKay's horse
was gone, along with a shotgun and some personal articles.
They got on the tracks, which were fresh and easy to follow,
and by that afternoon they were at Mickey Solner's jacale. His
woman and boy were there, and the horse was tethered in front
of the mud hut. Mickey Segundo, the boy, was honored to lead
such important people to his father, who was visiting with
Tudishishn.

McKay brought the horse along, and when they found
Mickey Solner, they took hold of him without asking questions
and looped a rope around his neck. Then they boosted him up
onto the horse they claimed he had stolen. McKay said it would
be fitting that way. Tudishishn had left fast when he saw what
was about to happen. He knew they wouldn't waste time arguing with an Apache, so he had come to me.

When I got there, Mickey Solner was still sitting McKay's
chestnut mare with the rope reaching from his neck to the
cottonwood bough overhead. His head drooped as if all the fight
were out of him, and when I came up in front of the chestnut,
he looked at me with tired eyes, watery and red from tulapai.

I had known Solner for years, but had never become close to
him. He wasn't a man with whom you became fast friends.
Just his living in an Apache rancheria testified to his being of
a different breed. He was friendly enough, but few of the
whites liked him—they said he drank all the time and never
worked. Maybe most were just envious. Solner was a white
man gone Indian, whole hog. That was the cause of the
resentment.

His son, Mickey the Second, stood near his dad's stirrup looking at him with a bewildered, pathetic look on his slim face.
He held on to the stirrup as if he'd never let it go. And it was

the first time, the only time, I ever saw Mickey Segundo without a faint smile on his face.

"Mr. McKay," I said to the cattleman, who was standing relaxed with his hands in his pockets, "I'm afraid I'll have to ask you to take that man down. He's under bureau jurisdiction and will have to be tried by a court."

McKay said nothing, but Bowie Allison, who was his herd boss, laughed and then said, "You ought to be afraid."

Dolph Bettzinger was there, along with his brothers Kirk and Sim. They were hired for their guns and usually kept pretty close to McKay. They did not laugh when Allison did.

And all around the clearing by the cottonwood were eight or ten others. Most of them I recognized as McKay riders. They stood solemnly, some with rifles and shotguns. There wasn't any doubt in their minds what stealing a horse meant.

"Tudishishn says that Mickey didn't steal your horse. These people told him that he was at home all night and most of the morning until Tudishishn dropped in, and then he came down here." A line of Apaches stood a few yards off and as I pointed to them, some nodded their heads.

"Mister," McKay said, "I found the horse at this man's hut. Now you argue that down, and I'll kiss the behind of every Apache you got living around here."

"Well, your horse could have been left there by someone else."

"Either way, he had a hand in it," he said curtly.

"What does he say?" I looked up at Mickey Solner and asked him quickly, "How did you get the horse, Mickey?"

"I just traded with a fella." His voice shook, and he held on to the saddle horn as if afraid he'd fall off. "This fella come along and traded with me, that's all."

"Who was it?"

Mickey Solner didn't answer. I asked him again, but still he refused to speak. McKay was about to say something, but Tudishishn came over quickly from the group of Apaches.

"They say it was Tony Choddi. He was seen to come into camp in early morning."

I asked McKay if it was Tony Choddi, and finally he admitted that it was. I felt better then. McKay couldn't hang a man for trading a horse.

"Are you satisfied, Mr. McKay? He didn't know it was yours. Just a matter of trading a horse."

McKay looked at me, narrowing his eyes. He looked as if he

were trying to figure out what kind of a man I was. Finally he said, "You think I'm going to believe them?"

It dawned on me suddenly that McKay had been using what patience he had for the past few minutes. Now he was ready to continue what they had come for. He had made up his mind long before.

"Wait a minute, Mr. McKay, you're talking about the life of an innocent man. You can't just toy with it like it was a head of cattle."

He looked at me and his puffy face seemed to harden. He was a heavy man, beginning to sag about the stomach. "You think you're going to tell me what I can do and what I can't? I don't need a government representative to tell me why my horse was stolen!"

"I'm not telling you anything. You know Mickey didn't steal the horse. You can see for yourself you're making a mistake."

McKay shrugged and looked at his herd boss. "Well, if it is, it isn't a very big one. Leastwise we'll be sure he won't be trading in stolen horses again." He nodded to Bowie Allison.

Bowie grinned, and brought his quirt up and then down across the rump of the chestnut.

"Yiiiiiiiiii. . . ."

The chestnut broke fast. Allison stood yelling after it, then jumped aside quickly as Mickey Solner swung back toward him on the end of the rope.

*

It was two weeks later, to the day, that Mickey Segundo came in with Tony Choddi's ears. You can see why I asked him if he had a notion of going after McKay. And it was a strange thing. I was talking to a different boy than the one I had last seen under the cottonwood.

When the horse shot out from under his dad, he ran to him like something wild, screaming, and wrapped his arms around the kicking legs trying to hold the weight off the rope.

Bowie Allison cuffed him away, and they held him back with pistols while he watched his dad die. From then on, he didn't say a word, and when it was over, walked away with his head down. Then, when he came in with Tony Choddi's ears, he was himself again. All smiles.

I might mention that I wrote to the Bureau of Indian Affairs about the incident since Mickey Solner, legally, was one of my charges; but nothing came of it. In fact, I didn't even get a reply.

Over the next few years Mickey Segundo changed a lot. He became Apache. That is, his appearance changed and almost everything else about him—except the smile. The smile was always there, as if he knew a monumental secret that was going to make everyone happy.

He let his hair grow to his shoulders and usually he wore only a frayed cotton shirt and breechclout; his moccasins were Apache—curled toes and leggings that reached to his thighs. He went under his Apache name, which was Peza-a, but I called him Mickey when I saw him, and he was never reluctant to talk to me in English. His English was good, discounting grammar.

Most of the time he lived in the same jacale his dad had built, providing for his mother and fitting closer into the life of the rancheria than he did before. But when he was about eighteen, he went up to the agency and joined Tudishishn's police. His mother went with him to live at the reservation, but within a year the two of them were back. Tracking friends who happened to wander off the reservation didn't set right with him. It didn't go with his smile.

Tudishishn told me he was sorry to lose him because he was an expert tracker and a dead shot. I know the sergeant had a dozen good sign followers, but very few who were above average with a gun.

He must have been nineteen when he came back to Puerco. In all those years he never once mentioned McKay's name. And I can tell you I never brought it up either.

I saw McKay even less after the hanging incident. If he ignored me before, he avoided me now. As I said, I felt like a fool after warning him about Mickey Segundo, and I'm certain McKay felt only contempt for me for doing it, after sticking up for the boy's dad.

McKay would come through every once in a while, usually going on a hunt up into the Nacimentos. He was a great hunter and would go out for a few days every month or so, usually with his herd boss, Bowie Allison. He hunted everything that walked, squirmed, or flew, and I'm told his ranch trophy room was really something to see.

You couldn't take it away from the man; everything he did, he did well. He was in his fifties, but he could shoot straighter and stay in the saddle longer than any of his riders. And he knew how to make money. But it was his arrogance that irked me. Even though he was polite, he made you feel far beneath him. He talked to you as if you were one of the hired help.

One afternoon, fairly late, Tudishishn rode in and said that he was supposed to meet McKay at the adobe office early the next morning. McKay wanted to try the shooting down southwest toward the malpais, on the other side of it, actually, and Tudishishn was going to guide for him.

The Indian policeman drank coffee until almost sundown and then rode off into the shadows of the Nacimentos. He was staying at one of the rancherias, visiting with his friends until the morning.

McKay appeared first. It was a cool morning, bright and crisp. I looked out of the window and saw the five riders coming up the road from the south, and when they were close enough I made out McKay and Bowie Allison and the three Bettzinger brothers. When they reached the office, McKay and Bowie dismounted, but the Bettzingers reined around and started back down the road.

McKay nodded and was civil enough, though he didn't direct more than a few words to me. Bowie was ready when I asked them if they wanted coffee, but McKay shook his head and said they were leaving shortly. Just about then the rider appeared coming down out of the hills.

McKay was squinting, studying the figure on the pony.

I didn't really look at him until I noticed McKay's close attention. And when I looked at the rider again, he was almost on us. I didn't have to squint then to see that it was Mickey Segundo.

McKay said, "Who's that?" with a ring of suspicion to his voice.

I felt a sudden heat on my face, like the feeling you get when you're talking about someone, then suddenly find the person standing next to you.

Without thinking about it, I told McKay, "That's Peza-a, one of my people." What made me call him by his Apache name I don't know. Perhaps because he looked so Indian. But I had never called him Peza-a before.

He approached us somewhat shyly, wearing his faded shirt and breechclout but now with a streak of ochre painted across his nose from ear to ear. He didn't look as if he could have a drop of white blood in him.

"What's he doing here?" McKay's voice still held a note of suspicion, and he looked at him as if he were trying to place him.

Bowie Allison studied him the same way, saying nothing.

"Where's Tudishishn? These gentlemen are waiting for him."

"Tudishishn is ill with a demon in his stomach," Peza-a answered. "He has asked me to substitute myself for him." He spoke in Spanish, hesitantly, the way an Apache does.

McKay studied him for some time. Finally, he said, "Well . . . can he track?"

"He was with Tudishishn for a year. Tudishishn speaks highly of him." Again I don't know what made me say it. A hundred things were going through my head. What I said was true, but I saw it getting me into something. Mickey never looked directly at me. He kept watching McKay, with the faint smile on his mouth.

McKay seemed to hesitate, but then he said, "Well, come on. I don't need a reference . . . long as he can track."

They mounted and rode out.

McKay wanted prongbuck. Tudishishn had described where they would find the elusive herds and promised to show him all he could shoot. But they were many days away. McKay had said if he didn't have time, he'd make time. He wanted good shooting.

Off and on during the first day, he questioned Mickey Segundo closely to see what he knew about the herds.

"I have seen them many times. Their hide the color of sand and black horns that reach into the air like bayonets of the soldiers. But they are far."

McKay wasn't concerned with distance. After a while he was satisfied that this Indian guide knew as much about tracking antelope as Tudishishn, and that's what counted. Still, there was something about the young Apache. . . .

                             *

"Tomorrow, we begin the crossing of the malpais," Mickey Segundo said. It was evening of the third day, as they made camp at Yucca Springs.

Bowie Allison looked at him quickly. "Tudishishn planned we'd follow the high country down and come out on the plain from the east."

"What's the matter with keeping a straight line?" McKay said. "Keeping to the hills is longer, isn't it?"

"Yeah, but that malpais is a blood-dryin' furnace in the middle of August," Bowie grumbled. "You got to be able to pinpoint the wells. And even if you find them, they might be dry."

McKay looked at Peza-a for an answer.

"If Señor McKay wishes to ride for two additional days, that is for him to say. But we can carry our water with ease." He went to his saddle pouch and drew out two collapsed, rubbery bags. "These, from the stomach of the horse, will hold much water. Tomorrow we fill canteens and these, and the water can be made to last five, six days. Even if the wells are dry, we have water."

Bowie Allison grumbled under his breath, looking with distaste at the horse intestine water sacks.

McKay rubbed his chin thoughtfully. He was thinking of prongbuck. Finally he said, "We'll cut across the lava."

Bowie Allison was right in his description of the malpais. It was a furnace, a crusted expanse of desert that stretched into another world. Saguaro and ocotillo stood nakedly sharp against the whiteness, and off in the distance were ghostly looming buttes, gigantic tombstones for the lava waste. Horses shuffled choking white dust, and the sun glare was a white blistering shock that screamed its brightness. Then the sun would drop suddenly, leaving a nothingness that could be felt. A life that had died a hundred million years ago.

McKay felt it, and that night he spoke little.

The second day was a copy of the first, for the lava country remained monotonously the same. McKay grew more irritable as the day wore on, and time and again he would snap at Bowie Allison for his grumbling. The country worked at the nerves of the two white men, while Mickey Segundo watched them.

On the third day they passed two waterholes. They could see the shallow crusted bottoms and the fissures that the tight sand had made cracking in the hot air. That night McKay said nothing.

In the morning there was a blue haze on the edge of the glare; they could feel the land beneath them begin to rise. Chaparral and patches of toboso grass became thicker and dotted the flatness, and by early afternoon the towering rock formations loomed near at hand. They had then one water sack two-thirds full; but the other, with their canteens, was empty.

Bowie Allison studied the gradual rise of the rock wall, passing his tongue over cracked lips. "There could be water up there. . . . Sometimes the rain catches in hollows and stays there a long time if it's shady."

McKay squinted into the air. The irregular crests were high and dead still against the sky. "Could be."

Mickey Segundo looked up and then nodded.

"How far to the next hole?" McKay asked.

"Maybe one day."

"If it's got water . . . Then how far?"

"Maybe two day. We come out on the plain then near the Datil Mountains and there is water, streams to be found."

McKay said, "That means we're halfway. We can make last what we got, but there's no use killing ourselves." His eyes lifted to the peaks again, then dropped to the mouth of a barranca that cut into the rock. He nodded to the dark canyon, which was partly hidden by a dense growth of mesquite. "We'll leave our stuff there and go on to see what we can find."

They unsaddled the horses and ground-tied them and hung their last water bag in the shade of a mesquite bush.

Then they walked up canyon until they found a place that would be the easiest to climb.

They went up and they came down, but when they were again on the canyon floor, their canteens still rattled lightly with their steps. Mickey Segundo carried McKay's rifle in one hand and the limp, empty water bag in the other.

He walked a step behind the two men and watched their faces as they turned to look back overhead. There was no water.

The rocks held nothing, not even a dampness. They were naked now and loomed brutally indifferent, and bone dry with no promise of moisture.

The canyon sloped gradually into the opening. And now, ahead, they could see the horses and the small fat bulge of the water bag hanging from the mesquite bough.

Micky Segundo's eyes were fixed on the water sack. He looked steadily at it.

Then a horse screamed. They saw the horses suddenly pawing the ground and pulling at the hackamores that held them fast. The three horses and the pack mule joined together now, neighing shrilly as they strained, dancing at the ropes.

And then a shape the color of sand darted through the mesquite thicket so quickly that it seemed a shadow.

Mickey Segundo threw the rifle to his shoulder. He hesitated. Then he fired.

The shape kept going, past the mesquite background and out into the open.

He fired again and the coyote went up into the air and came down to lie motionless.

It only jerked in death. McKay looked at him angrily. "Why the hell didn't you let me have it?! You could have hit one of the horses!"

"There was not time."

"That's two hundred yards! You could have hit a horse, that's what I'm talking about!"

"But I shot it," Mickey Segundo said.

When they reached the mesquite clump, they did not go over to inspect the dead coyote. Something else took their attention. It stopped the white men in their tracks.

They stared unbelieving at the wetness seeping into the sand, and above the spot, the water bag hanging like a punctured bladder. The water had quickly run out.

Mickey Segundo told the story at the inquiry. They had attempted to find water, but it was no use; so they were compelled to try to return.

They had almost reached Yucca Springs when the two men died. Mickey Segundo told it simply. He was sorry he had shot the water bag, but what could he say? God directs the actions of men mysteriously.

The county authorities were disconcerted, but they had to be satisfied with the apparent facts.

McKay and Allison were found ten miles from Yucca Springs and brought in. There were no marks of violence on either of them, and they found three hundred dollars in McKay's wallet. It was officially recorded that they died from thirst and exposure.

A terrible way to die just because some damn Apache couldn't shoot straight. Peza-a survived because he was lucky, along with the fact that he was Apache, which made him tougher. Just one of those things.

Mickey continued living with his mother at the subagency. His old Gallagher carbine kept them in meat, and they seemed happy enough just existing.

Tudishishn visited them occasionally, and when he did they would have a tulapai party. Everything was normal.

Mickey's smile was still there but maybe a little different.

But I've often wondered what Mickey Segundo would have done if that coyote had not run across the mesquite thicket. . . .

H. A. DeRosso

VIGILANTE

H. A. DeRosso was the Cornell Woolrich of the Western pulps. Many of his stories have the same phantasmagoric feeling of crime fiction's "dark saint."

Their lives were similar, too. Both men were loners, drinkers, and lost souls, Woolrich in the noisy isolation of Manhattan, DeRosso in the quiet loneliness of a small Wisconsin town.

Curiously, DeRosso's crime fiction was rarely as disturbing as his Western stories. While he was a very good suspense writer, his crimonious works were rarely as quirky and disturbing as his Westerns.

The following tale is a good example of how DeRosso could take a routine situation and imbue it with great passion and darkness.

Bill Leahy brought the word. "The Committee's meeting tonight, John."

John Weidler set down his newspaper and removed his spectacles. "Childress?" he asked.

"Yes."

Weidler carefully placed his spectacles in their case and cast a slight smile at his wife. He was glad that the two children were outside. He could hear their calls and laughter as they played in the backyard. John Weidler placed a hand momentarily on Martha's shoulder, then followed Leahy outside.

The evening air carried a crisp coolness and Weidler buttoned his jacket. They were silent as they walked along, the rasp of their shoe leather on the hard-packed ground the only sound.

Finally Weidler said, "It's come to a head this time."

Leahy nodded. He was a big man with a wide face and a violent redness to his features. For all his weight his step was light and soft—the tread of a stalking cat.

"He has asked for it," said Leahy heavily. "Matt Childress raised hell last night. Shot up half a dozen places, broke the windows of the Mercantile. When the marshal tried to arrest him this morning, Matt tore up the writ and threw it in the marshal's face. Matt sure did go and ask for it."

They walked along in the quickly gathering twilight. Virginia City was unnaturally quiet—such a quiet that it had never known. A far call from the Virginia City of a year ago—the Virginia City of Henry Plummer and the Innocents.

Weidler kept envisioning the old Virginia City that had been a tent city with its gambling houses and saloons and its roughly clothed, roistering miners and thieving, murdering Innocents. Full of wild, primitive laughter and full of sudden death.

A year had wrought a lot of changes in Virginia City. The tents were gone, replaced by frame buildings, though the saloons and gambling houses remained. It was a changed Virginia City with its muted laughter and vibrant life. A place where a man could settle down and raise a family. And the Vigilantes had made it so.

"What's the word from Nevada?" Weidler asked.

"Hang him," Leahy said bluntly.

"That will be going kind of far," murmured Weidler, a sudden coldness gripping him. He was a short, stocky man in his early thirties and there was the appearance of great strength in his arms and shoulders. He had a rather plain face with a blunt jaw and there was the hint of the bulldog in his features and in his bearing. He looked like a cold man.

"It's up to the Committee," said Leahy.

"This is going to be hard, Bill. Matt was one of us. He's not a bad sort when he's sober. Drunk, he's a wild man. We've warned him time and again, but it hasn't done any good."

"He's been bragging that the Vigilantes are through."

"We'll see about that."

"Matt has friends. They'll put up a fuss. You can bet on Tom Kincaid putting up for Matt."

"Yes, Tom will do that. The hell of it is—Tom is our friend, too."

"So is Matt Childress."

★

They came to Day & Miller's store, where the Vigilante meeting was to be held. Miners crowded in front of the store and they all had rifles but they were a quiet, somber lot. Weidler and Leahy nodded to a few of them and entered the store.

Two kerosene lamps had been lit and their shadowy, wavering light left heavy patches of black shadow in the corners and on the far walls. About twenty men were waiting. They were all morose and quiet, carrying about them a nervous silence as though wanting everything over with as soon as possible,

One of the men spoke. "I just saw Childress. Warned him to leave town. He laughed and said the Vigilantes are played out. That they won't dare hang a man for shooting up the town."

Every man's glance was on Weidler. He'd been one of the early organizers of the Vigilantes and he'd placed the noose around George Ives's neck when that first member of the Innocents had been executed. The men were very silent now, only the scraping of their boots when they shifted their weight marring the stillness. Weidler knew they were awaiting his words.

They would put much weight to what he'd say, Weidler realized. They had always looked to him for leadership and he had never failed them. But this time things were different. Matt Childress was a friend, not a thieving, murdering outlaw. His only fault lay in his inability to hold liquor.

Weidler felt the cold sweat stand out on the back of his neck. This was not going to be easy.

"There's not much to say," Weidler said tonelessly. "You all know Matt Childress's record. He's not at all bad when sober. He has no criminal record. But this is not the first time that he has shot up the town, destroyed property, and endangered the lives of citizens.

"And it's not the first time he has laughed at and ignored the law. He is a bad example. If he keeps on getting away with it, there will be others to follow his ways. He can't be reformed."

He paused awhile, searching his mind for more to say. He could go on and list Matt Childress's good points. In all fairness Matt had that much coming, but the time for loyalty and sentiment was past, Weidler told himself. He had to think of what Childress meant to Virginia City, not what he meant to John Weidler.

At length he went on. "Matt Childress is your friend—and my friend. But that should not prejudice our decision. Nevada has sent word that Matt Childress should hang and that is the voice of six hundred miners. Now that decision is up to us—the Executive Committee. We all want Virginia City and Montana Territory to be a law-abiding place where honest men can live in peace and security.

"You will vote 'Aye' or 'Nay.' "

It was Bill Leahy who broke the silence, saying, "Aye." One by one the others echoed Leahy's vote and the matter was done. Leahy walked behind the counter and took down a rope.

They acted quickly, anxious to get a distasteful thing done and out of the way. John Weidler led them out of Day & Miller's store. The group of armed miners were still there. Silent. Waiting. Some of them had lighted torches.

Weidler read their unspoken query and he bobbed his head in a wordless answer. They fell in behind the Committee.

Matt Childress was in Fielding's saloon, standing at the bar with Tom Kincaid at his side. Childress's face went white and he seemed to shrink a little when he spied Weidler, but only for a moment. Childress squared his shoulders and there was a tight smile on his pale lips as he waited for the Vigilantes to speak.

Kincaid had tensed, his face taking on the color of his red hair. Heat came to his eyes. They were friends, these men. They'd ridden through storm and cold to bring summary justice to the cutthroat Innocents. They'd worked side by side—John Weidler, Matt Childress, Bill Leahy, Tom Kincaid.

"We've come for you, Matt," said Weidler.

"This is a hell of a joke to play on a man, John." Childress's voice trembled a little.

"It's no joke, Matt."

Tom Kincaid pushed forward, facing Weidler. "Are you really going through with it, John?"

"Yes."

Kincaid's face worked and it seemed as though he was going to unloose a torrent of words. But no sounds came, although his eyes distended and a sneer curled his lips. His eyes were flat and ice-cold.

Childress's thick face was very white now. "You can't mean hanging," he said, forcing a quavering laugh. "I know I'm in the wrong and I'm damned sorry. I swear before God it won't happen again. I got something coming. Banishment, maybe— but not hanging!"

Slowly, wishing that it could be otherwise, John Weidler shook his head. He was thankful that he was a reticent man who could hide his emotions behind a cold exterior, or he could never have endured watching the life going out from Matt Childress's eyes and the way he leaned against the bar as though he could not stand alone.

"You'll give me a little time then?" Childress asked dully. "A little time to put my affairs in order and to write a few letters? And to see my wife?"

"You have an hour," said Weidler.

"But an hour isn't enough! She can't make it here in that time."

"One hour," said John Weidler, turning away.

*

They had taken Matt Childress to one of the back rooms of Fielding's saloon where the doomed man had been supplied with pen and paper. Weidler was outside in the cold darkness, leaning against the front of the saloon. There was a cold cigar in Weidler's mouth but he kept drawing on it as if unaware that it had died.

Presently Wayne Dunning came up. He was a young man who clerked in Day & Miller's store. "They've sent a rider for Elizabeth Childress. As soon as the meeting was over and the verdict known, the rider took out for Childress's place. His wife will sure raise hell if she gets here before the execution."

"A woman's tears have a way of moving a man," said Weidler, frowning. "Tears once saved Hayes Lyons and Buck Stinson and Ned Ray from the noose and left them free to murder and rob for almost a year. But she won't get here in time."

"She'll probably use Big Bay. That horse is the fastest thing around here."

"She won't make it. What bothers me is Tom Kincaid. I thought he'd take it much harder than he has. I wonder why he hasn't?"

The hour passed and Childress's guards came out of Fielding's saloon with the doomed man walking in their midst. In the torchlight Childress's face was pasty gray and his step was a trifle unsteady.

He looked at John Weidler out of wide, haunted eyes but Weidler would not meet the man's stare. Weidler led the crowd of men to the corral in back of Day & Miller's store.

The corral gate was swung open and a rope was tossed over the crossbar. A Vigilante came out of the back of the store, carrying an empty packing box, which he placed underneath the dangling noose. Bill Leahy and Wayne Dunning lifted Childress up on the box.

Childress's pale face glistened with sweat and his voice was raspingly harsh. "You can't mean this! You're all just playing a joke on me. You can't really mean to hang me for what I did last night! For getting drunk and having some fun? I'm not complaining. I deserve something for always getting out of hand and causing Virginia City a lot of trouble but I don't deserve hanging.

"I ain't ever killed but one man in all my life and he asked for it. I ain't ever robbed anyone. I've always been an honest man. Banish me. Cut off my ear or my arm but don't hang me!"

Bill Leahy had climbed up on the packing box beside Childress and Leahy fitted the noose about the doomed man's neck, and then signaled that the other end of the rope be tied to a corral post.

John Weidler stood by watching, the dead cigar still between his lips. For a while he could not believe that all this was real. But the torchlight and the milling men and Matt Childress's gray face were authentic enough and Weidler suddenly wished that all this were a dream that he might brush aside and forget upon awakening.

He hardly heard Wayne Dunning who kept whispering, "We haven't much time. She'll be here soon. We haven't much time."

★

There was a commotion within the crowd and Tom Kincaid came bulling his way through the armed miners. His face was very red and his eyes flashed. He bulled up close to Weidler, so close that the Vigilante leader had to fall back a step.

"Call it off, John!" Kincaid ordered.

Weidler shook his head.

"So you're really going through with it," Kincaid roared. "And

I held back. Thinking that you were just trying to put the fear of death in Matt. Let him know the feel of a rope around his neck and that would calm him. That's what I thought you were up to, so I held back. I didn't think you were kill-crazy."

Weidler chewed his cold cigar. "Take it easy, Tom. Take it easy."

"You'll hang Matt only over my dead body," yelled Kincaid, swinging a wild fist at Weidler. The Vigilante had been expecting the blow and he swayed his head aside and out of Kincaid's reach.

Bill Leahy came in fast and before Kincaid could try another blow Leahy had his pistol against the back of Kincaid's neck.

"Hold on, Tom," Leahy snapped.

Kincaid dropped his arms and his fists unclenched. He never took his stare off Weidler's face. When Kincaid spoke his lips curled back from his teeth as though the very words were unclean.

"You filthy, kill-crazy murderer! I always felt you had a bad streak in you, John, but I never would own up to it because I called you friend. I felt we needed a cold man like you to put an end to Henry Plummer and the Innocents. I never thought the killing craze would worm into you until you'd hang anyone just to satisfy your filthy craving.

"We need the Vigilantes. I was one of them, and I am not ashamed of what I did. But tonight you're tearing down all the good we ever built. You're blackening the name of the Vigilantes in a way that can never be forgotten. When histories of the Vigilantes are written you'll be marked down as a kill-crazy murderer, and all those associated with you will have to carry the same black brand."

Weidler took it all in silence. He stood there stolidly, the dead cigar clamped between his teeth, meeting Tom Kincaid's hot stare. Weidler's pulse was pounding and he could feel the throb of the vein at his temple.

He knew a coldness that filled him completely, the identical coldness he'd always felt at moments like these. Kincaid's words fell as from an alien world.

"One word from you and Matt could be saved," Kincaid went on. "Had you stood up for Matt, put in a good word for him, the Committee would never have voted as it did.

"It's an evil and dark day for Montana Territory when you've taken to hanging men for minor offenses. But Matt Childress

will be the first and the last. I can't save him. I know that. But
I'll see to it that you'll never hang another. Mind that, John."

Weidler turned his head and his stare away from Kincaid.
Matt Childress was mumbling brokenly, incoherently on the
packing box. Weidler felt a weakness creeping over his will.
The time had come and he had to make his choice—between
Matt Childress and a Virginia City that would be quiet and
still and peaceful, where a man could live and be proud of
his town.

And suddenly he realized that if he hesitated much longer,
he could not go through with it.

So he took the cigar from his mouth and said clearly, coldly,
"Men, do your duty!"

*

Afterward, when Childress's lifeless body was swaying in the
night wind, there came the thunderous clopping of a horse's
hoofs and a rider burst into the smoky torchlight. It was a
woman, and she flung herself out of the saddle before the horse
had halted. She stopped short when she spied the dangling
body.

Weidler was up against the corral fence with Bill Leahy and
Wayne Dunning on either side of him. They all watched Elizabeth Childress. She was a tall woman with a violently beautiful
face. They knew little about her except that she lived with
Matt Childress and he called her his wife. She stared at
Childress's body a long while, but no tears or cries came. She
spoke at last, her voice choking with grief.

"Oh, the shame of it," she cried as she knelt beneath the
dead man and clasped her arms around his stiffening legs.
"That Matt Childress should be hanged like a common felon.
Where were his friends? Why did they let this happen to him
who was a better man than all of them?

"Better that someone had taken a gun and shot my Matt
down. If I had been here, I'd have done that—rather than suf-
fer him to hang!"

She seemed to notice Weidler for the first time. The woman
rose slowly to her feet and she walked haltingly, stooped forward a little as if to see better. As she came close, Weidler saw
the tightness of her features and the way the cords stood out
on her neck.

He expected her to speak, to burst out in an orgy of denunciations, but she only stared at him, her lips working silently. Then she went back to Childress.

Weidler spat the shredded cigar from his teeth and walked away.

He found that Martha had put the children to bed and that she had a pot of boiling coffee on the stove for him. She didn't say anything but he could feel from her silent presence that she yearned for some comforting words to say to him.

He poured the coffee with fingers that were stiffly untrembling and, looking up, he caught her eyes and smiled a little.

"You'd better go to bed," he told her. "I'm staying up a while longer."

She left the room and he was instantly sorry she had gone. It felt so empty now—empty as he was himself. All he knew was a hollow feeling within him and a vast restlessness. He went to the kitchen door and threw it open, standing full in the soft sweep of the night wind.

He stood looking off at the sky but not seeing the stars or the moon or the scattered clouds flowing along with the wind. All he saw was Matt Childress's swaying body and the loathing and hatred in Tom Kincaid's eyes.

*

He was standing there in the chillness of the night when Bill Leahy came again.

"What is it, Bill?"

"Tom Kincaid is after you."

"He'll get over it."

Leahy placed a big hand against the doorjamb. His breathing had calmed. "He's taken on a load of drinks. He's in a bad mind, John. He's coming over here to have it out with you."

"He's drunk. He doesn't know what he's doing."

"But he's doing it just the same."

"Why has he got it in for me?" Weidler asked savagely.

"He blames you for Matt. Says if you'd put in a good word for Matt, he'd never been hanged. There's no telling Tom otherwise. I've tried for half an hour but Tom won't listen."

"Then I'll have to try," said Weidler.

"He's got a gun, John."

Weidler shrugged. Bill Leahy came in close and slipped

something into Weidler's pocket. He reached down and felt the cold metal of a revolver.

They had turned out into the street when they spied the man coming toward them. He walked with a rolling step much like a sailor's but Weidler knew that the roll of the walk was due to too many drinks.

Kincaid had stopped, his legs planted wide. His head was thrust forward and he raised a hand and pushed his hat back from his forehead. Recognition came to him for he laughed and said:

"Well, well, if it ain't Bloody John!"

"Hello, Tom," said Weidler easily. "I'm on my way to Fielding's for a drink. Will you join me?"

"Drink, hell!" exploded Kincaid wrathfully. Then he laughed again. "I won't join you in a drink but you sure will join Matt in hell!"

He had been holding his right hand at his belt and he suddenly flung up his arm. Weidler saw moonlight flash on the polished metal of Kincaid's pistol.

"Hold it, you damn fool!" Weidler cried, rushing forward. Kincaid laughed and his cold eyes looked down the sights of his gun but his bullet was wide.

Before he could fire again, Weidler was on him.

Kincaid was bringing his weapon up again but Weidler grasped the gun, holding it away from him. Kincaid lunged, grunting, and he drove the hard toe of his boot into Weidler's shin. Weidler released his hold and as he wavered on the point of unbalance, Kincaid shoved out his leg, sending Weidler sprawling.

He rolled over quickly to find himself staring in the bore of Kincaid's weapon.

Weidler hardly realized his actions. Perhaps it was the instinct of self-preservation that prompted him to act so automatically. For the gun in his hand roared, and as Kincaid staggered, it roared again.

Kincaid made a half turn and it looked as if he wanted to walk away when he said quite clearly, "Oh my God!" and fell.

*

They came running, the watching men, and they gathered around the fallen Tom Kincaid. Weidler's friends were about him, but he was heedless to their queries about his welfare.

Two words stuck to his mind as he walked away. Two words hurled at him by someone looking down at dead Tom Kincaid. "Bloody killer!"

A strange, cold loneliness settled down over Weidler. He knew that he'd never forget the double tragedy of this night. The memory of it would ever haunt him, but, looking about him, he saw that Virginia City was quiet now, a natural quiet, and that was consolation enough.

Marcia Muller

THE TIME OF THE WOLVES

Marcia Muller founded the contemporary school of female private eyes. She is finally getting the recognition so long (and inexplicably) withheld from her—a spot on the best-seller list, and kudos from most of the major suspense reviewers.

Marcia has not done much Western fiction in her career but, as you'll see here, she has a real affinity for the form, bringing her enormous skills as a storyteller to this mix of history and human observation.

"It was in the time of the wolves that my grandmother came to Kansas." The old woman sat primly on the sofa in her apartment in the senior citizens' complex. Although her faded blue eyes were focused on the window, the historian who sat opposite her sensed Mrs. Clark was not seeing the shopping malls and used-car lots that had spilled over into what once was open prairie. As she'd begun speaking, her gaze had turned inward—and into the past.

The historian—who was compiling an oral account of the Kansas pioneers—adjusted the volume button on her tape recorder and looked expectantly at Mrs. Clark. But the descendant of those pioneers was in no hurry; she waited a moment before resuming her story.

"The time of the wolves—that's the way I thought of it as a child, and I speak of it that way to this very day. It's fitting; those were perilous times, in the 1870s. Vicious packs of wolves and coyotes roamed; fires would sweep the prairie without warning; there were disastrous floods; and, of course, blizzards. But my grandmother was a true pioneer woman: She knew no fear. One time in the winter of 1872 . . ."

★

Alma Heusser stood in the doorway of the sod house, looking north over the prairie. It was gone four in the afternoon now, and storm clouds were building on the horizon. The chill in the air penetrated even her heavy buffalo-skin robe; a hush had fallen, as if all the creatures on the barren plain were holding their breath, waiting for the advent of the snow.

Alma's hand tightened on the rough door frame. Fear coiled in her stomach. Every time John was forced to make the long trek into town she stood like this, awaiting his return. Every moment until his horse appeared in the distance she imagined that some terrible event had taken him from her. And on this night, with the blizzard threatening . . .

The shadows deepened, purpled by the impending storm. Alma shivered and hugged herself beneath the enveloping robe. The land stretched before her: flat, treeless, its sameness mesmerizing. If she looked at it long enough, her eyes would begin to play tricks on her—tricks that held the power to drive her mad.

She'd heard of a woman who had been driven mad by the prairie: a timid, gentle woman who had traveled some miles east with her husband to gather wood. When they had finally stopped their wagon at a grove, the woman had gotten down and run to a tree—the first tree she had touched in three years. It was said they had had to pry her loose, because she refused to stop hugging it.

The sound of a horse's hooves came from the distance. Behind Alma, ten-year-old Margaret asked, "Is that him? Is it Papa?"

Alma strained to see through the rapidly gathering dusk. "No," she said, her voice flat with disappointment. "No, it's only Mr. Carstairs."

The Carstairs, William and Sarah, lived on a claim several miles east of there. It was not unusual for William to stop when passing on his way from town. But John had been in town today, too; why had they not ridden back together?

The coil of fear wound tighter as she went to greet him.

"No, I won't dismount," William Carstairs said in response to her invitation to come inside and warm himself. "Sarah doesn't know I am here, so I must be home swiftly. I've come to ask a favor."

"Certainly. What is it?"

"I'm off to the East in the morning. My mother is ill and hasn't much longer; she's asked for me. Sarah is anxious about being alone. As you know, she's been homesick these past two years. Will you look after her?"

"Of course." Alma said the words with a readiness she did not feel. She did not like Sarah Carstairs. There was something mean-spirited about the young woman, a suspicious air in the way she dealt with others that bordered on the hostile. But looking after neighbors was an inviolate obligation here on the prairie, essential to survival.

"Of course we'll look after her," she said more warmly, afraid her reluctance had somehow sounded in her voice. "You need not worry."

After William Carstairs had ridden off, Alma remained in the doorway of the sod house until the horizon had receded into darkness. She would wait for John as long as was necessary, hoping that her hunger for the sight of him had the power to bring him home again.

"Neighbors were the greatest treasure my grandparents had," Mrs. Clark explained. "The pioneer people were a warm-hearted lot, open and giving, closer than many of today's families. And the women in particular were a great source of strength and comfort to one another. My grandmother's friendship with Sarah Carstairs, for example . . ."

*

"I suppose I must pay a visit to Sarah," Alma said. It was two days later. The snowstorm had never arrived, but even though it had retreated into Nebraska, another seemed to be on the way. If she didn't go to the Carstairs' claim today, she might not be able to look in on Sarah for some time to come.

John grunted noncommittally and went on trimming the wick of the oil lamp. Alma knew he didn't care for Sarah, either, but he was a taciturn man, slow to voice criticism. And he also understood the necessity of standing by one's neighbors.

"I promised William. He was so worried about her." Alma waited, hoping her husband would forbid her to go because of the impending storm. No such dictum was forthcoming, however: John Heusser was not one to distrust his wife's judgment; he would abide by whatever she decided.

So, driven by a promise she wished she had not been obligated to make, Alma set off on horseback within the hour.

The Carstairs' claim was a poor one, although to Alma's way of thinking it need not be. In the hands of John Heusser it would have been bountiful with wheat and corn, but William Carstairs was an unskilled farmer. His crops had parched even during the past two summers of plentiful rain; his animals fell ill and died of unidentifiable ailments; the house and outbuildings grew ever more ramshackle through his neglect. If Alma were a fanciful woman—and she preferred to believe she was not—she would have said there was a curse on the land. Its appearance on this grim February day did little to dispel the illusion.

In the foreground stood the house, its roof beam sagging, its chimney askew. The barn and other outbuildings behind it looked no better. The horse in the enclosure was bony and spavined; the few chickens seemed too dispirited to scratch at the hard-packed earth. Alma tied her sorrel to the fence and walked toward the house, her reluctance to be there asserting itself until it was nearly a foreboding. There was no sign of welcome from within, none of the flurry of excitement that the arrival of a visitor on the isolated homesteads always occasioned. She called out, knocked at the door. And waited.

After a moment the door opened slowly and Sarah Carstairs looked out. Her dark hair hung loose about her shoulders; she wore a muslin dress dyed the rich brown of walnut bark. Her eyes were deeply circled—haunted, Alma thought.

Quickly she shook off the notion and smiled. "We've heard that Mr. Carstairs had to journey East," she said. "I thought you might enjoy some company."

The younger woman nodded. Then she opened the door wider and motioned Alma inside.

The room was much like Alma's main room at home, with narrow, tall windows, a rough board floor, and an iron stove for both cooking and heating. The curtains at the windows were plain burlap grain sacks, not at all like Alma's neatly stitched muslin ones, with their appliqués of flowers. The furnishings—a pair of rockers, pine cabinet, sideboard, and table—had been new when the Carstairs arrived from the East two years before, but their surfaces were coated with the grime that accumulated from cooking.

Sarah shut the door and turned to face Alma, still not speaking. To cover her confusion Alma thrust out the corn bread she had brought. The younger woman took it, nodding thanks.

After a slight hesitation she set it on the table and motioned somewhat gracelessly at one of the rockers. "Please," she said.

Alma undid the fastenings of her heavy cloak and sat down, puzzled by the strange reception. Sarah went to the stove and added a log, in spite of the room already being quite warm.

"He sent you to spy on me, didn't he?"

The words caught Alma by complete surprise. She stared at Sarah's narrow back, unable to make a reply.

Sarah turned, her sharp features pinched by what might have been anger. "That is why you're here, is it not?" she asked.

"Mr. Carstairs did ask us to look out for you in his absence, yes."

"How like him," Sarah said bitterly.

Alma could think of nothing to say to that.

Sarah offered her coffee. As she prepared it, Alma studied the young woman. In spite of the heat in the room and her proximity to the stove, she rubbed her hands together; her shawl slipped off her thin shoulders, and she quickly pulled it back. When the coffee was ready—a bitter, nearly unpalatable brew—she sat cradling the cup in her hands, as if to draw even more warmth from it.

After her earlier strangeness Sarah seemed determined to talk about the commonplace: the storm that was surely due, the difficulty of obtaining proper cloth, her hope that William would not forget the bolt of calico she had requested he bring. She asked Alma about making soap: Had she ever done so? Would she allow her to help the next time so she might learn? As they spoke, she began to wipe beads of moisture from her brow. The room remained very warm; Alma removed her cloak and draped it over the back of the rocker.

Outside, the wind was rising, and the light that came through the narrow windows was tinged with gray. Alma became impatient to be off for home before the storm arrived, but she also became concerned with leaving Sarah alone. The young woman's conversation was rapidly growing erratic and rambling; she broke off in the middle of sentences to laugh irrelevantly. Her brow continued moist, and she threw off her shawl, fanning herself. Alma, who like all frontier women had had considerable experience at doctoring the sick, realized Sarah had been taken by a fever.

Her first thought was to take Sarah to her own home, where

she might look after her properly, but one glance out the window discouraged her. The storm was nearing quickly now; the wind gusted, tearing at the dried cornstalks in William Carstairs's uncleared fields, and the sky was streaked with black and purple. A ride of several miles in such weather would be the death of Sarah; do Alma no good, either. She was here for the duration, with only a sick woman to help her make the place secure.

She glanced at Sarah, but the other woman seemed unaware of what was going on outside. Alma said, "You're feeling poorly, aren't you?"

Sarah shook her head vehemently. A strand of dark brown hair fell across her forehead and clung there damply. Alma sensed she was not a woman who would give in easily to illness, would fight any suggestion that she take to her bed until she was near collapse. She thought over the remedies she had administered to others in such a condition, wondered whether Sarah's supplies included the necessary sassafras tea or quinine.

Sarah was rambling again—about the prairie, its loneliness and desolation. ". . . listen to that wind! It's with us every moment. I hate the wind and the cold, I hate the nights when the wolves prowl. . . ."

A stealthy touch of cold moved along Alma's spine. She, too, feared the wolves and coyotes. John told her it came from having Germanic blood. Their older relatives had often spoken in hushed tones of the wolf packs in the Black Forest. Many of their native fairy tales and legends concerned the cruel cunning of the animals, but John was always quick to point out that these were only stories. "Wolves will not attack a human unless they sense sickness or weakness," he often asserted. "You need only take caution."

But all of the settlers, John included, took great precautions against the roaming wolf packs; no one went out onto the prairie unarmed. And the stories of merciless and unprovoked attacks could not all be unfounded. . . .

"I hear the wolves at night," Sarah said. "They scratch on the door and the sod. They're hungry. Oh, yes, they're hungry. . . ."

Alma suddenly got to her feet, unable to sit for the tautness in her limbs. She felt Sarah's eyes on her as she went to the sideboard and lit the oil lamp. When she turned to Sarah again, the young woman had tilted her head against the high back of the rocker and was viewing her through slitted lids. There was a glitter in the dark crescents that remained visible that struck Alma as somehow malicious.

"Are you afraid of the wolves, Alma?" she asked slyly.

"Anyone with good sense is."

"And you in particular?"

"Of course I'd be afraid if I met one face-to-face!"

"Only if you were face-to-face with it? Then you won't be afraid staying here with me when they scratch at the door. I tell you, I hear them every night. Their claws go *snick, snick* on the boards. . . ."

The words were baiting. Alma felt her dislike for Sarah Carstairs gather strength. She said calmly, "Then you've noticed the storm is fast approaching."

Sarah extended a limp arm toward the window. "Look at the snow."

Alma glanced over there, saw the first flakes drifting past the wavery pane of glass. The sense of foreboding she'd felt upon her arrival intensified, sending little prickles over the surface of her skin.

Firmly she reined in her fear and met Sarah's eyes with a steady gaze. "You're right; I must stay here. I'll be as little trouble to you as possible."

"Why should you be trouble? I'll be glad of the company." Her tone mocked the meaning of the words. "We can talk. It's a long time since I've had anyone to talk to. We'll talk of my William."

Alma glanced at the window again, anxious to put her horse into the barn, out of the snow. She thought of the revolver she carried in her saddlebag as defense against the dangers of the prairie; she would feel safer if she brought it inside with her.

"We'll talk of my William," Sarah repeated. "You'd like that, wouldn't you, Alma?"

"Of course. But first I must tend to my horse."

"Yes, of course you'd like talking of William. You like talking *to* him. All those times when he stops at your place on his way home to me. On his way home, when your John isn't there. Oh, yes, Alma, I know about those visits." Sarah's eyes were wide now, the malicious light shining brightly.

Alma caught her breath. She opened her mouth to contradict the words, then shut it. It was the fever talking, she told herself, exaggerating the fears and delusions that life on the frontier could sometimes foster. There was no sense trying to reason with Sarah. What mattered now was to put the horse up and fetch her weapon. She said briskly, "We'll discuss this when I've returned," donned her cloak, and stepped out into the storm.

The snow was sheeting along on a northwesterly gale. The flakes were small and hard; they stung her face like hailstones. The wind made it difficult to walk; she leaned into it, moving slowly toward the hazy outline of her sorrel. He stood by the rail, his feet moving skittishly. Alma grasped his halter, clung to it a moment before she began leading him toward the ramshackle barn. The chickens had long ago fled to their coop. Sarah's bony bay was nowhere in sight.

The doors to the barn stood open, the interior in darkness. Alma led the sorrel inside and waited until her eyes accustomed themselves to the gloom. When they had, she spied a lantern hanging next to the door, matches and flint nearby. She fumbled with them, got the lantern lit, and looked around.

Sarah's bay stood in one of the stalls, apparently accustomed to looking out for itself. The stall was dirty, and the entire barn held an air of neglect. She set the lantern down, unsaddled the sorrel, and fed and watered both horses. As she turned to leave, she saw the dull gleam of an ax lying on top of a pile of wood. Without considering why she was doing so, she picked it up and carried it, along with her gun, outside. The barn doors were warped and difficult to secure, but with some effort she managed.

Back in the house, she found Sarah's rocker empty. She set down the ax and the gun, calling out in alarm. A moan came from beyond the rough burlap that curtained off the next room. Alma went over and pushed aside the cloth.

Sarah lay on a brass bed, her hair fanned out on the pillows. She had crawled under the tumbled quilts and blankets. Alma approached and put a hand to her forehead; it was hot, but Sarah was shivering.

Sarah moaned again. Her eyes opened and focused unsteadily on Alma. "Cold," she said. "So cold . . ."

"You've taken a fever." Alma spoke briskly, a manner she'd found effective with sick people. "Did you remove your shoes before getting into bed?"

Sarah nodded.

"Good. It's best you keep your clothes on, though; this storm is going to be a bad one; you'll need them for warmth."

Sarah rolled onto her side and drew herself into a ball, shivering violently. She mumbled something, but her words were muffled.

Alma leaned closer. "What did you say?"

"The wolves . . . they'll come tonight, scratching—"

"No wolves are going to come here in this storm. Anyway, I've a gun and the ax from your woodpile. No harm will come to us. Try to rest now, perhaps sleep. When you wake, I'll bring some tea that will help break the fever."

Alma went toward the door, then turned to look back at the sick woman. Sarah was still curled on her side, but she had moved her head and was watching her. Her eyes were slitted once more, and the light from the lamp in the next room gleamed off them—hard and cold as the icicles that must be forming on the eaves.

Alma was seized by an unreasoning chill. She moved through the door, out into the lamplight, toward the stove's warmth. As she busied herself with finding things in the cabinet, she felt a violent tug of home.

Ridiculous to fret, she told herself. John and Margaret would be fine. They would worry about her, of course, but would know she had arrived here well in advance of the storm. And they would also credit her with the good sense not to start back home on such a night.

She rummaged through the shelves and drawers, found the herbs and tea and some roots that would make a healing brew. Outside, there was a momentary quieting of the wind; in the bedroom Sarah also lay quiet. Alma put on the kettle and sat down to wait for it to boil.

It was then that she heard the first wolf howls, not far away on the prairie.

★

"The bravery of the pioneer women has never been equaled," Mrs. Clark told the historian. "And there was a solidarity, a sisterhood among them that you don't see anymore. That sisterhood was what sustained my grandmother and Sarah Carstairs as they battled the wolves . . ."

★

For hours the wolves howled in the distance. Sarah awoke, throwing off the covers, complaining of the heat. Alma dosed her repeatedly with the herbal brew and waited for the fever to break. Sarah tossed about on the bed, raving about wolves and the wind and William. She seemed to have some fevered notion that her husband had deserted her, and nothing Alma would say would calm her. Finally she wore herself out and slipped into a troubled sleep.

Alma prepared herself some tea and pulled one of the rockers close to the stove. She was bone-tired, and the cold was bitter now, invading the little house through every crack and pore in the sod. Briefly she thought she should bring Sarah into the main room, prepare a pallet on the floor nearer the heat source, but she decided it would do the woman more harm than good to be moved. As she sat warming herself and sipping the tea, she gradually became aware of an eerie hush and realized the wind had ceased.

Quickly she set down her cup and went to the window. The snow had stopped, too. Like its sister storm of two days before, this one had retreated north, leaving behind a barren white landscape. The moon had appeared, near to full, and its stark light glistened off the snow.

And against the snow moved the black silhouettes of the wolves.

They came from the north, rangy and shaggy, more like ragged shadows than flesh-and-blood creatures. Their howling was silenced now, and their gait held purpose. Alma counted five of them, all of a good size yet bony. Hungry.

She stepped back from the window and leaned against the wall beside it. Her breathing was shallow, and she felt strangely light-headed. For a moment she stood, one hand pressed to her midriff, bringing her sense under control. Then she moved across the room, to where William Carstairs's Winchester rifle hung on the wall. When she had it in her hands, she stood looking irresolutely at it.

Of course, Alma knew how to fire a rifle; all frontier women did. But she was only a fair shot with it, a far better shot with her revolver. She could use the rifle to fire at the wolves at a distance, but the best she could hope for was to frighten them. Better to wait and see what transpired.

She set the rifle down and turned back to the window. The wolves were still some distance away. And what if they did come to the house, scratch at the door as Sarah had claimed? The house was well built; there was little harm the wolves could do it.

Alma went to the door to the bedroom. Sarah still slept, the covers pushed down from her shoulders. Alma went in and pulled them up again. Then she returned to the main room and the rocker.

The first scratchings came only minutes later. *Snick, snick* on the boards, just as Sarah had said.

Alma gripped the arms of the rocker with icy fingers. The revolver lay in her lap.

The scratching went on. Snuffling noises, too. In the bedroom Sarah cried out in protest. Alma got up and looked in on her. The sick woman was writhing on the bed. "They're out there! I know they are!"

Alma went to her. "Hush, they won't hurt us." She tried to rearrange Sarah's covers, but she only thrashed harder.

"They'll break the door, they'll find a way in, they'll—"

Alma pressed her hand over Sarah's mouth. "Stop it! You'll only do yourself harm."

Surprisingly, Sarah calmed. Alma wiped sweat from her brow and waited. The young woman continued to lie quietly.

When Alma went back to the window, she saw that the wolves had retreated. They stood together, several yards away, as if discussing how to breach the house.

Within minutes they returned. Their scratchings became bolder now; their claws ripped and tore at the sod. Heavy bodies thudded against the door, making the boards tremble.

In the bedroom Sarah cried out. This time Alma ignored her.

The onslaught became more intense. Alma checked the load on William Carstairs's rifle, then looked at her pistol. Five rounds left. Five rounds, five wolves . . .

The wolves were in a frenzy now—incited, perhaps, by the odor of sickness within the house. Alma remembered John's words: "They will not attack a human unless they sense sickness or weakness." There was plenty of both here.

One of the wolves leapt at the window. The thick glass creaked but did not shatter. There were more thumps at the door; its boards groaned.

Alma took her pistol in both hands, held it ready, moved toward the door.

In the bedroom Sarah cried out for William. Once again Alma ignored her.

The coil of fear that was so often in the pit of Alma's stomach wound taut. Strangely, it gave her strength. She trained the revolver's muzzle on the door, ready should it give.

The attack came from a different quarter: The window shattered, glass smashing on the floor. A gray head appeared, tried to wriggle through the narrow casement. Alma smelled its foul odor, saw its fangs. She fired once . . . twice.

The wolf dropped out of sight.

The assault on the door ceased. Cautiously Alma moved forward. When she looked out the window, she saw the wolf lying dead on the ground—and the others renewing their attack on the door.

Alma scrambled back as another shaggy gray head appeared in the window frame. She fired. The wolf dropped back, snarling.

It lunged once more. Her finger squeezed the trigger. The wolf fell.

One round left. Alma turned, meaning to fetch the rifle. But Sarah stood behind her.

The sick woman wavered on her feet. Her face was coated with sweat, her hair tangled. In her hands she held the ax that Alma had brought from the woodpile.

In the instant before Sarah raised it above her head, Alma saw her eyes. They were made wild by something more than fever: The woman was totally mad.

Disbelief made Alma slow. It was only as the blade began its descent that she was able to move aside.

The blade came down, whacked into the boards where she had stood.

Her sudden motion nearly put her on the floor. She stumbled, fought to steady herself.

From behind her came a scrambling sound. She whirled, saw a wolf wriggling halfway through the window casement.

Sarah was struggling to lift the ax.

Alma pivoted and put her last bullet into the wolf's head.

Sarah had raised the ax. Alma dropped the revolver and rushed at her. She slammed into the young woman's shoulder, sent her spinning toward the stove. The ax crashed to the floor.

As she fell against the hot metal Sarah screamed—a sound more terrifying than the howls of the wolves.

★

"My grandmother was made of stronger cloth than Sarah Carstairs," Mrs. Clark said. "The wolf attack did irreparable damage to poor Sarah's mind. She was never the same again."

★

Alma was never sure what had driven the two remaining wolves off—whether it was the death of the others or the terrible keening of the sick and injured woman in the sod house. She was never clear on how she managed to do what needed to be done for Sarah, nor how she got through the remainder of that terrible night. But in the morning when John arrived— so afraid for her safety that he had left Margaret at home and braved the drifted snow alone—Sarah was bandaged and put to bed. The fever had broken, and they were able to transport her to their own home after securing the battered house against the elements.

If John sensed that something more terrible than a wolf attack had transpired during those dark hours, he never spoke of it. Certainly he knew Sarah was in grave trouble, though, because she never said a word throughout her entire convalescence, save to give her thanks when William returned—summoned by them from the East—and took her home. Within the month the Carstairs had deserted their claim and left Kansas, to return to their native state of Vermont. There, Alma hoped, the young woman would somehow find peace.

As for herself, fear still curled in the pit of her stomach as she waited for John on those nights when he was away. But no longer was she shamed by the feeling. The fear, she knew now, was a friend—something that had stood her in good stead once, would be there should she again need it. And now, when she crossed the prairie, she did so with courage, for she and the life-saving fear were one.

★

Her story done, Mrs. Clark smiled at the historian. "As I've said, my dear," she concluded, "the women of the Kansas frontier were uncommon in their valor. They faced dangers we can barely imagine today. And they were fearless, one and all."

Her eyes moved away to the window, and to the housing tracts and shoddy commercial enterprises beyond it. "I can't help wondering how women like Alma Heusser would feel about the way the prairie looks today," she added. "I should think they would hate it, and yet . . ."

The historian had been about to shut off her tape recorder,

but now she paused for a final comment. "And yet?" she prompted.

"And yet I think that somehow my grandmother would have understood that our world isn't as bad as it appears on the surface. Alma Heusser has always struck me as a woman who knew that things aren't always as they seem."

John Jakes

THE WOMAN AT APACHE WELLS

> *John Jakes, like many of his contemporaries,*
> *started out in the pulps—or what remained of them,*
> *anyway. Jakes started selling stories in the early fif-*
> *ties, just as the pulps were breathing their last.*
>
> *Jakes went on to become one of the best-selling writ-*
> *ers in American history, his books inspiring several*
> *first-class TV miniseries.*
>
> *But much of his early pulp work—science fiction,*
> *heroic fantasy, crime, and Westerns—holds up very*
> *well today. too. And here's a perfect example.*

Tracy rode down from the rimrock with the seed of the plan already in mind. It was four days since they had blown up the safe in the bank at Wagon Bow and ridden off with almost fifty thousand dollars in Pawker's brown leather satchel. They had split up, taking three different directions, with Jacknife, the most trustworthy of the lot, carrying the satchel. Now, after four days of riding and sleeping out, Tracy saw no reason why he should split the money with the other two men.

His horse moved slowly along the valley floor beneath the sheet of blue sky. Rags of clouds scudded before the wind, disappearing past the craggy tops of the mountains to the west. Beyond those mountains lay California. Fifty thousand dollars in California would go a long way toward setting a man up for the rest of his life.

Tracy was a big man, with heavy capable hands and peaceful blue eyes looking out at the world from under a shock of sandy hair. He was by nature a man of the earth, and if the war hadn't come along, culminating in a frantic breakup at Petersburg, he knew he would still be working the rich Georgia soil. But his farm, like many others, had been put to the torch by Sherman, and the old way of life had been wiped out. The restless postwar tide had caught him and pushed him westward to a meeting with Pawker and Jacknife, also ex-Confederates, and the robbery of the bank filled with Yankee money.

Tracy approached the huddle of rundown wooden buildings. The valley was deserted now that the stage had been rerouted, and the Apache Wells Station was slowly sagging into ruin. Tracy pushed his hat down over his eyes, shielding his face from the sun.

Jacknife stood in the door of the main building, hand close to his holster. The old man's eyes were poor, and when he finally recognized Tracy, he let out a loud whoop and ran toward him. Tracy kicked his mount and clattered to a stop before the long ramshackle building. He climbed down, grinning. He didn't want Jacknife to become suspicious.

"By jingoes," Jacknife crowed, "it sure as hell is good to see you, boy. This's been four days of pure murder, with all that cash just waitin' for us." He scratched his incredibly tangled beard, unmindful of the dirt on his face or the stink on his clothes.

Tracy looked toward the open door. The interior of the building was in shadows. "Pawker here yet?" he asked.

"Nope. He's due in by sundown, though. Least, that's what he said."

"You got the money?" Tracy spoke sharply.

"Sure, boy, I got it." Jacknife laughed. "Don't get so worried. It's inside, safe as can be."

Tracy thought about shoving a gun into Jacknife's ribs and taking off with the bag right away. But he rejected the idea. He didn't have any grudge against the oldster. It was Pawker he disliked, with his boyish yellow beard and somehow nasty smile. He wanted the satisfaction of taking the money away from Pawker himself. He would wait.

Then Tracy noticed Jacknife's face was clouded with anxiety. He stared hard at the old man. "What's the trouble? You look like you got kicked in the teeth by a Yankee."

"Almost," Jacknife admitted. "We're right smack in the middle of a sitcheation which just ain't healthy. A woman rode in here this morning."

Tracy nearly fell over. "A woman! What the hell you trying to pull?"

"Nothin', Tracy. She said she's Pawker's woman and he told her to meet him here. You know what a killer he is with the ladies."

"Of all the damn fool things," Tracy growled. "With cash to split up and every lawman around here just itching to catch us, Pawker's got to bring a woman along. Where is she?"

"Right inside," Jacknife repeated, jerking a thumb at the doorway.

"I got to see this."

He strode through the door into the cool shadowy interior. The only light in the room came from a window in the west wall. The mountains and the broken panes made a double line of ragged teeth against the cloud-dotted sky.

She sat on top of an old wooden table, whittling a piece of wood. Her clothes were rough, denim pants and a work shirt. Her body, Tracy could see, was womanly all over, and her lips were full. The eyes that looked up at him were large and gray, filled with a strange light that seemed, at succeeding moments, girlishly innocent and fiercely hungry for excitement. Just Pawker's type, he decided. A fast word, and they came tagging along. The baby-faced Confederate angered him more than ever.

"I hear you joined the party," Tracy said, a bit nastily.

"That's right." She didn't flinch from his stare. The knife hovered over the whittled stick. "My name's Lola."

"Tracy's mine. That doesn't change the fact that I don't like a woman hanging around on a deal like this."

"Pawker told me to come," she said defiantly. From her accent he could tell she was a Yankee.

"Pawker tells a lot of them to come. I been riding with him for a couple of months. That's long enough to see how he operates. Only a few of them are sucker enough to fall."

Her face wore a puzzled expression for a minute, as if she were not quite certain she believed what she said next. "He told me we were going to California with the money he stole from the bank."

"That's right," Tracy said. "Did he tell you there were two more of us?"

"No."

Tracy laughed, seating himself on a bench. "I thought so." Inwardly he felt even more justified at taking the money for himself. Pawker was probably planning to do the same thing. He wouldn't be expecting Tracy to try it.

"If I were you, miss, I'd ride back to where I came from and forget about Pawker. I worked with him at Wagon Bow, but I don't like him. He's a thief and a killer."

Her eyes flared with contempt. She cut a slice from the stick. "You're a fine one to talk, Mister Tracy. You were there, too. You just said so. I suppose you've never robbed anybody in your life before."

"No, I haven't."

"Or killed anybody?"

"No. I didn't do any shooting at Wagon Bow. Pawker killed the teller. Jacknife outside didn't use his gun either. Pawker likes to use his gun. You ought to know that. Anybody can tell what kind of a man he is after about ten minutes."

Lola threw down the knife and the stick and stormed to the window. "I don't see what call you've got to be so righteous. You took the money, just like Pawker."

"Pawker's done it before. I figured this was payment for my farm in Georgia. Your soldiers burned me out. I figured I could collect this way and get a new start in California."

She turned suddenly, staring. "You were in the war?"

"I was. But that's not important. The important thing is for you to get home to your people before Pawker gets here. Believe me, he isn't worth it."

"I haven't got any people," she said. Her eyes suddenly closed a bit. "And I don't have a nice clean town to go back to. They don't want me back there. I had a baby, about a month ago. It died when it was born. The baby's father never came home from the war—" She looked away for a moment. "Anyway— Pawker came into the restaurant where I was working and offered to take me West."

"Somebody in the town ought to be willing to help you."

Lola shook her head, staring at the blue morning sky. Jacknife's whistle sounded busily from the broken-down corral. "No," she said. "The baby's father and I were never married."

Tracy walked over to her and stood behind her, looking down at her hair. He suddenly felt very sorry for this girl, for the life lying behind her. He had never felt particularly attached to any woman, except perhaps Elaine, dead and burned now, a victim of Sherman's bummers back in Georgia. He could justify the Wagon Bow robbery to himself. Not completely, but enough. But he coudn't justify Pawker or Pawker's love of killing or the taking of the girl.

"Look, Lola," he said. "You don't know me very well, but I'm willing to make you an offer. If you help me get the money, I'll take you with me. It'd be better than going with Pawker."

She didn't answer him immediately. "How do I know you're not just like him?"

"You don't. You'll have to trust me."

She studied him a minute. Then she said, "All right."

She stood very close to Tracy, her face uplifted, her breasts pushing out against the cloth of her shirt. A kind of resigned expectancy lay on her face. Tracy took her shoulders in his hands, pulled her to him, and kissed her cheek lightly. When she moved away, the expectancy had changed to amazement.

"You don't need to think that's any part of the bargain," he said.

She looked into his eyes. "Thanks."

Tracy walked back to the table and sat down on the edge. He couldn't understand her, or know her motives, and yet he felt a respect for her and for the clear, steady expression of her eyes. Something in them almost made him ashamed of his part in the Wagon Bow holdup.

Jacknife stuck his head in the door, his watery eyes excited. A big glob of tobacco distended one cheek. "Hey, Tracy. Pawker's coming in."

Tracy headed outside without looking at Lola. A big roan stallion with Pawker bobbing in the saddle was pounding toward the buildings over the valley floor from the north, sending a cloud of tan dust into the sky. Tracy climbed the rail fence at a spot where it wasn't collapsing and from there watched Pawker ride into the yard.

Pawker climbed down. He was a slender man, but his chest was large and muscled under the torn Union cavalry coat. He wore two pistols, butts forward, and cartridge belts across his shirtfront under the coat. Large silver Spanish spurs jingled loudly when he moved. His flat-crowned black hat was tilted at a rakish angle over his boyish blond-whiskered face. Tracy had always disliked the effect Pawker tried to create, the effect of the careless guerrilla still fighting the war, the romantic desperado laughing and crinkling his childish blue eyes when his guns exploded. Right now, the careless guerrilla was drunk.

He swayed in the middle of the yard, blinking. He tilted his head back to look at the sun, then groaned. He peered around the yard. His hand moved aimlessly. "Hello, ol' Jacknife, hello, ol' Tracy. Damned four days, too damned long."

"You better sober up," Jacknife said, worried. "I want to split the money and light out of here."

"Nobody comes to Apache Wells anymore," Pawker said. "Tracy, fetch the bottles out o' my saddlebags."

"I don't want a drink," Tracy said. Lola stood in the doorway now, watching, but Pawker did not see her. If he had, he would have seen the disillusionment taking root. Tracy smiled a little. Grabbing the money would be a pleasure.

"Listen, Pawker," Jacknife said, approaching him, "let's divvy the cash and forget the drink—"

Suddenly Pawker snarled and pushed the old man. Jacknife stumbled backward and fell in the dust. Pawker spat incoherent words and his right arm flashed across his body. The pistol came out and exploded loudly in the bright air. A whiff of smoke went swirling away across the old wooden roofs.

Jacknife screamed and clutched his hip. Tracy jumped off the fence and came on Pawker from behind, ripping the gun out of his hand and tossing it away. He spun Pawker around and hit him on the chin. The blond man skidded in the dust and scrabbled onto his knees, some of the drunkenness gone. Glaring, he slid his left hand across his body and down.

Tracy pointed his gun straight at Pawker's belly. "I'd like you to do that," he said. "Go ahead and draw."

Cunning edged across the other man's face. His hand moved half an inch farther and he smiled. Then he giggled. "I'm going to throw my gun away, Tracy boy. I don't want trouble. Can I throw my gun away and show you I'm a peaceable man?"

Tracy took three fast steps forward and pulled the gun from its holster before Pawker could seize it. Then he turned his head and said, "Lola, find the satchel and get horses."

Pawker screamed the girl's name unbelievingly, turning on his belly in the dust to stare at her. He began to curse, shaking his fist at her, until Tracy planted a hand on his shoulder, pulled him to his feet, and jammed him against the wall of the building with the gun pressing his ribs.

"Now listen," Tracy said. "I'm taking the satchel and I don't want a big muss."

"Stole my money, stole my woman," Pawker mumbled. "I'll get you, Tracy, I'll hunt you up and kill you slow. I'll make you pay, by God." His eyes rolled crazily, drunkenly.

Jacknife was trying to hobble to his feet. "Tracy," he wheezed, "Tracy, help me."

"I'm taking the money," Tracy said.

"That's all right, that's fine, I don't care," Jacknife breathed. "Put me on my horse and slap it good. I just want to get away from him. He's a crazy man."

Tracy shoved Pawker to the ground again and waved his gun at him. "You stay right there. I've got my eye on you." Pawker snarled something else but he didn't move. Tracy helped Jacknife onto his horse. The old man bent forward and lay across the animal's neck.

"So long, Tracy. Hit him good. I want to get away—"

"You need a doctor," Tracy said.

"I can head for some town," Jacknife breathed. "Come on, hit him!"

Tracy slapped the horse's flank and watched him go galloping out of the station yard and across the valley floor. Lola came around the corner of the building leading two horses. The satchel was tied over one of the saddlebags.

Tracy turned his head for an instant and when he turned back again, Pawker was scrabbling in the dust toward his gun which lay on the far side of the yard. Tracy fired a shot. It kicked up a spurt of dust a foot in front of Pawker's face. He jerked back, rolling over on his side and screaming, "I swear to God, Tracy, I'll come after you."

Lola was already in the saddle. The horses moved skittishly. Tracy swung up and said, "Let's get out of here." He dug in his heels and the horses bolted. They headed west across the floor of the valley.

They rode in silence. Tracy looked back once, to see Pawker staggering away from the building with his gun, firing at them over the widening distance. Until they made camp in the early evening at a small grove, with the mountains still looming to the west, Tracy said almost nothing.

Finally, when the meal with its few necessary remarks was over, he said, "Pawker will follow us. We'll have to keep moving."

She answered absently, "I guess you're right." A frown creased her forehead.

"What's the trouble?" He was beginning to sense the growth of a new feeling for this woman beside him. She was as silent and able as the hardened men with whom he had ridden in the last few years. Yet she was different, too, and not merely because she was female.

"I don't know how to tell you this right, Tracy." She spoke slowly. The firelight made faint red gold webs in her hair and the night air stirred it. "But—well—I think you're an honest man. I think you're decent and that's what I need." She stuck her finger out for emphasis. "Mind you, I don't mean that I care anything about you, but I think I could."

Tracy smiled. The statement was businesslike, and it pleased him. He knew that there was the possibility of a relationship that might be good for a man to have.

"I understand," he said. "I sort of feel the same. There's a lot of territory in California. A man could make a good start."

She nodded. "A good start, that's important. I made a mistake, I guess. So did you. But now there's a chance for both of us to make up for that. I'm not asking you if you want to. I'm just telling you the chance is there, and I'd like to see if what I think of you is right."

"I've been thinking the same," he said.

They sat in silence the rest of the evening, but it was a silence filled with a good sense of companionship that Tracy had seldom known. For the first time in several years, he felt things might work out right after all. Right according to the way it had been before the war, not since.

The next morning, they doubled back.

It was a five-day ride to Wagon Bow. The job was carried off at around four in the morning. Tracy rode through the darkened main street at a breakneck gallop and flung the satchel of money on the plank walk in front of the bank. By the time the sun rose he and Lola were miles from Wagon Bow. The only troubling factor was Pawker, somewhere behind them.

He caught up with them when they were high in the mountains, heavily bundled, driving their horses through the lowering twilight while the snow fell from a gray sky. Actually, they were the ones who caught up with Pawker. They saw him lying behind a boulder where he had been waiting. A rime of ice covered his rifle and his yellow boy's beard. His mouth was open. He was frozen to death.

Tracy felt a great relief. Pawker had evidently followed them, knowing the route they would probably take, and circling ahead to wait in ambush. It would have fitted him, rearing up from behind the boulder with his mouth open in a laugh and his avenging rifle spitting at them in the snow.

They stood for a time in the piercing cold, staring down at the body. Then Tracy looked at Lola through the dim veil of snow between them. He smiled, not broadly, because he wasn't a man to smile at death, but with a smile of peace. Neither one spoke.

Tracy made the first overt gesture. He put his thickly clad arm around her and held her for a minute, their cold raw cheeks touching. Then they returned to the horses.

Two days later, they rode down out of the mountains on the trail that led to California.

Bill Pronzini

NOT A LICK OF SENSE

Bill Pronzini's series of "Nameless" detective novels is one of the major suspense series of our time, a Balzacian look at a man's life and times in that most cutting-edge of cities, San Francisco.

But Pronzini has written extensively in the Western field as well. His historical mysteries are exemplars of the form. He also can do character sketches that are virtually without peer, as we see here in this handsomely wrought tale.

We come down out of the high country some past sunup, Lige driving the wagon too dang fast. Winter had played hob with the track; still had snow on it, too, deep in places. Every time a wheel jounced into a chuckhole or rut, the big old pineboard outhouse tied onto the bed swayed and creaked and groaned.

I kept hollering at him to slow down. Didn't do no good. When he latches onto some notion, he's like a mule with its teeth in a bale of hay. He don't have a lick of sense, Lige don't. I'm the Hovey born with all the sense; he's the one born with all the stubborn.

"Quit your bellerin'," he said once. "That outhouse ain't gonna bust loose and go flyin'. She's roped in tight."

"That ain't what's worryin' me."

"Won't shake apart, not as solid as we built her."

"Ain't that, neither, and you know it."

"All the more reason to get this here business over with quick. I still ain't sure we ought to be doin' it."

"After all the work we done? Lige, sometimes you're a pure fool."

"Wes," he said, "sometimes you're another."

I breathed some easier when we come to the junction with the county road. Off east was Antelope Valley and the Piegan Indian reservation. Little Creek was four mile to the west, and I had me a wish it was where we was headed right now. After four months up in the high country, we was near out of supplies. And I could scarce recall my last visit to Miss Sally's sporting house behind the Red Rock Saloon.

Lige turned us east. Wasn't near so cold down on the flats, though I could still see the frost of my breath and Lige's and our roan horse Jingalee's. No drifts of snow left on the ground, neither, like up to our place. You could smell things growing again, and about time, too. It'd sure been a long, hard winter.

County road wasn't near as bad off as the mountain track and Lige commenced to push Jingalee even harder. I hollered at him but he didn't pay me no mind. Not a lick of sense, by grab. That poor horse was showing lather already and we still had us a distance left to travel—

"Oh, Lordy Lord!" Lige said, sudden. "Wes, look yonder."

I looked. Man on horseback had just come trotting around a bend ahead. He was all bundled up in a sheepskin greatcoat and a neck muffler, his hat pulled down low, but I knowed him and that steeldust of his right off. So did Lige. Morgan Conagher, sheriff of Little Creek.

"What in tarnation's *he* doin' out here this early?" I said.

"Gonna ask us the same thing." Lige hauled back on the reins some and then give me one of his hot looks, all smoke and sparks. "You and your ideas," he said.

"Ain't nothing wrong with my ideas. You just let me do the talkin', hear?"

He muttered something and slowed us to a rocking stop as Conagher rode up alongside. He was a big 'un, Morgan was, and a holy terror with fists and six-gun, both. Smart, too, for a lawman. Unless a man was plain simple, he walked and talked soft when his path crossed Morgan Conagher's.

"Morning, boys," he said. "Cold as a gambler's eyeball, ain't it?"

"For a fact. Warmer than up to our place, though."

"Long time since I seen you two. Snowed in most of the winter?"

"Since the first week of December. How come you two be out riding this early, Mr. Conagher?"

"Spent the night at Hank Staggs' place in the valley. Little trouble out there yesterday."

"Serious?"

"Not so's you'd notice. Hank figured he had a gripe against a couple of Piegan braves. Turned out to be the other way around." Conagher took his corncob pipe outen a coat pocket and commenced to chewing on the stem. Pipe bowl was black, but I'd never seen him smoke the thing. Gnawing the stem seemed to satisfy him the same as tobacco. "Now that's a curious sight," he said.

"What is?"

"Thing you got tied in your wagon there. Looks like an outhouse."

"Well, that's what she is, all right."

"Can't mistake that half-moon cut in the door."

"No, sir, sure can't."

"Takin' it out for an airing, are you?"

Lige, who don't have no more humor in him than he does sense, just set there. But I laughed before I said, "Be a couple of jugheads if that's what we was doing, wouldn't we, sheriff? No, the fact is—"

"Fact is," Lige said before I could get anything else out, "we're takin' her over to Charley Hammond's place."

"That so?" Conagher said. "What for?"

Damn Lige for a fool! I give him a sidewise glance and a sharp kick with the toe of my boot, both by way of telling him to put a hitch on his fat lip, but he went right on blabbering.

"She don't set the ground right," he said, "and she's got chinks and warped boards. Wind comes whistlin' through them chinks on a cold night, it like to freeze you where you sit."

"Uh-huh."

"Well, Charley's the best carpenter in the county," Lige said. "So we figured to take her over and let him fix her up."

"Seems like a lot of work for you boys. Been easier to've had Charley bring his tools up to your ranch."

"Sure it would. But he's gettin' on in years and we're askin' a favor, so we come to the notion of bringin' her down to the valley instead."

Conagher nodded and chewed his pipestem, and I begin to have the hope he'd ride on and leave us be. But then he said, "How come you closed off the bottom end?"

"Sheriff?"

"Bottom end there. Closed it off with canvas, didn't you? Canvas over boards, I'd say."

"Well, now," Lige said, and then he just set there, the big jughead, on account of he couldn't think of no good answer.

"Tell you how it looks to me," Conagher said. "Looks like you boys built yourself a big packing case out of your outhouse. Now why would you go and do a thing like that?"

"Sheriff," I said, "it ain't no use tryin' to fool you. Lige and me done closed off that bottom end, right enough, but it wasn't to make a packing case. No, sir. It was something else entire we made outen that outhouse."

"Such as?"

"A coffin. We built us a coffin."

"Coffin?" Conagher frowned and chewed his pipestem and then he said, "Who for?"

"Old Bryce. Our hired man."

"Mean to tell me you got *him* inside there?"

"His poor froze-stiff remains, yes, sir. He up and died two nights ago. Had him the ague and it turned into new-monia and he up and died on us. Man weighed three hundred pounds, if he weighed an ounce—you know how big he was, sheriff. So there we was with a three-hundred-pound, six-foot-and-three-inch-high corpse and no way to give him a proper Christian burial."

"How come no way? Ground still froze at your place?"

"Froze hard as stone," I said. "That's one reason we couldn't plant old Bryce. Other one is, we didn't have no wood left to build a coffin. No lumber a-tall. Winter was so long and cold, we run out of stove wood and had to burn up the last of our lumber to keep warm."

"I thought you boys always took pains to provision yourselves against long winters. Got a reputation for laying in plenty of food, plenty of wood."

"That's just what we do, usual, Mr. Conagher. But this winter we got caught short. Had us a lean year, last, and the first blizzard took us unawares and next thing we knowed, we was snowed in. Why, we was just about ready to chop up that there outhouse and burn *it*. Would have if the weather hadn't finally broke. And then old Bryce up and died on us."

"Uh-huh."

"Big and tall as he was, why, he fits inside there just about snug. Couldn't of hammered up a better coffin from scratch—"

"Where you fixing to bury him?"

"Sheriff?"

"Old Bryce in his outhouse coffin. Where you intend to put him down for his final resting place? Town cemetery's in the other direction."

"Yes, sir, that's right, so it is."

"Well?"

Lige had that hot look in his eyes again; he kicked me down low on the shin where Conagher couldn't see. But I wasn't about to just set there like him. I said, "Potter's fishing hole."

"Bury a dead man in a fishing hole?"

"No, sir, not *in* Potter's hole. Near it. That was old Bryce's favorite spot in all of Montana. He spent every free chance he had down at Potter's fishing hole, and that's a fact."

"Uh-huh."

"Well, right before he croaked on us, he said as how he'd like to be buried down by Potter's fishing hole. Didn't he, Lige?"

Lige had enough sense to nod his head. Scowl on his ugly face said he was of a mind to gnaw my innards the way Conagher was gnawing his pipestem.

"Can't deny a man his dying wish," I said. "So me and Lige, we pulled the outhouse down and put old Bryce into her and closed off her bottom and now we're headed down to Potter's to find a shady spot to plant 'em both."

"How you figure on doing the planting?"

"Sheriff?"

"I don't see any tools in that wagonbed."

"Tools?"

"No pick, no shovel. Not even a hoe. Was you boys thinking of digging old Bryce's grave with your bare hands?"

"Lordy Lord," Lige said, disgusted, and spat out onto the road. Done it too close to Jingalee; roan horse hopped forward a couple of steps before Lige hauled him down again. When that happened, the outhouse lurched and swayed some—same as my insides was doing right then.

"Well?"

"Well, now, Mr. Conagher, sir—"

"Time you untied those ropes," he said.

"Sheriff?"

"You and your brother. Untie the ropes and we'll have a squint inside the outhouse."

"Ain't nothing to see except old Bryce's froze-stiff corpse—"

"Untie, boys. Now."

Wasn't nothing else we could do. Conagher was wearing his official holy terror look now and his hand was setting on the butt of his Judge Colt. Lige kicked me again, twice, while we was taking off the ropes; I just let him do it.

"Open up that half-moon door, Wes."

I opened it and Conagher poked around inside. A smile come to his mouth like a hungry wolf with supper waiting. "Well, well," he said. "Sure don't appear to be old Bryce's remains to me. What's all this look like to you, Lige?"

Lige didn't have nothing to say.

"Wes?"

"Well," I said, "I reckon it's jugs."

"Fifty or more, I'd say. Packed inside there nice and tight, with burlap sacking all around. What's in those glass jugs, Wes?"

I sighed. "Corn likker."

"Uh-huh. Corn likker you boys cooked up over the long winter, using up all your stove wood and spare lumber in the process. You and Lige and old Bryce, who's alive and kicking and tending to his chores this very minute. That about the shape of it?"

"Yes, sir. That's about the shape of it."

"And where were you taking all this corn likker? Wouldn't be over to the reservation to sell to some of the feistier Piegans, would it? Even though it's against the law to sell firewater to Indians?"

"No, sir," I said, "that sure wasn't what we had in mind. We was gonna sell it to the ranchers in Antelope Valley. Charley Hammond and Hank Staggs—"

"Charley Hammond don't drink. He's a Hard Shell Baptist, in case you don't remember. And Hang Staggs don't allow likker of any kind on his property. And Mort Sutherland's got a bad stomach. You figure to sell more'n fifty jugs of corn to Harvey Ames alone? Don't seem likely. Lot more likely you were headed for the reservation, and I reckon the circuit judge'll see it the same when he comes through next week. Meantime, boys, you'll be guests of the county. Close up the evidence and let's get on to town."

We closed her up. Lige said to Conagher, "You knowed, didn't you, sheriff? Knowed we wasn't taking her to Charley Hammond's, knowed we didn't have old Bryce's remains inside. Knowed all along she was filled up with jugs of corn."

"Well, I had a pretty fair notion."

"How?"

"Funny thing about that outhouse," Conagher said. "When you first rattled to a stop, and again when your horse frog-hopped, I heard noises inside. Good ears is one thing I can brag on, even in cold weather."

"What noises?"

"Sloshing and gurgling. Never yet heard an empty outhouse that sloshed and gurgled. Nor a man's froze-stiff remains that did, either."

Lige punched me in the chest this time. "You and your gol-dang ideas! You ain't got a lick of sense, Wes Hovey! Ain't got the sense God gave a one-eyed grasshopper!"

Well, hell, he didn't neither, did he?

Jon L. Breen

THE TARNISHED STAR

*This one of two stories in this collection with con-
temporary settings.*

*Jon Breen's reputation as a first-rate critic of the
suspense field has somewhat dimmed his luster as a
first-rate writer of suspense fiction.*

*You'll find here all the qualities that make his fic-
tion so vital and singular—fresh subject matter,
straightforward but resonant prose, and a passionate
take on the hypocrisy of human beings. This is an
excellent tale that should be nominated for a Spur
next year.*

The marshal stood in the dusty street, looked around at the
timid townspeople who had finally, after the shooting was
safely over, surged out of the buildings. He could have said
something to them. He could have said plenty. But that wasn't
his way. Instead, he removed the star from his chest, dropped
the star into the dirt, and climbed onto the buckboard that
would carry him and his new wife out of Hadleyville for the
second time that day. Tex Ritter's voice was heard reprising
the plaintive theme song: "Do not forsake me, oh, my
darling. . . ."

The lights came up in Plantain Point's state-of-the-art movie
theater. Most of us weren't of the generation or in the industry
that applauds movies, but I could tell from the murmurs that
High Noon hadn't lost any of its power in the forty-four years
since it was first released.

My name is Sebastian Grady, a relatively content resident
of one of the best retirement communities around. I'd come to

the screening with Charlie Fordyce, a retired lawyer who loves nothing better than to rile me up. My usual date for these screenings, Melanie August, can't abide Westerns, even great ones. As we pried our old bodies out of our seats, I thought Charlie looked troubled.

"What's wrong?" I said.

"Oh, nothing, I guess, Seb. I suppose it's just our age. The memory goes."

"Speak for yourself," I said as we made our way (I won't say tottered) up the aisle. "My memory's not going anyplace, and I turned ninety-six—"

"On New Year's Day, yeah, I know." When we got out to the lobby of the facility—the gift of a hot young writer-producer-director hyphenate whose grandfather was one of the residents—Charlie didn't join the senior-citizen rush to the refreshment tables, so I knew something must really be bothering him. We sat down in a couple of chairs considerately provided in the lobby for short-range walkers and Charlie continued, "You're ninety-six, but I'm barely eighty, and *my* memory. . . . Seb, there weren't different versions of this movie, were there?"

"There was a science fiction flick with Sean Connery that was mighty similar. *Outland,* I think it was called."

"No, no, I mean another version with Gary Cooper and Grace Kelly."

"It depends on what you mean by another version. There are always different working versions of a movie, ones they show preview audiences to test their reactions. There was one prerelease cut of *High Noon* where Tex Ritter came in with the song every time there was a break in the dialogue. About the fourth time, the preview audience started laughing, so—"

Charlie waved his hand impatiently. "It's nothing to do with Tex Ritter. It's that last scene. I distinctly remember Cooper not just dropping the badge but grinding it into the dust with the heal of his boot."

"Never happened," I told him.

"It *did!*"

"Nope. What you remember is how John Wayne always described that scene. He didn't like the picture much."

"Hmm!" Charlie said, not quite convinced but not disputing the matter, like it was a trial judge's ruling he might win on appeal. "I know that's supposed to be a great movie, Seb—I mean, it *is* a great movie, the photography and the acting and the music and the technical stuff and all that, but what's always bothered me about it is, I don't think it's true to history. It's not true to the memory of the kind of people who built the West. Those folks wouldn't have turned their backs on the marshal when trouble came. Seb, what the hell are you grinning about?"

"The Duke said that, too. Thought the picture was un-American."

"Well then, damn it, the Duke was right."

"Have you ever seen this picture before, Charlie, or did you just read an interview about it with John Wayne?"

Not to be diverted, Charlie went on with his jury summation. "The kind of men who won the West wouldn't have hid behind their lace curtains and their womenfolk and their trumped-up excuses at the first sign of trouble. They would have got their gun belts on and helped the marshal round up Frank Miller and his men. Are they going to turn coward like that all of a sudden, men with the kind of courage to settle the frontier, to deal with untamed deserts and Indians and wild animals and who-knows-what-the-hell else to bring civilization to a wild land?"

"Maybe they were just ready to enjoy some of that civilization they'd brought," I said.

Charlie shook his head. "Years later, maybe. Now, for sure. But that close to the time of frontier self-reliance? No way, Seb."

I wasn't sure whether I agreed with Charlie or not. I'd always found the townspeople who wouldn't help the marshal painfully believable. But anyway, I knew something Charlie didn't seem to: *High Noon* wasn't about the Old West at all. It *was* about years later—to be exact, Hollywood as it was in the early 1950s.

Seeing the picture again and having that conversation with Charlie set me to thinking back, specifically to the night of the Academy Awards for the best movies of 1952—what that usually means, you realize, is the best American movies in major release that aren't too arty and whose makers are popular (or at least not outcasts) in the industry. One of the Oscars that year presented not a whodunit so much as a who'd-do-it, but the answer just created more questions.

The date was March 19, 1953—that I had to look up; my memory's not that good—and it was raining in L.A. I'd actually attended my share of Oscar ceremonies over the years, and I would again, but that year I wasn't there in person and wasn't really sorry. You see, it was the first year they showed the Awards on television.

I was married to Greta at that time, and since TV had started coming on in a big way about five years before, we'd had one of the mellowest periods of our marriage, the numbing effects of the little box, I guess. When she found out the Awards would be televised, she had the bright idea we'd play host to an Oscar night party.

In exchange for inviting a few of my movie pals who were also insufficient fry to be on the scene at the RKO Pantages that night, I allowed to darken my modest suburban door Greta's brother Claud, who'd bought one of the first sets that came out after the war and had kept as close to the tube as an asthmatic to his oxygen ever since. Claud had been so warped by television, he seemed almost disappointed when Greta served us real food at a dining room table instead of one of those awful frozen TV dinners on metal trays in the hour and a half before we sat down to watch the show.

The other guests were what I thought would be a congenial lot. Vic Stemmerman was a scrawny, balding, intense sort of guy, a writer of B-grade oaters who'd been trying for years to peddle his own epic Western—we hadn't quite started calling them adult Westerns in those days. Vic's wife, Astrid, was an attractive if hard-edged fortyish blonde a few years older than he was. She worked as a film editor, one of the few important off-screen roles that, for one reason or another, women were considered capable of filling. Gabe Hanlon was an actor I'd known for years, whose big, muscular frame didn't quite fit with a chronic nervous state that had only got worse in the shaky political climate of fifties Hollywood—picture Arnold Schwarzenegger with a Woody Allen personality. Gabe's one-and-only, Stella Boyle, was a compact brunette, absolutely beautiful and not exactly dumb, who worked in what is now called continuity and whose blatantly sexist title in those days was "script girl." None of the kids were home that night—I can't remember why—so that was the group that sat down to an early dinner, anticipating the program's beginning at seven-thirty. Five guests may be an awkward number socially, but it was perfect for a little contest Greta would unveil with dessert.

My brother-in-law, of course, was the odd man out. While

the rest of us washed down our steaks and baked potatoes with martinis or scotch or California wine—we were pouring Petri, the brand that used to bring Sherlock Holmes on the radio— Claud stuck to his favorite tipple, a cheap beer called Brew 102. Claud was also the one without a partner—his wife, Minnie, understandably often took vacations from him—and the only one not connected to the movie industry. He appeared alternately fascinated and mystified by the shop talk flying around the dinner table, which at the moment was running to horror stories.

Stella: "So I told him, that's not the dress she was wearing in the previous scene, and he went after me like it was my fault. You know how he gets. Now John Ford's supposed to be some kind of ogre, but when the same thing happened on *The Quiet Man* over in Ireland, I hear he handled it very differently."

Vic: "I'm working on my tenth Jimmy Lariat Western without a break, and I'm getting stir-crazy. I used to work with a partner, Mack Redmond, but he wanted to move on and now I'm on my own, talking to myself down in the writers' ghetto. Scripting those things didn't really need two of us, I have to admit—we used to say he'd write every other bang. Now a Jimmy Lariat flick is a poverty row job all the actors and even the horses could do in their sleep, and it's starting to drive me nuts, so I tell the head man, let's show a little originality for a change. Just once, I tell him, let's have the girl's rancher father in league with the bankers and really *wanting* them to foreclose on him, see, because then he has an excuse to leave town with the loot from the payroll robbery he really planned with the owlhoot gang. So the guy across the desk says, 'Jimmy has to know who to shoot.' That's all he says for a minute, and we look at each other. Then he says, 'If Jimmy can't figure the plot out, how can the kids at the Saturday matinee?' Mack, wherever you are, you'd've loved it."

Astrid: "This damn director has it in his contract he gets to look over my shoulder while I'm cutting. The *last* person you want in the cutting room is the goddam director, especially that guy. When he looks over my shoulder, I don't think he's looking at the Moviola, if you know what I mean. So what's the result? Same picture. It just takes twice as long to cut and I get a sore fanny."

Gabe: "Who can remember what meeting you went to? Hell,

I could have gone to some pool party in 1944, and it could have
been a Communist cell meeting, and how would I know? They
weren't going to tell you. And maybe I went to a benefit during
the war for Soviet relief, and then it's supporting our allies
in the war and now it's associating with a Communist front
organization. What's a guy like me supposed to do?"

As you can see, Gabe was talking a different kind of shop
from the other guests, but his was a common topic of conversation those days, at least if you thought you could trust the
people you were with. Gabe wasn't the marquee star he wanted
to be but he was working regularly and hadn't been called
before any congressional committee. Still, he was living in fear.
That's what it was like in Hollywood of the late forties and
early fifties.

Silence followed Gabe's little outburst. The women all looked
sympathetic. Vic, who was unblacklisted but solidly left of center in his sentiments, muttered, "Don't get me started," poured
himself another glass of wine, and shut his trap firmly. Claud
was the one to break the discomfort, or maybe redirect it.

"So which picture's going to win tonight?" he asked brightly.

"Which one did you like, Claud?" Astrid asked him with a
bright smile, welcoming the change of subject.

"I haven't seen any of them," Claud said, and Astrid's smile
faded fast. Claud waded right in and made it worse. "You know
what? I don't think I've seen a movie in a theater in four or
five years."

"Ever since you got the TV, Claud?" I said.

"What a coincidence. I think you're right. Why don't you folks
work in the TV industry? That's where things are really
happening."

"Then why did the TV industry pay so much money to put
this awards show on, Claud?" I asked. The guy got under my
skin, and since he was family (sort of), I could show my irrita-
tion in a way my other guests could not. For years, Claud had
been prying all the inside industry dope out of me that he
could and then chiding me for being a name-dropper. After I
split with Greta, I never saw or talked to the guy again.

"Isn't anybody going to answer Claud's question?" Greta
asked, hostess polite but with a slight edge to her voice. She
didn't want her brother and me to get into it in front of outsid-
ers. She didn't have to worry, though. She always seemed to
think of me as what we'd now call a "loose cannon," but I would

have controlled myself in deference to our guests. "Which picture is going to win?"

"Some of the best pictures weren't even nominated," said Vic. "I thought *The Bad and the Beautiful* was pretty good, and *Singin' in the Rain* was terrific."

"Movies about movies never win," Astrid pronounced. "But what about *The Member of the Wedding*?"

"Too classy," her husband pronounced. "I don't know where they got some of the nominees. *Moulin Rouge* is good, though."

"And *The Quiet Man*," Stella chimed in.

"If I were going to go see just one 1952 picture," said Claud, "what would it be?"

"*High Noon*," said Gabe quietly. And suddenly there was agreement.

"A great picture," said Vic. "Proves something about Westerns, that they can really make a point and not just be fodder for the kiddies. If the studios see that, it might help me get *mine* off the ground."

"It won't win," I said. "Too political."

"The movies-about-Hollywood rule is against *High Noon*," Astrid said. "Just like those others."

"But it's a Western," said Stella, and three of my other guests looked at her patronizingly.

"There is an *editor's* movie," said Astrid, obviously trying again to direct the conversation away from politics. "Elmo Williams should win for editing if nothing else."

"I beg your pardon," said Gabe. "That is an *actor's* tour de force. The movie belongs to Gary Cooper. He was never better in his life."

Astrid nudged her husband kiddingly. "Well, come on, Papa, there aren't any producers or directors present, so isn't that your cue to say a piece for the poor ignored writer?"

Vic wasn't amused. He filled his glass again, peered at each of our faces in turn, and said, "You know what happened there, don't you?"

Astrid apparently realized she had headed him down a path she didn't want to travel, so she introduced another diversion, "Is Coop in town?"

"Nope," said Stella, who apparently kept track of such things. "He's in Mexico, shooting a picture."

"So if he wins, who accepts for him?"

"Carl Foreman," Vic suggested ironically.

"Also out of town, I understand," said Gabe, and a knowing look passed between the two of them.

"I'm betting the producer collects for Cooper," Astrid said. "Stanley Kramer."

Brother-in-law Claud, who had been sipping his Brew 102 and staying pretty quiet through all this, piped up, "I don't think so. That's not good TV." The other guests turned and looked at him like he'd just popped in from Mars. "It has to be an actor, another big star."

"Tex Ritter," said Vic.

"Hoot Gibson," I said.

"Jimmy Lariat," Gabe suggested. At least twitting my brother-in-law had got them off politics for the moment. But Vic wouldn't let it alone.

"You know where Carl Foreman, the writer of *High Noon,* is now?" Vic almost snarled. "He's trying to find a job in England. He's been blacklisted, can't work in his own country."

"Is he a Communist?" Claud asked.

"That's really not the point," Gabe said with strained politeness. "He may have been at one time, but so were a lot of people."

Greta didn't like the way the discussion was turning. This was supposed to be a party, not a debate. She threw me a these-are-your-friends kind of glare, and I did my best to throw back a that's-your-reactionary-brother-in-law.

"Hey," I said, "isn't it time for the chocolate Oscars?"

"So it is," Greta said. She disappeared into the kitchen and a moment later returned with a plate of five Oscar shapes wrapped in foil. She invited each guest to take one.

"I couldn't eat another thing," said Stella, "but I'll save it for later."

"No," Greta said, "you have to open it now."

"Aren't you and Seb having anything?" Astrid asked.

"No," I said, "this is just for our guests, to determine who wins the grand prize of the evening. So you don't have to eat it, but you do have to take the foil off."

The five of them complied and soon got the point. Between the foil and the chocolate was a slip of white paper, call it a Hollywood fortune cookie, that had the name of one of the five best picture nominees on it.

"Am I stuck with *Quo Vadis?*" Stella said. "Can't I trade for *The Quiet Man?*"

"If the person who drew it wants to trade," Greta said.

Claud held up his slip. "Sure. I'll trade with you."

"Sucker play, Claud," Gabe said. "*Quo Vadis* hasn't got a chance. Now I've got the winner, *High Noon.*" He looked to the Stemmermans.

"*Moulin Rouge,*" said Astrid with a shrug.

"Aw, I can't believe it," said Vic. "I might as well go home right now. *The Greatest Show on Earth.* Cecil B. DeMille. The last gasp of a dinosaur. So what's the prize I have no chance of winning?"

"You'll see," said Greta, "after they announce the winner."

It seemed for a moment that Greta had successfully diverted our little gathering back into the party it was meant to be. But her brother Claud promptly undid all her good work.

"Why is it always the writers that get blacklisted?" he asked with bland innocence.

"It's not!" said Vic, a little abruptly. "Of course, the Hollywood Ten got a lot of publicity, but it's actors and directors, all kinds of people in the industry. I guess the witch-hunters figure the writers have more of a chance to insert their views into a picture, so naturally they're on the front line, but it's not just writers." He filled his wineglass again. "Writing movies is a shitty profession anyway. I sometimes wish I could just turn my back on it, like Mack did, work on a novel, do some real writing."

"So Carl Foreman was lucky?" Astrid said.

"Hell, no, he wasn't lucky. He got in his last shot before he left, though."

"What do you mean?" Claud asked.

"He was called to Washington, D.C., by the House Un-American Activities Committee while they were filming *High Noon.* When they asked him if he'd ever been a Communist, he pled the Fifth Amendment, which meant he was guaranteed to be blacklisted by the industry—but not just yet. The movie wasn't finished. There was money on the line. So Foreman had a chance to sneak in some new scenes that heavily underlined just how much this little western town was like Hollywood. Kramer the producer and Zinnemann the director knew what he was doing and went along with it. He wrote a scene in the church, where the marshal asks for help and some of the parishioners talk a good fight but in the end nobody will face the outlaws with him. That's how Foreman felt himself when he went to his Hollywood friends. Some high-flown words, but in the end, no support. He wrote a scene where one guy who offers help to the marshal backs out when he finds out it will be the two of them alone against the outlaws. Straight from life. Straight from chickenhearted Hollywood." Vic took a breath, looked around a little embarrassed, as if he was afraid he'd said too much. You never knew whom you were talking to.

"Almost seven-thirty," my wife sang out, much too brightly. "Shall we move into the front room?" A lot of drinking had been going on, but we were all steady enough to make it to the midcentury video shrine.

Nowadays people hide their TV sets, but in those days every living room had the tube as its centerpiece. Greta and I urged our guests onto the sofa and easy chairs, all arranged to give a good view of the screen, and brought out chairs from the kitchen for ourselves. Our set was a blond-wood Philco, a twenty-one-inch job, big for that time.

On came the show with a clip from *Wings,* the first Oscar winner back in 1927, followed by a shot of a modern jet and the voice of Ronald Reagan, no stranger to Hollywood politics, who had the thankless job of standing in the rain outside the Pantages and introducing the proceedings. The broadcast was a bicoastal affair, a technological wonder at the time, with the action moving back and forth between the Pantages and the NBC Century Theater in New York. The emcees were a couple of guys with long-standing Oscar-hosting credentials. Conrad Nagel, who had been one of thirty-six founder members of the Academy back in 1927, was in New York, and on our coast was Bob Hope, who hadn't kicked off an Oscar show with one of his monologues since 1946. His disappearance and reappearance represented a kind of politics, too. The film industry had seen television as a bitter enemy, and anybody who appeared in the medium, as Hope had, was seen as a traitor in some quarters. But now that the film industry was, in effect, using television to assist in promoting its product, Hope was again a viable choice.

The comic, of course, got some laughs out of the big- and small-screen rivalry. There was even a grin or two in my living room when he said. "Television—that's where movies go when they die. How about that Jack Warner, he still refers to television as that furniture that stares back."

Vic Stemmerman wasn't enjoying himself, though. Once his

blacklist frustrations had been uncorked, he couldn't seem to stop. During the commercials, and sometimes during the musical numbers, he added more to his Carl Foreman story. "So before he decides what to do, Foreman has a meeting with the president of the Motion Picture Alliance for the Preservation of American Ideals, the Hollywood Red-baiter's club, better known in enlightened circles as the Hedda Hopper Gang. And who, pray tell, is at the head of this estimable organization? None other than John 'Duke' Wayne himself. You know, the guy who won us World War II."

"Vic, not so loud," Astrid said.

He lowered his voice to a harsh whisper, so if you really wanted to hear the show you could, but most of us were transfixed by Vic. "He didn't meet with Wayne to plead his own case. He wanted the Alliance to get off the back of a press agent who was a friend of his. For associating with Carl Foreman, the Alliance was going after the agent's clients. But Wayne, generous and kindhearted fellow that he is, said Foreman could save his Hollywood career. All he had to do was admit he was wrong, name a few names to show his sincerity, and he'd be back to work in no time. Foreman said no, and Wayne told him he was through in the picture business. Not even his plan of fleeing to Europe could save him—the State Department would pull his passport."

"Didn't happen, did it?" I said.

"Even the great Duke isn't that powerful. But he and his pals ran Foreman out of the country. And you should hear our great war hero on the subject of *High Noon*—most subversive Communist flick since *Song of Russia*. Written in the Kremlin."

Meanwhile, our ladies were doing what you're supposed to do when you watch an Oscar show, guessing the winners and commenting on the gowns. Gabe joined them—apparently the conversation's political bent had gotten too strong for his nervous system. Charles Schnee, who wrote *The Bad and the Beautiful,* snatched the screenplay award from Foreman and another blacklisted writer, Michael Wilson, but music and editing awards went to *High Noon,* encouraging our cheering guests that their favorite might go all the way. But John Ford won the directing award for *The Quiet Man,* and Stella Boyle gave a squeal of delight not appreciated by the *High Noon* partisans, especially when Duke Wayne came up to accept for the absent director.

"The Academy loves Ford," Vic said. "There's still a good chance at best picture."

"Westerns never win," said Astrid darkly.

"*Cimarron,* 1931," said the oldest person in the room (me, even then).

"Okay, now name another. Four directing Oscars now for John Ford and not *one* a Western."

"Best actor will tell us a lot," Gabe said. "If Coop wins that, best picture will follow."

"I hope you're right, because Cooper's gonna win," Vic said. "But who picks it up for him? It has to be somebody who's big enough to stand the political heat."

"Nobody's that big," Gabe muttered.

"What political heat?" Stella asked, sounding exasperated. "Nobody thinks Gary Cooper's a Communist, do they?"

"No," I said, "but Coop was the one big star to support Foreman—till Warners told him they'd invoke the 'morals clause' in his contract if he kept it up."

"Yeah," said Vic. "So he was the guy in the movie who was going to fight the baddies with the marshal until he found out everybody else was staying home."

I was getting a little annoyed with Vic's black-and-white view of things. "He might have gone to the wall, but Foreman couldn't ask it of him."

"Real heroes don't do heroic things because they're asked," Vic pontificated. "They do them because of who they are."

"You oughta give that line to Jimmy Lariat," Astrid said, "if he could remember that many words in a row. Or maybe that kind of dialogue was more Mack Redmond's line."

Vic threw his wife a poisonous look. This was proving a shaky night for the Stemmerman marriage. For the first time, it registered on me that Astrid was matching Vic drink for drink and they had both become more visibly intoxicated than the rest of us.

Then as now, the usual practice was for the previous year's best actress to present the best actor award, and vice versa, but Vivian Leigh was indisposed—we later found out she had suffered a sudden mental breakdown—and it was the old trouper Janet Gaynor who handled the chore of reading the nominees and announcing the winner. My living room was silent, all our eyes intent on the oblong box, a portrait of midcentury American social life. I think all of us were pulling for Gary

Cooper, whatever we thought about whether he had or hadn't supported Carl Foreman. It had been a great acting job, and any honor for *High Noon* made a kind of statement.

She announced the winner. Yup, it was Gary Cooper, for *High Noon*. The only question now: Who would come up to the mike and accept the award?

"I don't believe it," said Gabe. "What—what does it mean?"

"How can he have the nerve—?" Vic exploded.

"Shut up, Vic," said Astrid. "Let's hear what he has to say."

Holding Gary Cooper's Oscar, John Wayne faced the Pantages crowd and (thanks to the dreaded TV) the biggest Oscar audience in history. In that unmistakable, often-imitated delivery, he said, "I'm glad to see they're giving this to a man who has conducted himself throughout his years in this business in a manner that we can all be proud of him. And now, I'm going to go back and find my business manager, agent, producer, and three name writers—"

"Try looking in England, Duke, where you sent a pretty good one," Vic muttered, and Astrid promptly shushed him.

"—and find out why I didn't get *High Noon* instead of Cooper. Since I can't fire any of these very expensive fellas, I can at least run my 1930 Chevrolet into one of their big black new Cadillacs."

My living room fell silent until the next commercial. Then Vic said, "What a hypocrite."

Stella said, "He's just being a good sport." She must have loved him in *The Quiet Man*.

"He's big enough to admit he's wrong," Astrid offered.

"He's a loyal industry guy, showing his best face to an audience of millions," I opined, and I still think it's the best explanation.

"He's just honoring another right-wing Red-baiter," Gabe said, "wherever the script might have come from. Coo's a member of the Alliance, too, you know."

"What a hypocrite," Vic repeated.

"Who wants coffee?" my apolitical wife wailed.

Best actress was anticlimactic. We barely registered that Broadway star Shirley Booth won for *Come Back, Little Sheba* and stumbled on her way up to the podium in New York. But we still had our little best picture lottery going. With its commendable sense of history, the Academy had asked Mary Pickford to present the award. We all leaned toward the tube as she opened the envelope. Gabe was nervously humming "Do not forsake me, oh, my darling," maybe unaware he was doing it.

The winner was *The Greatest Show on Earth,* produced and directed by Cecil B. DeMille, a major financial success but (in my pretty well-informed opinion) the poorest movie ever to win top honors.

"Looks like you're the big winner, darling," Astrid said to her husband, not pleasantly.

Vic gaped at the screen. "I can't believe they could—aw, hell, what's my prize, anyway?"

"How about thirty pieces of silver?" Astrid said.

Vic stared at his wife. "What the hell are you talking about?"

"You know what I'm talking about."

Suddenly it was if the rest of us weren't even in the room. "Don't get on that subject, Astrid."

"Don't get on it? I've been trying to stay the hell off it all evening, but not you. It's blacklist this, blacklist that. It seems to me you'd keep off that subject without my having to keep nudging you."

"Mack wanted to get out of pictures, Astrid. He wanted to work on his short stories and his novels and his plays. He told me so plenty of times. And he'd already been named to the committee by three other people before I—"

Vic stopped himself, as if realizing he and Astrid weren't alone in the room. He looked around at each of us, looked down at the carpet.

Our other guests took the hint about the coffee—Claud even laid off his Brew 102—but Vic helped himself to another drink. Astrid accepted a ride home from Gabe and Stella, so we wound up giving Vic a bed for the night, a necessity to which Greta's reaction was anything but mellow. I don't think we ever gave Vic his prize for drawing the chocolate Oscar with the best picture winner. And, though I'm proud of my memory, I'm damned if I remember what the real prize was.

The last thing the Poverty Row oatersmith mumbled as I tucked him into the guest room bed was, "Jimmy's gotta know who to shoot." Even fortysome years later, it's hard to look back at that time and know who to shoot, but I'll add one interesting fact: Carl Foreman sort of liked John Wayne, even when the Duke was running him out of the country. I guess that's what you call star quality.

*

Author's note: The following sources were helpful in research for this story: Anthony Holden, *Behind the Oscar* (Simon & Schuster, 1993); Donald Shepherd and Robert Slatzer, *Duke: The Life and Times of John Wayne* (Doubleday, 1985); and Mason Wiley and Damien Bona, *Inside Oscar* (Ballantine, 1986).

James M. Reasoner

HACENDADO

In a full-time writing career that has spanned a couple of decades, James M. Reasoner has written well in virtually every category of commercial fiction.

His novel Texas Wind *is a true cult classic and his gritty crime stories about contemporary Texas are in the first rank of today's suspense fiction.*

Fortunately for the Western reader, James's Westerns are just as good as his crime work.

Here is a perfect example.

Cobb reached the border about noon. He reined in his horse on the slight rise overlooking the Rio Grande and thought about the problem facing him. The Ranger badge pinned to his shirt didn't mean a damn thing across the river. All it was good for was a target.

But he had been chasing Frank Shearman for nearly a week. He didn't much feel like letting the outlaw go now, just because Shearman had crossed the river.

Cobb heeled his horse into motion again. He rode down the slope and sent the animal splashing through the shallow, slow-moving stream.

Here along the river, Mexico was just as flat and dusty as Texas was. Gray and blue peaks rose in the distance, though, a rugged-looking range with deep shadows along its base. Shearman's tracks headed straight for the mountains.

Cobb was a big man, barrel-chested, with a week's growth of dark stubble on his face. He gnawed on some jerky and a stale biscuit as he followed the trail. The sun was hot, riding high in the sky overhead. The glare stabbed at Cobb's eyes.

He almost didn't see the men who rode out of a dry wash and started shooting at him.

Cobb swallowed the last bit of biscuit and grabbed for his gun. A bullet sang close by his ear as he palmed out the Colt and lined it on one of the two men charging toward him on horseback. Cobb triggered off a couple of shots, saw the vaquero rock back in his saddle and then pitch to the side. The other man kept coming, blasting away.

Cobb's horse was spooked by the gunfire. It tried to rear, but Cobb's strong arm on the reins hauled it back down. He aimed carefully, trying to ignore the whine of lead around him, and fired a third time.

The attacker was close now, only twenty yards away. Cobb heard his cry of pain as the bullet caught him in the shoulder. The gun in the man's hand flew out of his fingers. He sagged but managed to stay in the saddle.

Cobb holstered his pistol and slid the Winchester out of the saddle boot. Levering a round into the chamber, he lined the rifle on the man and called out, "Just hold it, fella! Sit still!"

The man's horse had slowed to a halt. Cobb walked his mount forward slowly, keeping the man covered. As he studied the man, Cobb saw that he wore the big battered sombrero and rough range clothes of a working vaquero, just like his sprawled companion. Neither man was particularly good with a gun. They had loosed plenty of rounds in his direction without hitting anything but air.

Reining in a few feet away, Cobb said to the man, "You speak English?"

"*Sí.*"

"Why the hell'd you start shootin' at me like that? It was right unfriendly."

The man glowered at him as he clutched his bloody shoulder. He was swaying slightly in the saddle, and his face was pale under its dark tan. "You are on the range of Don Luis Melendez, señor. Our orders are to shoot all who trespass on Don Luis's land."

"Damned unfriendly, all right," Cobb snorted.

The man's eyes rolled up in his head, and he fell from his horse, landing heavily on the ground. Dust billowed up around his crumpled form.

Cobb spat and said, "Hell." Cautiously he dismounted and rolled the man over with a booted foot. The vaquero was still breathing, but he was out cold. Cobb left him there and strode over to the second man. This one was still alive, too. The side of his shirt was bright red where the Ranger's bullet had torn through his body, but the wound was fairly shallow.

Cobb straightened from checking on the man and shook his head. Regardless of the fact that they had tried to kill him, he couldn't just leave them out here to die. He thought both of them might pull through if he could get them back to the hacienda of that Melendez fella they rode for.

The Mexicans' horses were nearby, watching him nervously. Cobb started trying to round them up. Damned if he was going to carry the wounded men on his back.

Cobb wondered how much of a lead Frank Shearman was going to have before this day was over.

*

Cobb had no idea where the ranch was located, so once he had the two unconscious men tied onto their horses, he kept following Shearman's tracks. Might as well, he thought. He couldn't ask the vaqueros for directions.

The land became more rolling as he approached the foothills. There was more vegetation here. Pastures of lush grass told him this was good cattle country.

In the middle of the afternoon Cobb rode up a ridge and topped it to see a cluster of adobe buildings in the small valley below. There was a large structure in the center with white-washed walls and a red tile roof. The outbuildings were plainer, more functional. Even at this distance Cobb could see the ornate wrought-iron gate that led onto the house's patio.

He had a feeling he had found the hacienda of Don Luis Melendez.

Someone on the place must have seen him coming, because several men hurried into a corral and threw saddles on horses. Cobb started down the slope, leading the horses bearing the two wounded men. He drew his rifle as the men from the ranch mounted up and rode hurriedly to meet him.

Cobb pulled his mount to a stop and lifted the Winchester as the men approached. Raising his voice, he called, "Howdy! Got a couple of hurt men here!"

The riders were vaqueros like the ones who had attacked him. They came to a stop a few yards away, and the looks they gave Cobb were icy and hostile. One man was dressed a little better than the others, and he edged his horse forward a step or two. Cobb pegged him as the foreman of the ranch crew.

The man had a weathered face and a drooping mustache. He gestured at the wounded men and said, "What happened to them, señor?"

"They came ridin' out of a wash and tried to shoot me," Cobb answered bluntly. "Figured I'd better stop 'em as best I could."

He saw hands edging toward the butts of pistols. The Winchester's magazine was full. They'd probably take him down, but some of them were going with him.

The foreman made a curt gesture and rattled off a command in harsh Spanish. Cobb understood enough of it to know that he was telling the other men not to shoot.

"We will take them to the house," the foreman said. "Don Luis will wish to speak with you."

Cobb nodded. "That's fine with me."

He moved his horse aside and let a couple of the vaqueros come forward to take charge of the wounded men. His grip on the Winchester remained firm. The foreman said solemnly, "It is not polite to ride up to another man's house with a weapon drawn, señor."

Cobb nodded toward the wounded men. "One of them told me their orders were to shoot strangers on sight. That ain't too polite, neither."

"You have my word of honor that no one will molest you, señor."

Cobb considered, then slowly slipped the rifle back in the boot. It was still close to hand, and so was his Colt.

He rode toward the hacienda, the foreman falling in beside him. The other men rode behind them. Cobb felt his back crawling, but he wasn't sure it was from being followed by angry Mexicans.

There was something strange about the hacienda itself.

As Cobb studied it, he saw that it looked like any other good-sized ranch headquarters on this side of the border. But one of the peaks behind it was casting a shadow over the house. The rest of the buildings were all still in the sun.

A trick of the light and the time of day, Cobb decided.

As the group of riders approached the wrought-iron gate, it swung open and a tall man strode out. He wore fine whipcord pants, a loose linen shirt, and tall black boots. The beard he sported was dark and neatly trimmed.

The hair on his head was white.

It was a striking combination, Cobb thought. The man was in his forties, still handsome and vital. But the gaze he turned toward the newcomer was quick and nervous. As Cobb and the foreman came to a stop in front of him, he asked sharply, "Who are you? What do you want with us?"

"Name's Cobb," the Ranger answered. "I'm a lawman trackin' an outlaw."

"You are a Texan." Don Luis sounded bitter.

The foreman spoke up. "He shot Pedro and Estaban, Don Luis."

"They started shootin' at me first," Cobb pointed out. "I was just defendin' myself."

"You had no right to be on my land," Melendez said. "You have no right to be on this side of the river."

Cobb nodded slowly. "Reckon you may be right. But I didn't come to cause you trouble, mister. I'm sorry about your men. If you want me off your land, I'll be glad to get on about my business."

Don Luis raised a hand and passed it over his face. His fingers shook slightly, Cobb noticed. The hacendado took a deep, ragged breath and said, "I apologize, Señor Cobb. You are right, of course. I should not have ordered my men to keep strangers away." He raised his head and met Cobb's level gaze. "Please, señor, accept my hospitality. I would like for you to remain here tonight."

Cobb shook his head. "I've got to be ridin'." He glanced around. The wounded men had been taken to the back of the house, no doubt to be carried in through a rear entrance. But the foreman and several of the vaqueros were still sitting on their horses behind him.

"I insist, señor," Don Luis said smoothly. "If you do not accept, I shall know that you are offended by my offer. I would not like that."

The foreman barked an order, and guns came out this time. Cobb heard the ominous sound of hammers being eared back. He looked back at Melendez. The man was smiling, but his eyes were as cold and hard as the mountain peaks in the distance.

"Looks like you got a guest, Don Luis," Cobb said curtly.

"Two," the hacendado replied. The smile remained on his face as he went on, "Another gringo rode in earlier today.

Somehow he had avoided my men. His name, he said, is Shearman."

★

Frank Shearman almost dropped his glass of wine as Don Luis Melendez strode into the big living room of the hacienda, followed by Cobb. The outlaw's eyes fastened on the silver star on silver circle pinned to Cobb's shirt. His hand moved toward his gun.

Melendez shook his head. "No gunplay, gentlemen," he said sharply. The foreman and a couple of vaqueros crowded into the room behind Cobb. "This is my home."

Shearman forced himself to relax with a visible effort and sank back against the cushions of the big chair in which he sat. After a moment a smile curved his thin lips. "Of course, Don Luis," he said. "I apologize for the rashness of my actions. Who's your new guest?"

"This is Señor Cobb," Don Luis replied. "I believe he comes from Texas, like you, Señor Shearman."

"Howdy, Frank," Cobb said, letting a grin play over his wide mouth.

"We know each other?" Shearman asked.

"Nope. But I've seen your picture on plenty of reward dodgers. I got to San Angelo a couple of days after you held up the bank there."

Melendez looked shrewdly at Cobb. "I see that your reason for crossing the border is Señor Shearman here."

"That's right. And if you'll allow me, Don Luis, I'll take him off your hands."

The hacendado shook his head. "As I told you, Señor Shearman is also my guest. I could not permit such a breach of hospitality as to permit you to arrest him."

Shearman's grin became cocky as he took in the situation. "That's right, Cobb," he said mockingly. "Where's your manners?"

"Left 'em back there with that deputy you gunned down in San Angelo," Cobb growled, the smile dropping off his face. Turning to Melendez, he said, "This man's a wanted outlaw, Don Luis. I'd appreciate your cooperation."

Don Luis shook his head. "I will hear no more about this matter, gentlemen. There will be no talk of business until after we have dined."

Movement in the corner of the room caught Cobb's eye. He looked over to see a small man gliding out of a doorway. The man was slender, past middle age, with a thin mustache and a few strands of hair plastered over his bald head. At first glance he was unimpressive in his servant's clothes, but something in the way he stared at Cobb made the Ranger frown. The man was so thin that his head resembled a skull as he bowed in Don Luis's direction.

"You wish a meal prepared for your guests, Don Luis?" he asked in a rasping voice.

"Yes, please, Jorge. And a glass of wine for Señor Cobb."

The servant poured the wine from a jug and brought it to Cobb. His fingers touched Cobb's as he handed over the glass, and the Texan was struck by how cold the man's hand was. He still didn't like the smile on the man's face, either.

Cobb kept an eye on Shearman as he sipped the wine. The outlaw might decide to take a chance on offending Don Luis if he thought he could get away with gunning down Cobb. Don Luis seemed to be staying between the two men, though—whether accidentally or by design, Cobb couldn't say.

As he glanced around the room Cobb saw that it was well appointed. There was a thick rug under his feet, and an equally elaborate tapestry hung on one wall. The furniture was low and heavy, built to last.

The sound of footsteps made Cobb turn his head. Two women came into the room through an arched doorway. Cobb's fingers tightened on the glass he held. He had already decided to play along with Don Luis, bide his time, and wait for a chance to grab Shearman. The presence of women was just an added obstacle to his plans. He didn't want any female getting in the way of a stray bullet.

He had to admit that these two dressed up a room, though. They were both slender, of medium height, and their lovely features showed a strong resemblance to each other. Mother and daughter, Cobb decided, the younger one in the full bloom of her youth, the older still a damned handsome woman. Melendez smiled broadly as they entered.

"Ah, gentlemen, allow me to introduce the two most precious jewels in my possession. My wife, Pilar, and my daughter, Inez."

Cobb just nodded to them and said, "Ma'am," letting the single word do for both of them. Shearman, on the other hand, stood up quickly, a broad smile on his face.

"Ladies," he said, reaching out to take Doña Pilar's hand. He bent over and kissed it, murmuring, "I'm charmed to meet you, madam, and your lovely daughter as well."

Cobb's mouth twitched. There was nobody smoother with the ladies than a damned outlaw.

He frowned as he looked closer at them. Both of the women were pale, their features drawn. It was probably a hard life for a female, out here in this isolated hacienda, but despite their attractiveness, Pilar and Inez looked like they were under some sort of strain.

Don Luis introduced Cobb and Shearman to his wife and daughter. Inez briefly said hello to Shearman, then moved over in front of Cobb. "Good evening, Señor Cobb," she said softly.

Cobb felt like a big awkward bear standing next to this pretty slip of a girl. He muttered something, and then Don Luis moved in and rescued him. "I'm sure Jorge has dinner ready," he said. "Shall we go into the dining room?"

It seemed to Cobb like there hadn't been much time to fix a meal, but the little majordomo called Jorge had probably already had dinner under way. It was late afternoon now, and as they went into the dining room Cobb could see the purple light of dusk through the big windows.

The long hardwood table shone, and it was piled high with food. Cobb hadn't seen such a spread since the last time he had gone to church. There had been dinner on the grounds after the preaching. The food there had been plentiful and good, but it wasn't served on such finery as was displayed here.

Don Luis took his place at the head of the table, with Pilar to his right and Inez to his left. Shearman managed to sit next to Pilar. Inez indicated with her dark eyes that Cobb should take the seat next to her.

Cobb settled into the high-backed chair, feeling like an old longhorn bull in a fancy parlor. He was more at home eating cold beans on the trail than sitting down to a meal like this. But there seemed to be nothing else he could do. That foreman and several of the vaqueros were just outside. Any ruckus would bring them running.

Jorge hovered near the table as the Melendez family and their two guests ate. The servant's hands were clasped in front of him, and the smile never left his face.

Cobb didn't like him, not a damn bit. Something about Jorge reminded him of diamondback rattlers he had seen lazing in the sun.

The sky outside darkened rapidly during the meal. Cobb had to admit that the food was good. Tender *cabrito,* warm tortillas, a crisp salad, plenty of beans, and more than enough wine. Every time his glass was empty, Jorge scurried forward to fill it. It was a good thing he was used to drinking good old Texas whiskey, Cobb thought. The wine didn't pack much of a wallop compared to the who-hit-John he usually drank.

Shearman kept up a running conversation with Doña Pilar, and Cobb could see that the woman was taken with him. For his part, he ate in silence, despite Inez's efforts to draw him into conversation. He didn't want to be rude; he just wanted to be out of here and on the way back to Texas with a bank robber and killer as his prisoner.

When the meal was finished, Don Luis leaned back in his chair and smiled at his guests. He had been drinking heavily throughout dinner, and he seemed more at ease now. The wine had helped soothe whatever was gnawing at him. He said, "Now, gentlemen, that you have enjoyed my hospitality, I will beg your indulgence while you listen to a story."

"Don't know that I've got time for a story, Don Luis," Cobb rumbled. "You said we'd talk business when dinner was over. I got a prior claim on this smooth-talkin' feller over there." He nodded toward Shearman.

"Come on, Cobb," the handsome outlaw said. "Let's not ruin a lovely evening."

Doña Pilar spoke up. "I do not understand," she said. "There is some . . . trouble between you and this man, Señor Shearman?"

"He wants to take me back to Texas and see me hung," Shearman replied. "He's a Ranger."

Cobb put his palms on the table. "That's right. And I intend to do it."

"Señor Cobb!" Melendez said sharply. "I will not allow this. As I said, I insist you listen to my story."

Cobb took a deep breath. If Don Luis yelled, plenty of help would come boiling in here. "All right," he said. He'd wait a little while longer.

Melendez took out a thin black cigar and lit it, not offering one to his guests. He said, "Gentlemen, I have quite a successful rancho here. I have worked hard, and I have seen my efforts bear much fruit. And the most succulent fruits of my life are Pilar and Inez." He smiled at them, then went on. "So you can see why I was devastated when they died last spring."

The room was warm, but Cobb felt cold knives stab into his nerves. What the hell was Don Luis talking about? A glance across the table told him that Shearman was just as shocked and confused.

Melendez went on after a second's pause. "If it had not been for Jorge, I do not know what I would have done. I could not have survived without my two lovely flowers. So I summoned Jorge."

Cobb looked at the servant and saw the superior smirk on his face. Suddenly he wasn't sure who was the master and who was the servant in this house.

"Jorge is a *bruja*. A . . . witch, I suppose you would say. He restored my wife and daughter to life and agreed to stay here with us, to keep them alive and vital. All he required in return was a small amount of tribute—and an occasional sacrifice."

Shearman was pale. He licked his lips and said, "Sacrifice?"

Melendez nodded. "That is why I have ordered my men to drive off any strangers who venture onto my land. I will not inflict my misfortune on innocent travelers. Whenever Jorge requires a sacrifice, I pay one of the peasant families who live on my land to provide it. I pay handsomely, gentlemen." He waved a hand. "However, there are times when providence dictates otherwise. Such as now."

Shearman pushed his chair back and stood up. "I don't know what the devil you're talking about, Melendez, but I don't like it. I'm riding on."

Cobb laughed abruptly. He had listened to Don Luis's yarn, and he knew what the hacendado wanted. "Forget it, Shearman," he said harshly. "These folks are figurin' to let that fella kill us both." He jerked a thumb at the still smiling Jorge.

"But . . . but that's crazy!" Shearman protested.

Don Luis shook his head. "Only one of you will be turned over to Jorge. The two of you will fight, and the loser will remain. The victor will be allowed to leave this rancho in peace."

Cobb didn't believe him for a second. If he and Shearman went along with this nonsense, both of them would wind up dead. He was sure of that.

"Shearman," he said softly, "we got to get out of here together, Shearman. It's our only chance."

The outlaw looked around, eyes wild. His hand darted toward the gun on his hip.

Cobb surged up out of his chair. The women screamed as he

grabbed the table and lifted it. The muscles in his back and shoulders bulged as he heaved, upsetting the table with a huge crash. He whirled, grabbing for his gun.

Don Luis shouted in Spanish. The door of the dining room burst open, and the foreman and his men came running in with their guns up and ready. Shearman twisted toward them, an incoherent yell on his lips as he started triggering his pistol.

He jerked backward as bullets slammed into him. The vaqueros cut him down mercilessly.

Sacrifices could always be found.

Cobb didn't bother firing at the vaqueros. He lunged away from the wrecked table, one long arm lashing out toward Jorge. The little man tried to leap away, but Cobb was moving with a speed born of desperation. He caught Jorge's collar and yanked him off his feet.

Cobb jammed the barrel of his Colt against the man's head and yelled, "Hold it!"

Don Luis screamed a command, and the foreman and his men stopped firing. The hacendado's face was haggard as he pleaded, "No, Señor Cobb! If you harm Jorge, Pilar and Inez will die again! He is all that is keeping them here with me."

Cobb clamped an arm around Jorge's neck and growled, "That true, little man?"

Jorge stopped his feeble struggles. He gasped for breath and then hissed, "You will die, gringo! I have powers—"

Cobb pressed down harder with the barrel of his Colt. "I'm a superstitious man, mister," he said heavily. "I believe if somebody blows your brains out, you die. And I don't believe anybody can bring dead folks back to life." His lips drew back from his teeth in a grin. "You want to try your powers against ol' Colonel Sam's here?"

For a long moment following Cobb's challenge, no one in the room moved or spoke. The Ranger gave an instant's glance toward Shearman's sprawled body and grimaced. He wouldn't be taking the outlaw back to Texas to hang. Justice had been served in a different way.

Finally Jorge said, snarling, "I will destroy you—"

"Do it," Cobb shot back. His finger tightened on the trigger of the pistol. "Do it damn quick, mister, 'cause I'm about to ventilate that bald head of yours."

Jorge sagged in his grasp then, a sob welling up from him.

"Tell 'em the truth," Cobb ordered, sensing the man's defeat. "Those ladies didn't really die, did they?"

Jorge shook his head. "I . . . I know about the healing herbs. Doña Pilar and her daughter were very, very sick, but they were not dead. I . . . I did what I could for them."

"And when they got better, you decided to cash in. You had Don Luis under your thumb, and you didn't want to let him out. You came up with this sacrifice business to keep everybody scared of you." Cobb tightened his grip on the man's neck again. "And maybe you enjoyed it some, too."

Jorge nodded as best he could.

Cobb shoved him away and looked at Don Luis. An awful realization had dawned on the hacendado's face. He understood now what his own fear had made him do, how he had given in to a human monster's demands. The word would spread through the peasants, the source of Jorge's sacrifices.

And there would be retribution, Cobb was sure of that.

"I'm ridin' out," he said, "and I'm takin' Shearman's body with me."

Jorge had sunk to his knees and was crying. The women were weeping, too.

"No one will stop you, Señor Cobb," Melendez said softly. "Please. Go."

Cobb slung Shearman's body over his shoulder and went.

He rode hard, not looking back as he left the hacienda behind him. He figured he would see the flames and hear the screams—

And there was always trouble enough for a Ranger, back on the Texas side of the border.

John Harvey

THE SKINNING PLACE

John Harvey's police procedurals are perhaps the best bridge yet between literary fiction and popular storytelling. They speak in a fresh, contemporary, and sardonic voice about all of us. And to all of us.

Harvey began his writing career as a writer of genre Western novels, mostly of the "spaghetti" variety that prospered in the wake of Sergio Leone's screen vehicles with Clint Eastwood.

John Harvey is poet, social observer, and relentless storyteller. His book-length story here displays all his many gifts.

One

There were three of them, two close by the river, the other eighty yards upstream. Blackfeet. The trapper watched them from the southerly bank, his eyes gray and curious. It had been a long time since they had invaded his trapping grounds, set out to steal his haul. The pair in the water were young, neither one of them a warrior; they stepped with care, anxious lest they draw attention to their thieving. Most men—most whites—would not have got within reach of them without being heard. Likely seen. But Aram Batt was not like most men, not even most mountain men. He eyed the elkskin pouch that hung from the neck of one of the braves and admired the way the smooth fur tapered down to shiny black hooves, the intricate quillwork around the neck. The other brave was decorated with twin stripes of yellow paint across his forehead, one dark and the other light, the sun and the moon, especial gods of his tribe.

A loose, flapping ornament hung down his back, attached by a narrow strip of hide to the thick, greased tail of his hair. It was fashioned from crimson and yellow beads surrounded by several inches of moosehair that curved widely away. Both men wore hide skirts with a roundel of beads and quills below the neck, a cross at the center. One wore elkskin leggings with white and blue thunderbirds along the inside; the lean, muscular legs of the other were bare.

The water was cold for each of them.

Aram sucked the last of his chewing tobacco from between his few back teeth and swallowed it silently.

They had reached the first of his traps, set below the waterline and partly covered with weeds and twigs. He had not checked them himself for five days and had good hopes of them being heavy with beaver. A lot of work, a deal of discomfort. He was not about to lose everything to a couple of thievin' Blackfeet!

As the brave in leggings bent toward the trap, Aram set his rifle along the branch of the tree to his left side and slipped his butchering knife from its sheath. Eight inches of steel blade worn into a curve at its center, razor sharp from the whetstone hanging in its buckskin case from the back of his belt.

The brave finished clearing his cover from above the trap and spoke to his companion, pointing excitedly down.

Aram ghosted between the alders, his moccasins softer than down.

The first thing the Indian felt was an arm, thin and wiry, fast beneath his chin and bending his head sharply back, choking him. Next was the punch of the blade as it punctured the tautness of skin below the arch of his rib cage. His arms flailed in struggle and a gurgle escaped his mouth as Aram's knife point sought his heart. He stumbled back against his attacker and already the air that hissed from his lungs was becoming pink with blood. Aram pulled on the haft of the knife but the brave fell away from him, juddering the bone handle from his grasp.

The second brave had jumped back, startled, feeling for the weapon at his belt. He stepped into the thresh of water and lifted the blade clear as Aram closed on him fast. He saw the points of the white man's eyes and his fingers faltered; he had seen his enemy's weapon go down below the shifting surface of the water; he saw now the broad flash of a tomahawk blade

as it rose from the white man's side. His right arm struck out
and missed the man's arm by a finger's length. He saw the
upswing of the tomahawk and arched his head back, stepping
awkwardly away.

Something bit into his leg, hard and deep, and his belly froze
like the skin of a dead fish. For seconds he did not know what
it was that had attacked him but Aram knew the brave had
stepped onto one of his traps. For five days beavers had avoided
it but not the Indian's heel as it stamped upon the metal disk
and sprung the steel jaws tight shut against the bone of his
shin. Tight and holding fast.

Aram saw rather than heard the brave scream.

The tomahawk was too far into its swing for him to adjust.
Instead of the head, it bit deep into the top of the shoulder,
the force driving the blade edge inches into the bone.

Aram heard the horse's hoofs splashing hard along the bank
of the river and turned away. Three paces took him to the
alder, the long-barreled .60-caliber Hawken. He drew it clear
and dropped on to one knee. The Blackfoot was galloping fast,
his body low against his pony's neck, cheek nuzzling the coarse
hair of its mane. Aram shut his mind to the cries of the
wounded brave and sighted along the barrel.

Not until he was twenty-five yards off did the Indian thrust
his body up in the saddle, his arm lifting a war club over his
head.

Aram felt the smoothness of the metal against his calloused
finger and knew in his gut that the shot was good even as he
made it. The pony went careening past and the dead rider
struck the water with an almighty splash, a hole big enough
to have stopped a buffalo above his breastbone.

Aram slung the rifle over his left shoulder and waded back
into the stream. He clamped his left hand down against the
Blackfoot's shoulder and wrenched the tomahawk blade free.
For an instant the eyes of the adversaries met and held. Brown
and gray. Pain faded from the brave's mouth and everything
was suddenly silent save for the splashing of the water and
the noise of the pony disappearing upstream.

Aram broke the silence with a blow that split open the front
of the Indian's head like kindling.

Back on the bank, in the cover of the trees, he waited to see
if there were more of his enemies to come. When he was certain
there were not, he set foot once more in the freezing river,

eddying red. Four of his six traps were heavy with beaver and he cleared them quickly, working with the precision of use. The traps would have to be reset upstream, baited with beaver scent, and covered in green. He leaned for several minutes against the smooth trunk of a paper birch, the bronze of the young tree sappy against his fingers. He listened to the breathless song of a vireo somewhere to his right and waited until he caught a glimpse of its red eye bright against the white stripe beneath the blue-gray cap of its head.

He would have wished things different, would have wished that the Blackfeet had not been there, intent upon pilfering what was his.

He had lived long enough to understand that however far a man set himself from his fellow men, such wishes were little more than pipe dreams to be dragged away on the thrust of another's ambition or greed. Even need.

Aram fingered open the possibles sack that hung from his neck and broke off a plug of chewing tobacco, working it between his teeth as he stepped clear of the thicket of trees and toward the clearing where his mules were tethered and chomping at the long-stemmed switch grass. Turning his head, he blinked into the early fall sun and saw for a moment the eyes of the Blackfoot as they had met his, the two yellows smeared across his forehead, sun and moon that had both gone out.

Two

Wes Hart had been in the saddle the better part of a week and it felt like the whole damned summer. He dropped to the ground and arched his back, pressing both hands into the spare flesh at the rear of his hips. The insides of his legs, where the leather patches covered the wool of his pants, were raw with sweat. Dust veiled his lean face, clogging his pores. He pulled the flat-crowned tan hat from his head and slapped it against his legs, shaking dirt down onto the straw-strewn floor. All the damn way from the coast through the Sierra to Virginia City! A handful of silver pieces in his saddlebags and one eye over his shoulder most of the journey. Him and Fowler, they'd left a couple of gunslingers on a spidery walkway out over the ocean at Monterey and they hadn't left them for dead.

It could have been, like Fowler had said between shots of bourbon, one hell of a mistake.

Hart had nodded, felt in his bones the truth of what the detective had said, and still been glad he hadn't turned his gun and pulled the trigger. It had been a missing kid job and though they'd found him in the end, they'd waded through a lot of blood to get there. Hart was sick with killing to the back of his craw. Which meant they were back there somewhere, the tall gunman with a Smith & Wesson .45 filed down to a hair trigger holstered at his left hip and a patch of dead skin over his left cheek and the slender Mexican with the bones of a girl and skin like burnished olive. Oklahoma and Angel Montero. They'd been hired by a gambler called Luis Aragon to kill a man who'd insulted his woman. It had got in the way of what Hart and Fowler had been doing and neither man felt like stepping aside. Not then; not after going through so much.

So it was that Hart had sliced the middle finger of Montero's gun hand down to the bone and Fowler had placed a couple of slugs in Oklahoma, one taking out his left kneecap and the other bursting through the top of his shoulder.

Enough to stop the big man for a time, but not forever. Maybe it was enough to warn him off, keep the pair of them from any ideas of revenge. Maybe they'd be sensible and set it down to experience and start over. Maybe the sun would forget to rise up in the east at dawn.

Hart and Fowler had split up short of the Sierras and if the gunmen were following, there was no telling which trail they'd take. Wes Hart had kept looking back, looking and seeing nothing that suggested he was more than alone.

He shrugged: Could be that was the end of it, after all.

The livery owner came scuffing from the rear stalls and took the gray's bridle, leading her away, sweat glistening on her coat. Hart gritted his teeth together and arched his body backward a few more times before lifting his saddlebags and rifle from the floor and walking toward the arched doorway that led on to the street.

Another hour and Hart was wearing a clean wool shirt— patched and deeply creased, but clean—leather vest and pants and boots that had been brushed at least. He'd soaked the worst of the trail dust and the worst of his trail aches away in one of the tall tubs at the Chinaman's and scraped at his stubble in front of the cracked mirror in his room at the hotel. His Colt Peacemaker had been cleaned and oiled and was tied down to his right leg, the safety thong dipped over the curve of the hammer. The double-bladed Apache knife he always carried was in its sheath inside his right boot, the tip of the haft almost visible above the edge of leather.

His hat was angled slightly over his right eye and his stride was long and purposeful as he crossed the street and paced seventy yards of boardwalk to the office of Herb Mosley, sheriff.

"Jesus Almighty! Ain't we seen the last of you yet?"

It wasn't the sheriff who spoke, but his deputy, leaning back against the wall close by the side window and scratching at the overhang of his belly as he did so.

Hart stared at Rawlings and ignored what he had to say. Mosley swung his stiff leg off the edge of the desk and pushed himself to his feet. A couple of paces using his walnut stick and he was gripping Hart's hand, something approaching a welcoming grip on his lined face.

"Good to see you, Wes."

"You too, Herb."

"Shit!" hissed Rawlings between his teeth and shrugged his way across the room.

"Ain't it time you checked up by the livery, Lefty?" said the sheriff. "They're still bitchin' 'bout that grain loss from the other day."

Rawlings grabbed a double-barreled shotgun from a pair of pegs sunk into the wall, gave a glowering look at Hart, and slammed the door behind himself as he went out.

"Still got a lot of charm, ain't he?"

Mosley laughed agreement and hobbled toward the stove at the back of the room, pouring coffee into a couple of tin mugs and handing one over to Hart without asking.

"Like I said before, Lefty'll do till I can find someone better."

"I guess you know your own business, Herb."

"Knew enough to offer the job to you, didn't I?"

Hart grinned. "An' I knew enough to turn it down."

"Thanks," said Mosley. "Thanks a whole lot!"

He settled himself back in his chair, leg stretched out straight, not bothering to conceal the wince of pain that caught him as he sat down.

"Still troublin' you some, huh?"

"Some! The bitchin' thing like to eat through me if I'd give it half the chance."

"Yeah."

Hart watched as the sheriff pulled open one of the drawers

alongside his desk and took out a bottle of whisky, pouring a
stiff shot into his coffee and swilling it around. He held out
the bottle toward Hart, who shook his head no, and the lawman stoppered the bottle and set it away.

"Guess you rode back this way for your share of the reward,"
said Mosley after a while."

"Could've had somethin' to do with it."

Hart and Herb Mosley had ridden out after a bank robber
called Henry George Barlow and finally persuaded him to come
in quietly. Since Barlow was dead at the time he wasn't in any
position to argue—and you can't come any quieter than that.
There'd been a three-hundred-dollar reward for Barlow dead
or alive, along with a tenth of any money that was recovered.
Neither Hart nor the sheriff had found as much as a damned
cent.

"Got a hundred an' fifty dollars waitin' for you," said Mosley.
"Put it in the safe at the bank."

"Let's hope no one takes it into their heads to make a with-
drawal before we do."

Mosley shook his head. "Not in this town they won't. Not as
long as I'm sheriff."

Hart nodded. "Long as they ain't what's known as famous
last words."

Mosley swallowed down some more of the coffee. "Finish this
an' we can get right on over. First thing you can do with it is
buy me a drink. They got some new whisky at the hotel, all
the way from Scotland. Tastes like nothin' I ever knowed."

Hart set his empty mug down alongside the stove. "You ain't
never heard nothin' 'bout those others involved in the Ely robbery along of Barlow? What was their names? Thomas an' . . ."

"High-Hat Thomas an' Cherokee Dave Speedmore."

"That's them."

"Caught a rumor 'bout Speedmore a couple of weeks back.
Stage held up between here an' Salt Wells, up by Fallon. Five
or six men an' the driver reckoned he heard one of 'em called
Cherokee. Figured him for a breed sure enough, but whether
it was Speedmore or not, ain't no way of knowing."

"He got money on his head? If it was him."

Mosley nodded, pushing himself up from his chair. "Same as
Barlow. Three hundred dollars. You get Thomas along with
him, that's a lot of loose change rollin' 'round your pockets."

Hart thought about it all the way to the bank and he was

still thinking about it when he and the sheriff were leaning against the hotel bar savoring the taste of good Scotch whisky.

"Why don't you leave it be? Goin' up against some gang for that kind of money, maybe it ain't worth it."

Hart shrugged. "Six hundred dollars ain't to be sniffed at, Herb."

"You ain't wantin'.'"

"Not now maybe. That ain't to say come six months I won't be on the ass end of winter without more'n the price of a beer between me an' nothin'."

Mosley tapped the end of his stick against the boards. "Man chooses to live his life the way you do, he has to take that kind of risk."

"I know it."

"Now if you was to take Lefty's badge you'd get paid regular . . ."

"An' end up as fat and foul-tempered as he is."

Mosley sighed and sank the last of his glass. "I guess you think that comes from workin' for an old cripple like me?"

Hart snorted: "One thing I can't stand it's some old man feelin' sorry for hisself. Wallowin' in self-pity like a hog in its own mire."

The sheriff looked at Hart carefully, judging the tone of his voice.

"When we went up against Barlow," said Hart, "you didn't handle yourself so bad."

"Bad enough it needed you to pull me out from under that bastard's gun. Ride back in an' finish things off on your own."

Hart shrugged. "No more'n the way things broke."

"Like hell! If ever I wanted proof as to how much older an' slower I got, that day set it all out for me like a picture book."

"You're okay. Now stop griping and get another drink down you before I get tired of spending this reward money."

Hart called over the bartender and had both glasses filled. He was thinking that Mosley was right; thinking also that a slug in the wrong place would slow him down to the point where a deputy's badge would be the most he could hope for. Then he'd be tied down to one place and likely forced to stick it out until some bunch of businessmen decided he wasn't worth his pay and tossed him out of office and onto the street. That was one of the penalties you paid for being a regular lawmen and settling down, you let yourself be the tool of other folk. Them as paid for the food you ate and the bullets you slid

into the chambers of your gun. Hell, there had been a time
when he thought to settle down, make a place for himself and
a family, kids . . . but that had been a long time back and
likely he'd been a different man. Although she hadn't thought
so. She'd have recognized him all too easily now, standing in
some bar with whisky in his hand and a Colt strapped to his
leg, fixing to ride out after some outlaw or other for bounty.

The whisky warmed the back of his throat. One letter in close
on ten years all he'd had from her and that he'd torn to pieces
still in the envelope, no part of it read but the scrawled-out names
of different places as it had followed him across the frontier.

He was better off on his own. His boot slid off the rail and
hit the floor with a thump.

"You okay?" asked Mosley.

"Sure I'm okay."

The sheriff raised an eyebrow quizzically. "Had this look on
your face, like you was a long way off . . . long way off an'
hankerin' for somethin'."

"You bet I'm hankerin' for somethin'." Hart threw back the
glass and wiped the back of his hand across his mouth. "Your
turn to set 'em up. I'm just gettin' the taste of this fancy
Scotch whisky."

Herb Mosley shrugged and did as Hart said, without ever
believing for a moment the words he'd spoken. Whatever was
eatin' into him wasn't about to be relieved for long by anything
that came out of a bottle. He doubted if it would be helped by
chasing up to Wells and throwing lead at a bunch of desperadoes either. But it wasn't none of his business, nothin' for him
to start working off his mouth about. He set his glass down
firmly enough and called for two more drinks.

Three

Jacob Batt pushed the door closed behind him and eased his
body back against the rough wooden wall. His face was drawn
and the skin around his eyes puffed and swollen; the pupils of
the eyes themselves were small and dark, surrounded by a
maze of red veins. It had been thirty hours since he had slept
more than a few minutes together. The underside of his boot
scraped against the ground, pushed hard against the stem of
the creeping weed that spread heavily across the ground close
by the house. The stink of stale cabbage water rose up from

leaves and stem and made him suddenly nauseous. He looked
at the weed as if for the first time, running from the water
barrel at the far side of the door to the pigpen beyond the barn.
Gill-over-the-ground: ground ivy. He vaguely remembered his
father trying to kill it, poison it, dig it up, and rid the farm of
its roots.

The ivy was still there, luxuriant, and his father was upstairs, dying.

He had been dying for forty-eight hours. Jacob's mother, Rachel, had found him out beyond the second pasture, rolled onto
the hard ground like a log. Together with Jacob's younger
brothers and his sister, Rachel had carried and dragged him
into the house, somehow lifted his six-foot-three frame up the
stairs to the rickety platform that held their marriage bed.
Lying there, his face gray and creased like a rotting flour sack,
she had been certain that he was already dead.

But the pulse still flickered against her fingers, against the side
of her face when she pressed it against his. His mouth opened and
the curved end of his tongue emerged like a snake from a dark hole;
the only sound was that of a man strangling slowly.

Rachel had sent the girl below to boil water in the huge
black pot, told Ben to saddle the pony and ride into town to
fetch Jacob from his work in the livery stable. She had not
moved herself, her strong and thin fingers locked in the
stronger fingers of the man she had married almost twenty
years before. Twenty years when they had built the farm with
those strong hands, cut and shaped each plank, lifted each
stone and dug out every trench and hole. They had driven the
first hogs on to the land, the bull and half a dozen cows, had
bartered as if with one voice for the goats; they had sown seed
as if with the same hand.

When Jedediah's fingers clenched involuntarily she started,
certain that it was the final seizure of death. But when the
grip relaxed again the crackling breathing was still there and
the horned eyelids continued to crinkle like a lizard's skin.

Rachel was there now, at his bedside, the room slowly filling
with the yellow stench of a slow and bitter dying.

Jacob hacked at the stem of the ground ivy with his heel
and stepped clear of the wall. Away to the left, where the
alders cropped the stream, he could see his sister, Rebecca,
astride her horse, long black hair falling loose to the middle of
her back. Neither rider nor animal moved other than the single

shake of the mare's head as a fly bothered her eyes. Jacob could see the horse's breath pluming up toward the branches of the young trees, the whiteness of his sister's hand as it gripped the coarse hair at the bottom of the animal's mane.

He tried to imagine what she was thinking but failed; how could he when he was uncertain what he was thinking, feeling, himself. The man upstairs had given him life, dragged him yelping and screaming into a world of mud and animals and hard work and mire: a world where the weeds grow hardier and stronger than any crops, where stock was as like to die from disease and the bitter cold of winter as it was to produce meat or milk or money. His father had hauled him into a life of poverty where soup was made from potato peelings and a few handsful of grain and the only word that counted, aside from that of Jedediah himself, was the Word of the Bible.

Each evening Jacob's father would make his family sit in the half dark and listen while he read to them by the hollow light of a tallow lamp that reeked of pig fat.

He had never forgiven Jacob for insisting on leaving the farm and going into town to work there—just as he had never forgiven his brother, Aram, for choosing the solitary life of a mountain man. His duty had been to take a wife and father children; toil over the land—go forth and multiply!

Jacob laughed bitterly: His father's multiplication rarely seemed to bring about an increase in numbers. His family had lived in near poverty, near hunger for so long that Jacob doubted if they gave it a second thought. It was not until he had gone to live and work in town and had found himself with wages in his pocket and the freedom to spend them on whatever he chose that Jacob himself had truly realized what he had escaped from.

He looked again as his sister stroked her horse's mane down by the alders. Maybe that was the way her thoughts were leaning. Maybe she was sitting there waiting for him to die, feeling the cords peeling off her and the young blood beginning for the first time to run through her veins.

Jacob heard his mother's shout and turned sharply, going back into the house.

*

The letter was wrapped around a piece of yellowing newspaper and folded inside a sheet of calico. It had been at the bottom

of the chest for more years than Rachel Batt could remember.
When she had bent low over her dying husband's head to hear
what were more or less the only words he spoke during all
those hours of dying, she scarcely understood what he meant.
Only later, later when the boys had straightened him out and
she herself had changed his clothes so that he lay there now
with dimes on his eyes and a patched, laundered night shirt
stretched along his long body, had she remembered the letter
in the old chest.

She read her husband's patiently scratched name and only
a few words more; near the beginning she recognized the name
John. After struggling with the crabbed lettering for some minutes, she passed the sheet to Jacob.

"He says we have to see John Quinton."

"Who's he?"

"Why him?"

"He's a lawyer. Up in town."

"In Fallon?"

"In town. Yes."

"What in the Lord's name . . ."

"Ben!"

"What we got to see some lawyer for?"

"Because your pa said so. Didn't you just hear your brother
say?"

"Jacob, what we got to go see some lawyer for?"

Jacob tapped the letter end and shrugged. "Find out when
we gets there, likely. Not before."

Ben sighed and swung his legs and all of a sudden the tears
he'd been holding back when the others had shed theirs came
springing from his eyes and he ran from the room and didn't
stop until he thrown himself against the corral fence and was
gulping great sobs of air.

                              ★

They buried Jedediah at the creek edge, close by the alders.
Rachel sang a hymn in a strong, low voice that echoed out over
the pasture and faded slow. The preacher threw back his head
and closed his eyes, pointed one hand at God, and closed the
other over his heart. He gave out a dollar's worth of words and
cut himself short when it seemed he might be giving more than
he'd been paid for. Ben read a few verses from his father's
heavy black Bible and then Rachel threw the first clods of

earth and the first stones down on to the rough-hewn wood of the coffin. Jacob, Ben, and the youngest, Saul, shoveled the dirt back into the gaping hole and closed it quiet. Rebecca cut flowers and strips of alder and set them in a glass jar at the foot of the grave, while Jacob and Ben took it in turns to hammer the wooden cross in above the head.

When the preacher climbed on his mule to begin his long ride back to town, Jacob harnessed the wagon and the whole Batt family, save the one who was now in the ground, rode in at back of him.

They had to see John Quinton, lawyer.

*

The shingle that fetched back and forth in the wind over the door read *John E. Quinton Attorney at Law*. Jacob turned the reins about the brake handle and jumped down, helping his mother and sister to the rickety boardwalk while the two boys clambered from the back of the wagon openmouthed. It was their first ever visit to town. They stood gawping at the buildings, some with a balcony that jutted out over the street, others with signs painted down their front walls advertising haircut and shave, laundry, and the best steak in the state.

Jacob hollered at them and they came running.

He opened the door and a bell jingled above the frame. Stairs led toward the first-floor office above a small dry goods store. Jacob hesitated for a few moments before climbing up. He was met at the landing by a thin man with a sepulchral face and a black suit that shone almost like glass, such was the thinness to which it had been worn.

"John Quinton?" said Jacob doubtfully.

"The same." The voice seemed to be coming from another man in another room.

"I'm Jacob Batt. This here's . . ." He turned to point a hand to his mother halfway up the stairs.

"He's passed on, then?"

"Huh?"

"Your father, Jedediah, he's passed on?"

"Yeah. He . . . how did you know that?"

The spidery fingers pressed their tips together for a moment in a web across his chest. "There would be no other reason for this visit." He glanced down the stairwell and nodded, as if confirming his impression. "Please come inside and sit down."

There were chairs for them all save Saul, who stood first on
one foot and then the other, fidgeting so much that finally
Jacob cuffed him and he stood still and sniveled instead, refusing to use his sleeve to wipe his runny nose.

Quinton offered Jacob and his mother some sherry wine to
drink and Jacob refused for them both.

"This letter," he said, drawing it from his pants pocket, "we
don't understand . . ."

"I shall explain." Quinton raised one white hand in the air
and clenched it shut as if trapping an insect that no one else
had observed. He bent his back to a small safe and after several moments pulled a wide brown envelope out from under a
bundle of dusty papers. He held it toward the open door and
blew along both sides of its surface, before sitting down and
showing the envelope to the family.

"As you will see this is still sealed and dated, just as it was
when Jedediah left it in my keeping a little over ten years ago."

"Jedediah! How could he . . . He was never in town."

John Quinton smiled like a candle going out. "That is not
quite accurate, Mrs. Batt. He visited me in my office and inquired how best to go about making out this document . . ."

"What the hell is . . . ?"

"Jacob!"

"What is that thing you got there?"

"This . . ." Quinton smoothed his fingers along its edge ". . . is
the last will and testament of your late father, Jedediah Batt."

"Will! What will? Pa didn't make no will. If he had we'd've
known about it. Ma, you know anythin' 'bout a will?"

Rachel shook her head, hands clenched tight in her lap. She
was on the verge of tears without knowing why. Rebecca gazed
at the envelope in the lawyer's hands as if somehow it might
prove the answer to some of her unknown dreams.

"Why the hell . . . why would my pa bother with a will? All
he's got is that farm back there an' a parcel of land just big
enough to keep us on. Not big enough for that. He ain't had
no call to make no will. It don't make sense!"

Quinton dimmed his tallow smile and reached inside his
desk drawer for a bone-handled paper knife. He broke away a
knot of deep red sealing wax and inserted the end of the blade
inside the crack of the envelope; slowly he drew the blade along
the stiff brown paper. The sheet he extracted was written in
his own hand, using a quill pen, and signed by Jedediah Batt

at the bottom. Red drops of wax spun away from the name to
the foot of the page like long-dried blood.

The lawyer read the will as if reading it for the first time,
his thin lips moving slightly as he spelled out the words inside
his head.

"You gonna tell us or . . ."

"It seems that the farm and its land were not, indeed, all
that your father had to bequeath."

"What?"

"It seems. . . ."

"Damn! I heard what you said. What the hell's it mean?"

"Jacob, your language since you came to town to work is
shameful!"

"Ma, let it go. Come on, Quinton, let's have it plain and
clear."

"Very well." The lawyer glanced at the page again before
laying it on the desk and setting one clawed hand firm upon
it. "Jedediah Batt was the owner of gold to the approximate
value of one thousand dollars. It is lodged in the branch of the
Nevada Mining Company Bank here in Fallon."

During the silence that followed, all eyes in the room were
on the lawyer as he rubbed his right hand down the shiny
lapel of his suit and waited. Rachel's mouth opened and closed,
opened and closed. Rebecca's heart beat so fast she was certain
everyone in the room could hear her excitement and she
flushed crimson. Jacob felt a grinding pain at the front of his
head, as if a heel were pressing and twisting hard into him,
driving him down into the dirt.

"There's been a mistake . . . there has to be . . ." Rachel's
words, when they came, were faint to the point of being almost inaudible.

Quinton shook his head, swiveled the will toward her. "There
has been no mistake."

Rachel looked down at the paper and recognized her husband's signature; she shook her head with a shudder and
pointed to Jacob, asking him to read the will aloud.

This he did haltingly, stumbling over the legal terminology
and having to be corrected by Quinton. But of the sense there
was no doubt. One thousand dollars' worth of gold was waiting
in the Fallon bank and—Jacob choked on the part the lawyer
had not mentioned. The sentence which said to whom that
money was left.

Aram Batt.

He tried the words and found them lacking.

Aram Batt.

John Quinton nodded, exactly.

Rachel hugged herself and shivered; Rebecca began, silently, to cry. Ben and Saul failed to understand what their brother was saying.

Jacob threw the will down onto the desk and whirled aside. He bunched his fists and drove them into the partition wall, making it shake. "Aram!" he shrieked. "Aram! My God, he hated Aram! Hated him, despised him for doing what he did. Going off into them damn mountains livin' like some lone animal!"

Rachel squeezed herself tighter and felt the truth; her husband had not hated his brother, he had envied him.

"This ain't true!" shouted Jacob, launching himself at the desk so suddenly that Quinton was certain he was being attacked. "It can't be! Can't be! All them years we sweated an' starved out on that stinkin' place and he leaves his gold to someone we ain't never seen. He ain't never seen him himself since afore I was born." Jacob's fists hammered the surface of Quinton's desk. "It ain't goin't happen. It ain't. There's got to be some way of makin' it different. Gotta be!"

Quinton gripped the sides of his chair and nodded his bony head up and down.

"What?"

"There's two possibilities," said the lawyer clearly. "First off, he could relinquish his claim in law, leaving the gold to you an' your kin. Second . . ." His fingers formed a cage below his chin.

". . . he would be disqualified if the same fate had befallen him as your father. If he were proved dead, the gold would pass on your father's family."

"Proved dead?" said Jacob, straightening.

"Uh-huh, proved dead."

⋆

Jacob lifted his mother down from the front seat of the wagon. Her face was like gray stone, her eyes hardly moved. Since the news in the lawyer's office she was numb, going through the motions of life merely. As soon as she got back inside the house she set to the fire, going about her accustomed tasks automatically, without thought or feeling.

Ben and Saul chopped wood and fetched water.

Jacob unharnessed the mules and went in search of his sister.

He found her where he knew she would be, close by the alders, close by their father's grave. She was kneeling at its foot, shredding the already fading flowers between her young fingers.

Jacob stood back of her, wanting to touch the nape of her neck where it showed between the long fall of her dark hair but not daring to.

"It weren't necessary," he said, "not none of this. Weren't necessary. We could've moved from this place to somewhere better. Built a proper home, bought good stock, held our heads up. Lived in the world not outside it like paupers."

Rebecca bent her body forward toward the mound of earth and tears fell across it but they were tears for herself, not for the man who lay covered. *In the world not outside it:* her brother's words stung her brain.

Jacob looked through the alder branches. He didn't know where his uncle might be, knew only that he had to find him and for one reason. He had lived too long without getting his hands on the wealth that could have made his growing different; things were going to change and they were going to change because he was going to make sure they did. That gold wasn't being wasted on some damn trapper who had no need of it. It was going to be his, his and his sister's.

Jacob, not looking, stretched his fingers down until they touched softly the small bare patch of skin at the base of Rebecca's neck. Not looking, she moved her hand toward his and held it warm and firm against her.

Four

Hart came down on Fallon from over four thousand feet, the trail winding its way in a zigzag pattern from where the Carson river bellied out around Lahontan. Eventually the road broadened and leveled and he was riding easy with the river to his right and short-stemmed grass never rising above the gray's fetlocks. The air was cold and clear and back of the plain he could see the graying overhang of the Stillwater Range—he knew that south of those mountains and out beyond them there was little but the salt flats and the desert. A land of seemingly endless wilderness only broken by the bitter scrub of cholla and prickly pear, the fishhook thorns of the barrel cactus, and dwarfed paloverdes. A land fit for the desert tortoise and the horned lizard, bull snakes and diamondback rattlers, not for men. Hart had gone out into the desert one time, ridden after a prospector whose family had paid fifty dollars to have him found and brought back to civilization. When Hart had finally found him, he'd been chewing on some prickly pear, sharing its flesh with a desert hog, while a family of woodrats skulked just out of reach of his boot and looked fierce and hungry. His eyes seemed to have swollen to almost twice their proper size and inside that white and yellow expanse, the pupils were little more than kernels of darkness. Hart tried reasoning with him for just as long as it took to realize that the man was as close to being crazy as anyone he'd seen. He waited until the prospector had finished his meal and then sapped him on the side of the head with the barrel of his Colt and flung him over the pack mule he'd brought out with him. He delivered him that way and collected his fifty dollars and before he could spend one half of it, the prospector had looped his leather belt around his neck, tied the end over a door frame, clambered unsteadily onto a chair, and kicked it away from beneath him.

Hart hadn't seen him like that, he'd no more than heard about it in passing, a scrap of conversation that came to him across a barroom, but it caught at him like one of them fishhook thorns and refused to let go for a long time.

Now that he was riding back toward Fallon, it all came back to him again and he tried to convince himself that if he'd left the man out there in the desert he'd have died soon enough anyway. Nothing wrong with the logic of that, except that if he'd died out there with the cactus and the hogs, he just might have died happy.

Hart reined in the gray and tilted his hat back on his head. To hell with it!

If the damned fool wanted to hang himself that was his own business, weren't it?

He unwound the strap of his hide water bottle from the pommel of the saddle and took two deliberately short swallows. He could see the outlines of the town now, dark violet shadows that squatted on the plain. Setting the bottle back, his fingers touched the smooth wooden stock of the Henry lever-action rifle that was held in a bucket holster under the left flap of the saddle. Turning, he reached down into one of his saddlebags and pulled into sight the sawn-off ten-gauge he liked to have with him whenever he reckoned he might be going up against odds that needed a little equalizing. With the twenty-eight-inch barrels cut to half their original length, the weapon had a wide blast pattern that was deadly over a short distance, capable of stopping four or five men in an enclosed space. He pushed a couple of fat cartridges from their box and broke the gun, slotting them down firmly into the barrels.

Above, the sky broke for a moment to reveal a pale yellow sun. Hart slid the sawn-off back into the saddlebag and loosely fastened the strap. His tongue clicked against the roof of his mouth and his knees pressed against the mare's sides.

"C'mon, Clay," he said in a soft voice. "C'mon. We got us work to do."

*

The main street was wider than most and a three-legged dog lay sprawled in the middle of it, summoning up the effort to get to the other side. A supply wagon was offloading outside the general store while its team of six mules hung their heads and swished their tails at passing flies. A woman in a wheelchair propelled herself slowly along the south side of the broadwalk, a neat black bonnet fastened over her white hair and a small ginger and white cat curled in her lap.

Hart noted the whereabouts of the three saloons, the sheriff's office, and the dining rooms as he passed through town on his way to the livery stable. He left Clay with a sallow-faced old-timer who sported a brace of bent and buckled bullets from his watch chain. Saddlebags slung over his left shoulder, Hart headed back up the street, keeping to the north. The window of Zack Moses Hardware and Grocery delayed him a few moments with the advertisements pasted across it. Hart considered the merits of Sim D. Kehoe's Model Indian Clubs, Ten Pins and Balls for muscular and physical development—"No Clubs genuine unless Stamped with my Name"; Van Buskirk's fragrant Sozodont for the cleansing and preserving of teeth; Dr. Sage's Catarrh Remedy at fifty cents a bottle—"$500 reward for a case of Cold in the Head, Catarrh or Ozena which is cannot cure"; and most interestingly Helmbold's Buchu

Leaves—gathered by the Hottentots of the Cape of Good Hope especially for H. T. Helmbold—guaranteed to cure infections of the bladder and kidneys, brick dust deposit, loss of memory, difficulty in breathing, dimness of vision, pains in the back, and eruptions on the face.

Hart figured he'd get along without buchu leaves for a while longer and broke his thirst in the Salt Flats Saloon. That done, he crossed the street to the sheriff's office.

Merle Wringer was one hell of a lot different from old Herb Mosley back in Virginia City and it wasn't just a case of having two good legs and some fifteen to twenty years on his side. He looked up from his desk as Hart stepped into the office, eyes blue and alert, beard and mustache fair and neatly trimmed. His cotton jacket was beige and spotless, his tan pants were clean and pressed. The leather of his gun belt shone and the butt of the Smith & Wesson in the holster was so polished it was a wonder his fingers didn't slip off it when he made his draw.

He got up from his chair and stepped around the desk, extending a hand toward Hart in what he made into one fluid movement.

"Sheriff Wringer, Merle Wringer."

"Wes Hart."

The sheriff's mouth sucked in a little at one side and his eyes blinked quickly as if the name triggered off something he couldn't quite catch.

His grip didn't falter.

"Just rode in, huh?" the sheriff said, looking at the trail dust that still clung to Hart's clothes.

"Yeah. More or less."

Wringer nodded and released his hand, stepped back but not too far. He was still trying to place Hart's name, remember if and where he had seen his face, his mind flicking back through the dozens of flyers that came in with every visit of the stage.

Hart realized what was going on, was accustomed to it— Mosley back in Virginia City had been the same—lawmen most places were the same. Man who looked the way he did, wore a gun the way he did, well, he asked for a certain degree of suspicion.

"Somethin' I can do for you?" Wringer asked.

"Uh-huh. Hear there was a holdup on the stage line a while back, somewhere between here an' Salt Wells. . . ."

"Two or three of 'em this six months."

"Well, way I heard it, feller by the name of Speedmore could've been tied up in one of 'em anyways."

"Dave Speedmore?"

"Uh-huh."

"Cherokee Dave Speedmore?"

"That's what he calls himself."

"You know him?"

"Not personal."

Wringer nodded again, glanced pointedly at the pearl-handled grip of Hart's Peacemaker, with its design of an eagle gripping a snake between mouth and claw. "Just through the reward poster, huh?"

Hart's lids blinked down over the faded blue of his eyes. "You find anythin' wrong with that?"

Merle Wringer slowly drew a handkerchief from the side pocket of his coat and unfolded it carefully, wiped it across his mouth. "No," he said. "Not for them as can't see no better."

"Meanin' what?" The edge bit through Hart's voice and his muscles tensed.

"Meanin' if you don't even halfway understand there ain't no point in me sayin'."

"Sayin' what? Spit it out!"

The kerchief was refolded and slipped from sight.

"Sayin' what, damn it?"

"Ridin' out after a man an' fixin' to gun him down no better'n a dog seems a strange way of choosin' to make a livin'."

"Maybe he ain't no better'n a dog."

Wringer stared at Hart hard. "Who's to say that?"

"What?"

"Who's to make that judgment, stranger? You? You the one to say this man's life ain't worth worryin' over, nor this, nor that? Judge an' damn jury both! Ain't it time this country got somethin' better in the way of justice than that?"

"Meanin' you?" Hart spat out.

Wringer pulled aside the lapel of his coat and showed the shiny badge pinned to his shirt. "I was elected legal. I represent what law there is. Speedmore or anyone else gets the same chance from me—he gets a spell in jail an' a fair trial and then whatever the jury decides."

"An' if he don't take kindly to that idea?" sneered Hart.

"Then I'll do what I have to."

"You'll kill him."

"If I have to."

"Then what's the big difference? There sure ain't none for Speedmore."

Wringer opened and closed the fingers of both hands, tightening them into ball-like fists. His breathing was still steady but louder; he was remaining unruffled but it wasn't easy. For his part Hart was almost needlessly annoyed by the lawman's manner, his arrogant sureness that he was right, even the uncreased cleanness of his clothes succeeded in getting under Hart's nerves.

"You know the difference," the sheriff said after a couple of moments. "The difference is this badge. The difference is that I was elected. The difference is I ain't goin' out there huntin' down some man for money like he was antelope, I ain't trappin' him like he was beaver." He touched one finger lightly to the front of the badge, as if not wanting to smear it. "There's somethin' here that make it more than just animal—hell, no, what you an' others like you do, that's worse than animal. They kill out of need: with you an' your kind it's greed. Sheer bloody greed! You an' every other bounty-huntin' trash I ever clapped eyes on!"

Hart's hand was fast on the butt of his Colt and his eyes were no more than slits. His breath had jammed in his throat. His mouth was open. Wringer stared at him with a mixture of anger and disgust full in his face. He hadn't bothered to make any kind of a move toward his own gun. It was as if he was daring Hart to break down to the level he expected of him.

Seconds passed with no more than the uneasy breathing of both men and the faint sounds from the street. Then there were steps on the boardwalk coming nearer and a fist hammered against the door.

Wringer made no move; Hart neither.

The knocking repeated, more urgently.

Wringer's eyes flicked away from Hart toward the door; Hart let out a deep breath and his body relaxed a fraction.

"Come on in!"

The man who stepped inside was medium height, middle thirties, his belly was sagging a sight more than it ought to, and his bare arms were as well muscled as a logger. When he spoke he filled the office with the fumes of whisky and cigars.

"Everythin' okay here, sheriff?" He looked at Hart anxiously, then at Wringer and back to Hart again.

"Fine, Howard. What's the trouble?"

"It's . . . er . . . you know the Batt kid? The elder one, come to work up at the livery?"

"Jacob?"

"Yeah, him."

"What about him?"

Hart uncoiled his body, slid his fingers back from his Colt .45; he moved back from the desk into the corner of the room and took an interest in the posters tacked to the wall at the same time as listening to the conversation and trying to calm himself down. He was angry with himself for getting riled up so fast and for no real good reason. Merle Wringer hadn't said anything he'd not heard a couple of dozen times before; hadn't said anything he hadn't felt himself.

"Got himself into a poker game at the saloon an' lost a little money. 'Bout all he had to lose, I guess. Went out in a temper an' come back with coin enough to buy a bottle of rotgut. Don't know where he got it from, but he sure didn't have time to earn it. He's been sittin' back in the corner swiggin' it down an' growlin' at anyone who comes near. If someone don't get him out of there fast he's goin' to cut up real nasty."

Merle Wringer nodded in an understanding sort of way and moved back toward his desk. He reached into a drawer and pulled out a small billy club, then tucked it down into the back of his pants. It made an unseemly bulge at the rear of his coat, just about the only thing out of place about him.

"How 'bout Speedmore then, sheriff?" Hart lost interest in the posters and set himself between the lawman and the door.

"It'll wait." Wringer moved as if to step around him.

"But you are goin' to help, ain't you? Tell me what you know?"

Wringer moved forefinger and thumb back along his upper lip and let it have another moment's thought. "Maybe. When I get back."

Hart nodded. "Mind if I tag along?"

"Why the hell should you want to do that?"

"Figure I might learn somethin'. Like to see a man do it nice an' legal."

Wringer narrowed his eyes and said: "You goin' to step out of my way?"

Hart almost grinned. "You fixin' to arrest me if I don't?"

Wringer's hand faded toward his pistol and the man from the saloon took a pace into the center of the room, but Hart just laughed shortly and took himself away from the door.

When the sheriff was up to it, Hart said: "You goin' to tell him you're arrestin' him before you sucker him with that club you've got hidden, or after?"

Wringer sighed and didn't bother either to answer or turn around. He set off down the boardwalk, the saloon man close on his heels. Hart took one last look around the sheriff's office and marveled that he was so trusting as to leave it unattended with a bounty hunter in the vicinity. Then he pulled the door closed and followed the pair down the street.

Fifty yards along there was a loud shout from the saloon and then a couple of pistol shots and the shatter of glass. It seemed as if Sheriff Wringer might be too late and his billy club might just not be enough.

Five

When Merle Wringer arrived outside the saloon the echoes of the two shots were beginning to fade. There was a lot of noise coming through the batwing doors, mostly folk talking too fast and too excited, though through it Wringer reckoned he could hear the half-choked sobs of someone in a lot of pain.

He unbuttoned the front of his coat and moved one lapel back so as to show his badge clearly to anyone who might have reason to be interested. His right thumb shifted the safety thong from the curved hammer of his Smith & Wesson .45 and the palm of his hand pressed hard against the shiny butt.

Wringer glanced once over his shoulder, noting that Hart was coming down the street without any kind of hurry.

He drew a breath, held it several seconds before releasing it slowly as he stepped toward the doors. His left hand pushed one side back and held it and he went through, not too fast, not too slow. if there'd been some kind of school or academy that taught lawmen and peace officers to enter buildings in which there was likely a crowd of angry and frightened folk along with a man who'd used a gun and was maybe going to use it again, they'd have taught Merle Wringer to do it exactly the way he did.

Cool, calm, authoritative, and dependable.

He stood in the doorway, badge on his shirt and gun in his holster, visible for all to see. Most of the talking shut off fast, most folk stopped moving. A shape detached itself jerkily from the shadows of the back of the saloon and a third pistol shot roared out. Merle Wringer was hurled backward, a hole spreading from the center of his forehead. He was dead before his back cracked against the edge of the boardwalk.

Hart jumped fast against the front wall of the building, fingers diving for his Colt as he did so. For several moments there was little sound other than the squeak of the left-side door as it came back and forth on his hinges. His mind raced: The town's sheriff was dead and as far as he could tell there weren't any deputies around who were about to take his place and finish what he'd set out to accomplish. There was, on all accounts, a young kid inside there with a bottle of rotgut whisky inside him and a gun in his hand and likely three more shells left in it. That hole in Wringer's forehead could have been a fluke, but even it if was, Hart didn't relish walking in on someone who was running that kind of luck.

And it seemed the boy's luck had surely changed since his earlier game of poker.

"What . . . what you gonna do?" shuddered the man at the other side of the door. He spoke to Hart without once taking his eyes off the way the blood was spiraling away from the black hole at the top of the sheriff's head, running around one eyebrow, and settling in a widening pool alongside his left ear.

Hart shook his head; he didn't know what he was going to do.

One thing for certain, though, anyone as fussy about appearances as Merle Wringer had been sure couldn't have complained about the way he got shot.

"What you gonna . . . ?"

"What makes you think I'm goin' to do anythin'?"

"You . . ." The man looked at him, at the drawn gun. "You sure look as though you're fixin' to do somethin'."

"Right. Not end up the way your sheriff just did."

"That all?"

Hart glanced down and grinned grimly. "For him, it'd be more'n enough."

Men were approaching from both ends of the street, a few on horseback, the others running until they were within some thirty yards of the saloon, after which they slowed and stared. Hart figured if they saw him standing there with the Colt in his hand they were liable to draw the wrong conclusions and he wasn't about to set himself up for a potshot in the back from some public-spirited citizen. Slowly he released the hammer and slid the pistol back down into its holster.

A lot of questions were getting shouted around and not many

of them were getting any answers. Inside the saloon everything seemed to have gone awful quiet and for now seemed to be staying that way—maybe it was something to do with the way the late sheriff's well-polished boots were sticking through under the door.

A burly man with a storekeeper's apron and a black jacket that was several sizes too big for him pushed his way through the half circle of onlookers and went to the edge of the boardwalk.

" 'Lo, Zack," said the man standing opposite Hart.

"Hell's goin' on here, Howard?"

"Batt kid's drunk in there an' shootin' off a gun."

Zack Moses attacked the underside of his black beard like it was giving him a sudden and terrific itch. "Batt did this? Jacob Batt? From the livery?"

Howard nodded solemnly. "That's the one."

Zack gestured upward with both hands and shook his head from side to side. He looked at Merle Wringer's face and made a move toward it, as if intent upon closing his vacant eyes. Halfway down he realized he might be making himself too much of a target and stepped back.

"Ain't no one gonna do somethin'?" called somebody in the crowd.

"Let's get in there an' get the murderin' bastard!"

"String him up!"

"Ain't no more'n a fool kid!"

They pressed forward, emboldened by their own rhetoric but not so much so that any one of them was prepared to step up out of the street.

"What you goin' to do, Zack?"

"Yeah, c'mon, Zack. You mayor of this town or ain't you?"

"How 'bout it, Zack?"

The storekeeper turned toward the crowd angrily, his head jutting out and his right hand gesturing heavily. "You want I should go in there myself, maybe? Walk into a drunk with a gun? A drunk who can shoot like this one can? You say I am the mayor, and that's a fact. I am not sheriff. Wringer was elected sheriff, not me."

"He sure ain't gonna do a lot now, Zack."

"All right! All right! Some of you who are so strong with the voices, you go ahead. Go on now. Go ahead!"

Zack Moses stood back and swung his arm toward the batwing doors and every eye followed his gesture; no one did a lot else.

"We could rush the place," someone over to the side suggested. "He ain't goin' to get all of us."

"Okay, Casey, you lead the way," called someone else.

Casey shut up.

"How 'bout you, mister?" Zack Moses asked of Hart, who'd stepped a dozen feet back along the boardwalk and was waiting and watching to see what happened.

"How 'bout me?"

"You look the kind of man who could handle this."

Hart shrugged. "Maybe."

"We'll make it worth your while."

"We?"

"The town."

"Uh-huh. How much does the town reckon to pay for the man who shot its nice clean lawman?"

Zack scratched his beard some and said: "Ten dollars maybe."

Hart looked at him and laughed.

"Twenty?"

"I ain't wastin' my time bargaining. You want it done, you pay for it right. Otherwise, sort out your own problem your own way."

Zack glanced around the crowd and the quiet, watching faces; he wet his lips and smoothed back his hair. "Wringer, he got seventy-five dollars a month only for doing his job. You want we should give you that much, more, for one piece of work?"

Hart looked at the saloon doors, then at the still-darkening hole in the peace officer's head. "Give me a month's pay. I'll be your new sheriff. Only thing, I'm retirin' come mornin' and you don't get no refund. How's that?"

It didn't take Moses long to decide. He shrugged his heavy shoulders and nodded agreement. Hart went quickly forward, deftly unpinned the badge from his shirt, and fastened it to his own. He asked Howard if there was another entrance and found out there was a door at the rear that was usually kept locked.

"You got the key?"

Howard shook his head. "Hangin' up over the bar."

"Fine!"

"You could bust in easy enough."

"Yeah, an' get shot doin' it. If that door's near where he is, he ain't going to stay sittin' there while I knock the door in."

"Don't seem too happy 'bout folk walkin' in through the front, neither."

Hart acknowledged the truth of that by stepping over its proof and setting his eye close against the smoke-smeared window. There were eight or nine men that he could see, most of them sitting around the center of the room and none of them looking any too anxious to make a move. There was someone off on his own toward the back and Hart figured that to be the boy, though he had no way of being sure.

He stepped away and gave it a little more thought: If he set himself up in the doorway he was likely to get the same treatment as the late Merle Wringer; if he went in shooting there were more than few likely to get in the way and stop a stray bullet. He shrugged and looked around at the crowd.

"Howard, get somethin' good and heavy. Somethin' that'd make a mess of that." He pointed at the window.

After a couple of minutes he moved toward the door, keeping off to one side. "Son!" he called. "You hear me in there?"

He waited out the silence.

"I said you hear me there? You, Jacob Batt."

Nothing.

"You know you just killed a man? Killed the sheriff? You understand that?"

Howard was standing by with a three-legged stool raised by one powerful arm.

"Jacob! There's a new sheriff now. You got to answer for what you done. Throw down that gun, boy. Throw it down!"

There was a shout from inside but the words were so slurred that Hart had difficulty in distinguishing one curse from another.

"I'll give you a count of ten to throw down that gun and start walkin' toward the door. You ain't moved by then, I'm goin' to have to come get you. You understand me?"

There was another flurry of curses, which Hart took as meaning that Jacob understood. He also hoped that everyone inside would have the sense to throw themselves flat as soon as the ten was reached. He made sure Howard understood what he had to do and started counting out loud, slow, and clear.

". . . eight . . . nine . . . ten!"

The stool went crashing into the window, shattering most of the glass and sending it inside in a scattering spray. Hart waited for the kid's first shot and dived through the center of the batwing doors. He thrust his left arm up in front of his face as he went through and used that hand as a lever to push his body into a rolling movement that took him away from the broken window and the focus of Jacob Batt's attention. He came up fast and smooth as Jacob was sending a second, delayed, shot after the first. Apart from an old man who was sitting at a table with both hands pressed down onto the top of his head and both eyes closed tight, everyone else had hit the floor.

At the back of the room Jacob Batt stood up and made a couple of shaky steps forward. The pistol in his hand didn't look any too steady and he waved it vaguely in Hart's direction. There was likely only one shell remaining; he'd had time enough to reload after his first shots, but Hart didn't think he would have bothered. If he'd tried, his fingers might not have been steady enough to slot the shells down into the chamber.

One shot was all he'd needed to account for Wringer, though, and Hart wasn't forgetting it.

His Colt had come clear when he stood up and his thumb held the hammer back, arm extended halfway so that the barrel was aiming at the unstable figure at the end of the smoky room.

"How 'bout it, Jacob? How 'bout chuckin' down that gun and comin' with me?"

Jacob Batt leaned forward so far that Hart thought for a moment he might fall flat on his face; but he righted himself enough to stay upright and then Hart heard a sound that he recognized as laughter mixed with drunken fear and bravery both. The arm holding the pistol dipped and the fingers shuffled themselves around the butt, but he didn't let go. Hart kept his Colt level and began slowly to walk forward. He pushed a table out of his way with his left hand, edged a chair aside with his leg—kept on going at the youngster without deviation. When there was no more than a dozen feet between them, Jacob Batt's laugh broke into a cackle and tears sprang from his eyes. He opened his mouth in a curse and swung up his gun.

Still walking forward, Hart shot him through the right shoulder.

Jacob was swung right around by the tearing force of the bullet, his gun pitching against the back wall. His cackling laugh choked short and was replaced a moment later by a scream of rage and pain.

Hart dropped his left hand onto the back of the boy's collar-less shirt and jerked him around. His face was white and his neck was spotted with tiny splashes of blood. Blood ran down his arm and dripped away from his fingertips.

The small pupils of his eyes were clouded over with disgust, whether at himself or Hart there was no way of knowing.

He looked down at his shoulder and made a small moaning noise.

There was a bunch of men standing just inside the doorway and some of them were starting to shout for the kid's neck to be stretched right there in the room. It hadn't taken long for Merle Wringer's precious law and order to die with him.

Jacob kicked out a leg toward Hart's groin and took him sufficiently by surprise to catch him on the inside of the knee. Hart stumbled back a ways and lifted the Colt. He waited for Jacob to come for him and laid the side of the barrel along his left temple. Jacob hardly called out as he sank down.

Hart scooped up the kid's pistol from the floor and pushed it down into his belt. Then he dropped his own gun back into its holster and lifted Jacob off the ground. He could just manage to carry him over his left shoulder.

The crowd was no longer close by the doorway, it was thick across half the saloon. Even if those at the front had wanted to stand aside, the pressure of the ones behind wouldn't have allowed them. Hart looked around for Howard and couldn't pick him out. Zack Moses, though, was over toward the side, close to the front.

"Okay, mayor," said Hart, "suppose you get that key from back of the bar an' open up the back door here."

Zack stood out front of the crowd but still hesitated from going farther.

"Less'n you want a lynchin' on your hands."

A man with stubbly red hair jabbed a finger toward Hart. "You done your bit, stranger, now hand him over to us."

"Yeah! We know what to do with the likes of him."

"Hangin's what he wants!"

Hart had seen men hang. Seen them from close enough to smell the stink and count the minutes it took until they finally choked to death. He could hear now, through the shouts of that mob, the thud of the trap doors as two men he'd taken in had been hanged in Fort Smith. One of the men had gone fast but the other lacked the weight to make it either a quick or an easy ending. Hart remembered the way his neck had seemed

to stretch and his youthful face had twisted sideways with the
pressure of the rope; his tongue had darkened and thrust from
the corner of his open mouth and his eyes had bulged from
their sockets until he had thought they must burst bloodily
away. A harsh gargling sound had stuttered through his mouth
and spittle had flown out over those of the crowd who were
pressed in fascination against the front of the scaffold. A cheer
had risen up and a bugle had begun playing off-key. It had
been a long time before he had finally died.

"Hangin's what the no-good little bastard wants!"

Hart threw his Colt faster than most eyes could follow and
pistol-whipped the redhead across the face. He screamed and
fell back against the men behind him, his cheek torn open by
the pistol sight, the broken flesh above the cheekbone already
beginning to swell.

"Mayor?" called Hart.

Zack Moses hurried behind the bar and took down the key.
He half ran to the rear door and unlocked it, standing aside
to let Hart and his prisoner through.

There were more of them spread across the street, but the
sight of the Colt in Hart's hand and the rumor of what he'd
done with it inside the saloon kept the mob's anger down to
shouts and threats. Jacob Batt was starting to come to when
they got inside the sheriff's office. Hart dumped him across
the desk and turned the key in the front door's stiff lock. He
was turning back toward the desk as Jacob tried to push his
dazed way off it. He managed to get up on one arm before
falling off the side and crashing face first onto the boards. From
the crunching sound that came muffled from the floor, Hart
figured Jacob had broken his nose.

He opened the door that led back to a row of three empty
cells, found the ring of keys in a drawer, and unlocked the
center cell. He dragged Jacob into it and locked it behind him.
By then the mayor was hammering on the door and asking to
be let in. Hart made certain there wasn't time for anyone else
to get through at the same time.

He didn't know for certain what Zack Moses had come to
say, but anyway he didn't give him a chance to say it.

"Right. There's things that want doing and fast. First off I
want my seventy-five dollars. Then a bottle of good whisky and
two lots of food, one for me and one for him back in there. Get
a doctor in, too, to get his arm patched up and look at his face.

You'd best pay someone you can halfway trust to keep him
guarded up in here after tomorrow morning 'cause that's when
I'll be riding out." Hart saw his saddlebags were still on the
floor where he'd left them, he glanced along the shelves to
make sure there was ammunition enough for his guns. "Best
get me some ten-gauge shotgun shells from that store of yours.
That should just about do it." He nodded toward the door. "Tell
your townsfolk out there that any of 'em thinks they're goin'
to get good and drunk tonight and bust that boy out of here
for some lynchin' party's goin' to get 'emselves shot dead."

Zack Moses scratched at the underneath of his beard and
gestured wordlessly.

"While I'm wearin' this badge I'll run things legal as I know
how. May not be Merle Wringer's way but that ain't goin' to
be worryin' him none. Not anymore."

Zack Moses went about his errands and Hart sat behind the
sheriff's desk and began searching through the piles of flyers
to see if he could come up with anything useful about Cherokee
Dave Speedmore or High-Hat Thomas. He was more than
ready for something to eat and after that he'd settle down with
the whisky and get himself a good night's rest. Action enough
for one man for one day, he reckoned—on his pay at least.

Six

Right or wrong, Hart slept the sleep of the just: not even a
fleeting image of Kathy to disturb it. It was as if the act of
tearing apart her letter, unread—the one she had for some
unknown reason sent chasing him across as many as three
state lines—had ripped her, at last, from his mind. Now he
woke and was instantly alert; he tossed aside the blanket
under which he'd slept and swung his legs around on the cot
bed that Merle Wringer had used by the side wall of his office.
There was water in an enamel jug and Hart poured some into
a chipped china basin from which blue patterns of flowers had
begun to fade and wear. He locked his fingers under the water
and lifted it to his face, feeling the thickening stubble around
his mouth and jawline. He poured more of the water into the
sheriff's coffeepot, scattered in some ground coffee, and pushed
several sticks of kindling into the center of the stove, where
they were soon persuaded to catch from the smoldering embers.

He was whistling cheerfully when he checked his prisoner

in the small cell, continued to whistle through the barrage of
abuse the youngster threw at him. Jacob's shoulder had clearly
bled again during the night; the bandage the doctor had
strapped on was dark with concentric circles on it. His face
looked a mess: the bone of his nose had broken midway and
the attempt to reset it had been painful and not exactly satis-
factory. The lump on his temple was still the size of a small
egg, only now it had colored up a distinctive shade of purple.

Hart promised Jacob he'd send out for some breakfast presently, as well as empty the bucket that was beginning to stink
out the cell.

He locked the communicating door in case and lifted the lid
from the coffeepot to see how far the contents were from being
brewed. As soon as he had a strong cup inside him, he'd dig
out the mayor and turn in his badge, hand over the task of
guarding Jacob Batt to whoever had been appointed, take a
leisurely breakfast, and see what he could turn up about the
two men he was looking for.

It all worked out as he'd planned. At least, it was seeming
to. He was wiping a chunk of corn bread around his plate,
mopping up the last of the bacon fat before it congealed, that
and the final traces of yolk from his three eggs. The bread was
almost in his mouth, not quite, when he realized that someone
was staring at him. Outside the window of the dining rooms,
her face a wide oval clearly visible underneath the painted
lettering across the glass.

Hart sensed the intensity of the stare and set the piece of
bread back down. He readjusted his chair and tried again; but
even though he could no longer see her, he knew she was still
there, and that presence was unsettling enough to take the
taste away from the last of his breakfast.

He swilled down the remnants of his mug of coffee, lukewarm only by now, dropped some coins on the table for his
bill, and went out onto the street.

The girl had disappeared.

Hart shrugged and turned toward the livery stable. He
wanted to make sure that his horse would be good and ready
as soon as he'd made whatever inquiries he could.

The old man was sitting bent-backed by the stove, a piece of
stale-seeming pie untouched on a barrel head beside him. He
was drinking black, bitter tea from an enamel mug and pol-
ishing the bullets that hung from his watch chain. When Hart

walked in he glanced up and scowled, then went back to his task.

"Must be pretty special," said Hart.

The livery man growled something that might have been agreement.

"Guess you didn't just find 'em lyin' around?"

The old-timer moved his head to one side so that he wouldn't spit down on Hart's boots by three or four inches. "Dug 'em outta me when they got me back to Coloma on a wagon. Been layin' up in the hills three days in the snow. Leg was bust an' most the time I weren't conscious at all. Hadn't been for that damned snow I'd've bled to death if the blasted thing hadn't took bad an' festered up on me."

Hart set one foot on a bale of hay. Horses shifted restlessly in the stalls along the far wall and he knew without looking that Clay was one of them, the mare sensing his presence, recognizing his voice.

"Forty-eight?" he said.

"Forty-nine." The livery man swallowed a mouthful of tea and grimaced. "Got me a strike off toward the American. Damn gold so bright when you set a pick end against it you'd've thought it'd drive you blind."

"Lot of folk, it did just that," said Hart.

The man looked at him. "True ain't the word, feller."

"What happened?"

"Bunch of 'em jumped me just around dark. Couple of fellers'd been talkin' a while, claimed they was passin' down to Coloma to meet up with some friends. They was ridin' raggedy-assed mules an' managed to stink worse'n them mules did. If either of 'em'd washed or shaved in a moon I'd've been surprised. Had some tea brewin' an' gave 'em some—only seemed right. One of 'em was handin' me back the mug when they jumped me. He let the mug fall an' grabbed my hand while the other one, he laid about my head with a shovel. Soon as I was down there was two more of 'em. Lord alone knows where they sprung from. I did my best to fight the buzzards off, but never stood no chance. When there was blood thick across my eyes so's I couldn't hardly see, I figured it was time to make a run for it."

He paused long enough to wet his lips with more tea, glancing at Hart and making small nodding movements with his head.

"One of 'em pulled his gun an' put four slugs in me. Two in the back of the leg, one under the shoulder blade, other up here close by the side of the neck. They come over an' looked at me and laughed an' left me for dead. When they was sleepin' I dragged myself as far as I could down the hill, but never got too far. Sometime durin' the night snow set in an' I was stuck. Prospector an' his kid, they found me three parts buried under an' dug me out. Loaded me up and took me down to town. Heard him say to his kid it was likely a waste of time an' I'd die for sure but it was the Christian thing to take me anyway."

He grinned, broken-toothed.

"That doc sure did a good job. Dug these beauties out of me an' set 'em on the edge of the bed. You keep 'em, he says, remember how close you come to dyin'. Well . . ." He fingered the buckled bullets almost tenderly. ". . . I wore 'em since an' I ain't forgot. Ain't passed a day without I ain't said my thanks."

Hart wondered whether he thanked God or the prospector or the doctor—maybe it was all three.

The old-timer pitched what remained of his black tea onto the dusty floor and stood up about as straight as he could. "Guess you'll be wantin' that gray of yours?"

"Give me an hour."

The man swung his head. "Thought you was all finished here. Jacob's in the jailhouse, ain't he?"

"Long as some mob don't take it into their heads to drag him out an' lynch him."

"That was last night. Merle Wringer layin' there with the blood runnin' out of him. They won't feel the same this mornin'. I know the folk in this town. They ain't hog-wild like you might think."

"Uh-huh," Hart nodded. "An' the boy? He worked for you, didn't he?"

"Jacob? Yeah, he did. Come bustin' out of that hole of a place his pa kept him slavin' on all the hours God sends and most of them as belongs to the other feller. It was like bustin' out of hell, I guess. He worked hard and long for me on account he weren't used to no other way. But there was always somethin' strange about him. Somethin' dark, I reckon. Like there was some strange feelin' just under his skin an' itchin' to get out. When I heard he'd gone loco in the saloon I weren't surprised."

"I thought he was more drunk 'n loco."

The old-timer spat. "Whisky was no more'n the excuse, I reckon. He'd've gone strange soon enough one way or another. Specially after what happened."

"How d'you mean?"

"He was workin' here one day and they sent for him. His pa was sick an' like to die. Stayed back there till it happened. Buried him along with the rest of his kin then come back into town. I figured he'd be a deal happier with the old man gone and under, but maybe it did no more'n turn his head. I don't know. He weren't easy to figure. Now I guess, one way or another, he'll end up swingin' from a rope."

Hart shrugged. "Could be."

The livery man moved toward the stall where the gray mare was pushing her head over the door. Hart patted her, stroked her, and she nuzzled against him.

"An hour then?"

"That should do it." Hart began to walk away then changed his mind. "That stage holdup . . ."

"Which one?"

"Out by Salt Wells. Not too long back. You happen to know who drove that day?"

"Likely Charlie Spencer. If it was, you can find out soon enough. Got a small place on the northern edge of town. If he's out with the stage his missus'll be there. She'll tell you what she can. They're both good folks. Charlie an' Ethel."

Hart touched his fingers to the underside of his hat. "Much obliged."

"Okay. I'll see your mare's ready."

Hart nodded and turned and as he did so he caught a glimpse of the girl's face, oval and pale, shrouded with black hair, as it pulled out of sight past the livery door.

"Hey! . . ."

But when he got there she'd ducked around the side and he could hear her feet running along the dusty alleyway. Hart headed up to where he might find Charlie Spencer and some more information about Dave Speedmore.

Both the Spencers were at home. Charlie, who turned out to be a paunchy sandy-haired man of around fifty, was doing his best to stop the lean-to from leaning too far, while his hound dog tried to distract him into a game with an old bone. Ethel, who was taller than her husband, likely ten years younger, sharp-faced and shrewd, was fixing the last of a batch of meat and potato pies for the oven. She had flour on her cheeks and the front of her apron, a smidgen of it at the very tip of her nose. Charlie kissed it off as he came in and she was too embarrassed in front of a stranger to tell him off for walking into the house without first scraping all the mud from his boots.

They asked Hart to take a seat, gave him a cup of weak coffee and a chunk of oatcake, and Charlie told him all that he knew. It didn't turn out to be much except for one thing. He thought there might have been half a dozen of them, though he couldn't be sure. The one he heard called Cherokee was wearing a gun belt studded with diamonds that were as fake as a Saturday night whore (Ethel reddened and fidgeted with her cup, reaching around to pet the dog) and a black hat with a white feather sticking up out of the brim. He was a breed certain enough and looked mean enough to scalp a man as long as his hands were already tied behind his back. He didn't recall much about the others, never heard no other names, not a lot about them that would help him to pick them out again.

But then there was this one thing: just when they were riding off he heard one of them shout to the others, "Meet you at the hollow."

Hart set his cup down on the floor, the coffee only half drunk. "Any idea where it might be?"

"Didn't at the time, only the other night we was talkin' 'bout somethin' miles away from this and of a sudden Ethel . . ."

"I remembered this place I rode out to one time when I was no more'n a girl . . ."

"Weren't no more'n ten year ago, an' she was up there with Reno Walker, sparkin'." Charlie laughed. "Woman her age!"

Ethel flushed again, but this time with pleasure. "You didn't reckon it strange when I was sparkin' with you, Charlie Spencer, and most folk wouldn't have thought you had anythin' left in you!"

"See here . . . !"

Ethel shook her head and waved her hands and calmed him down. "This ain't what Mr. Hart's come callin' to hear, Charlie, an' you know it."

"Go on then. You tell him what you remembered."

Ethel turned in her chair. In place of the flour on her nose there was now a small piece of oatcake at the edge of her mouth. Hart wondered if Charlie would eat it off.

"We rode out to this place between here and Salt Wells. Off

between two stumpy hills to the southwest. There's a creekbed that's dried up eleven months of the year and we rode along it, climbing all the time. Half an hour, maybe more, we come to this valley snug between the hills, choked in on three sides. Never know it was there unless you happened on it by chance."

"Or someone told you where to look," put in Charlie.

"Or that," Ethel agreed.

"It was called the Hollow?" asked Hart.

"That's what Reno called it. Said a bunch of rustlers used to use it as a way station for horses they were taking across into California."

"Reckon he was telling the truth?"

"There was an old shack up there, but it was half tumbled down. Bits of fencing like there might have been a corral of sorts." She glanced over at Charlie, as if for confirmation. "Yes, it could have been used for what Reno said, I suppose. Though I never heard no one else 'round here call it by that name. You, Charlie?"

Charlie shook his head.

"This feller, Reno—he still around?"

Ethel laughed: "Reno Walker never did stay in one place too long. I guess that's why I got hitched to Charlie here instead." She reached a hand across and laid her long fingers on his arm, just for a moment. "Not that I'm sayin' I regretted it, mind."

Hart stood up. "Thanks for the coffee, ma'am. An' the information. Thanks to you, Charlie, too."

The couple stood up.

"There's more in the pot," Ethel urged him, but Hart declined, hoping she wouldn't notice that he hadn't drunk more than half of what she'd given him.

Hart hesitated at the door, then stepped back. "Charlie, do me a favor, will you?"

"If I can."

"Take a look out through that window there. You see a girl hangin' around? Young thing with dark hair."

Charlie looked through one window and Ethel the other. The girl was across the street, trying to find something of interest in the miserable front garden of one of the Spencers' neighbors.

"She somethin' to you?" asked Charlie.

Hart shrugged. "She seems to think she is. Been followin' me since first light."

"Why don't you ask her what she wants?"

"Every time I see her she runs away. Makes conversation a mite difficult." He looked toward the rear of the house. "Mind if I slip out that way? See if I can't loose her off'n my tail."

Charlie nodded. "Help yourself."

Hart cut a path across Charlie's patch of ground and circled around so as to hit the main street some hundred yards farther back and just about up by the jail. There were still one or two things he had to collect before taking his leave of Fallon for a spell. He'd ride out the way Ethel Spencer had described and see just what was going on in the place she'd heard called the Hollow. If it was some kind of staging post for horse thieves, or just a general hangout for no-goods and desperadoes, he still might pick up something about the men he was looking for.

The two fellers Zack Moses had put into the jailhouse in his place were deep into a game of checkers and he could have sneaked up on them and taken their guns from their belts before they'd noticed.

He hoped for Jacob Batt's sake that what the livery man had said was true and the town's lynch fever had passed in the night like a bad dream. It certainly seemed peaceful enough, no more than a handful of folk on the street, and most of the storekeepers loitering outside their doors looking for custom.

Hart heard Jacob's cursing from the back and opened the partition door long enough to bid him good morning and farewell.

Laughing at the boy's threat to burst out of there and take a knife to his throat, Hart shouldered his saddlebags, waited to watch a few moves on the checkers board, and let himself out onto the boardwalk.

There she was right in the middle of the street, only this time she wasn't running the second she saw his face. She was standing with her legs spread apart and the cheap cotton of her skirt hung tight against her thighs. Her black hair was pushed back from her neck at one side and her eyes were squinted up although there wasn't any sun. Both arms were stretched out in front of her as far and as straight as they could go and her small fingers could just about grip the Colt .45 that she was pointing right at Hart's chest.

"What you fixin' on doin' with that?" asked Hart, quite still.

"You bastard!" she said in her soft little girl's voice. "I'm goin' to shoot you dead!"

Seven

Hart stared at the face, at the dark eyes that seemed to be set just a fraction too wide apart; he watched the upturn of the mouth, the unchanging fall of hair, the fineness of the nose. The hands were steady, white to the bone with effort; her arms showed no signs of dropping but in time they would. A Colt Peacemaker .45 weighed two pounds, four ounces. Anyone could buy one for seventeen dollars, mail order. All you had to do was buy some shells and point it at someone and given skill or luck it was accurate at up to forty yards.

The girl was no more than ten yards away from Hart and he guessed she meant what she'd said. She'd sure been tailing him around long enough to make up her mind.

Strange, standing there with that pistol in her hands and the hammer cocked, she no longer looked timid as an antelope.

Hart sighed: It weren't so strange.

"Who are you?" he asked.

The tip of her tongue appeared momentarily between her lips. She gave a quick shake of her head as if to say that don't matter none and her hair came back over her shoulder and fell against her pale cheek.

"What's your name?"

The tongue pushed farther, curling down.

"What's he to you?" Hart's head nodded backward.

She opened her mouth as though she could no longer breathe through her nose. The tongue disappeared. A woman was standing watching them from the far side of the street, wicker shopping basket held in both hands and resting against her legs. Not moving, doing, or saying anything, watching like it was some kind of free show.

Back inside the jailhouse, Hart reckoned they were still playing their game of checkers.

"He your feller?"

"No!" The word almost spat from her mouth.

"What then?"

"He's kin."

"Close kin?"

"He's my brother."

"Uh-huh. That's why you're goin' to kill me, huh?"

"Yes!"

"On account of stickin' him in there." Another backward nod.

"Yeah!"

"You know what would've happened to him if I hadn't done that, don't you?"

"Sure I do. He'd've got away."

Hart shook his head. "He'd have got lynched. You'd be cuttin' him down right now."

"No."

For a second her fingers tightened farther around the gun and Hart thought it was going to fire; but at the last second she relaxed just a little and sucked hard on the side of her cheek instead.

He wondered how much longer he had to keep her standing there before her arms got too tired.

He said: "You wanted him to get clear?"

"Of course I did. What d'you think?"

"He killed a man."

"So . . . ?"

"Killed the sheriff. Shot his head clean away. With a gun like that. That what you want to do?"

"Yes!"

"You sure of that?"

Her head moved to one side and swung back. "You miserable bastard, I'm goin' to kill you just as you stand there!"

Zack Moses was walking slowly along the boardwalk and had come into the corner of Hart's vision. The mayor was toting a double-barreled shotgun and fixed to use it. If he did he was about as likely to cut Hart in two from that angle as he was the girl. Besides, Hart didn't want to see her shredded to pieces in front of his eyes.

He gave Moses a quick look that warned, keep out of this, and hoped that the girl didn't notice and get panicked into pulling home on that Colt trigger.

"You ever killed a man before?"

" 'Course not!"

"Killed anything?"

"You're goin' to be my first."

Hart kept his breathing even; her arms were beginning to sag at the elbows. He didn't know if she realized that yet herself and thought that when she did she might decide to fire the gun before it was too late.

"What you aimin' to do after you've killed me?"

She blinked back at him, the wind that had begun to push down the street from the northeast sliding her hair over to the corner of her left eye.

"You fixin' to get him out of there, Jacob?"

"I ain't goin' to leave him there to rot or hang just for . . ."

"Then you're goin' to have to kill a whole lot more folk after you've killed me."

"I . . ."

"You know that, don't you. You know there's two men sittin' tight guard on your precious Jacob inside and if you kill them there'll be others when you get out." Slowly, almost imperceptibly, Hart was beginning to walk forward as he spoke. "Maybe you can get a gun for Jacob an' he can kill a few with you. Pretty damn good at that is Jacob. Killin' folk. You saw what happened to the sheriff I guess, Jacob blasted half his head away. From maybe thirty yards, too. Sheriff never had a chance to draw his gun. You knew that as well, didn't you. Merle Wringer never as much as got his gun out of his holster before your ever-lovin' Jacob blew him all the way to eternity."

"I . . . I . . ."

The arms were near bent into a V shape and the barrel of the gun was lowered almost to the point where it would have shot away one of Hart's kneecaps if it had been fired. There were no more than six or seven feet between them and Hart could see the tight lines alongside her mouth and extending either side of her eyes. Her shoulders were beginning to shake.

"You ain't goin' to' fire that gun, are you?"

Hart took another pace forward and her arms jerked awkwardly upward, like the arms of a puppet whose strings were almost out of control. He lunged for the gun, turning his face and chest aside as he went forward. There was a blast of fire and Hart fell sideways, taking the girl with him. One of his hands was locked around her wrist, and the Colt fell into the dirt of the street as she struck the ground.

"You bastard! You rotten bastard! You . . ."

Hart moved onto one knee and pulled her half-up with his left hand.

"You bastard!"

He slapped her across the side of the face, once, with the inside of his right hand.

She choked on her next shouted word, gasping for air. Tears tried to force their way from the backs of her wide eyes. Hart waited and watched and for a couple of moments he thought she was going to hurl herself against him and sob, but she was made of different stuff.

Rebecca screwed her fingers tight into her fists and rammed

her fists into the tops of her legs. She twisted her head till her hair was back over her shoulders. There wasn't a tear on her face, nothing but frustrated anger, hatred in her eyes.

Folk were coming cautiously across the street and back of them the two guards had left their checker board to see what the shooting was about.

Hart stood up, lifting the pistol she'd been threatening him with from the ground. He broke the gun and unloaded it, letting the shells fall into the palm of one hand. He dropped the shells into the front pocket of his vest and tossed the Colt back down toward the girl.

"You want to have another try, go get yourself some more ammunition. Only next time, don't waste your breath talking. Aim the thing and squeeze the trigger. For you there ain't nothin' else goin' to work."

Rebecca stared up at him, surprise modulating the anger and tension of her face and body.

From the depths of the jailhouse, Jacob's shouts of rage and anger filtered jaggedly out onto the street.

Hart pushed his way through the circle of onlookers and headed up toward the livery stable, leaving a couple of dozen gawping people in his wake.

*

He was wearing a green wool shirt that was buttoned almost to the neck, his leather vest buttoned in a couple of places also; a light brown scarf was wound loose below his chin and the brim of his hat was pulled down till it all but covered his eyes. The wind was coming down between the hills, skimming a layer of dust with it. None of the grass or the spare scrub was thick enough to hold the land. After a couple of hundred yards following the upward trail of the creek, Hart reined in and found a red and white kerchief down in one of the saddlebags and knotted it at the back of his head, lifting the front up over his mouth. He touched his spurs lightly into the gray's flanks and they continued their slow, winding climb. Just when he was beginning to think that the land was never going to level out and that Ethel Spencer's memories had played her false, Hart saw the start of a widening away from the narrow run of the creek.

He rocked his body in the saddle and the mare climbed with

more vigor until they came to a place where the terrain closed in on them again.

Hart let the mare drink what little water was running down from the hills, a slow and haphazard trickle down along the worn channel of the creekbed. He took the water bottle from the pommel, slid down the kerchief, and set his back to the wind and dust as he drank, washing the coating from the roof of his mouth and the back of his tongue.

"Hell, Clay, you reckon we're goin' to find this Hollow place or not?"

The mare turned her head, tossed her mane, and resumed her search for water. Hart glanced up at the antics of a bluebird, enjoying the wind and using it to good effect, celebrating each new insect taken on the wing with a shrill, triumphant threefold whistle.

He remounted and continued the climb, but now it was markedly less steep and he could see a band of light between the closing of the hills up ahead. For the first time in maybe half an hour or more a smile drifted across his face. He urged the mare toward the gap and pretty soon he could see for himself it was the way Ethel Spencer had described it.

The land had suddenly bellied out into a grassed valley broad enough to have held a good-sized herd of horses. At the far end was the shack that she'd spoken of, only from where Hart was sitting it looked to have been repaired some and a new tin chimney stack was poking up from the center of the flat roof. The broken-down corral had been mended and now it held eight or nine horses. A couple of saddles were draped over the top fence and here and there other bits of tackle were hanging.

If Ethel and her former suitor had ridden up there right then, they might have figured the place a little too occupied for much sparking to get done.

The man on the hillside some eight feet above the level of Hart's head moved out from the partial cover of the scrub oak and levered a shell into the barrel of his rifle.

Hart sat perfectly still, making no attempt to go for his Colt, making it clear that he was doing anything but. He was getting a little tired of having guns pointed at him, but he figured that whoever had been left up there on guard was a shade more likely to press the trigger home than young Rebecca Batt.

He held tight rein on Clay with his left hand, the palm of his right curled about the top of the saddle pommel, listening to the lookout scrambling down the slope back of him. He knew he was there when the firm barrel end of the Winchester jabbed deep into his back.

"The Colt," the guard said. His voice was gruff and deep as if it was coming from a long way off; from the Winchester that was still poking a hole alongside his spine Hart knew that to be an illusion.

He used thumb and middle finger to slip the safety thong off the pistol hammer, then lift the gun clear by the butt, and swing it slowly sideways until it was held out at arm's length.

"Let it go."

He let it go. From the corner of his vision he glimpsed the man duck forward to pick it up. There was a half chance of freeing his right boot from the saddle and taking a kick at the man's head, if that landed he could hurl himself sideways from the saddle and dive on the feller before he got a chance to use his rifle.

That way he might get clear but he sure as hell wouldn't get inside the Hollow. He'd already seen enough to know that if Speedmore wasn't holed up inside, someone else outside the law was there in his place.

Hart let the moment pass and the guard shifted back out of his range of sight.

"Ride down to the place. Easy. Try anything funny an' I'll blow a hole in your back bigger'n a buffalo's head."

Give or take a little exaggeration, Hart believed him.

They moved down the valley at a slow walk, the mare scenting the other horses in the corral and throwing back her head once or twice. A black stallion ran up and down inside the fence, showing off. When they were almost level with the corral the man behind Hart gave a two-toned whistle, repeated twice. The shack door took a couple of minutes to open and when it did the men who came out were armed fit to stand off a sheriff's posse.

One was a chunky-looking Mexican with a long drooping mustache that left his mouth a long way behind and all but tickled his neck. He had crossed ammunition belts over his sloping chest and a gun belt with two holsters sagging a little loose over his hips. Neither of the pistols were in their holsters; both were in his hands. The man alongside him was thin and gray and wearing the brightest yellow shirt that Hart had seen in a long time. He had a shotgun hefted across the crook of his left arm and a couple of pistols tucked down into his pants belt.

"Who the hell's this, T. J.?"

"How the hell should I know?"

"Then what's he doin' here?"

"Don't know that either. Why don't you ask him?"

Yellow-shirt grinned lopsidedly and stepped forward. "Maybe I will."

He poked the shotgun up through the air and motioned for Hart to get down from the saddle.

When he was on the ground, the guard came forward and led the mare off to the side, looping her reins around the end of the corral.

"You got his gun, T. J.?" said the Mex.

"Sure I got his gun—what you take me for?"

The Mexican cleared his throat noisily but held it in his mouth. "Why you think I ask?"

The guard cursed and lifted the Colt .45 from his belt. "Pretty damned fancy, huh?"

"Lemme see," called the Mex.

"Go to hell!" snarled the guard and jammed the Colt back into his belt.

They were, thought Hart, a pretty friendly bunch.

"Who are you, mister?" asked yellow-shirt, but before Hart got a chance to answer, a voice from inside the shack called: "Get him in here!"

There wasn't any arguing. The three men watched Hart closely as he went toward, then through the door. Inside there were two pairs of bunk beds, one against the right side wall and the other back of the door. A couple of bedrolls were stretched out on the floor, the first close up by the stove at the center of the room and the other on the opposite side of the door to the bunks. To the side of the stove there was a rectangular table with a lot of nicks along the edges as though someone had sat there with a knife and made what he figured were pretty patterns. A large black pot was on the stove, hot water bubbling gently. Close beside it was a coffeepot whose red enamel was half chipped or blackened away.

The lower bunk on the side wall was occupied by a man lying along it clothed and darning a brown wool sock. He was taking his time to get it right, hardly looked around when Hart entered the room.

At the table another man, this one with a scar sweeping down from below his right ear to below the collar of his check shirt, was reading what looked to be an old newspaper. Wire-framed spectacles were pushed down to the end of his nose and he squinted through them at the small, smudged print.

Beside the stove, one boot standing on someone's blanket, was a half-breed Indian with high cheekbones and shiny skin, a pair of dark eyes that seemed oddly luminous in the subdued light of the cabin. He had a cup in his hand and looked as if he'd been in the act of pouring himself a fresh helping of coffee.

It was, Hart reckoned, a nice homely scene; not at all like the squabbling that had been going on outside.

The man he figured for Cherokee Dave Speedmore looked him up and down and nodded to himself, reaching the lid of the coffeepot and going on with what he'd been about to do. The guard said something about being half frozen by the damned wind and reached down a tin mug from where a line of them had been hung from nails hammered into the back wall. He lifted the pot from the stove and helped himself.

Still one man was tending to his darning and another was finishing a column in the newspaper.

Still no one else had asked Hart to explain just what he was doing riding in on their hideout with a Colt at his hip and a Henry in his saddle scabbard, looking like he knew how to use either or both of them if he had to.

It occurred to Hart they weren't asking on account of they figured they already knew. It wasn't the first time he would have been mistaken for a lawman and if he got out of there it wouldn't be the last.

"That his gun?" said Cherokee suddenly, catching sight of the carved pearl handle sticking up above the guard's waistline.

"Yeah, I . . ."

"Give it here."

"I took it, I . . ."

"Here!"

The guard shrugged his shoulders with evident annoyance but he pulled the pistol from his belt and handed it across nonetheless. Off to the side, the Mexican sniggered loudly. Cherokee examined the Colt carefully and nodded in admiration.

"Those men over in the state capital are fools," announced the man seated at the table, removing his spectacles with a sigh and folding the newspaper carefully in half and then half again. "Fools and swindlers both."

He turned in his chair and looked up at Hart, looking at him properly for the first time. Hart could see the livid welt of his knife scar, even in profile. It sent the memory of the two gunmen Fowler and himself had left out in Monterey racing across his brain. He wondered where they were right then; wondered if they'd gone after Fowler or himself. Maybe they'd just set it down to experience and gone on about their business.

Maybe not; right now it didn't seem too important.

The man on the bed finished his darning and swung his legs around from the bunk. "What we got here?" he asked in a pleasant voice, as if Hart had stopped by to pass the time of day over a cup of coffee.

Cherokee Dave Speedmore drank a little more of his own and passed the cup down to the bunk.

"Thanks," the man said, wiping at the underside of his blond mustache before he drank. Two swift swallows and he passed the cup back.

"That his gun?" he asked, nodding at the Colt in the breed's hand.

"Yeah."

"He totin' anythin' else?"

There was a moment's uncertain pause.

"Rifle in his saddle," said the guard.

"Uh-huh." The man pushed himself up from the bench and it took him some time to get to his full height. Most tall men stop at a couple of inches over six foot but not this one. When he was standing as tall as he could, he was forced to bend his head some to stop from banging it against the roof.

Hart guessed this was High-Hat Thomas. Stick a fair-sized Stetson on him and he'd pass for one of them tall buildings he'd seen over in San Francisco.

Thomas stuck a hand out toward the breed.

Cherokee let him have the gun.

Thomas admired it for a few moments. "Where's your badge, mister?" he asked, looking at the Colt, not at Hart direct.

"I ain't got no badge."

"No badge, huh?" Thomas was still looking at the gun, watching the snake struggling inside the pearly beak of the eagle, writhing inside its pearly claws.

"No."

"Just happened on this place by chance, huh? Takin' a ride for your health? Passin' the time of day?"

"Somethin' like that." Hart nodded.

High-Hat Thomas smiled wryly and moved faster than Hart had figured he might. The butt end of the Colt smashed down against Hart's forehead and his knees began to buckle under him. Black jetted up over his eyes. He stuck out a hand but there wasn't anything for him to catch hold of. Thomas swung the gun a second time and the butt connected with the top of the head this journey. The black was deep red and as Hart fell he tried to open his eyes but the lids seemed to be gummed shut. He heard something he half realized was the sound of his own body striking the floor and then the side of his head collided with the base of the stove and he neither felt nor heard anything at all.

The Mexican laughed and cleared his throat again, only this time he turned his head and spat it out through the open door as if wanting to prove that he was house-trained.

High-Hat Thomas wiped a smear of blood from the pearl grip of Hart's Colt and tossed it back to Cherokee, who stuck it into the front of his gun belt.

"Search him," Cherokee ordered while Thomas went back to his bunk. "Go through what he's wearin', then his saddle things. An' make sure anythin' you find you bring in here."

The men grumbled and got on with their task.

Cherokee finished that cup of coffee and started another. High-Hat found a shirt that needed some stitches in the seams under one arm. At the table, the scarred man had put his glasses back on and was reading a dime novel about Billy the Kid.

Eight

In his dream he was sitting in a restaurant with red and white check tablecloths and candles burning dimly from where they'd been stuck into the tops of wide-bellied bottles. Wax was clogged in deep rills against the sides. The light flickered and in his dream Hart blinked. Kathy was in the restaurant as well but she wasn't with him. She was sitting off to the side and there was a man with her, though Hart couldn't see who he was because his back was turned.

Hart tried to figure out where the place was and he guessed it had to be Frisco again on account of the clothes that people were wearing and the size of the interior.

There must have been food on his plate but he didn't know what it was, didn't know if he'd been eating or not; he couldn't look down to see on account of a pain in his head and another, keener pain that jolted every now and then between his ears, cutting against bone.

He called her name and at first he thought she couldn't hear him because his voice refused to rise above a whisper. But then she turned her head slowly, like in a dream, toward him and her eyes were dark fire, accusing him. Accusing him and he didn't know what of. He wanted to turn his head away but his own pain held him there and he was forced to watch as the skin around the eyes gradually started to slip away and shrivel. He had to watch as Kathy's mouth opened in a smile and the lips peeled back to reveal teeth that were blackened and broken and that rotted and fell from her face. Soon all that seemed to remain were the eyes: the accusation.

Hart's hands were working, tearing something, paper, tearing paper, tearing a letter, her letter, a letter asking him . . .

"Hey!"

The icy water splashed into Hart's face and his head jolted with a painful gasp, the dream washed away.

"Hey! Wake up, you bastard!"

Hart's eyes flickered open and he winced a second before the Mexican's hand crashed into the side of his jaw and drove him back against the wall.

The crown of his head was throbbing with an insistent, repeating ache and he knew that the swelling above his eye had to be the size of a duck egg, though a different color.

His hands were tied behind him and his legs were roped tight together at the ankles, knees drawn up toward his chest. He didn't know how long he'd been unconscious, but it had been time enough for the gang to go through his belongings with care. On the table behind the Mexican he could see the sawn-off Remington ten-gauge, his Henry rifle, and the double-action Starr .44 that was a souvenir of his time fighting for the Confederacy in the War Between the States. At first he thought they'd failed to find the Apache knife he kept stashed in his boot, but then he realized that both boots had been pulled off and thrown under one of the bunks and the knife blade was sticking up from the far end of the table, just back of where Cherokee Dave Speedmore was sitting, a sneer cutting hard across his face.

High-Hat Thomas was sitting over the door, a chair reversed under him. None of the other men were in the cabin.

"You better do some talkin'," said the Mexican threateningly.

Hart glanced up at the round mustachioed face and laughed.

The Mexican punched him in the mouth.

Cherokee laughed.

"You the law?" asked Thomas. He managed to look tall sitting down.

"You know everythin'."

"Answer the question!" shouted the Mexican and aimed another blow at Hart's head, only this time he held it back.

"I ain't the law," said Hart. "You didn't find no badge, did you?"

"That don't have to mean nothin'," suggested Cherokee.

Hart shrugged. "Suit yourself."

"You could be a Pinkerton, one of them?" High-Hat Thomas's voice was quieter than the rest, more reasonable. Hart didn't trust it; he'd been at his most reasonable immediately before he'd pistol-whipped him unconscious.

"Sure," agreed Hart, "I could be, but I ain't."

"Then what you doin' here?" asked the breed.

"Ridin' through?" suggested Hart.

"Very funny!" snorted the Mex.

"Not as funny as lookin' like a greaser on the front of some trashy book," said Hart.

The Mexican punched him in the mouth. He was still swinging when Cherokee got off the table and grabbed his arms, pulling him away.

Hart spat some blood from between his lips and didn't bother about it splashing down the front of the Mexican's pants.

"Why, you . . . !"

"Take it easy! Hold off, for God's sake!"

Cherokee spun the Mexican around and propelled him back against the table. The Mex's hand made a move toward the gun at his right hip and Cherokee's face tightened into a mask. He had his own pistol out and pushed up under the Mexican's ribs before the other man could clear leather.

"I ought to blast you away!" Cherokee hissed.

The Mex managed a halfhearted sneer but one side of his mouth was quivering and his eyes were a lot wider than they had been moments before.

"Forget it," said Thomas, winding himself up from the chair.

The tall outlaw moved between the two, lifting Cherokee's pistol with his forearm and waiting until the hammer had been released and the gun was back in its holster.

"Go help with the horses," Thomas said without turning his head.

"You said . . ."

"I said, go help with the horses." Thomas's voice was still soft and reasoning. Underneath he was hard as well-honed steel.

The Mexican gave a token scowl and stomped out of the room.

High-Hat Thomas leaned back against the table and forced Hart to look a long way up if he was going to see his face at all. Cherokee was off to the side and seemed anything but patient. Hart wondered where the others were and what needed doing with the horses; it could be they had a raid planned and that Hart's presence was holding them up. They could even think he'd got wind of whatever they were planning and had come snooping around for that reason.

One thing was certain: No one was about to believe that he'd happened upon the Hollow by chance.

Hart moved his head slowly from side to side and asked for something to drink. Thomas poured half a cup of lukewarm coffee and bent double, holding it to Hart's mouth. A couple of mouthfuls was enough. Thomas pulled the cup away and leaned back against the table and waited.

One of the men outside was whistling a hymn.

Hart said: "I was down in Fallon. Couple of days back. Had a little trouble with the sheriff down there." He paused and caught a quick look pass between the two men. "Seemed to think playin' stud with a marked deck weren't right. Some fool ranch hand made a fuss about bein' cheated out of his money and the sheriff he comes over to the saloon an' accuses me of cheatin' and tells me to ride out of town within the hour."

"What you do?" asked Cherokee.

"What would you do if a man accused you of cheatin' at cards in front of witnesses?" Hart looked from one to the other. "I killed him, of course."

"You shot the sheriff?"

"That's what I said."

"Down in Fallon?"

"That's right."

Cherokee started to laugh, a low, deep sound that began in

his belly and worked its way up slow and gradual. Thomas levered himself up from the table and stood, head hunched down, in front of where Hart was tied on the floor.

"This lawman you claim you killed, tell me about him."

Hart shrugged, thought for a couple of minutes. "Near as I recall, he was dressed pretty smart. Clothes looked like they come right out of the store an' onto his back. Real neat little beard he must've had trimmed in the barber shop every damn mornin'. Struttin' around with that badge on him like some peacock."

The door opened and the newspaper reader with the scar down his neck came into the shack; he went across the room and around the stove and stood close by the back wall.

Hart carried on with his story. "So there he was all shinin' like the Fourth of July an' fixin' to use that Smith & Wesson he had at his hip, I beat him to it, that was all. Cleared that Colt of mine and let him have it right between the eyes."

"Between the eyes?" queried Thomas.

"Well," Hart shrugged, "mite above 'em, tell the truth."

"Tell the truth!" scoffed Cherokee. "You wouldn't recognize the truth if it was crawlin' up out your own ass!"

Hart leaned back toward the wall and looked at Thomas. "Never mind what he says. What I'm sayin's gospel. You send one of your men down into Fallon an' ask 'em what happened to Merle Wringer. They'll likely take you out the cemetery an' show his grave marker. Maybe even got my name on it."

"Your name," said Thomas softly. "Now you forgot to tell us exactly what that was."

"Batt," said Hart. "Jake Batt. Jacob, my pa, had me christened."

There were a few moments of silence inside the cabin. Outside the whistler had found another tune much like the first and you could hear horses, restless and close.

"You believe any of this shit?" asked Cherokee.

Thomas shook his head. "Not a deal."

"You, Bailey?"

The scarred man grinned. "What I heard wouldn't even make the back page of the *Butte Times and Express*."

Cherokee came closer to Hart and pointed a finger at his face. "Mister, you best start prayin' up a few last words while you got the chance."

The breed leaned his body away and his long fingers found

the butt of Hart's Colt peacemaker, where it was sticking up from his belt. The triple click of the hammer coming back was underscored by the sound of a horse and rider coming along the valley at a canter.

"Mescal?" Cherokee turned questioningly toward the center of the room.

Thomas gestured that he had no way of knowing.

Bailey went back around the stove to the door and threw it open. "Yeah," he said. "It's Mescal right enough. Looks pretty lathered up 'bout somethin'."

Hart couldn't hear everything the newcomer said, but he heard enough to pick out the news that the sheriff down in Fallon had walked into the saloon and got himself a slug through the brain pan.

"You see it?" called Cherokee.

"Saw the earth an' read me the marker."

Hart allowed himself the beginnings of a grim smile.

"How d'it happen?"

"Hell, I didn't stay long enough to find out. Some of those boys down there, they was actin' mighty jumpy with strangers. Followin' me all 'bout the place like they was 'bout to get tar an' feathers an' see me out the hard way."

"You don't know who killed him, then?"

"Only what I heard."

"Yeah?"

"Some feller put one in him from thirty yards in bad light, near inch perfect."

"What feller?"

"Hell, I don't . . . wait a minute, Bird, some such . . . no, wait on . . . Batt, that was it. Fool name if ever I heard one. Batt, that was the feller. Did us one hell of a good turn when he blowed that lawman away, no mistake about that."

Cherokee and High-Hat Thomas were staring down at Hart and their expressions were starting to change. The breed extended his arm and pointed the pistol at Hart's face and squinted up his eyes along the barrel. He laughed a guttural laugh and used his thumb to release the hammer.

"It does seem like you might've been tellin' the truth after all."

"Surely does," added Thomas. "Only that still don't say how you got up to the Hollow."

"Easy," said Hart. "I was on the run from a bunch of fellers whose idea of a little fun was throwin' a rope around my neck an' stretchin' it from the nearest tall tree. I headed off into the livery stable an' this old-timer in there, he shook me by the hand for shootin' the sheriff and told me if I didn't have nowhere to run to come up here."

"Why here?"

"Said it was used as a relay by a bunch runnin' stolen horses. Ten or more years back. Deserted now, he said. Good place to lie low."

Hart looked at the men and waited.

"Makes some kind of sense," allowed Thomas.

Cherokee grudgingly agreed that it did; he seemed more than a little disappointed that he wasn't going to be allowed to blast Hart's skull into fragments and scatter it all along the cabin wall.

"What we goin' to do with him?" asked Bailey from the doorway.

"You got any ideas?"

"He's that good a shot, why not let him ride with us?"

"You out of your head?"

"What we got in mind, one more gun won't go amiss."

"You goin' to trust him with a gun?"

"Sounds like he puts it to good use. Hell, he's already got rid of the sheriff for us. Ought to give him a vote of thanks for that anyway."

"He can have a vote of thanks," said Thomas. "But he ain't gettin' a cut of that bank money. We're splittin' that too many ways as it is."

"I never said nothin' 'bout givin' him no share. Take him along for the ride. He proves as useful as his mouth is, we might want to take him in for whatever we set up next." He pushed the back of his boot against the jamb of the door. "Don't see what we got to lose."

High-Hat Thomas agreed that they'd call the boys together and talk about it, which they did. Finally it was agreed that Hart could ride with them into Fallon, but his hands would be roped to the saddle all the way to the edge of town and he wouldn't get his fingers around a gun until they were close by the bank itself. One of them would be watching him all the way in and at the first sign of a sneaky move they'd take his head off from the back with the first shot. If he played it right he'd get a place to sleep for a few days and maybe even an offer to join up. If not, that was his lookout.

The Mexican voted no all the way along the line, saying they should string him up like the folks down in Fallon had wanted to do, except that he wanted a little time alone with him first so that he could work on his nose and his *cojones* with a blade.

Cherokee might have been tempted to go along, but there was still something about Hart that made him curious and he knew that once he was hanging from a cottonwood with his balls stuffed in his mouth he wasn't going to be saying very much.

So they loosened the ropes at Hart's feet and wrists and gave him some stale bread and a few bits of fatty bacon, with some more weak and cold coffee to swill it down. He didn't know exactly how he was going to play it when they finally rode back into Fallon, but he knew it wasn't going to be the way Cherokee and High-Hat had got it planned.

Whatever happened, he wanted time to teach the Mexican some lessons and he hadn't forgotten there was a pretty price that he intended to collect riding on at least two heads.

Nine

Aram Batt slid his hands into the water and pulled the twin lengths of branch clear. The river eddied around his arms and he paused long enough for it to settle. His fingers felt the cold of steel beneath the cold of water. The trap had shut but the beaver had gone; all that remained was the furry stump of his foot where he had gnawed it off to make his escape.

Aram sighed, shook his head, and reset the trap. There was time enough before the coming of the snow and ice for him not to worry overmuch about one hide more or less.

Better that the creature should escape of its own accord than that it should be stolen by the Indians.

Since the occasion when he had come upon two of them in the act of unloading his traps and left them dead in the river—their lookout making a bloody and sudden third—he'd scarce seen sign of a Blackfoot at all. Least, what signs there had been were distant ones and unlikely to disturb him overmuch.

Back on the bank, he set the four beavers on the back of his mule and took the time out to break off a chew of tobacco from his possibles sack. He touched the clay stem of his pipe and promised himself a good smoke when he got back to the shanty. He was feeling wolfish and his mouth began to water at the thought of the side of antelope that was waiting for him. Two hours he'd spent tracking her down, laying in wait until the moment when that lovely head thrust up into the sights of his .40-.60 Hawken.

He'd savored it as he pulled the trigger and he did so again now, heading back through the underbush, moving gradually away from the main stream of the river.

The place he'd built was fashioned from skins stretched over a framework of slender poles that had been bent skilfully to make a sloping, semicircular shell. Inside this his belongings were packed and covered—tea, flour, salt, coffee, the dried meat he had left, and the nuts and wild plums that he'd collected and kept in old tins.

In front of the shelter was the remnants of a large fire, the center of which would still be smoldering and hot. At either side of the fire were the graining block on which he worked the skins and the frame upon which they were then stretched.

So far it had been a goodish season, nothing like the old days when the Rocky Mountain Fur Company and the American Fur Company were dividing things up between them. Big profits to be made and every trapper worth his salt was signed up with one outfit or the other and some of them ready to kill a man who worked for the opposition if he showed his face in the wrong territory.

Now those days were over and everything was starting to change. Aram was freelancing again and spent both seasons out in the wilderness with his own company. Wouldn't see another white man, most likely, till he made it back down to the trading post at the fort a couple of days ahead of the worst weather. It'd be fine when he got there and he'd enjoy the warmth and the sound of other voices coming from other heads than his own. He'd eat hot food and drink bad liquor and after maybe a week he'd be hankering after the mountains again, the sounds of water moving through the trees and the chatter of birds, the silence.

Aram got the fire going and rinsed his mouth with water. He bit into a piece of hardtack and chewed on it while unloading the mule. His long-barreled rifle he leaned against the side of the shanty carefully, never letting it far out of his reach.

Soon he was sitting down on a makeshift stool and tamping cut tobacco down into the base of his pipe. When he got it lit and was drawing the strong smoke down into his lungs he thought—for no reason that was apparent to him—of his brother, Jedediah. He wondered how he was getting on working that miserable patch of land of his where nothing seemed to grow and the hogs and the cattle took fever most winters and never survived 'round till spring. Stuck there with that wife of his—too good for him by half—and all them damn kids.

Aram tapped the end of the pipe stem against those few teeth he had remaining at the bottom of his mouth.

Kids must be pretty old by now. Men and women, more or less. Eldest flown the coop and gone, he shouldn't wonder.

Never knew with Jedediah, though. Strange old bastard with his Bible and his psalm-sayin' and hymn-singin' and the like. What the hell a woman like Rachel wanted to get herself tied down to a lifetime of psalms and hymns and misery, Aram had never understood. He'd have shown her a better time if she'd come up into the wilderness with him. Least she'd've laughed once or twice. He doubted if Jedediah permitted laughing.

All them times his brother would try to get Aram to go into partnership with him. Come on with me and we'll get us a good stake of land, build a place, we can raise crops and cattle and kids. Make a life for ourselves and our young 'uns. It's what men got to do, Aram. You know that. You read it in the book, heard it from the preacher. Go forth and multiply.

Multiply, shit!

Only thing that brother Jedediah succeeded in multiplying was his kids. Never seemed to be so damn fruitful when it came to stock or anything that was meant to sprout up out of the land. Never enough money to buy clothing or boots or even nails to fix up the house. Stop the wind getting in and tearing it down. Stop the cold. The rats. Stop death.

It occurred to Aram that sometime his brother had to die. He wasn't a young man any longer and the life he'd chosen had worn him hard. Could be he'd pass on and Aram'd never know about it. They weren't likely to pass the news up there by the Missouri, that was certain.

When it came for Jedediah Batt to leave for the promised land not a lot of folk were going to shed a tear or wave him on his way and wish him good luck.

Aram grinned to himself and sucked on his pipe, satisfied. Weren't no one special going to be mourning him, neither, but then that was the way he chose it. That was what he'd wanted. Lots of the other trappers, they bought an Indian squaw and took her into the mountains with them. She made the food and kept the place clean and at nights she was warming enough, that was pretty certain. Aram knew of some men, took a squaw they bought for a parcel of hides and spent four or five winters with her without ever exchanging as much as a single word. Just a succession of gestures and grunts and that was all it took.

Not for Aram: He'd gesture and grunt to himself.

He wanted company, someone to talk to, well, he'd strike up a conversation with the mule. Least it wouldn't quote the Bible back at him, try telling him how to live his life.

Hell! He knew how he wanted to live his life and he was doing it. Weren't nothing or nobody going to come along and make him change.

Ten

They'd sent Bailey and the Mexican in ahead. Hart rode with the main group: Cherokee and High-Hat Thomas at the front, then Mescal and the guard who'd first got the drop on Hart and whose name turned out to be T. J. Bodine; next came Hart with yellow-shirt close at back of him—though today his shirt was dark blue and his name was LaRue. All of them were well armed and none of them was going to hesitate before pulling the trigger. They'd got the word that there was going to be close to a couple of thousand dollars in the Fallon bank and they wanted to hit it while the money was still there. Their idea of hitting a bank seemed to involve getting as many men inside as possible and scaring the hell out of everyone in sight. While that was going on, a couple of others would brandish their weapons up and down Main Street and keep other folks clear.

As a plan it lacked subtlety but that wasn't going to prevent it from working.

It had worked over at Ely, when the bunch had taken the Mining Company bank and shot two of the staff, leaving the manager dead and a clerk crippled. On that occasion they'd ridden clear with eight hundred dollars. This time the stakes were higher and they were going to make all the more certain that no one stood between them and the money.

With the sheriff in Fallon a few days dead and likely nobody in his boots, there wasn't anyone who was likely to stop them. Unless it was Hart.

"Hey, now!" LaRue called from behind him as if somehow he'd read his thoughts. "Remember I got this gun drawn and you covered. All the way down to the wire!"

Hart glanced over his shoulder at the thin, balding man who sat in the saddle grinning his lopsided, gap-toothed grin. "Yeah," he nodded, "I'll keep it in mind."

LaRue scowled and spat and Hart swung away. In less than half an hour they would be in Fallon.

★

The bank was right across the street from Zack Moses' store. It was a pretty imposing-looking building, with a balcony jutting out from the upper story so that it covered the boardwalk and slim pillars pushed down from underneath the balcony edge into the dirt of the street. There were glass windows set at either side of the front door, three more windows, curtained, above.

There was just enough wind to shift the sign where it hung over the sidewalk.

Bailey was sitting on a rocker close by the door, enjoying the comforts of the chair that was generally used by the bank's manager when business was slack. Bailey was able to make use of it this particular morning on account of the bank being about as busy as hell come Sunday. Three or four farmers were in town to negotiate a loan or pay some of their mortgage; the local manager of the stage line was checking that his men's wages had arrived in time to be collected and taken out to the surrounding way stations the next day; old Mrs. Parsons had brought in the profits from her rooming house and was set to add them to her savings account.

It was a busy day and busy enough without the sudden influx of extra custom that Cherokee Dave Speedmore and the rest of his bunch were intent on providing.

Bailey stretched his legs, one boot hooked over the other. He had his wire-frame spectacles on the end of his nose again and he'd picked up a local newspaper and was going through it column by column. He was also keeping a check on how many folks were going in and out of the bank, whether anyone who looked useful with a gun was hanging around too close, and what signs there were of a new lawman being in town.

The Mexican was thirty or so yards lower down and on the opposite side. He was leaning back against the side wall of the barber shop, hat sloped over his eyes and the toe of one boot making slow patterns in the dust. No one was about to interrupt and ask just what he figured he was doing.

His and Bailey's mounts were tethered close by, their reins looped over the barber's striped pole. The hitching rail in front of the bank was full and when the gang arrived they were going to find themselves squeezed across to the far side of the broad street.

One horse, one mule, and one brightly painted rig waited already outside Moses' store, their respective riders inside making purchases and talking with the mayor about the need to appoint a new peace officer to replace Merle Wringer just as soon as possible.

Zack Moses placated them and assured them the town council was making inquiries about the most suitable replacement. He was sure they'd have a man in the job by the time he was needed. Sure of it.

Zack rubbed a hand across his stomach and glanced through his store window as a tall rider in a steep hat went slowly past, checked his mount, and turned.

Yes, they'd get their new sheriff soon enough.

★

Cherokee rode alongside Hart and quickly pulled back the long coat he was wearing to reveal the pearl-handled Colt. He lifted it toward Hart's body and smiled. "I still ain't sure I shouldn't pull this trigger right now an' leave you in the street for dead."

Hart glanced around. "Do that, you're liable to get yourself a mite more attention than you need."

Cherokee swiveled the pistol on his finger and handed it toward Hart, butt first.

"One false move . . ." he said, letting the threat ride.

"Yeah," said Hart, "I know."

High-Hat Thomas dropped to the ground and threw his reins up to LaRue. He waited for Cherokee, T. J., and Mescal to dismount, and the three of them went over to the bank together, pushing the door open nice and easy like they were customers much as any others.

Once they'd gone from sight, Hart knew he had to wait a couple of minutes, hitch his horse across the street, and keep the north end clear of trouble. The Mex was handling the south. LaRue held the horses.

Bailey folded his newspaper carefully, looked over at Hart,

and gave him a short nod that might have been either warning or greeting, there was no way of knowing. He took off his spectacles and slipped them into his pocket, patted his holster a couple of times for luck; then he, too, entered the bank.

Hart stood close enough to Zack Moses' store to shout out a warning that the mayor was half certain to hear. But Moses was busy persuading a woman to buy a new pair of button-down shoes and he wasn't paying heed any longer to what was going on out front. Hart turned away from the store and saw that LaRue was watching him carefully from the saddle. Down the street the Mexican had shifted his position a little; his hat was no longer down over his eyes and he was watching a couple of men arguing about cattle prices just below where he was standing.

Up toward the end of town a tall feed wagon was trundling toward the livery stable, drawn by a team of four long-eared mules.

When Bailey entered the bank, the others were all in their positions. Cherokee was standing over by the side wall, opposite the counter and its two clerks, pretending to read the official notices pinned to the bulletin board. T. J. and Mescal were leaning against the end of the counter nearest to the door. T. J. figuring out some arithmetic on a scrap of paper. High-Hat was close to the door, a look of expectation on his face and one hand hovering awful close to his pistol.

Bailey looked at all three men, set his glasses back on his nose, and headed for the manager's office.

He knocked on the door, took half a pace back, and waited.

Sy Enderby opened the door with a patient smile and a warm handshake. "What can I do for you?"

"You the manager here?" Bailey's voice was so soft that Enderby instinctively lowered his head toward the speaker.

"Yes, I am. Sy Enderby, that's me. Anything I can do will be a pleasure. That's the way we like to do business."

The manager beamed and Bailey smiled quietly and kept hold of the man's hand.

"Just one thing."

"Go ahead."

"Open the safe."

The hand that wasn't gripping Enderby's suddenly produced a small derringer and stuck the twin barrels against the banker's right ear.

Cherokee threw back the flap of his long coat and produced Hart's sawn-off Remington and poked it in the direction of the counter.

"Don't nobody move or you're dead!"

Four men and one woman standing at the counter spun around and stared. One of the men began a move toward his belt and stopped as the shotgun angled around to cover him. The woman opened her mouth in a shrill scream.

"Shut her up!" Cherokee nodded to T. J. and jabbed the shotgun toward the woman.

T. J. took three steps and slapped the woman around the side of the head with the knuckles of his right hand. She gasped, sobbed, looked as if she might scream again. The outlaw drew back and clipped her under the chin hard enough to drive her back against the counter edge. When she bounced forward, he rammed the butt end of his pistol into her teeth and laughed as she sank down spitting blood.

"Get them drawers empty!" ordered Cherokee, pointing at the two clerks. "Fill a couple of sacks an' do it fast!"

Mescal moved around behind to make sure it was done.

Bailey had moved the manager over to the safe and was standing close behind him as he fumbled nervously with the lock. The derringer was still at his head, this time resting immediately behind the ear.

Out on the street the Mexican was still watching for trouble and had his back toward the bank. Hart started to walk into the middle of the street, not running but not going slow. LaRue swiveled his horse through a half circle, hand tight on his gun butt.

"Where the hell you reckon you're goin'?"

"In there."

"Like hell you are! Your job's out here on the street."

Hart kept on walking, past LaRue now and almost at the boardwalk.

"I'm warnin' . . ."

"Forget it, LaRue!"

Hart half turned and his hand was hovering over the pearl handle of his .45. LaRue clearly wasn't about to forget it. He went through with his draw and got the tip of the barrel almost clear of the leather before a slug from Hart's Colt ripped through the flesh at the top of his right arm and exited with a fierce spray of blood that showered over the nearest mounts.

The gun fell away from the balding man's hand and Hart jumped toward the bank door. As he did so he was conscious of the Mexican turning and shouting in his direction, but he could wait.

High-Hat Thomas had whirled fast at the gunshot and had the door half open, his gun hand poking through. Hart chopped down on it with the barrel of the Colt, and the force of the blow vibrated along his own arm.

Thomas went numb to the elbow and the pistol was forced from his fingers. Hart shouldered the door inward, taking Thomas back against the wall. Hart jumped through the doorway just as Cherokee was swiveling around the shotgun.

Hart swung up his arm and shot the breed through the head. It was an almost exact replica of the shot that had killed Merle Wringer, only this time there was no doubt it was aimed and true.

The Remington slid toward the floor as Cherokee was driven back hard against the wall. Hart snatched it up and lifted it with his left hand, covering Mescal and T. J. with the .45.

"Freeze!"

"Bastard!" called T. J., but froze anyway.

Thomas was looking a little groggy over by the door, and Hart pushed the Remington in his direction.

"You, too, High-Hat."

Thomas cursed him and stood there swaying.

"You folks," Hart said to the bewildered customers, "hit the floor! Now and fast!"

They did as they were ordered but they weren't quick enough. Bailey swiveled the bank manager around in front of him so that he formed a shield and rammed the little .22 right inside his ear.

"Okay, feller. Now how you fixin' to play this one? You drop them guns or this man here's gettin' a bullet through the brain.

Hart hesitated, feet running toward the door outside, and he guessed they belonged to the Mexican.

"Your choice," said Bailey, beginning to move his shield along behind the counter toward the door.

There wasn't enough of him showing to aim for and Hart didn't want to be the cause of the manager's death if he could help it. He slowly began to lower both weapons as Bailey continued on his way.

"Let's go!" Bailey called to the others. "Let's move it!"

Hart was midway to the floor.

With a holler the Mexican appeared in the open doorway. He was armed and coming straight for Hart with anger bright in his dark eyes. He got one pace through before there was an almighty roar from the street and a couple of barrels' worth of 0-0 gauge shot from Zack Moses' gun drove into his spine and the back of his neck.

"Jesus Christ!" sang out T. J.

Hart came up straight quick as a whip but not quick enough to prevent Bailey from squeezing back on the trigger of the derringer and sinking a .22 slug into Sy Enderby's skull.

Hart leaned his body to one side and brought up the Colt fast. Bailey let the banker fall and made a dash for the door, twisting the up-and-over barrels of the small pistol around as he went.

Hart shot him twice, splintering the left kneecap and breaking the shinbone of the other leg. Bailey hit the floor face first and rolled over toward the wall. T. J. made a rush at Hart, who ducked under his blow and brought the barrel end of the Colt up into his jaw.

High-Hat Thomas made it through the door while this was going on and found himself face to face with Zack Moses and a long-barreled shotgun that had just been reloaded. Behind the mayor were the getaway horses and behind them were half a dozen of the local citizenry, armed and looking pretty damned angry. Mescal sprang after High-Hat and was welcomed in the same way.

LaRue was writhing on the ground with a short, fat man standing over him, a rifle close to the top of the outlaw's balding head.

Hart pushed T. J. ahead of him and down into the street. He stood in the doorway to the bank and hoped to hell that the folks out there knew whose side he was on. From the looks on their faces and the way they were fingering their guns he wasn't any too sure.

He lifted both arms wide of his sides, Colt and sawn-off held well clear of his body. "Glad you got here in time to stop the Mex, Mr. Mayor."

Zack nodded and lowered the shotgun toward the ground. "Didn't think you'd be comin' back to visit so soon."

Hart shrugged. "Didn't have a deal of choice."

"You still ain't wearin' no badge, though."

Hart grinned. "Didn't seem to make a whole lot of difference."

Zack Moses started to say something and then his face changed expression fast. Hart read the warning and turned on his heel in time to see Bailey crawl through the door on his hands and knees, the derringer between his fingers and pain clear in every move.

Hart watched Bailey balance on one hand and try to bring the pistol up. He swung back his right leg and kicked out, the underside of his boot smashing into Bailey's face, its heel cutting a line through the cleft of his chin. Bailey was lifted up onto his knees and his eyes shut tight so they didn't see the round-arm swing that brought the cut-down barrels of the Remington into the side of his face like a hammer.

There was a fierce, sustained cracking sound and Bailey rolled along the boards and slumped down into the street.

"That see it done?" asked the mayor.

Hart nodded. "I guess so."

"Let's get these beauties in the jail and then you and me can have a drink, maybe. You look as if you could use one. We'll talk about what's happened. I guess it'll be a good story."

Hart slipped the Colt back into its holster and stepped in behind Mescal and Thomas on their way toward the jailhouse. LaRue was being carried and T. J. was being dragged more or less by the hair.

Short of the jail Hart turned and looked back down the street. Rebecca was standing over near a water trough, her long black hair shrouding her face, hands at her sides. She was quite still, staring into Hart's face for as long as he stood where he was. After he'd turned away he could still feel her eyes piercing his back; even the door of the jailhouse didn't help.

Eleven

She was sleeping up in the hayloft at the livery stable, curled in upon herself tight as she could. The blanket that was covering her showed only the fingers of one hand, one side of her face, the dark of her hair. Hart stood by the top of the ladder and looked down on her for several moments without either moving or speaking.

When he was kneeling over her, he held his hand ready to cup across her mouth.

She sensed his presence—not him but someone—and swung awake, her arm jerking up as she lifted her body off the straw.

Hart's hand muffled her shout and above it the dark eyes were wild with fear: surprise.

"It's okay. Just take it easy. Calm down."

She wriggled her mouth against his hand sufficiently to sink her small teeth into his palm, small and sharp like a young animal's.

Hart winced and cursed inside his head but clung on.

"I ain't goin' to hurt you."

She struggled and beat her fist against his arm, the side of his head. Hart knocked it away and kept his temper checked. He could feel her warmth from sleep; the pressure of her face against his hand was strange, not unpleasant.

"I want to help you."

She bit him again, but without as much force.

"I'm goin' to take my hand away and I don't want you to scream. You got that?"

She nodded beneath his hand.

"Okay."

Hart lifted his hand from her face and she didn't scream. She dived both hands for his face, nails seeking out his eyes. Hart blocked both arms upward and she scratched twin lines up his forehead and into his hair.

"Bitch!" he hissed and trapped both wrists and flattened them against the straw, twisting her around as he did so.

"I said I wanted to help."

"Like you did Jacob?"

"Your brother got what he deserved."

"And those men yesterday. Them at the bank. I suppose they deserved it, too?"

"Sure they did."

Rebecca shook her head and fought with him again till he slackened his grip and allowed her to turn back around and sit up; he wasn't letting go of her hands yet.

"Yesterday ain't nothin' to you."

"Why did you do it?"

"I said it ain't nothin' to you."

"You rode into town with those men. Pretended to be one of them. Then you turned on them."

"It weren't like that."

"That's not what folks around here say. They say you joined up with 'em and then back-shot 'em for the reward money."

Hart showed his anger on his face; his fingers tightened on

her wrists until she called out. "If that's what they're sayin',
they're wrong. They don't know what happened. I didn't have
no choice but to come ridin' in with 'em. An' I sure as hell
didn't back-shoot anyone. Didn't shoot anyone I didn't have to."

"But you did do it for the money?"

"Some of it, sure. Couple of 'em had a price on their heads.
Reckon I can collect it as well as the next."

She seemed to have calmed down, her voice was less shrill
and her breathing had steadied. He let go of her wrists and
watched her carefully. She crossed her arms across her chest
and rubbed at them where he had held her.

"You do do things for money, though? Things like that?"

"I guess so."

"All kinds of things?"

"I ain't bustin' that brother of yours out of jail, if that's what
you're thinkin'."

She gave a quick shake of the head. "It weren't that."

"What then?"

"I want you to find my uncle."

"Find him?"

"Uh-huh?"

"How come?"

"My pa died. Just before you took Jacob to jail. He left a lot
of money we didn't know about. Left it all to his brother, Aram.
Lawyer says there ain't nothin' we can do about it."

Hart didn't feel it sitting right, not the way she was telling
it. "You want me to fetch him so's he can claim this money,
that it?"

"Yes."

"What?"

"Yes, that's . . ."

"That's all there is? You love this uncle of yours so much
you can't bear to think of him workin' his fingers to the bone on
some dirt farm somewheres not knowin' about all this money?"

Rebecca turned away and he grabbed her shoulder and spun
her back to face him. "What's the truth of it?"

One of the horses below stamped his feet and then kicked
against the back of his stall; the others shifted around restlessly. The first light of day was starting to filter through the
narrow gaps in the roof, and the kerosene lantern that hung
below was beginning to fade.

"Uncle Aram, we ain't seen him for years. I ain't only seen

him the once when he come visitin' and then he was an old
man, least to me he was, an' I was no more'n a little girl. He
lives up in the mountains, somewhere off in the wilds. Hates
folks, hates towns, anythin' like that. Pa was always tryin' to
get him to come an' live with us, but he wouldn't."

"He a mountain man?"

"He's a trapper, I know that."

"But you don't know where he is? Where anyone can find
him?"

She pushed her thumb against the center of her lower lip.
"Jacob does."

"Jacob's in jail."

"You can talk to him. He'll tell you where to find Uncle
Aram."

"Always supposin' I intend to."

"We'll pay you."

Hart laughed: "You got money?"

"We will have."

There was enough light now to see her face clearly and he
was surprised at the mixture of youth and pain that he saw
there. Rebecca, in her turn, was staring at him with much of
the intensity of before.

"This why you've been followin' me around?"

"Partly," she admitted after several moments.

"I thought you wanted to kill me."

"I did."

"Now you want me to go find your uncle?"

"Yes." She swung her back around and tossed her head so
that her hair flared out for a second over her shoulders and
revealed a glimpse of a cream-white neck.

Hart had a moment's impulse to reach forward, slip his fingers beneath her black hair, and touch that neck.

He didn't; he said, "How you fixin' to pay me when you ain't
got no money?"

"I told you, we will have."

"Who's we?"

"My kin."

"Uh-uh." Hart shook his head. "You mean your uncle."

"But it's our money. All of us. Uncle Aram'll understand
that."

Hart grunted. "Not many folks are so understandin' when it
comes to money. Kin more than most."

"Maybe our family's different."

Yeah, thought Hart, I guess maybe it is at that.

"You'll do it?" she asked, a trace of excitement jarring her voice.

"I'll talk with Jacob. I'll go that far and see what happens."

*

As soon as Zack Moses was up and about, Hart went over and talked to him about the Batt family and also about the possibility of getting some kind of payment from the town council for saving their money from being stolen from the bank. Moses put him on to John Quinton and Hart found the attorney asleep in the back room of his office above the dry goods store and waited long enough for Quinton's spidery fingers to fix himself a cup of coffee and set his brain working. He found out as much as he could about the Batt will and what the attorney told him supported the facts of Rebecca's story. That done, Hart stepped over to the jailhouse and had words with the temporary acting sheriff, a former stage line guard who'd been fired for persistent drunkenness. The stink of cheap whisky was rampant in the office and the lawman hadn't bothered to hide the empty bottles that were already beginning to line the side wall beneath the gun rack. If he carried on that way, Hart thought, nothing would be easier for Jacob than to sucker the sheriff out of his keys and get himself good and free. Right now, that weren't none of his business.

Hart watched carefully as the man signed the two reward applications Hart had filled in, then took them from him and slipped them down into his back pockets, ready for the mails. If he left them in the office with the sheriff they'd likely still be there when he got back from searching for Aram Batt.

Supposing he did get back.

Supposing he ever went.

"Your prisoner . . ." Hart nodded toward the rear of the office.

"Whichever one? Damn jail's so crowded since you come back to town we're having to keep a couple of them bank robbers locked in a shed."

"Won't harm 'em none. It's Jacob Batt I'm talkin' about."

"What about him?"

"I want to talk with him an' I ain't so keen on too many other folk knowin' what about. You reckon you could see your way fit to bringin' him out here and leavin' us alone for a while?"

The sheriff shook his head and the action made him belch, the stench of whisky fumes filling Hart's lungs. "Can't no way do that. That man's my responsibility. Anythin' happen to him an' . . ."

He cut short and stared down at the five-dollar bill Hart had just placed in his hand.

"Buy a lot of whisky," Hart said.

The sheriff scratched his head, grabbed the bill before it disappeared, and mumbled: "Guess you can look after him pretty good, you bringin' him in in the first place an' such. But no one's gotta hear about this, you understand?"

"I understand. Have him in here one hour from now."

Hart left the sheriff to think about the bottles he was about to buy to replenish his supply and went looking for Rebecca Batt. As usual when he was in town, she wasn't hard to find. More or less as soon as he emerged from the jailhouse, she was there right across the street, staring that same damn stare.

"Did you talk to him? To Jacob?"

"Not yet."

"But . . ."

"It's all arranged for later."

"You could've talked to him then. You could . . ."

"Could have, but there's some things more important."

"What kinda things?"

"Breakfast. My stomach's playin' hell with me an' I aim t'eat before I do anything else." He caught hold of her and spun her round. "Come on!"

"Where d'you think I'm goin'?"

"You're havin' breakfast with me. Now move it!"

"I ain't doin' no such thing," she complained as Hart propelled her forward.

"Yes, you are. I know damn well if you ain't sittin' alongside me, every time I look up I'm goin' to see that face of yours starin' at me through the window. Nothin' puts me off my food quicker than someone starin' at me while I eat. Even you."

Rebecca shrugged and allowed herself to be hurried along the street to the dining rooms. It wasn't until she was midway through her plate of ham and eggs that she looked up at Hart and asked: "What did you mean, even me?"

Hart shook his head and carried on chewing. "Nothin'. Didn't mean nothin' at all."

But the way she continued to look at him, her head slightly to one side, suggested that she didn't altogether believe him. Hart did his best to ignore her, concentrating on his hash and eggs and coffee, knowing that down inside he didn't believe it either.

★

Jacob Batt was a mixture of fierce anger and driving urgency: He clearly would have liked to rid himself of the cuffs about his wrists and the length of chain by which the sheriff had attached him to the leg of the heavy desk. Since he wasn't going to be able to do that, he used his energies to convince Hart he should head up toward the North Platte River and locate Aram Batt.

"You can tell him what Pa did for him. Tell him if he comes back he's got all that money waitin'."

"Suppose he don't want to come back? Suppose he don't want the money?"

"What kind of a man d'you think he is?"

"Them mountain men—never can tell. Got to be somethin' strange, choosin' to live the way they do, never seein' another white man maybe for months at a time."

"Aram ain't all like that. He's close kin."

"So the both of you keep sayin'. Sure don't seem to have brung him close yetaways."

"Pa's money weren't there before." There was no missing the bitterness in Jacob's voice.

"I still don't see how I get paid for all this. The Platte ain't just a day's ride, you know. More like a week on the trail without a break."

"Uncle Aram," Rebecca put in, "he's bound to pay you good for tellin' him. You can work that out with him. I guess you'd get, oh, couple of hundred dollars easy. More maybe."

"An' if he don't want the money?"

"All he has to do," said Jacob, "is come into town an' see lawyer Quinton, sign a paper, an' . . ."

"An' release the money over to you," Hart finished for him.

"That's right," affirmed Jacob.

"Then we can pay you ourselves," said Rebecca.

" 'Course, that's what you're hopin' he'll do, ain't it? Sign the money over. That's the only way you'll get what you reckon's rightly yours, ain't it? Less'n old Aram turns up dead."

"You'll do it?" said Rebecca a shade breathlessly.

"He'll do it," said Jacob, contempt in his voice. "He's the kind'll do anythin' for money."

"That's right." Hart nodded, stepping away. "Even money from the likes of you."

He knocked on the door and the sheriff came back inside, looking a little more glassy-eyed and walking a mite less steadily than he had before. Hart waited to make sure that Jacob was set back in the cell without trouble and then ushered Rebecca out onto the street.

"You best get back to your ma. You done what you had to do."

"I can't leave Jacob here alone."

"Sure you can. It's a time before the circuit judge gets to these parts. You can ride in an' visit, bring him stuff from home. You won't do no good hangin' round Fallon; no good's goin' to come to you either."

She looked at him and pursed her lips tight together. Hart knew he was wasting his breath to argue further. She'd do what she wanted to do, advice or no advice. He touched her lightly on the shoulder and she jumped like she'd been stung. He left her there outside the jail and went down to Zack Moses' store to get supplies for his journey.

Twelve

Aram was thinking about the time he'd come up against the Blackfeet at Pierre's Hole. That had to be back in '32 when he was still a young man and the bristles on his beard were soft as the underbelly of a dove. He'd not been with the Rocky Mountain Fur Company long, eight, nine months at most, when all hell seemed about to bust loose.

When they'd reached the rendezvous at the end of the spring season, there'd been trappers there so thick it was like watchin' the waves pump down the ocean till they hit the shore. Not only Rocky Mountain men, but them from the American Fur Company, half a dozen smaller outfits, a few ragged-assed freelancers. Only three things got talked about among all that carousing and celebrating that always greeted a season's close: The first was what had been took and how—after that the men were full of the way the Blackfeet were whooping themselves up into a state of bloody glory and the rumor that the Hudson's Bay Company from up north were aimin' to push down south of the Missouri and muscle in on trade down there.

It wasn't clear which the trappers feared most—the invasion

of a new group of men into an already overcrowded area, or the last-ditch attempt of the Indians to keep the whites out of their hunting grounds.

The beaver were going to be trapped out inside another ten years if things escalated from what they were and then, Indians or no Indians, there'd be damn all to hunt for anyhow. There were buffalo on the plain, sure enough, but chasing them wouldn't occupy all the men who were going to be fighting to make a living. That left deer and elk and antelope, maybe bobcats and wolves, but they promised slim enough pickings.

Anyhow, the rendezvous ended without anything being settled one way or another and Aram rode out from Pierre's Hole with a bunch of Rocky Mountain men, some fifteen in all, led by Milton Sublette and a Boston merchant by the name of Nathaniel J. Wyeth. They hadn't got above eight or so miles and made camp, when these Blackfeet rode up and asked for a parlay.

Sublette agreed and sent a small group of men out under a flag of truce. Aram watched them ride out and remembered being surprised at them as Sublette had chosen—he'd heard enough of them cursing the stinking savages the night before to know they weren't best suited to talk peace.

From where he was watching, he couldn't see clearly what happened, just the sudden movements and the sound of shooting and the realization that the negotiators had killed one of the chiefs while they were exchanging greetings.

Well, all hell did bust loose right about then. A rider went galloping back to the Hole to fetch the rest of the trappers still there and the Indians lit out for a batch of trees and the firing began in earnest. The battle, for that was more or less what it was, went on all day and by the time dusk approached there were five trappers dead and three times that many wounded. Most counts called for a couple of dozen dead Indians, which amount became greatly increased in the later telling. Aram himself reckoned the true total of dead Blackfeet was nearer to seven or eight.

It could have been the end of himself as a trapper. He was not much more than a boy and scared as all hell let loose. He'd near enough been forced to rope himself to a tree to keep from running, wave after wave of Indians bearing down on them, and then, later, when they were trying to smoke them out of the trees, it had seemed there was a warrior behind every trunk, an arrow singing through every patch of air.

But he'd stuck and when it was over (for then; if it would

ever be over) and the men were shouting and bragging and
drinking, he'd felt different. Sure, they blasted all hell out of
the painted bastards! Sure, they'd stood together an' seen every
charge come to nothing. Hadn't they gone through that timber
like an army, driving out everything in sight?

No, they hadn't: A rumor that another eight hundred Blackfeet were approaching had been enough to make the trappers
withdraw and at that point the Indians slipped away and the
battle had faded to an inconclusive end.

No one was saying that, not during the celebrations. There
were hunks of cowmeat to eat, sizzling hot and still tasting of
blood. Any amount of raw corn whisky to drink. One of the men
broke out his fiddle and another found a three-string banjo and
pretty soon a few of the men who came from the Appalachians
were step-dancing while the rest whooped and hollered. A big,
red-haired, red-faced man went weaving and swaying in between the dancers, whirling a Blackfoot scalp around his head
and shouting: "I tickled this bastard's fleece but good!"

Thinking back on it now, sitting there under his shelter of
skins, Aram knew the foolishness of it. Blind stupidity. At the
time he had been sucked in and likely would be again if it
ever happened. Now, though, the big companies no longer kept
armies of trappers working the rivers. Now it had gone back
to a clutch of men working alone, selling what they caught for
themselves, and getting little enough for their labors. One half-
year rendezvous after another there were less of the old boys
there; more and more the meeting at Fort Bent or Fort Laramie was a telling of tales of them as had passed on. And each
time Aram looked around for the youngsters who were coming
to the life as he had done; and each time they were not there.

He felt old and strange, almost extinct. Like the buffalo. Like
the beaver. Something he recognized as civilization was
spreading fast and wiping them all out.

It was what his brother had always said, but what he knew
of Jedediah, the way of life he'd made for himself, was little
improvement upon what Aram had up on the Platte. Build a
place and stock it with a wife and children, cattle and hogs.

There was a moment, drawing hard on his clay pipe, when
Aram felt a loss of what he'd never had: his own flesh and
blood. As he felt that, the memory of Rebecca rushed back to
him like the fall of water down a mountain cliff in sunlight.
The child, no higher than his knee, running toward him, black

hair spraying around her face, arms reaching out till he caught her and swung her high in his arms.

Aram could feel her tiny, bird-bone body, the warmth of her breath on his face and neck, the scream of fear and excitement as he whirled her around and around.

He set down his pipe and stood up.

Old fool that he was, sitting there and making himself homesick for what was never his home. Feeling regret for kids he'd never had. Never wanted. Just a stupid old fool!

Aram looked around his camp site, then up at the sky. The clouds were getting that much lower every day, dull and gray and heavy like they was laden with snow. He looked west beyond the Laramie River and the fort that of course he couldn't see— the tops of the Rocky Mountains were white and getting whiter. Pretty soon South Pass would close and there'd be no one else journeying through from the Colorado River, the Great Salt Lake. All the old rendezvous were out there, scattered beneath those snow-topped peaks: Henry's Fork, Bear Lake, Cache Valley, Green River, Pierre's Hole, Popo Agie River—Aram swung his head slowly from the southwest around to the north, remembering.

To hell with it!

There was work to be done before the snow came. One of his snowshoes wanted mending; the sewing on the birchbark canoe needed resealing with pine pitch; his leggings were beginning to split at the seams. Let him get to it and enough of this foolish daydreaming. Let him get to it now!

Thirteen

Fort Laramie had begun life as a way station in the 1830s. Originally it had been used by the Rocky Mountain Fur Company for their caravans of wagon and pack mules and later it was used by the American Fur Company for the same purpose. The original building had been fashioned from timber, a log stockade that provided protection for those inside its surroundings. This was replaced in the early 1840s by a thick adobe wall, which was extended when the army took over the fort in '49. Inside the walls was a fair-sized barracks, cabins for the officers and their families, a warehouse and armory, a double corral, a billiard room and two bars, and several trading rooms.

Despite the fact that the army maintained a company of men stationed there, the fort was to some degree open to civilians and a large amount of the trading that went on within its walls was conducted by folks whose connection with the military was simply that of money or goods.

When Wes Hart rode through the tall gates under the watchful eye of the sentries, there was nothing out of the ordinary about his arrival. He had his Indian blanket draped over one shoulder and spread wide to cover as much of his chest and back as possible; a scarf was tied over his hat and under his chin, pulling the brim tight to his ears; scuffed leather gloves retained some feeling in his fingers. The mare's breath went before her like furls of silver-gray. He didn't seem any different from any other lone rider seeking warmth and something warm for his stomach, maybe someone to talk to, a place to throw down his blanket and feed his horse.

It wasn't long before he was standing with his back to the stove in the sutler's store, enjoying the warmth that was slowly coursing back through his body. All the way from South Pass the wind had threatened strong and there'd been more than a hint of snow in the way the clouds hung low over the peaks to either side of his trail. If he was going to get Aram Batt out of there before the weather closed them in, he didn't figure he had more than a couple of weeks, three at the most. There should have been longer, the trapping season had more than twice that time to go, but no one had bothered to tell that to the sky.

'Course, he could put up at the fort and wait for Aram to come slowly in, pack mules laden with furs behind him. Thing was, if he did that they'd be forced to winter where they were and there'd be little chance of getting back to Fallon before the spring thaw.

Hart had spent his time with the army and he wasn't about to volunteer for more. He didn't think the hardtack that passed for food in winter would have garnered any more taste or become any less stale. He could still remember the sergeant down in Apache country who splintered his two front teeth right across biting down through the day's chow.

No, he wanted to find Aram and argue him out. He'd even considered taking him out at gunpoint if the trapper refused to see reason—though if he did that the chances of his getting a rake-off from the proceeds of the will were less than healthy.

Not for the first time, he wondered why he'd taken the job at all. Some girl with strange staring eyes and her brother who'd shot and killed a sheriff when he was drunk and would just as happily do the same to Hart if he ever got a gun in his hands. He wasn't even getting paid for certain; he'd financed the trip on the promise of what he was due for capturing Cherokee Dave Speedmore and his buddy, Thomas. Zack Moses had been pleased enough to trust him for that.

Not for the first time, he asked himself what there was in Rebecca Batt's eyes that reminded him of Kathy. The way he'd seen her accusing him in his dream. Dark eyes boring and burning. The letter that had finally caught up with him and that he'd torn apart and never read. He hadn't helped her, hadn't even bothered to find out what she'd wanted, and now he was helping Rebecca instead.

Hart clapped his hands together behind his back and rubbed at the fingers. He'd been standing long enough; it was time to get to work, ask questions. He bought himself a regulation tot of liquor to warm his insides and set to it.

One man passed him to another and eventually he was sitting on a molasses barrel across from a gnarled-faced old-timer who went by the name of Wolf. Called that, one of the others had said, on account of he ain't never had enough to eat—if that was the truth, Wolf's skinny frame hardly bore it out. Under the worn and greasy hide leggings and fringed buckskin jacket, he didn't seem a lot more than skin over bones. His face had sunken in at the cheeks and the hairs of his scrappy beard were almost pure white save where they were stained with tobacco juice and spittle. His eyes had faded almost away.

"Aram Batt, you say. What you wantin' that old buzzard for?"

"D's that matter?"

"Sure enough does. Young feller like you, wearin' a gun like that you got there. Maybe Aram be best off if you never find him." He chuckled a little and a line of saliva started to run from one corner of his mouth. "Never took to other folks much at the best o' times, did Aram."

Hart shrugged. Outside he could hear the orders being barked out on the cold air as the wood patrol set out. "Got news for him. Message from kin."

Wolf chuckled again and wiped at the spittle with the back of his hand, smearing it through his beard. "Mister, you sure ain't Wells Fargo!"

"Never said I was."

"What then?"

"You know him good?"

"Trapped with him maybe seven, eight seasons. Run them blasted savages out o' Pierre's Hole when we was both wet an' slippery back of the ears. Yeah, I know him."

"Okay then. He had a brother, Jedediah, settled over to the west of here. Family. Eldest son called Jacob. They sent me after him."

"You said he had a brother?"

"That's right. Died an' left Aram money. All he's got to do is ride back with me to collect."

Wolf allowed himself another laugh and scratched at something that was biting at his scrawny leg under his leggings. The patrol wagons trundled toward the gate, dogs running after them across the parade ground and yelping.

"Don't know how much money it is, mister. But it's got to be a whole lot before Aram's gonna ride anywhere with you. I'll tell you that."

Hart shrugged. "That's up to him. All I'm paid to do is tell him what's his due. Rest is up to him."

Wolf looked at Hart through his weakened eyes like he was trying to get a better idea of whether he was likely to be telling the truth. He didn't want to set his old friend up for some kind of trap; then again, if this feller was telling the truth, he didn't want to stop Aram from getting enough money to pack in his trappings and live the rest of his life in comfort. Not that Aram would thank him for that though—hell, he wouldn't have done so himself until a couple of years back when he was forced to admit that his body just couldn't cope with the life anymore. Now he was grateful for whatever came his way.

He looked at Hart and sniffed loudly. "Got a plug of tobacco?"

"I'll get you one."

Wolf nodded, looking embarrassed. "Price of a drink?"

Hart stood up. "Whisky do you?"

Wolf grinned, gap-toothed and more saliva escaped into his beard. Hart headed toward the bar and pretty soon after he'd come back, the old man was telling him two or three places that Aram favored for his fall season. Hart pulled out a piece of paper and borrowed a stub of thick pencil and, with Wolf's help, drew a map of the area between the North Platte and the Sweetwater rivers. There was an abundance of creeks and most of the area was thick with untouched forest, save for where the army had

started making inroads in its searches for winter fuel. There were
Blackfeet still there, though their numbers were falling off with
each year. Those who remained were living off their wits more
than ever and fighting the trappers who still worked the region
for whatever was worth catching.

It sounded like two dying breeds fighting a rearguard action
against the inevitable.

Hart wondered how much persuasion it would take to get
Aram Batt to see things that way.

*

Aram pushed another piece of wood into the bole of the fire and
wriggled it around, watching the heart of it redden and expand
as the flames grew stronger and the scent of pine hissed upward.
He squatted back on his haunches and rubbed the tops of his
thighs, desperate to rid them of the cold. Hauling traps out of
freezing water was something he'd done as a matter of course
almost since he could remember. He had seen and heard of others
going down with attacks of rheumatism so bad they were as good
as crippled. Amos Jennings one time dragged himself close on
three miles with half a dozen beaver on a line behind him, legs
so bad he could no more walk than fly.

He shook his head from side to side and cursed the water
and his fool limbs for being so damned weak. Old and weak.
That's what he was.

"That's what I am, God damn it to hell!" Aram was standing,
trying to ignore the pain in his legs, brandishing a fist above
the treetops. "Old an' weak like . . . !"

Something came low through the flat sound of his own voice
and he stopped short. A few seconds to listen carefully and then
he was back in the shanty, lifting the tomahawk from the ground,
and sliding the haft down into the loop of his belt; knife and
pistol were already at his belt. His cold hands gripped the cold
barrel of the Hawken and he turned back to the fire. The rheumatism in his legs was forgotten. No point in trying to extinguish
the blaze, not now. With a final glance around his camp, Aram
slipped out of sight between the tall lines of timber.

*

Hart was in the third day of his search of the trapping grounds.
So far all he'd come up with was a mess of Blackfeet sign and

a line of Newhouse traps set back along a narrow creek that he guessed would eventually empty into the Sweetwater.

For the best part of an hour now he'd been slowly closing in on the smoke and scent of someone's campfire. The mare was hobbled back on the tree line and Hart was softfooting it over ground slippery with fall leaves that had held their coating of frost. Red and yellow-brown fringed with silver; webs flittered between the black branches of trees like silver rain. He wore his Indian blanket over a wool coat, scarf close around his neck. The safety thong had been pushed free from the hammer of the Colt at his hip and the Apache knife loosened inside its boot sheath.

Every few minutes he paused and listened—the crackling of the fire was just audible now, carried on the wind. Nothing more. The undergrowth was thickening and there seemed to be no sign of life within it. Hart pursed his lips, swiveled his head. Nothing. He didn't like it, didn't believe it. Carefully setting one foot before the other, he snaked his way toward the faint sounds of burning until he could see the orange glow through a haze of crisscrossed branches.

He wet his bottom lip with his tongue and almost immediately the moisture froze. He worked the fingers of his right hand, making the fingers move independently, then opening and closing them into the palm as fast as the skin of his gloves would allow.

"Okay, Aram," he said inside his head. "I'm comin' in to get you."

He moved a yard closer, then another, another. A thick trunk blocked the line of his approach and he changed direction left to pass it. A mesh of branches made him duck low, bend almost double. As he began to straighten he smelled something other than the pine of the fire. He . . .

An arm whipped tight about his throat like supple iron and he was dragged backward. The sudden moving flash of steel and a knife blade dived for his throat. Hart threw himself backward, the knife slashing inches from his neck, passing over a layer of his scarf without catching. He felt it cut into the weave of his blanket and jammed his right elbow back hard. The grip about his neck faltered but didn't unlock. He knew the blade was trying for his ribs. He threw up his left arm and went for his attacker's head, at the same time swiveling fast and trying to turn himself inside the man's grasp. He used his elbow again, elbow and knee, forcing it between the man's legs, and succeeding in ramming it against the muscle of the thigh.

He'd lost sight of the knife, didn't know where it was.

That bothered him.

Hart managed to free his left arm and he sent the forearm jarring against his attacker's chin; his right fist punched with all the force he could muster into the middle of the face and he toppled back against one of the trees. Hart's own knife was in his hand and its point was close against the wrinkled skin of the man's Adam's apple.

They stared at one another, both breathing hard.

It was long moments before either spoke.

Finally Hart said: "Had you for an Indian."

"I'd been an Indian, you'd've been dead."

"Maybe," Hart spat grudgingly.

There was another silence.

"Figured you for Blackfeet, too."

"You mean you didn't look?"

"Weren't about to stick my head out an' let whoever it was see me first."

"You could've killed me."

"Should've. This time last year I would've. Last year, hell! Left three braves dead in the creek less'n a few weeks back."

"Guess I should be grateful?"

"For what? Me gettin' old?"

Hart shrugged. The point of his knife was still all but resting against Aram's throat. "Happens to all of us."

"If I'd done like I was supposed to, wouldn't've happened to you an' that's a simple fact."

"Then I'm glad you didn't."

"Huh! Maybe you are. Don't help me none. S'posin' you was some Indian sneakin' 'round my camp to see what he could steal. I wouldn't be here now. Not alive an' talkin' I wouldn't."

"Then I guess we both got reasons to be grateful."

"Huh! Maybe."

Hart drew back his arm, turned the knife in his hand, and slipped it back down inside his boot. The blade with which he'd been attacked was on the ground close by his left boot; he set the boot firmly on it.

"Who are you, anyhow?" said Aram. "What fool business you got creepin' up on a man that way?"

"Depends who you are, old man."

"How come?"

"What name d'you go by?"

Aram glanced at the knife under Hart's boot. He shrugged and sighed. "Aram. Aram Batt."

Hart allowed himself the beginning of a smile, just the faded blue of his eyes and the corners of his mouth. "Then you're the one I want to see. Got news for you, from your kin. Might be good news. If'n you take it that way."

"You come all the way out here to find me?"

Hart nodded.

"Must be some important message."

"I reckon."

"What name you travel by?"

"Hart. Wes Hart."

"Could be a good thing I never cut your throat, Wes Hart. Even if you did ask for it."

Hart nodded and moved his boot. He picked up the trapper's skinning knife and handed it back to him. "Any food back with that fire?"

Aram Batt looked at him closely, nodded slowly, and led the way back to his camp.

*

It had been a time since Hart had eaten bobcat, and if he had his way it would be even longer before it happened again. The meat was tough and sinewy and tasted bitter as gall. He sat close by the fire, chewing away and making a token attempt to disguise his lack of enjoyment from his host.

While Aram had been preparing their food, Hart had told him about his brother's will and what had taken place back in Fallon. The old trapper had listened with obvious interest, but his only comments had been in the form of questions, seeking to flesh out what Hart was telling him.

When there was nothing more to come, Aram spat into the flames and reached into his possibles sack for his pipe and tobacco. Hart figured he'd talk when he chewed things over well enough in his mind, so was more or less content to sit and chew the tough meat and wait.

"Guess you don't reckon much to our cookin', huh?" laughed Aram.

"Cookin's fine. It's this damn bobcat I ain't so sure of."

Aram laughed louder and wiped the edges of his mouth. He

tapped the bowl of his clay pipe against his foot and sucked hard on the stem, striking a match and relighting the tobacco.

"That cat's pretty damn good for this time of the year. Let me tell you, boy, I done ate some strange things out here in my time. I ate crickets an' ants and one time when I was caught in snow up to my ass I wrapped my feet in a blanket and stewed up the soles of my moccasins! Either that or die of hunger." He glanced across at Hart. "That's the way it is up here."

"Yeah," agreed Hart, looking around. "Yeah, I can see."

Aram tried not to notice how bad his legs were paining him and did his best to disguise the twisting and drawing that was attacking the joints. Hart saw the pain shoot through the old man's eyes and tried not to notice it either.

"You know how he died? Jedediah?"

"Uh-uh. Way I heard it, he just took to his bed and passed on. Don't know no more'n that."

Aram shook his head almost savagely. "Hell of a way to go! Stinkin' poor and all that gold sittin' in the bank wastin' away."

"Weren't hardly doin' that."

"Never mind! Jedediah was, wastin' himself on that no-good land an' for what?"

Hart knew for what: Kids and a wife were what. *I want to marry you. For you to come and live here. For us to have kids.* *Standing in the kitchen of the home he had built for them, the one she had refused to live in. Staring at him, freckles across her nose and beneath her eyes, just staring, unsmiling. A strand of brown hair caught across her face.*

"Kathy, for Christ's sake, you don't understand!"

"No, Wes, it's you that doesn't understand."

He understood; knew.

"Wastin' himself for what?" Aram repeated, as much to himself as his visitor.

Hart shook his head. "I don't know," he lied.

Aram nodded. "You got a wife, kids?"

Hart looked into the fire, shook his head again.

"Never think about it?"

"Guess I did that much. Time back. Most men do, I guess."

Aram smiled and toyed with his pipe. "Like me, huh? Rather live your own life. Be your own man. Ain't so good gettin' tied down. Kids an' such, they're okay but they weigh you down. Stop you doin' what you want in your heart to do. Ain't that the way you see it?"

Hart spat into the edge of the fire. "Somethin' like that."

Aram stood up, wincing despite himself. "Figured it was. I'll fix us some coffee. 'Fore we ride."

Hart's head jerked upward in surprise.

"Ride?"

"Sure. What you said, Jedediah's wife an' kids, they got themselves a tough row to hoe. Specially with that fool Jacob gettin' himself stuck on a murder charge. Guess I better ride back with you an' see how things are. Get that money out from the bank an' hand it over to them as needs it most."

"You wouldn't be thinkin' of stayin'?"

"Stay there? Me, Aram Batt, settle down on some worthless farm for the rest of my days? What in tarnation you take me for?"

Hart smiled and leaned back, watching the old man fetch the coffeepot to the fire, trying hard as he knew not to show how bad the rheumatism was biting into him.

"Wouldn't mind seein' that little girl. Dark-haired little thing. What was she called?"

"Rebecca."

"That's it, Rebecca. Cute little thing she was. Held her in my arms an' swung her around till she laughed fit to bust." He started to rub his leg and stopped just in time. "How'd she grow up? Still cute?"

"Kinda."

"Yeah," Aram said quietly, "Always figured how she would be. Cute an' dark. Even be good to see her again after all this time. Rebecca." He set the pot on the side of the fire and looked across at Hart. "Damn it, hoss, that girl's my niece. Ain't got too many of those."

Fourteen

They stopped over at Fort Laramie and got as good a price as they could for the skins. Aram and Wolf fell over one another in greeting and set to a night's drinking that left Hart behind after the first couple of hours. Neither man got to sleep until the sergeant on night duty had given them the assistance of the billy club he kept for such special occasions. When Hart roused up at first light and went to look for them, he found the two trappers lying outside the guardhouse door, wrapped in one another's arms against the cold and snoring blissfully.

"Sweet, ain't they?" grinned the Irishman standing sentry.

"You didn't lock 'em up?"

"No reason when they're like that."

Hart nodded agreement and got the corporal to give him a hand in separating the two of them and shaking them back to consciousness. Aram woke slowly and grudgingly to a buffalo-sized hangover, a bump on the back of his head, and a tongue that was as yellow and bitter as a dried snake.

"Had yourself a time, huh?" said Hart, propping the trapper back against the guardhouse wall.

"Sure hung one on!"

"You surely did. Now you reckon you can drag yourself off to the washhouse, or I got to sling you over my shoulder an' carry you?"

Aram answered by levering himself gingerly away from the wall, stepping with care over Wolf's legs, and heading toward his destination with a straight back, his head in the air, and his route about as straight as a ship tacking into a headwind.

Hart watched him go, exchanged a laugh with the sentry, and tagged on behind.

Less than an hour later they were loaded up with supplies, most of which were tied to the back of the mule Aram was taking along with them. His other mule and his traps and equipment were being stored with Wolf, who promised to look after them until Aram returned.

"If'n you don't make it back this way again," Wolf had said, "I'll just take 'em out meself and trap a few pelts for you."

They'd all enjoyed the lie and played along with it, even as Aram assured his old friend that he'd be back for the spring season without fail. He may even have believed it.

They ate as much breakfast as they could cram down into their stomachs and rode out into the cold stretch of flat terrain that would take them toward South Pass. The hills ahead of them looked gray and forbidding enough, to say nothing of the snowcapped peaks that towered behind. The clouds were a little higher than the past few days and it was beginning to look as if the first serious fall of snow might just hold off until they'd forked southwest and found the trail across the Salt Lake Desert.

After that they'd drop down south of Cherry Creek Mountain and look to stop over at Ely, the place where Cherokee and High-Hat had taken the bank belonging to the Mining Company and got their names onto the reward posters for the first time. After Ely, they'd follow the high trail between Diamond Peak and Summit Mountain until they finally dropped down beyond the Shoshones and skirted Dry Lake. The road to Fallon was straightforward and easy from there on in, up through Frenchman and Salt Wells with the scent of the Carson River accompanying them all the way.

It was a hard ride, long and arduous and made only a mite easier by having company. For whatever reasons, both Hart and Aram seemed to shut in upon themselves as soon as they were in the saddle, keeping conversation down to what was essential, and thinking their own unspoken thoughts.

Only at night, wrapped in their bedrolls and with the fire between them, did they talk about themselves, mostly the trapper going back over the incidents of his life and exaggerating as much as any frontiersman ever did. Hart talked a spell about the time he'd ridden with the Texas Rangers, of the strange encounters with the wife of John Wesley Hardin, and how he'd been present that time in Florida when the Rangers stepped out of their own jurisdiction and arrested Hardin on the train while it was waiting to pull out of the station. He talked about the short time with Billy Bonney in the Lincoln County War and the even shorter spell as a United States deputy marshal. Of Kathy or the place he built for her, he never said a word.

Aram didn't speak of the time he swung his niece, Rebecca, in his arms either.

They weren't any different from most men of their kind in that, no better, no worse.

They didn't hear about Jacob until they were talking with a peddler a couple of miles outside of Ely. He told them how the boy had tricked the guards in the jailhouse into unfastening his cuffs and leggings so that he could go to the outhouse and grabbed one of their guns. He shot the two without hesitation and pushed both their bodies—one dead with a bullet through his brain and the other wounded in chest and neck—into the privy and stole guns and a horse. He emptied a half-dozen shots through the plate glass of the mayor's store and rode up and down the main street a few times firing at will, folks diving off the sidewalk for cover and all bloody hell let loose. Before Jacob Batt finally lit out of town there were two women nursing surface wounds, a seven-year-old kid with a slug jammed hard against his shinbone, a dead dog whose brains had been splattered all over the saloon wall, a badly maimed horse, and a lot more broken glass.

He'd shown again pretty soon. A trader on his way toward Fallon had been held up at gunpoint, his supplies strewn all over the road while the youngster took what he wanted. The man had handed over every cent he had with him and been lucky to escape with his life.

Three days later Jacob put a bullet through the back of a stagecoach guard and broke the arm of the driver before robbing the passengers and bursting open the strongbox and taking three hundred dollars.

A deputy had come close enough to him a couple of days after that to get a leg wound for his troubles. Since then there'd been a lot of rumors and not a deal more. Some folks reckoned Jacob had quit the territory altogether, others swore he'd been seen in the vicinity of his family's farm and was hiding out there; he'd been reported as far north as the state line and as far east as Ely.

The peddler didn't know which story was more like to be true than the rest; he just prayed he wasn't goin' to run into Jacob on the road.

"Young feller like that, must want to make hisself into another Billy the Kid, some such like that. Don't you reckon, mister?"

Hart didn't know what he reckoned for certain, except that he didn't see Jacob striving to make a reputation for himself as an outlaw and killer. He figured there was something else going wild inside the youngster's head, some strange mixture of frustration and anger that was all bound up in being forced to work all the hours that God sent among hogs and crops that refused to grow right—that and knowing there was money and plenty he reckoned was his except he couldn't get at it. Couldn't get at on account of it belonged legally to his Uncle Aram.

Close alongside Hart, Aram Batt was more or less reading his thoughts. "He know you're fetchin' me in?"

"Knows I'm tryin'."

"An' he can figure out when?"

"I guess."

Aram shifted his pipe across from one side of his mouth to the other. "Then he'll be waitin' for us. Somewhere along the trail."

Hart shifted in the saddle. "Welcome party."

Aram half laughed, removed his pipe stem from between his lips, and cleared his throat off to the side. "Sort of."

Neither man spoke for another mile or so and then Aram asked: "Supposin' you'd rid out to the Platte an' found me dead—what'd've happened to the money then?"

Hart didn't answer right off. "Jacob's next in line for it, the lawyer reckoned."

Aram set his face into the wind and said, unblinking, "Then the sort of welcome party he's got in mind for me is to blow my brains clear out my old head."

Hart looked over at the trapper but didn't say anything. There wasn't a deal to say. He'd already voiced the same thought inside his head a while back. The way Jacob was acting he'd got the taste of blood in him and he couldn't let go. Hart had seen it in other men before; seen it in Billy Bonney at times—the Kid's mouth would like to froth with saliva like a mad dog eaten up with rabies. It was one hell of a journey to bring a man just to get him killed.

"You know," Aram said, "I lived a long life an' a good 'un. Wouldn't have suited most folk but for me it was fine. Ain't never done nothin' I can't face lookin' at when it comes my time. Ain't done nothin' I come to regret bad inside. While I ain't about to say I'm done through with livin', I had more'n my time by most counts and if I pass on today or tomorrow, that don't matter too much. But I'll tell you—I don't want to go if it means one of my own kin's goin' to set me under the ground. You understand that?"

Hart nodded; he understood. He said so.

Aram said: "You know what this Jacob looks like, huh?"

"Yeah, I know him."

"More'n I do. That Rebecca I might know, though I doubt that. The boy I don't reckon I could place." He looked square at Hart. "You know him, you give me a chance. You let me know, too."

"Okay," said Hart. "You got my word on it. I ain't about to ride you back to your kin to see you shot, don't you worry none 'bout that. 'Sides," he added, with an attempt at a laugh, "you don't make it to that gold, how'm I goin' to get paid?"

★

Frenchman wasn't much more than a trading post with a few hangers-on scattered about it. Sod houses and dugouts, they made a rough circle about the only frame building, one story the width of a fair-sized saloon with another half story down into the dug cellar. The bottom section was used for storing corn and flour and supplies and in the worst of winter the animals were crowded in there so that the freezing wind wouldn't catch their blood and stop it in their veins. The main floor was divided into three, the major part of which was a bar and store and dining room, a long scarred and rough-hewn table standing on trestles down most of its length. The rest of the place was split off into the living quarters of the proprietor and his wife and a few bunk beds and straw mattresses that were rented out to any passing travelers with a dollar to keep out the night and the cold.

The place had belonged these past seven years not to a Frenchman at all, but to a fifty-year-old immigrant whose original home was somewhere in the heart of the Austro-Hungarian Empire and whose original name had long fallen into such disuse that he was hard put to remember it himself. With a stubbornness that was typical of the older settlers to the new, most folks insisted on calling him Frenchie, on the lines that any man who spoke American with a broken tongue could as well be from France as any other godforsaken place in the world. The Old World, that is.

Frenchie had taken on the place and worked hard to carve some kind of living from it; he'd taken on the name because he didn't want to offend those folks whom he depended upon for his bread and money; he'd taken on a part Yakima squaw whose tribe had thrown her out and who'd turned up at the trading post dragging a few belongings behind her on a travois and followed by a yelping one-eyed black-and-white dog.

She'd stayed.

The first two winters had been hard and to get through the second they'd butchered the dog and stewed it slow over the fire with turnips black from the fierce frost.

Gradually other folks had stayed instead of forever passing through. When the post had grown too small they'd either moved on or built for themselves places around the perimeter, huddled there for warmth or protection or both.

When Hart and Aram rode in there was snow in the air and the clouds sealed the land down like sheet iron. They hitched their mounts to the rail and pulled off their saddlebags and went inside, slapping their arms across their chests. Inside the lanterns were already lit and the stink of tallow was high and keen. A game of checkers was in progress close by the stove and an aging woman sat the far side of it, almost resting her stockinged feet against its base as she cradled a glass of beer between her hands and dreamed about some past that had never happened.

Hart went to the bar while Aram stood and looked carefully about the long room. Four or five others were sitting or squatting, drinking or staring at the walls.

Frenchie said there was meat stew, and when Hart questioned him further about the meat he shrugged his heavy shoulders and looked evasive. Other than that, there were potatoes hot in the oven, pie filled with some canned fruit that had lost its way between St. Louis and San Francisco, and the best coffee in this part of the state.

Hart bought a couple of beers to break the dust from their throats, two shots of whisky to warm their bellies, and ordered two platesful of stew and potatoes, pie to follow, and sure, he'd try the coffee if it was that damned good.

Aram had piled their belongings close by the center of the dining table and was sitting up to it, the fringes of his buckskin jacket silver with frost. Hart gave the other customers the once-over as he carried the drinks from the bar, but failed to see a face that he recognized.

"Food comin'."

"Tha's good."

Hart snorted. "Wouldn't bet on it!"

Aram nodded and wiped a layer of grease off the glass before sampling the whisky. It burned into the back of his throat like a knife and made the corners of his eyes water instantly.

"Makes his own, huh?"

Aram glanced at the Yakima woman near the stove. "Gets his squaw to piss in a pot an' keeps it buried underground while it collects a little flavor!"

Hart looked at the fat-armed woman stirring the contents of a blackened pot and laughed. "Wait till you get a taste of this stew."

"I have to?"

"Lessn' you want to ride through the night an' get your balls froze off."

Aram shook his head. "Might find use for 'em yet."

"We'll be out of here come sunup. Ain't many miles to go."

Aram sipped suspiciously at the beer. "I'll be glad when it's over."

★

The stew tasted better than they'd figured. Whatever meat it was, there were so few sinewy pieces of it floating on the thick surface that their origin scarcely mattered. But it was rich in something, and both men ate with relish, heads bent over their plates and spoons working greedily.

They were so intent upon what they were doing that neither of them noticed the slim figure detaching himself from a small group seated over by the side wall. His face was smeared with a mixture of grease and dirt, and through it the beginnings of a stubbly beard were pushing hopefully. His clothes were ragged and patched and as grease-lined as his face. At a quick glance he might have been an old man—but for the straightness of his body and the keenness of his eye. He slipped between the two men with whom he had been drinking and talking in a desultory fashion. Angling himself away from the wall, he slid a hand inside the folds of his heavy coat; the pistol that emerged was the only clean, shining thing about him.

Spoon to his mouth, Hart sensed the danger before he saw it. His body automatically rocked sideways, clearing the way for his right hand to make its clawing move toward the Colt at his hip.

The spoon clattered down into the plate and stew splashed across the table.

Hart yelled a warning and flailed a left hand toward Aram's head, trying to snatch him clear.

The fingers of his other hand hit the pearl handle of the Colt and began to pull it clear of the smooth leather.

Jacob fired once and Aram was kicked hard against the table, driving it forward into Hart's midriff. The thick edge struck against the back of his wrist and jammed the hand fast.

Jacob was one pace farther to the left and heading for the door. He had his arm extended and he was paying Hart no heed, intent upon doing the job he'd come to do, dispatching his long-lost uncle to his six foot and more of earth.

Hart's voice broke through the startled clamor of the room and he tried to push Aram off the bench and down to the floor. Even as he touched the trapper's shoulder he felt the body leap beneath his fingers as Jacob's second slug tore into him.

He kicked the bench away behind himself and leaped to his feet. The youngster had all but gained the door.

Hart's hand was free and the Colt came up fast and smooth.

"Hold it!"

Jacob kept on going.

"Now!"

The boy's hand grabbed at the handle of the door.

Hart squeezed evenly on the trigger and a .45 slug exploded through the back of Batt's left thigh, an inch or two above the knee. It broke away a section of bone and burst through the side of the leg, ricocheting off the inside of two walls.

Frenchie's wife was standing with her hands pressed against her heavy breasts, mouth and eyes wide open, staring.

Frenchie had yanked his sawn-off out from below the beer cask on the bar and was wondering where to aim it best. One or two of the other men had drawn weapons and most of them had taken whatever cover the interior afforded.

Aram Batt was stretched across the long table, his face resting half in the plate of stew. His eyes appeared to be closed, and his mouth was twitching open and closed like a fish claiming air.

Hart went around the table fast.

Jacob had somehow got himself propped against the wall alongside the door. One knee and the side of one boot were pressed against the floor, and his face and one hand were against the logging of the wall.

Hart couldn't see where the other hand was.

He went up behind him and swung his boot, hooking away the boy's legs from under him.

He struck the ground with a crash and rolled over, face up.

The Yakima woman screamed like an arrow piercing soft flesh.

Jacob's other hand still clung to the gun.

Hart waited till it was angled up toward him and kicked at the bone immediately at the outside of the wrist.

The fingers flew open and the pistol looped useless away.

Jacob's eyes flickered and closed as his head turned away.

Aram's head fell from plate to table, and the plate smashed on the ground.

Instinctively, Hart half turned. Jacob had the knife from his belt in his hand and leaped for Hart's back. The point of the blade cut through the sleeve of his coat as Hart's body ducked and his upthrust elbow, following through, drove into Jacob's jaw and sent him staggering back toward the wall.

Hart saw for a second the madness in the boy's eyes and leveled the Colt. The lower half of Jacob's face disappeared in a sprawling welter of blood and fragmented bone that sprayed out over the space between them, splattering Hart's hand and gun, his outstretched arm and his face.

When Jacob Batt slid down the wall and stretched across the floor, most of the back of his head seemed to have disappeared, too.

Fifteen

Frenchie's wife spent a lot of time fussing over Aram with half-chanted words and herbs and yellow mud that she packed tight over his wounds. It didn't look any too good to Hart, but Frenchie assured him that his woman was a good doctor, and Aram himself, between frequent bouts of unconsciousness, seemed to approve of what was being done. He'd seen trappers treated in similar ways by their squaws enough times to know their cures were as likely to succeed as the efforts of any half-trained white doctor who was doing the job on the side as a way of getting some extra money into his barber shop.

The boy's two bullets had avoided anything vital. The first had made one hell of a mess of Aram's upper left arm, and the other had mangled its way through the ribs on his right side without busting more than one or two of them.

Other men might've suffered more, specially accounting for their age, but Aram's hide was as tough as the weathered skins he traded in, and his constitution was akin to that of an ox.

They spent four days at Frenchie's, Aram mending all the while and Hart trying hard not to let the inaction sink him down into a bout of morbid depression. He hated doing nothing, putting up in one place—especially when that place was as one-eyed as Frenchie's trading post. Ever since he'd ridden off from home as a kid he'd kept moving, never allowed himself too much time to think. He'd tried once to change—thought seriously about it any road—and that had only made him travel more when it was over. A good horse under him and the land wide and deep farther than the eye could see. Tall red grasses and the startled yellow of sunflowers and other than that nothing but the expanse of sky.

'Course, he knew things were changing all around him. Fences and boundaries and the man who invented barbed wire being treated like the nation's hero instead of what he really was. You hem men in and you coop them up and tell them how many acres they can farm and they get greedy; they get like the land, smaller and more petty, and they know they ain't free.

Sitting there under the low roof and amid the stink of the

tallow lamps, Hart felt himself close to sick. If he'd stayed with
Kathy, he wondered, if she'd stayed with him—was this what
it would have been like? Would they have found themselves
clemmed together the way these folks had? Or the way Jedediah Batt and his family had worked themselves dead or half
crazy trying to fight a living off bad land? Would their kids
have been like that—like Jacob and Rebecca—if they'd married
and settled on some patch of prairie?

He sat there brooding, drinking too much whisky, and trying
his damndest to convince himself that it would have been so.
That he was better off as it was. On his own. No ties. No kin.

And Kathy?

Was she better off?

Hart stood abruptly, knocking the rickety chair back against
the wall. He kicked out at someone's mongrel dog that got in
his way as he stalked to the bar, seizing the neck of an open
bottle and tipping the contents down his throat. When his eyes
were watering and his breath was all but stopped, he pulled
the bottle away and stared around the room, as if daring anyone there to say anything, to challenge him.

When no one did, he aimed another kick at the dog, which
backed off and growled deep in the rear of his throat. He saddled his mare and rode her hard for the best part of an hour,
so that when they returned both man and horse were lathered
with sweat despite the cold.

Aram was on his feet inside the building, walking gingerly,
but walking.

"Stop your frettin', hoss," he greeted Hart, " 'nother day an'
we can ride."

"Who's frettin'?" snapped Hart and helped himself to some
food from the iron pot on the stove.

Aram shrugged his right shoulder, winced, tried not to laugh
on account of that would hurt him, too.

By evening Hart had calmed down some, the whisky laying
thick on his tongue and on his brain. He sat with Aram and
played a few games of checkers, his mind half concentrating.

"Want to talk 'bout it?"

"What?"

"Whatever's eatin' into you."

Hart gave a short shake of the head and made his next move.

Aram sucked on his pipe some and decided that with his
opponent playing the way he was a little side bet wouldn't
run amiss.

"Times in the winter," Aram began, almost as if he was musing aloud, "get to feel so damned cooped up it's all I could do not to bust down the walls. Would have 'cept I knew I'd freeze to death inside half an hour. That calmed me some. That an' some rotgut whisky—take it like you do for an achin' tooth."

"Tooth you can pull out," interrupted Hart.

Aram nodded, acknowledging it to be true.

"Some folks," he went on, "they ain't fashioned to live like others, with others. Settlin' down." He poked the end of his pipe toward Hart for emphasis. "Take me an' Jedediah. No reason for it, far as I could see. But we was different right from the start. Ran different ways since we was kids. Always wanted different things. From the age he was movin' out into the land, Jedediah, he always hankered after a place of his own, kids an' crops an' hogs. Tried to get me to come in with him, reckon he wanted that more than most. Him an' me buildin' together, family."

Aram spat neatly into the palm of his hand and rubbed it along his pants leg.

"Never wanted to build, not me. Him, he never wanted nothin' else. Couldn't see nothin' else. Wouldn't. That's why he was the way he was with the gold. If he'd let his family know that was there, they'd've known they could get off the land. Leave and strike out elsewhere. Jedediah, he didn't want that. Needed 'em all with him, workin' the land, strivin' an' toilin'. That money, it'd've changed all that. For the better. Jedediah, he didn't want for things to be better. Not that way."

Hart thought for a while and then said: "Reckon that explains the boy here, Jacob?"

"Helps to. Maybe he was more like me—or you—his pa's way of life weren't his but he didn't see no other way out. Even when he got himself that job in the livery, he was still tied to his fam'ly. Findin' out the gold was there and what'd been keepin' him strivin' shoulder to shoulder all through his young years weren't needed, that could've spun his mind so's he turned real wild."

Aram tamped down the tobacco in his pipe.

"But who's to say for sure? Jacob could've been born with that streak in him, born wild. Mean. Who's to say?"

Hart remembered the wild, crazy look in the youngster's eyes when he had been doing his damnedest to shoot his uncle dead; he remembered, too, the dark, intense stare of the girl, Rebecca—if Jacob was touched with insanity, then what of . . .

"Your move," said Aram, breaking across his thoughts.

Hart glanced down quickly, moved too fast, lost again.

"I ever thank you for what you did that day?" asked Aram, leaning back in his chair.

Hart shook his head. "Had too many other things on your mind. Like stayin' alive."

"Well, I'll thank you now."

"Okay. You want to play another game?"

"You want to lose again?"

Hart shrugged: "Why not?"

"Money on it?"

Hart laughed. "I ain't that much of a fool."

"Glad to hear it, hoss. Plumb glad to hear it. Put your mind to it, you might stand a chance of comin' close to winnin'."

The old trapper toyed with his pipe, sipped at his glass of beer, and tried not to notice the pain that was shooting from his shoulder. Hart hooked one boot over the other and concentrated on the game, secure in the fact that come morning they'd be in the saddle and back on the road to Fallon. For a moment and no more, his mind snagged on the thought of the two gunmen from Monterey, nursing their wounds and their wounded reputations, maybe back there somewhere searching him out. But Aram nudged him and he jolted the thought clear and settled down to checkers, determined to take at least one game before the night was over.

*

The day was bitter and the sky seemed to have taken over the land. Hart's Indian blanket was thrown over him and his scarf held his hat over his ears. Gloves retained a semblance of feeling in his hands. The ground over which they rode was brittle as iron; the vibrations jerked through their saddles and jolted their spines as they rode.

Neither man spoke a deal, shouted comments as abrupt as possible all that passed between them until they climbed down and passed coffee strongly laced with whisky from hand to hand.

When they reached Fallon the main street was bare of people; nothing stirred save a couple of shingles hanging over the sidewalk and rattling in the wind. Kerosene lamps burned dully in the back of a store or two, even though it was still an hour into the day. But for that the whole place could have been dead, deserted. In the time that Hard had gone it was as if an epidemic had swept through the town, clearing everything with it.

"Some welcome!" Aram reined in his mount and shifted one leg painfully in the saddle. He pushed back his skin cap and shook his head as he looked up and down the length of the street.

"Sure makes you feel at home, don't it?"

Hart touched the mare with his spurs and guided her along to the front of Zack Moses' store. He dropped to the ground, looped his reins over the rail, and waited for Aram to do the same.

Zack beckoned them in from behind the plate glass of his door, the ravages of Jacob Batt's escape having been repaired. The stove was well stoked, and a couple of men, neither of whom Hart recognized, glanced around from their game of cards, nodded a hasty greeting and returned to their play.

"You must be Aram?"

"S'right." The trapper held out his hand, and Zack gripped it with a degree of warmth that was surprising.

"You come then?"

Aram looked about him. "Seems that way."

"Figured you would."

"How come?"

"Money's money."

Aram hawked up phlegm and, failing to find anywhere to deposit it, swallowed it back down. "An' shit's shit!"

Zack wrinkled his nose as if he could suddenly smell it and turned toward Hart. "The boy . . ."

"We know."

Zack glanced from one to the other. "Bust out from them fools in the jail an' shot up the town like he was Quantrell or Bloody Bill Anderson."

"Yeah, we heard."

Zack nodded and pointed a finger at the trapper. "Wouldn't be at all surprised if he didn't come lookin' for you now he's on the run. He . . ."

"He did," Hart said flatly.

"Did? He come after you? But you only this minute got back into town."

"Didn't wait that long," said Aram. "Figure to meet his old uncle back up the trail."

Zack's mouth opened but he didn't say anything, just looked and waited.

"Know Frenchman?" Hart asked.

"Sure."

"Kid was there. Could've been chance, could've figured for

certain that was the way we'd come. Either way, don't matter. Snuck behind Aram here and put a couple of bullets into him."

"You okay?" asked Zack, concerned.

"Here, ain't I?"

"Looks like." He looked back at Hart. "What happened to . . . to Jacob?"

"Didn't give me a lot of choice. Tried to stop him with a slug in the leg but he weren't goin' to give up."

"Killed him, huh?"

Hart nodded.

"Only way when they run wild like that. Shame is you never done it when you had the chance back here in town, time he shot the sheriff."

Easy to say now, thought Hart. "Maybe," he said, anxious to change the subject.

"What you figurin' on doin'?" Zack asked Aram.

"Go see this here lawyer, find out about Jedediah's will, maybe take a look at this gold that's supposed to be in the bank. Ain't never seen that much gold all of a time. Then I guess I'll ride out an' meet with my kin."

"Ever see 'em before?"

"Long time back. Jedediah's wife and the eldest kids, Jacob an' Rebecca, they—"

"She's been hangin' around town again," Zack broke through, speaking more to Hart than the trapper. "Just moonin' about the place like she was lookin' for somethin' she'd lost 'cept she didn't know what it was. Tried speakin' with her, told her she'd be best off back at home with her ma, but all she did was stare at me with them eyes of her'n an' I figured it best to tend my own affairs."

"Where is she now?" asked Aram.

"Home, I guess. Ain't seen her around these past few days."

"How'd she seem 'bout her brother bustin' loose the way he did?" Hart asked.

"How d'you think? She was pleased as could be. Hell, she was fixin' to kill you one time for gettin' him locked away."

Aram and Hart exchanged glances, puzzlement on the trapper's face.

"Ain't no way of tellin' how she'll cope with him bein' dead." Zack bent closer to the stove to warm his hands, rubbing them together energetically.

"Got me a spare room out back," Zack said after a few moments. "You're welcome to share it for a time till you figure out what you're aimin' to do."

Hart looked at Aram, who nodded agreement. They fixed a fair price with the mayor and busied themselves unpacking their belongings and taking them through to the room. Aram said he'd take the animals up to the stable and get them fed and watered and bedded down.

"How 'bout this attorney? Quinton."

"Tomorrow'll do for that. Him an' the bank."

"Okay. While you're doin' that, I'll take a ride out to your brother's place. Tell 'em 'bout Jacob. Ain't no sense in you bein' the bearer of bad news."

"Maybe it's my task."

"Uh-uh. More like mine. I was the one as killed him."

Aram started to say something and then changed his mind. He showed his agreement with a quick gesture of the hand and a tightening of the mouth, then turned aside and got on with what he was doing. Now that he'd arrived, he wasn't any too anxious to meet up with the family his brother had fought for so long to keep together and that he himself had already been instrumental in breaking apart.

Sixteen

The ground ivy by the front of the house was rimed with frost. The sky was iron-gray and so low it seemed you had but to reach up to touch it. Rachel Batt was inside the kitchen, flour on her hands and dying on her mind. First her husband, Jedediah, and now . . . it was weeks since she'd seen her son, Jacob. Weeks since Ben had come back with the wagon from town telling her that there wasn't going to be any more credit from the store and that Jacob had bust out of jail and killed more folks doing it. The posse had ridden by the farm more than once, their horses trampling down the winter vegetables and eating what little feed was left for her own stock. But Jacob had never shown his face and Rachel had no idea where he was save that something inside her said that he was already dead.

The pain of twenty years of living pressed hard on her temples till she thought they must burst, break inward, and shatter.

They did not. The farm was still there, the kitchen, the mixing bowl, flour, and water. Outside there were children to feed when the work was done and clothes to wash and patch and mend. There was their dwindling stock to pen and feed. Everything to bed down against the cold and a few hours of huddled warmth that would crack like ice at the first step of light.

She wiped her arm across her forehead and saw Rebecca pause for a few seconds' rest, the wooden pail from which she was feeding the hens heavy in her hand. The stupid hens clucked and pecked about her feet but Rachel knew that Rebecca scarcely saw them. She wondered if the girl had seen Jacob since his escape; if she saw him now. Wondered if Rebecca saw him as she saw him herself, his body stretched over some anonymous snowy ground, crows jerkily clamoring.

She was closing the oven door when she heard the horse approach, one rider. She turned, almost dropped the pie, burned her forearm against the inside of the oven, and bit down into her lower lip hard enough to draw a trickle of blood.

Through the steam and dirt of the windowpane she saw that it was not Jacob. Not anyone that she knew. Rachel saw Rebecca run toward the barn. She wiped the edge of her hand against the glass and looked at the man, tall in the saddle even though his head was stooped against the swirl of the wind. He wore a striped blanket over his coat with some kind of Indian design patterned on it, there was a rifle butt sticking up over his saddle, gloves on his hands, and the bottom of a holster showing through the folds of the blanket. The breath of man and horse plumed out on to the air.

Rachel thought he was a peace officer, maybe a United States marshal.

She didn't know for sure.

Jedediah's old pistol was in the kitchen drawer; the rifle with which Ben had been learning to shoot was resting on two pegs above the door.

She glanced again at the man and knew it would be no use.

Ben came running hard from the pigpen, feet skidding here and there on the hard, uneven earth. He crashed through the door and came to a halt breathlessly against the kitchen table.

"It's okay, Ben."

His eyes swiveled nervously, purposefully toward the rifle over the door.

"No. It's all right."

"You don't know . . ."

"Shush!"

The man had dismounted and left the gray to stand or wander in the yard. Rachel guessed that Rebecca was still in the barn and wondered if she had the two younger boys with her. Hart knocked on the door with a gloved hand, and before the woman could answer he had stepped inside.

He recognized Rebecca's features in her mother's face, but not the eyes; saw something of Jacob in the uncertainty and aggression of the fifteen-year-old. He told them his name.

"You the marshal?"

"No, ma'am."

"What then?"

"Jacob an' Rebecca, they didn't tell you about me? I'm the one as went to find their Uncle Aram."

She crossed her left arm under her breasts, clutching the elbow of the right. "Never heard your name. Don't reckon they . . . she ever said it."

"No matter."

Rachel's fingers twisted and pushed. "You come to tell us you couldn't find him?"

"No, ma'am, I found him."

"But he wouldn't come with you?"

"He came."

The eyes of mother and son stared at the window onto the yard, but it was bare of anything save the slow movement of Hart's horse. Ben's eyes lingered a moment more on the rifle that was at the stranger's back and out of reach above the door. He wondered about the pistol in the drawer and wished he knew if it were loaded.

"He ain't fixin' to visit his kin?"

"He'll be out right enough. Wanted to talk to the attorney back in town, get things clear in his mind before he talks with you."

"He come for the money," she said with resignation, not looking into his face.

"That money's ours!" called Ben and moved across the room toward the kitchen table.

"Ben!" She seized his arm and spun him around, flushes of anger and fear red against her sallow cheeks.

"When he comes out," Hart said, "he'll settle the matter with you then."

Rachel's mind turned slowly. She gradually let go of her son's arm and turned her head toward the tall stranger. He read her question in her resigned eyes before she spoke.

"Why d'you ride out? Not just to tell us Aram was in town.

Not to get paid by us 'cause you know we ain't got nothin', not even what we need. There's somethin' else, ain't there?"

Hart spoke slowly, flatly. "Yes, ma'am, there's somethin' else."

Rachel cried out and grabbed her son and pulled him against her chest. For several minutes she rocked against him, her mouth open and struggling for breath, body heaving. But there were no tears in her eyes.

"How did it . . . ?"

"He was back along the trail. Place called Frenchman. Hid up till he could pull a gun. Put two bullets into Aram before . . ."

The fifteen-year-old ran straight at him and Hart swerved to the side and parried a fist. He seized the boy by the arm and twisted hard, bringing it up between his shoulder blades and turning till Ben's face was pressed hard against the tabletop.

"Before I could stop him."

"And Aram?"

"The old man had his back to him. Never stood a chance. It's a wonder he ain't dead."

Rachel wrinkled up her eyes. Ben struggled and tried to kick backward, but Hart increased the pressure, and the boy yelped and went still, face burning.

"Jacob?"

"I called a warnin'. Twice. He weren't goin' to heed. Put a bullet through his leg but he still come at me. Didn't allow me no choice."

"You shot him."

"Yeah."

"Killed him."

"Yeah."

There was nothing but cold in Rachel's heart. The words did no more than confirm what she already felt . . . knew. Hart looked at Ben and released his grip, standing back and away. The boy remained where he was for some moments before going to the back of the kitchen, holding his aching arm. He looked at Hart with a sullen hate. There were steps outside close by the door but no one came in.

"Did he . . . ?"

"Died right off. Doubt he felt a thing. His uncle and me, we saw he got buried good an' deep."

"There weren't no marker?" Rachel's face seemed to wobble and Hart watched for the tears to come.

"No, ma'am. Stone, but no marker."

He looked at her and the tears failed to run.

"Ben," she said, "go fetch your sister. She has to be told. Tell her to leave the boys. I'll tell them later."

She had to tell him twice before he dragged his feet, sullenly, from the room. When Rebecca came into the kitchen her cheeks were bright from the cold, and her long black hair was pinned close to the back of her head. She stood silent while her mother told her what news Hart had brought. She looked at her mother's face all the while, impassive, but Hart knew that in her heart she was looking at him. Only for a second did she turn her face toward him, and her eyes were black stone.

"You'll tell Aram to come by as soon as he's able?"

"Yes, ma'am."

There was nothing more to say. Steam rose up in coils from the sides of the oven door and struggled with the wind that bit beneath the door and through the gaps in the window frames. Mother and daughter stood close to one another, not touching. Hart turned aside, closed the door back of him, picked up the gray's reins, and slotted his left boot into the stirrup. From the barn Ben watched him mount up and ride out, watched till he was a shadow that moved past the alders into the graying mist that rose up off the land along the creek.

★

Aram was waiting for Hart in the rocker that Zack Moses kept close by the stove. The mayor was up at the bank and he'd left the trapper in charge of the store. It tickled Aram's fancy to be a store clerk, and he was sore disappointed when the only customer who came in was Hart.

"How'd she take it? 'Bout the boy?"

"Fine. As if she weren't surprised at all."

"Then I guess she weren't."

Hart nodded and pulled off his gloves, pushing them down into the front of his gun belt. He had taken off the blanket and thrown it over a barrel of blackstrap molasses. His hat was tilted back from his forehead.

"You ridin' out there?"

Aram nodded, without looking any too certain.

"She said for you to come."

The trapper nodded again. "I'll do it." He seemed to think of something by the way his eyes narrowed and his head turned to one side. "How 'bout the girl? How 'bout Rebecca?"

"What about her?"

"Was she there? How'd she take her brother bein', well, dead the way he was?"

Hart shrugged. "Never said a word."

Aram shook his head like he didn't understand. "Recall when she was no more'n a button, shiny black button, she come runnin' into my arms an' . . ."

Either the memory deserted him or he realized he was talking too much in front of another man. He began to fidget with the possibles sack that dangled from his neck.

"Want me to ride out with you?" Hart offered.

"No call. Kind of you, but no, there ain't no need. I'll walk down the livery soon as Moses gets back from the bank. Ride out."

Hart nodded and pulled a chair by the stove and sat across it, straddling it. "You went by the bank yourself?"

"Yeah. Saw that Quinton, queer bird. Gold's there an' it's worth every cent as was said an' more."

"You figured out what you're fixin' . . ."

"Ain't my money. Not by any kind of right I understand. It's theirs, Jedediah's fam'ly. Figured I'd take out enough to pay for your time, see me through the winter. All the rest is theirs."

"After the winter," Hart said, "you goin' back?"

Aram turned his head slow and looked at him and didn't say a thing. Less than an hour later he was on his way out to the farm.

★

He sat stock-still in the saddle down past the tree line and looked at the pitiful place. Twenty years of his brother's life till it claimed him and now it was taking his kids, Jacob runnin' mad and the others. . . . He didn't know about the others, just about what growing up on a farm like that might do to them. There was folk who said it was the best way, would make you strong enough to withstand anything that came to pass. But Aram didn't know if that was true. Not for all folk it weren't. Not for Jacob—realizing he'd been slaving all those years over stubborn ground for nothing had broke his reason like a boot on a brittle branch not yet formed true.

The others: Aram wondered about the others as he saw them moving like shades about their tasks. He wondered about his niece, about Rebecca. If only . . .

The cold was tugging at his shoulders and his bad leg was aching like someone was prizing at the bone with the blade of a knife.

He saw the smoke drifting up toward the flat, imprisoning gray of the sky. He touched his heels to the horse and it began to walk slowly forward.

Rachel was waiting. She'd seen him away off down the creek, past the bare alders. There was coffee brewing and a slice of pie she'd saved and reheated against his coming. She'd changed her dress and set a brush to her hair and now she sent the youngest to fetch Rebecca and Ben to the house. She wasn't certain what it was she expected from this man who had been a stranger to her for so many years, existing as a moving shadow she sensed always at the back of her husband's thoughts, moving and free.

Aram tethered his horse and came into the house. Rebecca wasn't there. She had tossed her head at her mother's message and run off across the yard, past the vegetable patch and out toward the place she loved, the line of alders that overlooked the crisp, shifting creek.

Aram could see her dimly through the window, her hair no longer pinned but loose and catching in the wind.

He pulled his mind from her and back to the thin, sallow-faced woman who had been his brother's wife. His hands accepted the coffee, the pie; he ate and talked sparingly, telling her something of his life out by the Platte, a little about the setting of traps, the stretching and scraping of skins. The boy, Ben, asked him about Indians and he told him a couple of tales about the Blackfeet that caught the boy's excitement and that were three parts true. Warmth flowed from the stove, from the sparse conversation; Aram forgot for those moments the hours of hard, grinding, thankless work that went on endlessly to make them possible. He warmed to his brother's memory, his wife and kids. He told Rachel what he'd decided about the money. Told her impulsively and was disappointed when she heard him with a barely stirred silence, as if it was no more than she had expected.

"Will you stay with us, Uncle Aram?" called one of the youngest.

Aram looked at Rachel. Her face expressed nothing he could readily understand.

"Please, Uncle Aram!"

The old trapper looked at the woman again and she nodded a brief agreement.

Aram said: "Be pleased to stay, long as that's what everyone wants." His eyes turned toward the window.

"She'll come around," said Rachel. "She always was a strange child, an' since Jacob . . ."

"I'll ride back to town, settle things with this attorney. Sign paper an' such. Pack up what little I got an' come back out. Tomorrow, most like."

He was standing now, close to the door. He moved by the window and looked out. Rebecca was leaning against one of the trees, one hand resting on the bare branch close by her head.

"Leave her be," advised Rachel.

Aram nodded, but it was not what he wanted. What he wanted was a young girl to come running across the yard toward him, hair flying out behind her, and her arms outstretched. He nodded again and let himself out of the house. She had scarcely moved, save that her arm was back down at her side. Aram's hand toyed with the reins, but the pull was too strong. He began to walk across the hard, ridged ground, away from the stink of stale cabbage that rose up from the ivy by the door, out toward the gray-blue of the stream, the line of alders broken only by the girl's body.

If she heard him—and she must have heard him—she gave no sign. Aram watched the wind catch her hair and lift it up and saw the white of her neck an instant and something caught his breath. He spoke her name and she leaned away from the trunk but nothing more.

He knew that when she did finally turn to him everything would be all right. Like it had been that time long before; like it had never been. The wind across his eyes made them smart.

"Rebecca," he said.

He was close behind her. His hand reached out, fingers at her hair, touching lightly against her shoulder, her neck.

"Rebecca."

He felt her body begin to turn and began to smile his welcome. Swish of black hair. The blade slid into his flesh below the jaw and cut. Aram jerked back, stumbling. Her eyes, dark over him. The knife lovingly honed. He was on his back on the hard, ridged ground and Rebecca was standing over him, her arms stretched out but not in greeting.

Aram's body twisted like an animal caught in a trap, drowning.

The red mouth below the harsh stubble of his beard buckled wide.

Seventeen

Hart saw the stage from the ridge of land he was riding west. It was moving at a steady pace along the main trail that would see it into Fallon by the middle of the day. A few desultory flakes of snow turned on the air as he watched. He guessed it would be one of the last making the journey that side of winter. His breath was like fine gray cloud. He pulled at the reins and moved the mare along the ridge, dipping down into the tree line some quarter mile farther. By then he could see the thin spiral of smoke that came from the Batt farm.

They had already come from town for Rebecca. Found her hunched by the far side of the creek, ice clinging to her eyelashes, the ends of her hair. She looked at them when they spoke to her and never seemed to hear a thing. Zack Moses and the three men he'd deputized stood by helplessly while the boy, Ben, struggled across the yard with his mother.

They stared at one another, Rachel and Rebecca, mother and daughter, and neither seemed to recognize the other. Rebecca's empty, staring eyes and her mother's empty womb.

Rachel held out her hands and the girl took them and allowed herself to be lifted from the ground. She shivered with the exposure to the cold, but never seemed to notice. Zack Moses hung his head and damned and cursed and told Rachel there wasn't anything they could do but take her into the jail and lock her away until they could arrange some kind of trial. With the weather closing in hard the way it was, they might not see the circuit judge until the thaw.

Rachel looked at the mayor and allowed that she understood. She didn't seem to know the girl anymore, hold any claim on her.

"Mind, you can come into town an' visit whenever you want," he called when they were all mounted.

Rachel nodded slowly and turned her back.

In his heart, Zack was already wishing that the girl had turned her knife on herself after killing her uncle. He was to wish that all through that long winter. And Rebecca was to remain in her cell, eating little yet enough, a stony rebuke to something Zack Moses never understood.

Hart had seen the slow procession down the town's main street before he had left, folks lining the sidewalk to point at her and stare, calling out the vilest names they could bring to their tongues. Rebecca had not seemed to have heard or seen a thing. Now he was riding in the wake of the preacher, set to make a farewell to the man he tracked down and persuaded to come back with him into what some folks were pleased to call civilization.

The ceremony was in progress by the time Hart arrived. Rachel Batt stood close by the foot of the long opening her sons had labored long to hew from the frozen ground. The rough wooden coffin rested to the side, resting at an awkward angle against the loose clods of earth that were already fringed and blotched with white.

Ben Batt glanced up at Hart as he walked over from the creek and seemed about to move toward him. The preacher's words rose and fell. At the head of the coffin lay a skimpy bunch of winter flowers. Hart stood, bareheaded and bowed, keeping his distance.

It was soon over.

Hart walked to the graveside and reached for one of the shovels, intent upon taking his share of throwing the heavy earth down over the man he'd ridden with and begun to think of as a friend. His gloved hand had no sooner touched the shaft of the shovel before Ben snatched it from him and began furiously to work, clods raining down upon Aram's coffin like hammers.

Hart gave the family—what remained of it—a final, slow look. He guessed that with Aram dead, even with no papers signed, their father's hidden wealth would find its way eventually to them. He knew he had no claim to any of it now; he could never ask Rachel for the price of bringing Aram home.

He turned on his heel and walked to where the gray was biting at the bark of the alder. No one as much as watched him go. The faint sound of his spurs, a small metallic ringing, was almost the only one to accompany him on the trail back to Fallon.

Zack Moses was waiting for him at the edge of town. From the expression on the mayor's face, Hart knew that Zack was waiting to intercept him, and he knew that the news wasn't good. His immediate thought was that something had happened to Rebecca; he, too, reckoned she'd take her own life.

But it wasn't that.

Zack's face made clear that he'd had enough of what this fall had already brought, and the winter was going to be hard as cold hell on earth.

He spoke to Hart without ever managing to look at him straight. "Couple of men got in on the stage."

Hart let out a long, slow breath and knew the rest before he asked.

"Lookin' for me?"

Zack Moses found a reason for examining the cuff of his coat. "Yeah."

"One around the same age as me, same height. Got an odd patch of skin on his face here." Hart gestured toward his own left cheek. "Other one's younger, smaller, Mexican."

"That's them."

Hart nodded, gave a short sigh, let the mare walk around through a halfcircle.

"You know 'em?"

"We met."

"They ain't friends?"

Hart shook his head. "No, they ain't no friends of mine."

"Trouble then?"

"Seems that way."

Zack scratched at his belly, shifted the weight of his body from one foot to the other, fidgeted with the buckle of his belt.

"What's gripin' you?" Hart asked.

"Town's had more'n its share of killin'. Don't seem—"

Hart jabbed a finger at him fast. "You think that, you go tell 'em. Ask 'em to climb back on the stage and ride out of town. Explain to 'em the cemetery's full and besides there's a town ordinance about blood on the streets."

"Hey, now! I didn't mean—"

"Like hell you didn't!" The gray tossed her head at the anger in Hart's voice. "I didn't notice you objectin' to a little shootin' in the streets when I stopped that bunch from takin' everythin' as was in the bank. Not when I brought in Jacob Batt neither."

"I know, I—"

"You just want me to face up to 'em somewheres else."

The mayor's hat was in his hands and he moved the brim through his fingers, looking down. "There's another alternative."

"Spell it out!"

"You could turn around. Ride off an'—"

"And have 'em come chasin' after me."

"They wouldn't have to find you."

"Bullshit! They found me here an' they'd find me again. They both reckon they owe me an' there won't be no restin' till that debt gets paid, one way or another. It don't happen here then it's some other street, some other town, some other mayor champin' at the bit and runnin' off at the mouth 'bout how his precious town's bein' driven back into the dirt by gunslingers and roughnecks both."

"Wes, I . . ." Zack fiddled with his hat a little more and ground a heel into the dirt. "You know I'm grateful for what you done. Know you could have been sheriff here an' welcome. The town ain't about to forget about the bank, nor the Batt boy neither. That other stuff, the old man and the girl, they weren't down to you."

"Maybe not," said Hart without believing it.

"But if you ride into town now and they're laid up waitin' for you, there's innocent folks might get hurt."

"Damn it, Zack! Where the hell d'you think you are? Innocent folks always get hurt!"

The mayor turned away, set his hat back on his head, and shrugged his coat collar up to his neck. The snow was still holding off, but it wouldn't be long now. The wind was keen as a knife edge.

"I just wanted to save what I could." His voice was low and resigned.

"I know. I know these two ain't worth a two-cent damn either. But they ain't goin' to go away. Their guns ain't about to disappear." He leaned down from the saddle and gripped the mayor by the arm. "I'll do what I can to make sure no one else gets involved. You see if you can keep folks off the streets until it's done."

Zack Moses nodded his thanks and stood aside as Hart set his horse in motion.

"They went by the saloon," he called after Hart.

"Yeah," Hart said back, "they always do."

*

Oklahoma was leaning his right elbow against the bar counter, leaving his left hand free to tease the butt of the Smith & Wesson holstered by his left hip. There was a sizable butcher knife held in a sheath on the opposite side of his gun belt. His fingers drummed unevenly on the counter and from time to time he glanced toward the batwing doors, as if expecting some kind of signal.

His shirt was worn and creased and fraying at the collar and cuffs and the wool vest was patched and torn at the back. His boots were scuffed and needed mending. There wasn't above five dollars in his pants.

Since Hart and Fowler had put him and the Mex temporarily out of business over in Monterey, work had come hard and pickings had been slim. News like that traveled pretty damn fast where it mattered and when folks wanted their killing done they went elsewhere first. Jobs that didn't involve using a gun were the kind Oklahoma didn't take to and he had Hart to thank for making his kind of work more difficult to get. Hart and that blasted bourbon-soaked detective with the fat belly and beard! Shot him twice, shoulder and knee. The one had healed up pretty good but the knee gave him trouble when he walked, when he climbed onto a horse, when he turned over on his bedroll—whenever he did any damned thing.

Killing Hart wouldn't make the knee any less trouble, but it would make Oklahoma feel a whole lot better otherwise.

Angel Montero, he felt the same. Hart had sliced the middle finger of his right hand close to the bone, and that was Angel's gun hand—his working hand. It was still stiffer than it ought to have been, the flesh that had regrown around the knuckle was more or less devoid of feeling, and that kind of numbness didn't help him with the speed or accuracy of his gunplay. His thin and handsome face turned this way along the street, then the other. He was sitting outside the saloon on a rocker someone had left there, feet pushed out against one of the posts that held the balcony in place over the sidewalk. His pistol was close to his injured hand, the hammer all but touching his palm. The palm itched. Itched to kill Wes Hart. The nastier, the slower and bloodier, the better.

That done, he could ride back west with an easy conscience and pick up things where he'd left them off.

There wasn't a soul on the street save for a woman hauling two sacks of flour from one of the stores over to her buckboard and a couple of men leaning against an empty hitching rail a hundred yards off, swapping yarns about who knew what.

Angel Montero wondered what a gunfighter like Hart found to do in a place like this. He'd heard some gossip about a girl

over in the jail who'd cut the throat of some older feller Hart
had brought back to town, but that didn't seem to make a
whole lot of sense.

He shifted in the chair and angled the brim of his sombrero
more steeply over his narrow eyes.

Inside, Oklahoma slid his tongue around his cracked lips and
downed what had remained of his whisky. He banged the
empty glass down on the counter and called for another. He
was still glancing from time to time at the door, still waiting
for a signal from outside.

The barkeep's hand shook just fractionally when he poured
the drink, and bit by bit the saloon cleared itself until Oklahoma and the bartender shared it with a sleeping cat and a
one-eyed miner whose drunken stupor kept him from realizing
what was about to go down.

Hart had seen the Mexican keeping watch outside the saloon
and taken his horse around the back of the town, coming in
near the livery. He left Clay there and walked easily, carefully
down to the rear of Zack Moses' store. His sawn-off Remington
was resting on the makeshift bed. Cartridges were in his saddlebag. He loaded the gun, checked his Colt .45, took off his
flat-crowned hat, and set it back on again. The shotgun disappeared beneath the folds of his Indian blanket, gripped tight
in his left hand. The right hand swung free, the fingers curled.
The thong that held the bottom of the holster to his leg was
secure, the safety loop pushed clear from the pistol hammer.

Hart had one final glance around the room and left the way
he'd come. He'd remember the back door into the saloon, the
one he hadn't been able to use the time Jacob Batt had put a
slug clean through the sheriff's brainpan.

Likely this time he could.

His feet were quiet as he approached the rear of the building.
He was hoping that if it spread out onto the street, Zack Moses
would have had time to clear folks out of danger.

As he neared the saloon he remembered what he'd said to
the mayor about innocent people; he remembered the look of
anticipation that had lit up the trapper's face before Aram had
made that final ride out to meet up with his brother's wife and
kin. He recalled the ugly rictus of death that had stared up at
him from the coffin before it was nailed shut and loaded onto
the wagon ready to take back out to the farm for burial.

He didn't want to think about the girl across the street in
the jailhouse but he did.

His fingers closed on the rounded handle of the rear door.

He leaned his ear to the wood but couldn't hear the least sound from inside. Oklahoma might not still be inside; he could have guessed wrong and he might never have been there—that might not have been what Angel Montero's presence outside meant.

He wasn't going to find out by standing where he was.

His hand turned against the catch and at the last moment he threw the door open wide and went in fast. He saw the gunman slumped against the bar, saw him jerk upright and start to spin around, saw his hand drive for his gun.

To Hart it all seemed to happen very slow.

He was making his own draw, waiting, wanting to see Oklahoma's face. He wanted Oklahoma to see him. He didn't mind getting rid of trash, but he wanted them to see what was going down. Oklahoma's mouth hung open and the Smith & Wesson seemed to jump into the palm of his left hand.

Hart narrowed his faded blue eyes into the narrowest of slits and squeezed back on the trigger.

Two shots cannoned out across the almost deserted saloon.

Oklahoma was thrown back against the bar, his arms jolted wide, the pistol tumbling through his fingers. His eyes had jammed shut and his mouth was still open, though wider now.

Hart heard a sharp scraping from outside, feet on the boards, running.

Blood looped out of Oklahoma's open mouth.

He shucked the blanket from the barrels of the shotgun.

Angel Montero slammed one half of the batwing doors inward and leaped in, firing. He got off two shots while Hart stood his ground and adjusted the angle of the gun. The Mexican skidded on the sawdust-strewn floor and tried to duck, or turn, Hart would never be certain which. A volley of ten-gauge shot hurtled into Angel's thigh and ribs and face and sent him crashing against the wall alongside the door. He hung there for a couple of seconds before his body slammed down hard and his nose broke with the force of landing.

Hart put up the shotgun and swung around the Colt.

The Mexican's body jerked and convulsed, arms and legs working like a swimmer trapped way beyond his depth.

There was a shout from the street, then another.

Oklahoma was huddled close to the bar and the cat, delicate on white feet, was sniffing suspiciously at the blood that puddled about his head.

Angel's body was not yet still, his boots dancing some strange fandango, toes rattling the wood of the floor.

Hart levered back the hammer of the Colt and put a bullet through the side of the Mexican's brain. Gray and pinkish red squelched against the wall, and Angel's right boot clattered a last time. Zack Moses' face, anxious, appeared over the center of the doors. Back of the bar, the barkeep was helping himself to the stock. Hart slid his Colt back into its holster, slipped the safety thong in place. He let the blanket fall back over the Remington. For a moment he held Zack's gaze.

There was little to do; less to say.

He didn't think he'd see Fallon or its mayor again, not after today. In time he'd stop thinking about the dark-haired girl locked in the jail and the trapper who'd trusted him and ridden back to civilization and the bosom of what family he had. As for the two men he'd just killed, Hart had all but forgotten their names already.

It was time for moving on.

Wendi Lee

WINSTON'S WIFE

Wendi Lee has written seven Western novels, a historical novel, and two books in a private-eye series.

She has also written dozens of articles and short stories for rock and roll and comic book publications.

She has an easygoing, sometimes wry style that works equally well on the range or in the concrete canyons of the city.

Over the past few years she has begun to win a great deal of praise from mystery reviewers who should also give her Westerns a try.

Jefferson Birch had been reluctant to take this case, especially when Annabel Winston asked him to look into her husband's disappearance, then proceeded to offer him her entire savings. Birch should have saved himself the trouble of looking for Joe Winston by explaining to her that men who disappear into the night, with a packed bag and all the savings, usually didn't want to be found. But he hadn't had the heart to turn her down when she began to cry in front of him.

Birch had been working at a ranch near Sacramento the day Annabel Winston came knocking on his bunkhouse door. Except for Birch, the bunkhouse was empty, his bunkmates having already gotten up with the sun and gone. Birch and the other cowhands had just come in off the trail the day before. During the last ten miles of the trail, Birch had gone after a stray calf and twisted his ankle rescuing it from a ravine. On orders from the trail boss, Birch was resting up.

Whoever was timidly knocking at the door would not go away, and Birch finally limped over to answer it, expecting the foreman to be standing there, asking if his ankle felt good enough to do a little branding. Instead, he opened the door to find a woman waiting there.

"Mr. Birch? Jefferson Birch?" she had asked. Her eyes widened at the sight of him in his longjohns.

Birch had the presence of mind to shut the door quickly. "I apologize, ma'am," he called out through the door as he reached for his denims and stepped into them. "I'll step outside when I'm respectable."

Inside the bunkhouse, Birch hobbled over to a tin mirror nailed to a wall above a beat-up basin with a few inches of water in it. He ran a hand over his whiskers, deciding not to take the time to shave, splashed water on his face, and combed his wet fingers through his hair. Grabbing his least dirty shirt, he paused to test his ankle. The swelling had gone down and he was able to slip both his boots on.

Birch wondered if he had really seen an attractive lady outside the bunkhouse or if maybe it had all been a dream. Shrugging, he opened the door and stepped outside.

She was still there, wearing a gray traveling dress now thick with dust, a little indigo bonnet perched on her fair hair. Two spots of color were fading from her cheeks, remnants of the embarrassment she must have felt when she saw Birch standing before her in all his longjohn glory.

"I apologize again, ma'am," he said.

"Nonsense," she replied, her slender hands twisting her thin, dark blue gloves. "It was my fault. I should have allowed someone to accompany me out here, but I was so eager to find you that I. . . ." She stopped, lowering her eyes and smiling slightly. "I didn't think," she finished.

"What's so urgent?"

She looked up at him, gazing directly into his eyes and introduced herself as Mrs. Annabel Winston. "I heard about you through Arthur Tisdale, who is acquainted with my parents and who is currently back East on business. I want to hire you to find my husband. He's been gone almost a year, and I haven't heard from him in almost six months."

After leaving the Texas Rangers several years ago, Birch worked for Tisdale's investigations agency from time to time.

Mrs. Winston gave Birch the details: One year ago, they had been living on a small farm outside of Redding. One day, her husband came back from town, very excited. He had run into an old friend who had been living up North, panning gold on Oregon's Rogue River. Winston wanted to go up there himself to pan a little gold. When Annabel expressed her concern about pulling up stakes to pursue a dream, her husband had decided it would be better if he went alone.

"I begged him to think about it for a few days, but he was packed and ready to go the next morning," Mrs. Winston said, blinking rapidly. She turned and paced a bit in front of Birch to collect her thoughts. "I received a wire from him a few weeks later, telling me that he'd bought a stake on the Rogue River not far from Klamath Falls. He wrote about once a month, telling me that the claim was almost worthless. Then three months ago, he stopped writing."

"Are you afraid something's happened to him?" Birch asked.

She nodded, small frown lines marring her smooth forehead. "I just hope I'm not too late."

"Why did you wait so long?"

She lowered her eyes, a hesitant look on her face. "Well, I waited about two months for a letter, hoping that he might be sick, or out of money and ashamed of telling me. About three weeks ago I contacted the marshal of the nearby town of Gold Hill. He was very kind, making inquiries on my behalf. Unfortunately, Marshal Stanley learned next to nothing. There were a few miners who recalled my husband, but Joe hadn't stayed around long enough for anyone to get to know him. It was as if one day he was there, and the next day he was gone."

So Birch had taken the money she offered, along with a photograph of her husband that had been taken just before he left for Oregon. Joe Winston had a stern nose and small, fierce eyes. He had a look about him as if life had disappointed him one too many times. Birch gave notice to his boss and saddled up his horse, Cactus. When he left the ranch, the weather was sunny, warm, and dry. When he reached Oregon two days later, the rain was dripping off his hat and Cactus was restless to find shelter.

Gold Hill was a small but growing town, built by men who wanted to profit from the gold miners who populated the banks of the Rogue River. Restaurants offered outrageously priced meals; general stores stocked supplies that cost twice the going rate; and saloons, with working girls who insisted on miners buying a drink before sitting down, advertised overpriced, watered-down drinks. All of these businesses ate away at the greenhorn miners' hard-earned gold. If a man lasted long enough, he learned to avoid Gold Hill like a poisonous snake.

Despite the abundance of businesses intent on parting a miner's dust from his pouch while providing a good time, Gold Hill didn't look like a very inviting place. The rainy season had churned up the main street, and the air was chilly with the promise of another deluge. Birch huddled deeper into his whitewashed canvas coat, glad that he was wearing his thick wool shirt underneath.

It was late afternoon when he dismounted and tethered Cactus to the hitching post outside Marshal Stanley's office. Inside, Birch was grateful for the warmth of a potbellied stove. A rangy man in his midforties sat in a chair with his boots propped up against the lip of the stove, a steaming tin mug in his hand.

Birch took off his hat. "Marshal?"

The man bobbed his head to acknowledge that he was, indeed, Bill Stanley. "State your business, stranger."

Birch introduced himself and explained why he was in town. Stanley straightened his chair and stood up, placing his mug on the stove's surface.

"You want some coffee?" he asked, already reaching for an empty mug on his desk. Birch wrapped his fingers around the full mug. Stanley pulled up another chair and indicated that Birch should sit. "I'm sorry that Mrs. Winston hired you. I've already talked to the other miners who had stakes near Joe Winston, and they said that he left after six months. No one knows where he went."

"I'm sure you did the best you could, Marshal," Birch said, "but it must be hard for you to devote much time to a missing miner when you have to keep order in this town."

"Well, I can't stop her from throwing her money away," the marshal said with a shrug.

Birch was curious. "What do you think happened?"

Stanley sighed. "Probably what happens to most of the men who come here to mine. They give up."

"So why didn't he go back to his wife?"

"Ashamed of failing. They either go off to make a new life or they kill themselves."

Birch digested the information. He had had some dealings

with miners a few years ago, and he knew that they could also be very jealous if a fellow miner struck it rich. "Is there any possibility that he may have been killed?"

"It's unlikely. I already looked into it," Stanley explained. "Most miners aren't very bright. I think the fever makes 'em stupid. If another miner had killed him for his stake, he would have moved right onto it. No one was mining his stake. The miners I talked to said that Winston was barely eking out a living." Stanley leaned back in his chair and stretched. "No, I think he just packed up and moved on."

When Birch finished his coffee, he thanked the lawman and got directions to the river. It was almost dark when he arrived at the first claim. A dubiously makeshift shack with a ragged blanket for a door sat about twenty-five feet from the riverbank. Birch stayed on Cactus and called out. A moment later, a large hand pulled the blanket aside and a bear-sized man shambled out, shotgun resting easily in his hand.

"I'm looking for information on a fellow named Joe Winston. He disappeared from his land a few months ago."

The miner sullenly squinted up at Birch. "Don't know anything."

Birch looked around the site, noting the beat-up gold pan and the rusted coffeepot on the campfire. He took a silver dollar from his pouch, casually flipping it in the air and catching it. "That's too bad. I was hoping to find someone who could give me some information."

The miner licked his lips, his eyes darting from the coin to the riverbed, which was, no doubt, played out. He ran his forearm across his mouth. "Look, stranger, I don't know much. Honest. I hardly knew the man. He didn't spend much time with the rest of us miners. But I can tell you that someone's working Winston's claim now."

Birch was surprised. "Marshal Stanley was here just the other week and was told that no one wanted it."

The miner gave a short laugh. "None of us wants it, that's for sure. No, this is some greenhorn from down South who took it over. Claims Winston sold it to him and he has the papers to prove it."

"You think he got a bad deal?"

"Depends on what he came up here for," the miner replied, amusement evident in his eyes. "If he's here for his health, that's one thing. If he's here to get rich from panning that sorry lot, he's out of luck. When Winston left, a few of the other miners snuck onto his claim to try it out. But they left the poorer for it."

Birch tossed the silver coin to the miner. "Where's this claim?"

"About three miles downstream. Just follow the Rogue."

It was full dark when Birch came to a dying campfire. The sound of a rifle being cocked brought Cactus to a standstill.

A man's voice called out, "This is my claim, stranger. I hope you're just moving on." There was a quaver to the voice, betraying how young and inexperienced the owner of the voice must be.

"I'm just looking for information on Joe Winston," Birch said.

There was a silence, then the sound of the rifle being uncocked. A black man stepped into the light of the campfire, rifle at his side. He was no more than twenty, his face ravaged by smallpox, and his prominent Adam's apple bobbing up and down. "I only met him three times."

"Where?" Birch asked.

"Bodie. I was working at a saloon, cleaning tables and sweeping up at night. Saved me enough to buy a stake."

"Bodie's a pretty good mining town," Birch said.

The young miner's shoulders slumped. "You have to have a lot of money to buy a stake near Bodie. And it's a rough area. Didn't like all the shootin' goin' on. So when Winston came through town and offered to sell his stake, I took him up on it."

"Any luck?" Birch asked.

The question brought a hooded expression to the miner's eyes. "Winston didn't warn me that it was played out. I thought I knew everything I needed to know about mining. I'd overheard lots of miners talk in Bodie when they'd had a few too many whiskies and I stored up the knowledge." He rubbed the back of his neck with a grubby, calloused hand. "But I guess learnin' and doin' are two different things."

"I'm sure things'll get better for you. You happen to remember where Winston was staying in Bodie?"

"Far as I know, he's still there," the miner replied. "Place called the Nugget Hotel."

Birch thanked him and rode off, certain that the young miner had found a lode. He was a day's ride from Bodie, but he pushed himself and Cactus to ride on into the night. As the dawn lit the sky, Birch found himself at the edge of the boom town.

With a population of ten thousand and more than fifty saloons, Bodie had a reputation as a dangerous town. Newspapers back East reported more killings per week in Bodie than in any other gold rush town in the West. Knowing that violence could erupt at any moment, in any place, Birch kept his eyes open for signs of trouble. He wasn't long finding it. As he passed by the Gold Stake Saloon and Gambling Parlor, he heard the crack of gunshots from inside. Birch spurred Cactus to a trot in time to see two men stagger outside and fall face down onto the dusty street, smoking guns in their hands. A third man walked out of the saloon to examine the two dead men. Then he wadded up a handkerchief and pressed it to a bullet wound in his upper arm.

In the center of Bodie, most of the gambling parlors were clustered on one side of the main street, and the hotels on the other side. The Nugget overshadowed the rest of the buildings; it was not only a hotel, but a restaurant, saloon, and gambling parlor as well. The facade was a bright red and blue that looked freshly painted.

The inside was a different story. Birch took time to glance around the lobby. The faded elegance of its imported blue wallpaper and worn, polished hardwood floors were second to the crystal chandelier, with several of its prisms missing, that hung just above and beyond the registration desk. Birch walked up to the registration desk, where a clerk looked at him expectantly.

"I'm looking for Joseph Winston."

The clerk shook his head, disappointment and suspicion replacing his previous expression. "No one here by that name."

Birch frowned. "May I see the registration book? He may be listed under another name."

"I'm afraid I can't help you, sir," the clerk replied, now with his nose in the air.

Before Birch could explain why he was here and maybe offer a small bribe for a look at the book, a bell rang. Room 10 needed assistance. With an irritated glance in Birch's direction, the clerk left his station unattended. The book sat on a swivel stand to the far left of the counter. Birch quickly looked through the signatures for the past few days. One set of names stood out: Mr. and Mrs. J. Swinton registered in room 7. It was the only name that was entered day after day.

Before Birch started toward room 7, a man walked into the lobby. He was dressed like a gambler, with a dark suitcoat over a fine linen shirt and brocade vest. When the man doffed his bowler at a passing woman, Birch recognized him as Mrs. Winston's prodigal husband. He approached.

"Mr. Winston."

The man's eyes widened in recognition of his name. "I'm afraid you have the wrong man," he said, glancing around the lobby to make sure no one overheard their conversation. "My name is Swinton." He began to walk toward his room.

"No, I'm sure I have the right man," Birch replied, lengthening his stride to catch up. Winston quickened his pace, trying to ignore Birch. "In fact, I have a photograph right here." Birch reached into his vest pocket to draw out the portrait.

Winston stopped in front of his room and grabbed Birch's arm to stop him. "Not here," he said with a hiss, opening the door and drawing Birch into the room.

Inside, gray daylight filtered into the room through grimy windows. It was actually two small rooms. The one in which Birch stood was a sitting room shabbily furnished with a small sofa, a wingback chair, and a desk and chair in the corner. There was barely enough space to take three strides from the door to the opposite wall.

A second chamber, presumably the bedroom, could be seen through an open doorway. Birch guessed that it had a separate entrance. He remembered passing a door in the hallway that was only a few steps away from the doorway through which Winston and he had just entered.

A young woman appeared in the doorway between the two rooms, dressed in an ivory silk robe, her heavy, dark hair tumbling all around a lace shawl collar. Birch took off his hat in her presence. Her best features were her translucent blue eyes, accentuated by slender dark brows that arched delicately above.

She moved farther into the room, the robe swirling around her like silky water, and looked at Birch with open curiosity. From her expression, it was clear that the couple rarely had visitors. "John?" she asked.

"Grace," Winston said nervously. He cleared his throat. "Grace, why don't you get dressed. I bet you haven't eaten a thing all day." Grace lowered her eyes and went into the other room. Winston strode over to the desk, opened a drawer, and brought out a half-empty bottle of whisky and a none too clean glass. Not bothering to offer a drink to Birch, he poured himself a generous amount and gulped it down. "How did you find me?"

"The man who works your claim."

Winston's laugh was bitter. "I didn't think he'd still be there. Seemed too soft for that sort of work. Besides, the stake's played out."

Birch wisely refrained from contradicting him. "He seems to enjoy the role of miner right now."

The woman called Grace came into the room again, this time dressed in lace-trimmed muslin. Her hair was pinned up with tortoiseshell combs and her cheeks were lightly rouged.

"Where are your manners, John?" she said sternly. "Aren't you going to introduce us?"

Winston grunted. "This is my wife, Grace. Gracie, this is . . ."

"Jefferson Birch, ma'am."

"We have some . . . business to take care of." Birch met Winston's eyes and caught the warning in them. "Why don't you go down to the lobby and wait for me. I'll take you out to a nice restaurant in a little while." His eyes had softened as he watched her leave, then hardened again when the door closed.

"All right," he said to Birch. "I'm Joe Winston. What do you want?"

"It's not what I want," Birch replied mildly. "It's what your wife wants. Your first wife, that is. I take it that girl thinks she's married to you."

"As far as I'm concerned, she is my wife." Winston took a tobacco pouch out of his coat pocket and began to roll a cigarette. He shook his head. "I have nothing to give Annabel. What does she want, money?"

"She was concerned about you. She's taking in sewing and laundry to make a living, and she spent her hard-earned money hiring me to find you." Birch watched Winston's impassive face.

Winston lit his cigarette and inhaled deeply. "I don't want to go back to Redding and the farm. I want to stay here. I was a terrible miner, but I'm a good gambler." He withdrew a fat poke from his inside vest pocket and shook it to drive home his point. "I took the little gold I came away with from the claim and turned it into a decent living. Now I play poker and monte, occasionally roulette."

"So you don't feel any obligation to either woman, not even

to get a divorce from Annabel in order to make Grace an honest woman."

Winston laughed cruelly. "Grace hasn't been honest since the day she set foot in Bodie. And as far as Annabel is concerned, I don't feel anything anymore for her. I stopped loving her the day she told me she wouldn't sell the farm to pay for my gold claim."

Birch was having a hard time listening to Winston. Clenching his jaw to keep from saying anything he might regret, Birch jammed his hat on his head and stood.

As he made his way to the door, Winston asked, "You won't tell Annabel where I am, will you?"

Birch paused, then turned. "You won't object to a divorce, will you?"

Winston shrugged. "If she can find me, I'll happily consent to a divorce."

Birch couldn't contain himself any longer. He strode over and grabbed Winston by his lapels, hauling him to his feet. An uppercut to the chin knocked Winston across the sofa, head over heels.

The knuckles of his right hand smarting, Birch departed without another word. He was halfway down the hall when he heard the shot. Racing back to the room, he found the bedroom door partially open. Through the open door to the sitting room, he could see Winston slumped in the sofa, blood staining his brocade vest. He heard a sound behind him.

"Don't turn around, Mr. Birch," she said. Her voice was shaking.

"Mrs. Swinton—" he began.

She cut him short. "No, call me Grace. I came back to the room to get my evening bag and I heard most of your conversation." Birch could hear the sorrow seeping into her voice.

"I'm sorry, Grace."

She hesitated. "You were only doing what you had to do. The person for whom I grieve is his wife. No matter what he told you about me, Mr. Birch, I would never . . ." Her voice broke and he could hear the sob caught in her throat.

"But why did you kill him?" he asked, wanting to turn around and look at her again. "Why not just leave him?"

"John, I mean Joe, wasn't an easy person to leave. I don't know what life with him was like for his wife, but he didn't always treat me well. Maybe that's why it was so easy—" She trailed off again, then added in a stronger voice, "I'm sorry, Mr. Birch. But I had to do it."

He felt the blow to the back of his head before he sank into unconsciousness.

★

Birch wasn't sure how long he was out. When he opened his eyes, the room was almost dark. Standing up cautiously, Birch staggered into the sitting room. Winston was still there, still dead. Grace was gone.

He was surprised that there hadn't been more of an uproar when the shot had been fired earlier. Then he remembered he was in Bodie, where a person was killed just about every hour. People had probably gotten used to minding their own business.

Birch pondered what to do. Grace was obviously gone. He thought about sending for the law, but he didn't much like the idea of putting them on the trail of a woman betrayed. In a fit of passion, Grace had killed a human being. Then again, Winston wasn't much of a human being, having lied to one woman and hidden from another.

If she was caught, there was a chance that she would be found not guilty. But justice was a tricky thing. She might also be sentenced to life or even hanged.

Birch touched the back of his head and winced. He squinted at his fingers, but he couldn't see blood. She hadn't broken the skin, but he would have a nice-sized goose egg for a few days. Birch closed the hotel room door and walked down the hall. The registration desk was empty. He crossed the quiet lobby and left the hotel.

It wasn't until he was heading out of Bodie that he realized he'd made his decision. He hoped Grace left Bodie to start a new life. Meanwhile, it was difficult to know what to tell Annabel Winston. He finally decided to tell a small lie, that he had come to Bodie a day late, that Joe Winston had been shot by a person or persons unknown. He wanted to spare Mrs. Winston the sordid details. She didn't deserve what had happened to her.

Birch reached into his vest pocket for his bandanna, but it was missing. In its place was a poke. He pulled it out and examined it. Although it was not as full as the one he had seen earlier on the dead man, it was definitely Winston's bag. It was filled with gold and silver coins.

Birch could only guess that Grace had taken a few coins for her escape, but had left the rest with Birch to give to the new widow. Dying was probably the only unselfish thing Winston had ever done. The money would enable two women to have a better life than when he was alive.

It was a better legacy than Joe Winston deserved.

Joseph Gores

GUNMAN IN TOWN

*"Goodbye, Pops" remains one of the best short stories
ever published in the crime field.*

But Joseph Gores certainly didn't stop there.

*Over the past quarter century he has produced
many books and stories that have become benchmarks
for the entire field.*

*His DKA novels, for example, remain state-of-the-
art in the private-eye field. His recent novel* Dead Man
is an exemplar of the modern, stripped-down thriller.

*Gores has worked extensively in television and mov-
ies, and that visual style can be seen here.*

At the brow of the hill I pulled Dan up, swung a foot out of
the stirrup, and hooked a knee around the saddle horn. It was
coming on the evening cool, with a chill wind rising off the
valley floor. On the far side the redwoods stood out thin and
sharp on the ridges; above them, flat-bottomed layers of mist
sliced off the hills like knife cuts. Thin rows of elms divided
the fields, and a train trailed out long ends of lonesome black
smoke.

I hadn't seen the valley in close to eight years. It didn't look
to have changed much, but I had. Getting out a crumpled sack
of Bull, I rolled a cigarette. Then I'd been a kid of sixteen with
a hand-tooled Mexican saddle my uncle had given me, no horse,
and no other kin not dead; now I was a man, on my way to
old Mexico. A man with a score to settle in Parson's Valley.

I shifted the long blue .44 strapped low on my thigh. It had
been Uncle Rob's gun. Dying, shot down in a muddy Skagway
street, he had been more concerned with me squaring my Par-

son's Valley account than in squaring his own with his killer. *Get back down there, Dunc. It's . . . damned important.*

So here I was.

My cigarette was gone. I straightened in the saddle and touched a heel to old Dan's lean belly, and he took me down the rut gouged in the sloping side hill. Parson's Valley, where I had sworn to shoot two men. I still could remember the first time I'd seen it in the dusk of an April evening. . . .

★

The white frame post office had a false front, as did the ladies' dry-goods store across the street. The teamster drew in his rig and pointed at the general store, next to the bank on the corner, which had WILLIAMSON'S painted above the door in new black letters.

He loosed a dirty brown stream of tobacco juice at the road. "You ask there, boy. That's where I heard about the job."

Horses crowded the rail in front of the saloon, and a team was pulled up longways in front of Sommer's Feed Store. At Williamson's I went by two beak-nosed, unsmiling Indians to drop my heavy saddle on the stoop. Behind the counter a steer-solid fellow of about eighteen counted bills into the drawer of a tall silver cash register. He had a square, tanned face and meaty hands sprouting from his tight cuffs.

"Teamster told me a fellow named Cutter Hennessey needs a man."

He looked me over, then grinned. "Man? Well, I guess you'd do as a hired boy to clean up after his cows. Half a mile back the road, take the dirt track goin' up the side hill through the poplars. That's it—if you ain't too proud to shovel manure."

"I done worse."

He let me get to the door, then added: "Better be ready for some Bible-thumpin' from that wife of his. An' stay away from his daughter, Ruthie. They don't call him 'Cutter' for nothin'."

"Girls don't bother me none—I ain't but sixteen."

"This one'll bother you."

By the time I saw the lamp glowing homely-like from the Hennesseys' kitchen window, the light had faded from behind the high rounded hills standing up against the horizon. A pair of muddy boots waited in bent-topped patience beside the rough cement stoop.

"Well?"

The dour woman who answered my knock wore a severe black dress with a red and yellow apron over it. Her cheeks looked as soft as a piece of tanned saddle leather.

"Is this Cutter Hennessey's spread, ma'am?"

"And if it is? He owes no man."

"Yes, ma'am. I heard he needs a boy to help around the place."

From behind rimless glasses, her pale eyes moved over me like a horse buyer's hands over a colt at auction. "Lord knows there be'n't much work in them limbs of yours."

"Oh, I can work, ma'am. My pa always said I'd just growed too fast for the meat to catch up with the bone."

"Where is your pa, boy? And the Lord punishes them as lies."

"He's dead, ma'am. Whole family's dead 'cept for my Uncle Rob."

"Then why ain't he took you in?" Her hands formed a tight moving ball under the apron, like a pair of squirrels in a gunny sack.

I thought of Uncle Rob down at Sacramento two days before, when he'd given me the saddle: *Come back when you've got a horse to put under it, kid, and we'll ride North.* North to the Klondike, where gold had been discovered, sending men to Seattle in droves for the coastwise steamers to Alaska. Uncle Rob: a tall, hard, lean man, a gambler by profession and a gunman by reputation. Take in a snot-nosed kid like me?

"He . . . goes his own way, ma'am."

"Hmph." Her eyes went behind me, to the saddle. "Fancy tooling like that costs a sight of money."

"I didn't steal it, ma'am."

"That waits to be seen. Cutter's at the barn."

I turned away from the rich bread and meat and pie smells that drifted from the bright kitchen behind her. At the barn, through the open upper half of the Dutch door, I could see eight good milk cows with their heads thrust between sliding boards that could be fastened close against their necks. A bulky man in a red and black mackinaw and blue jeans was milking one of them.

Seeing me at the door, he gestured at the kerosene lamp hanging from a nail in the rough crossbeam. "Let a man see you, boy." I stepped forward in the light. "Reckon you're looking for work?"

"Yes sir. My name's Russ Duncan."

"It's up at five and to bed by nine, 'cause they's a sight of chores to be done." He smelled faintly of cow dung and sweat. Reddish hair stuck up in tufts from his head, and his eyes were a pale blue. "And we read the Book reg'lar between times. Understand?"

"Yes sir."

"Then we'll get on, boy." His smile was like the smile of a bear trap laid open under the leaves and smeared with grease so no trace of human smell is left on it. "We'll get on jest fine."

That night at supper I met Ruthie for the first time. I remembered young Williamson's saying that she would bother me. She did. Her oval face was framed in honey-swirled hair, and her slender, willowy body was that graceful it made my knees weak.

"This is our Ruthie," Old Lady Hennessey said proudly.

Ruthie dropped me a very grave and graceful curtsy. "How do you do, I'm sure."

"I'm pleased to meet you, ma'am."

I had the loft room all to myself, with a straw-filled pallet that was sure a heap softer than the stubble fields at harvest time I'd gotten used to. Once alone there, I thought on the lamp's slanted light glinting through Ruthie's golden hair, and the laughing way she'd looked at me from the corners of her eyes.

In the weeks that followed I got used to that look; too used, maybe. The trouble was she'd follow me around on the chores. Nothing bad happened, but it could have, especially one afternoon when I was up on the horse trail that wound off the bald knob of pasture into the silent redwoods. Something rustled behind me and I turned slow, fearful I'd been trapped by a moseying bear in search of a honey tree or red vinegar ants. But it was Ruthie.

She came close and leaned past me to stare down at the fine, sharp rise of thin trees on the slopes below.

"You like to come up here alone, don't you, Russ?"

"I . . . sure, I guess so." I could feel my face coloring up as it always did when she talked to me.

"What do you see when you look down there?" she asked. "Do you see castles or knights in armor or—"

"Mostly nothin', I guess." I had picked out a drifting eagle, keen-eyed for rabbits or squirrels or anything small that moved and could be made to die. "Sometimes a baldy like him."

She gave a light giggle, and came closer. "You're so serious, Russ." She tossed her head, so the honeyed hair swirled around her shoulders. The movement emphasized the maturing curves beneath her tight jeans. "Don't you like me, just a little?"

She was only a foot from me; my arms went around her as if it were the most natural thing in the world. She shut her eyes and swayed tight against me and we were kissing, hard. Then she suddenly pulled away and laughed again, and then was gone, back down the path in a swirl of golden hair.

I suppose old man Hennessey couldn't help but notice the way I kept watching her all during supper that night. After she and her ma had gone into the kitchen with the dishes, he tilted his chair back and hooked his thumbs through his belt. Those pig eyes fixed on me.

"Boy, what were you doin' up on the hill today?"

"I . . . looking for a calf that had strayed off, sir."

Down came his chair with a jolt that shook the room. "If I thought you'd been messing around with my Ruthie . . . Your sort of trash—"

"I ain't such trash!" I burst out. "Just 'cause—"

He came erect as fast as a rattler striking, his face a match in redness with his hair. One hand swept up along his side, bringing with it a long, slim-bladed knife from somewhere on the way up. He jabbed the point out to within an inch of my eyes, sending me stumbling backward away from it.

"Just shut your mouth, boy. And look on this blade, and remember it. And remember I ain't gonna tell you twice 'bout my Ruthie!"

After that I just couldn't get Ruthie alone, even though school was out and she was home all the time. I figured it was her pa's doings during the day; and after dark, most evenings, she'd go into town for visiting with her girlfriend, Mary Helen Hawkins. But on the Fourth of July, old man Hennessey said that she could go to a barn-warming with Mary Helen, and I got all steamed up. That would be a good time, I decided, to get her off alone. Getting that horse to put under my saddle— even getting to Alaska—didn't seem as important anymore as being alone with Ruthie.

That night I cleaned up at the watering trough back of the barn, tallowed my boots, and wore the britches I'd pressed under my mattress the night before. The new pine floor of the barn was just right for dancing, and they had a man up from

Santa Rosa to call the squares. I tried to get Ruthie alone, but she kept putting me off; and then she disappeared entirely. I went outside looking, determined and puzzled. It was out back by the haystacks that I found her.

"What do you want?" she finally answered petulantly from the offside of one of the stacks. She sounded breathless and almost angry.

I stepped into the shadow where the moon was no longer in my eyes, and there she was, with her hair loose and her eyes bright and her dress rumpled. And there was young Williamson, big and blond and grinning in the shadows behind her.

"What are you and—and *him* . . ."

"You didn't really think I was coming into town all those nights to see Mary Helen, did you?" she asked. Then Williamson busted out laughing.

I leaped at him blindly, without any thought but to tear him apart. His heavy fist met me, swinging me around; then his heavier boot drove into my kidneys. I went down like a neck-shot buck, tried to roll, caught another heavy boot in the ribs.

"Don't start nothin' you can't finish," Williamson grunted.

I got one frozen glimpse of Ruthie behind him; Her eyes were huge and her breasts were heaving with excitement.

"Kick him again, Carl!" she whispered fiercely.

He did. In the face that time. I went out. When I was able to sit up again, they were gone.

I probably would have left Parson's Valley right then, just pulled out with nothing but my saddle and the few dollars I'd saved, except that the harvest was due and I felt I owed Old Man Hennessey that. As far as Ruthie went, I just avoided her: Nothing kills romance sooner than knowing a girl's seen you getting whupped and has egged on the man who did it.

But one September night when I came in after chores, Hennessey's ham of a fist met me at the door. I fetched up against the bannister across the room and he swarmed over me, his face as mean and angry under its scraggled upright shock of red hair as a boar hog's in rutting season.

"I told you what'd happen if you laid hands on her!"

"Wait a minute! I ain't—"

He grabbed my hair and slammed my head against a stair runner. I tasted bitterness; things got fuzzy. I guess I was fighting back, not really knowing what I was doing; for suddenly he skipped away and that knife appeared in his fist.

"Raise your hand to me, you Satan's hound? Git up them stairs and pray it's a weddin' tomorrow and not a lynchin'!"

I sat at my loft window, working a loose tooth with my tongue, staring at the few high stars that had poked holes in the darkening night. There I was, faced in the morning with a wedding or a lynching, and not sure which would be worse.

Williamson had gotten Ruthie in trouble, of course, and together they had lit on me as the likeliest prospect for the blame. While I was thinking on that, hooves clattered and the dark shapes of mounted men passed around the house. I could pick out the Williamsons, father and son, Sommers from the feed store, and Jed Slocum.

They all went into the kitchen, and after a while I got curious about what they were planning for me, so I got what money I had from the bureau, crawled out of the window, hung by the drain spout, and just could reach the shed roof with my stockinged toes. It was a short jump from there to the big cottonwood tree, and an easy drop to the ground.

I hunkered down under the kitchen window, listened to ten minutes of jawing, and decided it would be a lynching if young Williamson had his way. I got my boots from the stoop and got out of there.

Trotting down toward town, I tried to think it through. I couldn't make it out of the valley afoot before they'd catch up; and stealing a horse would get me hung quicker than I probably would be anyway. That left the train. But the train into Parson's Valley only passed through town on its way to Settler's Gap at the end of the valley, and then turned around and came back again. If it was *in* Settler's Gap already . . .

It wasn't. I stopped and asked Gus March, the telegraph operator in the depot. He was a small, cocky, white-haired old gent who'd been more friendly to me than most others in town.

"She'll be through at six in the morning for the Gap, Russ," he said. His shrewd, faded eyes twinkled at me. "Why, you figger on mebbe leaving town or something, boy?"

"Me? Why, no, I . . ." I already was backing away from the window.

"Reason I asked, I heard young Carl Williamson say . . ."

But I was away by then, off the planking beside the depot and into the darkness. If old Gus mentioned my question to Hennessey or to any of the others who'd been in that kitchen palaver, they'd have men waiting at Settler's Gap for me.

Unless . . . I got into an empty woodshed a quarter of a mile down the track from the depot. Unless I hid there until the train came *back* from Settler's Gap, and caught it then. They wouldn't expect me to do that. I got behind some cords where I couldn't be seen by anyone just glancing in casually, and waited for morning.

But about daylight, through a gap in the wall, I saw old Cootie Davis heading for Hennessey's place in his buckboard, with his two old blue tick hounds in the back. They'd checked and found me missing then, and those hounds would bring them right to this shed long before the train came back from Settler's Gap.

So when the train rattled by at 6 A.M., I ran out across the loose cinders of the roadbed and swung aboard the caboose. It was empty, so I hunkered down in a seat and listened to the regular beat of the rails underneath, and wondered what I would do when it got to Settler's Gap.

Next thing I was sitting up and knuckling my eyes, in a panic from falling asleep. But then I looked out the window, and my heart gave a fiercer jump than I'd thought possible.

A lone rider just was breaking from a stand of blue spruce halfway upon the hillside. He was a big, erect man who knew how to ride, giving easily with the fetlock give of the powerful black stallion under him. Lather foamed the horse's neck, and its eyes had the wild, sideways look you'll never see in a gelding or a mare. Floury dust had whitened the rider's boots and brown suit, and I knew him long before I saw his squinted blue eyes or hard jaw.

Uncle Rob swung out of his saddle to catch the handrail on the back platform, and stepped off that stallion as natural as stepping off a boardwalk. He faced me down the swaying aisle of the car, his shadow cast long and thin before him by the morning sun.

I could only think of one thing to say to him: "What about your horse?"

"Never mind that horse, boy. He could outrun this train from here to Sacramento if he'd a mind to. Did you do it to her?"

"How did you know about that? How come you to be here?"

"Gus March was a faro dealer for old Bill Briggs at the Bryant House in 'Frisco, till they closed it down in '81. He taught me what I know about cards and he sent me a wire last night." His hard blue eyes fixed on my face. "I asked you a question, boy."

"I never touched her. I thought I wanted to marry her."

"Right," he said. It was his last word on the subject.

At Settler's Gap, while the train was turning around, he went out and talked to some men there. He had people like Gus March that he knew all up and down the state, men he'd gambled with or prospected with or fought with—or, sometimes, against. On the way back he just lounged in his seat, telling stories that were exciting enough to be lies but weren't. Then the flaked and faded PARSON'S VALLEY sign slid past our window, and he stood up with a lithe movement and bit the end off a black cigar and canted it between his teeth, just so, as if to tell Parson's Valley that there was a gunman in town now.

Folks were crowded up thicker than currants in the bottom of the jam jar when the train stopped, with kids and yapping dogs ducking in and out of the crowd like mountain jays at a logging camp picnic. I felt a moment of panic as we stepped out on the rear platform; a shout went up and young Williamson came swarming up the steps with a length of new hemp already formed into a noose.

"Here he is!" Oh, he was awfully eager to stop my mouth, he was. But he never got the chance.

Uncle Rob's right hand came out from under his coat with that terribly long blue .44, and laid it alongside Carl's head with a hollow, juicy sound like biting into an apple. Carl went back down the steps again even faster than he'd come up, rolled over once, and lay still. Uncle Rob kicked the rope down on top of him.

"Hey!" yelled Cutter Henessey, starting across the platform. "We want that boy for raping my daughter! We aim to string him—"

"Whoa, Hoss," Uncle Rob said; and his voice, soft and chill, stopped Henessey like a charge of shot. "The boy says he never laid a hand on your daughter."

"*His* word against the *decent* folk of this town?" shrilled Old Lady Hennessey from the crowd.

"I would of had another name for you, ma'am," said Uncle Rob politely.

Just then a voice broke in from the crowd, "Hey, ain't you Rob Duncan from down around Sacramento way?"

"The same. The boy here is my nephew."

Old Man Hennessey gave back a hasty step, and there was a general sort of shuffling in the crowd. Uncle Rob didn't move, just stood there with his eyes ranging over them as if looking for something.

I know now what it was: a man with the guts to act even if the crowd didn't back his play; but there wasn't any such in Parson's Valley that day. The tension suddenly went out of Rob and he thrust the .44 back under his coat.

"Move this burner out," he yelled down at the engineer. "The comedy's over!"

The train lurched and clanked, and the platform started to slide away. I saw Ruthie at the edge of the crowd, shrunk back against her ma as if she wanted to be invisible.

"Hey, wait," I said to Uncle Rob, suddenly brave. "I want to make her stand out and accuse me to my face. I want—"

He gave me a strange look. "You come back and settle things up later, Dunc."

"I'm gonna shoot that Hennessey and Williamson for what they done to me. I—"

"Lots of time to square accounts, Dunc," he said easily, taking the cigar from his mouth for the first time since the train had stopped. "Tell me, you ever been to Alaska?"

"You know I ain't."

He grinned and settled back in his seat. "Neither have I."

*

I made camp five miles from town, hobbled my horse, and chawed some jerky for supper. Afterward I rolled up in my blanket and laid with my head on the saddle, listening to an occasional snort from old Dan and watching the stars. I was glad that Rob had urged me to come back and square things up, even though I still didn't understand why it had suddenly become so important to him that I should. Revenge would taste good.

I rode into Parson's Valley about midmorning on a Saturday. I'd timed it for then: Unless he'd changed considerable, Hennessey would be in for supplies and the week's banking. The town had grown some, even had a Chinese restaurant; but Williamson's store still was there, and in fact had expanded into the place next door.

When I walked in, a heavy blond man came from behind the counter, rubbing his beefy hands on a soiled white apron. He had a drinker's eyes, and a white, shiny scar on his temple. He stood a good three inches shorter than I did.

He smiled at me. "Can I help you, stranger?"

I hit him, as hard as I could, in the gut. He went down, gagging. I stepped over him behind the counter, where they'd always kept an old Colt Peacemaker. They still did. I checked that it was loaded, then dropped it clanking on the floor beside him. His hand crawled toward it like a spider after a housefly.

"Go ahead, make your play," I said. "A man hadn't ought to never start nothing he can't finish."

The hand quit moving. Carl Williamson even seemed to quit breathing.

Then a fleshy woman came from the back of the store with two towheaded kids, the older one, the boy, just about the right age. Her years with Williamson had done more to Ruthie than I ever would have wanted.

"Ru . . . Russ?"

Her voice was small and scared, the voice of a woman whose man might be taken away from her. I looked back to Williamson; he still hadn't moved, just laid there holding his breath, his eyes sick from the fear of dying. He made me feel a little sick myself.

"Who else owes him that?" I asked.

I walked out of the store and down to the rail where I'd left Dan. It hadn't been anything like I'd expected. I was reaching for the reins to untie him when I saw Hennessey. Just like that, coming out of the bank, just as I'd seen him in a thousand lonely campfires.

Only not quite the same. He'd shrunk considerable. Then I realized; I was seeing him with a man's eye now. He would have walked right by me to his buckboard if Ruthie hadn't busted out on the porch of the store.

"Pa!" she cried in an anguished voice.

Swinging toward her, his eyes lit on me just long enough to see more than a stranger about to get on his horse. All of a sudden something happened in his face. Not fear. Just . . . oldness.

He was only three feet away, close enough for his right hand to make that practiced lightning move that would have flashed out the thin-bladed stiletto from its boot sheath. And for a moment, as his eyes stared into mine, he thought he was going to try it. Then the moment passed, and the eyes faltered and finally the fear was there, as it had been in Carl's face.

I jerked the reins free from the hitching post and swung into the saddle atop the big black stallion that just by his presence told Parson's Valley that a gunman was in town.

I looked down into Hennessey's face, and suddenly I laughed. "You're getting fat, dirt farmer," I said. "And you're going bald."

Then I rode on out of there, because I finally knew what Rob had known all along. That if I hadn't come back the hate always would have been there, bright and shiny, to be taken out and polished like a miser's gold, until finally it would have poisoned me as a dead coyote down deep in a well poisons all the water in it.

"You had that old ace lying back there in the hole again, didn't you, Rob?" I said aloud. The icy-nerved gambler who rode in my memory had staked his pot on the way he'd figured I'd play my hand.

Old Dan threw his head to turn an eye on me as if to ask just what the hell went on; then he broke into his flowing gallop. All of a sudden it was a fine morning, with none of the past left in it like cold coffee in the bottom of the cup. Instead, the long and dusty road to Mexico stretched before us, full of a lot of miles we'd never covered before.

Dan and I went South.

Livia Washburn

HOLLYWOOD GUNS

Livia Washburn has managed to work in both the Western and the detective genres simultaneously.

Her novels about Hallam are set in the Los Angeles of the silent-movie era and involve the stuntman in fair-clue mysteries with a distinctly Western air about them.

The Hallam books should be on the shelves of anybody with an interest in Hollywood, private-eye fiction, and realistic Western fiction.

Hallam's Colt jammed just as he was about to shoot William S. Hart.

Hallam said, "Dammit!" and glared down at the revolver. Bill Hart, who was directing as well as starring in the picture, merely shrugged his shoulders and called, "Cut!" in that deep, resonant voice of his.

"Sorry, Bill," Hallam said as he drew back the hammer of the Colt and studied it. "Looks like the sear's busted."

"Don't worry about it, Lucas. The script called for you to miss me anyway," Hart pointed out. He held out his hand. "Mind if I take a look?"

Hallam handed over the Colt, knowing that Hart was a Westerner like himself and not some play-acting dude from back East. Hart handed the weapon back after a moment's study of it and agreed with Hallam's conclusion.

"I imagine that old hogleg's seen a lot of use," he said.

Hallam grinned, hefting the Colt. "Had it, man and boy, nigh onto forty years."

"I have a pair of six-shooters that belonged to Billy the Kid. Did you and young Bonney ever cross paths, by any chance?"

Hallam shook his head. "He was a few years before my time. Not much, mind you."

Nearby, an assistant director sweated and watched the two older men talking. He was wearing an open-throated sports shirt and jodhpurs, which were quite a contrast to the dusty range clothes worn by Hallam and Bill Hart. In the wilds of Bronson Canyon, where the company was shooting today, the AD looked more like he was in costume than Hallam and Hart did.

They looked right at home.

"Excuse me, Mr. Hart," the AD finally said. "Are we going to try to set up for another shot?"

Hart glanced around at the crowd of people, momentarily forgotten as he and Hallam had looked at the broken gun. He looked back at Hallam. "Feel like doing the scene with another gun, Lucas? We could start from the top so there wouldn't be any problem with continuity."

Hallam removed the battered, broad-brimmed hat from his head and ran his fingers around the inside of the band, wiping away the seat. His craggy face with its drooping gray mustache was thoughtful. "Wouldn't really seem right," he said after a moment.

Hart nodded. "That's what I thought. Man gets used to his own gun." He turned to the AD. "Might as well get the chase out of the way, Marty."

The young man nodded and hurried off to confer with the camerman and round up the riding extras who would be needed to film the scene. Hallam slid the Colt back in its holster and said, "Reckon it won't matter while I'm just ridin'. I can get it fixed tomorrow."

"Are you going to take it to Old Bob?" Hart asked.

"Where else? Old Bob's the best damn gunsmith in Hollywood."

★

The sign painted on the window of the little shop read HOLLY-WOOD GUNS. The place was far out on Sunset, on the edge of town in an area where the rents were low. Inside, it was musty and a little gloomy, but as Hallam opened the door the next day, he thought that it was one of his favorite places in California.

There were guns everywhere you looked in the front part of the store, rifles and shotguns in racks along the walls, handguns of all kinds in glass-topped display cases. A wooden counter ran through the middle of the room. The back section was cluttered with metal racks and workbenches and guns in various states of disrepair. That was where Old Bob did his gunsmithing. There was also a small back room where ammunition was stored.

Hallam had never heard Old Bob called anything else. He didn't know the man's last name. But he was a familiar figure as he sat on a tall stool behind the counter, fiddling with a little nickel-plated .25. He was a small, wizened man in his sixties, with a few strands of hair plastered across a bald head and a wispy growth of whiskers on his chin. His dark eyes lit up as he saw Hallam come into the shop.

"Well, if it ain't the actor!" he said mockingly. "How's the picture business, Fairbanks?"

Hallam grinned, used to the old codger riding him. Of course, Bob wasn't that much older than Hallam himself. But, hell, Hallam didn't mind being a codger.

He hauled out the broken Colt and laid it on the counter. "Got a busted sear," he said. "Reckon you can fix it?"

Old Bob snorted derisively. "Can I fix it? Of course I can fix it!" He picked up the Colt and sniffed it, wrinkling his nose. "Don't you ever clean this damn thing?"

Hallam ignored the question and said, "Time's money. How soon can you have it ready?"

"You picture people," Old Bob said with a growl. "Hurry up, hurry up. That's all you do. Then you stand around."

Hallam put his hands on the counter. "How long?"

Old Bob shrugged and said, "Give me a couple hours."

Hallam nodded. He turned to leave the shop, but he paused in front of a small stretch of wall where there were no gun racks. Instead, the wall was covered with yellowed newspaper clippings, some of them dating back to the 1870s. Hallam always got a kick out of reading them. Old Bob had one interest besides guns, and that was outlaws.

The stories had been cut out of papers all over the country. Evidently Old Bob had traveled a lot in his younger days. The clippings told of bank robberies and stagecoach holdups, train

robbers and shootists and road agents. All the famous desperadoes were there—the James boys, the Daltons and the
Youngers, Bill Doolin, Bitter Creek Newcomb, Jake Fentress and
his back-shooting brother Leroy, the Wild Bunch, Ben Thompson, King Fisher, John Wesley Hardin. . . . Nearly every outlaw
Hallam had ever heard of was up on that wall, represented by
the colorful writing of the journalists of those wild days.

Hallam had crossed paths with a few of those lawbreakers,
had traded lead with some of them. In fact, one of the clippings
contained a group photograph of the posse that had rounded
up a gang of train robbers in Arizona, and Hallam was right
there, a lot of years younger and serving as a deputy. Old Bob
had been excited to meet one of the men pictured in his collection, and it had been an even bigger thrill when Hallam had
brought Al Jennings around to meet him. Hallam didn't know
the Oklahoma bad man well, but he had made a few pictures
with him.

"Relivin' past glories, Lucas?" Old Bob asked from his seat
behind the counter, and the irascible tone was gone from his
voice now.

Hallam shook his head. "Them days weren't so glorious, most
of the time. Lots of hard work and gettin' shot at."

"You still a detective?"

"When somebody wants to hire me," Hallam answered with
a nod. He divided his time between movie work and being a
private detective, and between the two jobs, he made a
decent living.

Old Bob shook his head. "Must not be much of a challenge,
chasin' crooks these days. The country's grown up a mighty
sorry crop of desperadoes."

"Oh, there's still a few wild and woolly ones out there," Hallam said.

"Not like the old days," Old Bob insisted.

"Hell," Hallam said with a grin, "what is?"

With a wave of his hand, he went out the door and wandered
down the street.

There was a diner a couple of blocks away, and he settled
in there to drink several cups of coffee and read a paper that
a previous customer had left behind. There was a lot of tension
in the world, as usual. That seemed to be something that just
went with modern times. Back East, in New York and Chicago,
the gangsters were shooting each other up, also as usual. Hallam was glad he was in sunny Southern California.

There was crime out here, too, though. As he scanned the paper he saw stories about a man going insane and shooting his wife and in-laws, a payroll robbery in Glendale, a gun battle between two rival groups of rum-runners, and a swindle that had left several people penniless. Only the lunatic had been caught. The cops were still looking for the folks who had pulled all the other jobs.

Hallam turned the pages to the trade news. A new studio had opened for business down on Poverty Row, and he was sure they'd be grinding out Westerns, just like all the other Gower Gulch outfits. Good news for him and all the others like him, the riding extras and the wranglers and the stuntmen who had found a home in the moving pictures.

It was hot in the diner, the one fan not stirring up much air. Hallam was used to heat, though, having lived in the Southwest most of his life. Hollywood was nothing compared to the deserts of Texas and New Mexico and Arizona. The time passed fairly quickly, and when he checked his turnip, he saw that he ought to be heading back to Old Bob's to check and see if the Colt was ready.

Before, the old man had been alone in the shop. This time when Hallam came in, there was another customer, a tall man in a suit who was studying some of the pistols in the display cases. He glanced up at Hallam and then went back to looking at the guns.

Old Bob was sitting stiffly on his stool, and he didn't return Hallam's nod of greeting. He was probably feeling touchy again, Hallam thought. "Got that Colt ready yet?" he asked.

Old Bob squinted at him. "What's that name again?" He held up a hand as Hallam frowned. Before Hallam could say anything, Bob went on, "Oh, yeah, I remember now. Fentress, ain't it? Had a Colt with a busted sear."

Hallam nodded slowly. "That's right."

"Got 'er ready for you, Mr. Fentress." Old Bob reached under the counter and pulled out Hallam's Colt. "Be five dollars," he said as he handed it over.

Hallam took the gun and pulled out his wallet, gave a five-dollar bill to Old Bob. "Thanks," he said.

"Welcome," the gunsmith grunted. Hallam turned to go out, but Old Bob stopped him by saying, "You wouldn't be any relation to Leroy Fentress, would you?"

Hallam shook his head. "Never heard of him."

"Thought you might've been. I seen ol' Leroy not long ago."

Hallam smiled politely. " 'Fraid I don't know the man, friend." He left the shop after nodding politely to the other customer.

Hallam walked to his flivver, parked at the curb nearby, got in, drove away. He turned at the next corner and went around the block. There was a vacant lot behind the shop called Hollywood Guns. Hallam parked next to it, then reached into the glove box and took out a box of shells. He thumbed the cartridges into the cylinder of the Colt.

He wished there was more cover leading up to the back door of Old Bob's place. There was only one window on the rear wall, though, and it was fairly grimy. He'd just have to chance it.

Hallam got out of the car, went toward the building at a run.

He lifted a booted foot and drove it against the back door, his heel slamming into the panel beside the knob. The wood splintered and the door smashed back against the wall.

Hallam went through low, the boom of a gun filling his ears. He saw the muzzle flash off to his left and dove to the floor, rolling and tracking the Colt in that direction. He just had time to hope that Old Bob had done a good job repairing it before he triggered off two fast shots.

Both of them hit their target, smashing into the chest of the man crouched in the shadows of the back room and driving him back against the wall. The pistol he held slipped from his fingers and thudded to the floor. The man slid down the wall into a sitting position. His eyes were staring at Hallam, but they weren't seeing him. All the life was gone from them.

Hallam was back on his feet before the echoes of his shots had died away. A thick curtain covered the opening in the partition between the back room and the rest of the shop. Hallam bulled through it, his eyes scanning the room and finding the man who had pretended to be a customer. The man had a pistol out now and was trying to find something at which to fire it.

Old Bob was still on the stool. Hallam kicked out, upsetting the stool and sending the old man flying. He crashed behind the relative safety of the counter as Hallam leveled the Colt at the other man and yelled, "Hold it!"

The man jerked his gun toward Hallam and got off a shot. The slug whined past Hallam's head and punched through the partition behind him. Hallam fired once. The heavy bullet from the Colt caught the man in the shoulder, shattering bone and shredding muscle. The man flopped to the floor, his gun spinning away. He gobbled in pain for a few seconds before shock knocked him out.

From the floor behind the counter, Old Bob looked up at Hallam and asked, "T'other one?"

"Dead in the back," Hallam said shortly. His face was grim as he looked at the sprawled figure of the second gunman. "What the hell was that all about?"

Old Bob got to his feet, brushing himself off. He reached under the counter and brought out a bulky machine gun. "Feller got too attached to his gun," he said. "Thing kept jammin' up on him, so he brought it in to be fixed before him and the other one took off. They was on the run, somethin' about a payroll robbery they pulled in Glendale. Been layin' low for a few days, but the cops were closin' in on them. They were goin' to try to head back East, where they come from. Right talkative pair. 'Course, they figgered to kill me when they left, so's I couldn't send the cops after 'em."

Hallam shook his head. "Damned foolish."

"That they were," Old Bob agreed.

Hallam glared at him. "I'm talkin' about *you*. Startin' a shoot-out in here like that."

"Hell, boy, I knew you'd pick up on it when I called you by Jake Fentress's name. I just threw in that bit about Leroy so's you'd know there was one hidin' in the back. Knew you'd remember the Fentress boys and understand what I was gettin' at."

"I'd've looked a mite embarrassed if that gent had turned out to be a real customer." Hallam grimaced. "I'm gettin' too old to be goin' around bustin' in doors and wavin' guns around. Besides," he added, "what if them two had dropped me, instead of the other way around? Then there'd be two of us dead."

Old Bob shook his head slowly. "I knew you could take 'em. Ain't I been tellin' you? These owlhoots today ain't real desperadoes! Now, if it had been Frank and Jesse James, or the Daltons . . ."

Hallam just shook his head and went to see if he could keep the wounded man from bleeding to death before the cops and the ambulances got there.

Deborah Estleman

FOOL'S GOLD

This is one of the first pieces in a career that is gathering momentum even as you read these lines.

Deborah Estleman shows a skill with words and drama well beyond her "new writer" status.

She has a nice feel for people and place, and instinctively knows how to tell a dramatic and engrossing story.

A cold rain stole its way into camp, patting the rimrock boundary of Number 15 below Discovery on Deadwood Creek. The three prospectors, drenched from an eleven-hour panning effort involving two downpours, five punctured rubber boots, and a thimbleful of gold, knew it was raining again only when the droplets spat into the campfire and sizzled.

Gordy Lamar, a weather-aged man with stooped shoulders brought on by decades of panning gravel bars for gold, wrapped a hand around the soot-blackened handle of the graniteware pot and poured the only cup of coffee he was allotted for the evening. He took a swig and winced. "Boys," he said wearily, "we ain't done nothin' more'n keep ourselves in weak joe and thin sourdough for nigh on to four damn weeks."

Harold Shedd bolted from his seat. "Are you saying I'm not carrying my weight?"

Shedd paused then and threw a confused look toward the felled log where he had been sitting. Exhausted, he slumped back down. His build, though muscular, had been no match for the rigors of squatting in frigid Black Hills streams to scoop up gravel and water with a steel pan the size of a washbowl. "Sorry, old man." He lit a cheroot, drew in the smoke. "It's damned hard to sit here like a drowned rat while our neighbors upcreek are in town celebrating that lode they discovered today."

"Think nothin' of it, lad. We're all a bit edgy."

Pete Maguire, slightest of the three men both in size and brains, seemed entranced by the crackling flames that licked at the rain. "Sounds like bacon fryin', don't it?"

"It sure does, Pete," Gordy said, sighing. "It sure does."

The blaze died down until all that remained was a deep orange glow cloaked in translucent ash. Instinctively, the men pulled closer to the bed of embers and absorbed its last heat.

Gordy watched Shedd, who was gazing into the darkness toward the claim's northern perimeter. At length, the former cleared his throat like a politician about to deliver a speech. In Gordy's case, it did not gain the attention of his audience. He spoke anyway.

"We knew we were gonna be latecomers to these here hills. We figured it'd be worth the gamble, what with all the misery we'd done been dealt. Well, it ain't been. And unless we do somethin' different, it ain't gonna be. Maybe we need to try our hand with a rocker. I've got the rheumatics in my back somethin' fierce, you know, and a rocker would sure enough cut down on the squattin'."

Pete said, "I've heard of them rockers, but I never did see one."

Gordy settled back against a boulder. "Well, Pete, a rocker is this box made of wood that looks sorta like a yonker's cradle—"

"Rocker, hell," Shedd broke in. "If you're not willing to work on the pump that's setting out there going to waste, then you're sure as hell not willing to spend the time on a rocker."

"I've told you before, Shedd. It's dangerous work, and whoever left that broke-down piece of junk out there must've figured out the same thing, so why don't you quit your bellyachin' and put that energy into somethin' worthwhile."

Shedd turned toward Gordy, stroked blond chin stubble below a diabolical grin. "Oh, I've got a worthwhile plan, old man. Easy, too." Shedd lowered his voice. "We salt the mine."

The trio looked to the north toward the place that held an old mine shaft Pete had found hidden by an overgrowth of brush and saplings, a sentinel of crumbling timbers and sluice boxes guarding its mouth. The tunnel had proven barren then, just as it likely had to another unlucky group of prospectors years before. Gordy, Shedd, and Pete had sealed it off; the mine had not been mentioned since.

"Have you taken leave of your senses?"

"Come on, Gordy, think about it. Those highfalutin' investors from back East are nothing but sharpers and they have a hell of a lot more money than we'll ever see. I say the only break we'll get is the one we make for ourselves."

Shedd trotted to his bedroll under the granite outcropping canopy and returned with a double-barreled shotgun and a small, honey-colored leather pouch. "My ten-gauge Whitney's perfect for the job." He stoked the fire for light, then took a cartridge from the pouch and quickly pried off the case head. "I'll show you how it's done."

"I know how it's done and I ain't interested." Gordy placed a steady hand on Shedd's arm. "Let's keep our wits, boy. We'll hit pay dirt soon and then this'll all be behind us."

"Pay dirt, hell. We can't even hit pay *grub,* and we're starving to death because you're too damned stubborn to see when you've been whipped." He jerked the drawstring of the pouch with his teeth, grabbed the Whitney, and started for the makeshift shelter. "Chew on *that,* old man, when you're trying to sleep with a growling belly for a bedmate."

After a moment, Gordy said, "Come along, Pete, we'd best get some shut-eye."

★

The next morning, each man looked as if he had aged a year for every hour slept. Pete fetched water for coffee while Shedd and Gordy built a fire. The men didn't speak.

When the coffee was almost done, Gordy pointed to the pot. "See how it gurgles and pushes up through the spout? It's percolatin', goin' anywheres it can when it can't fit the space no more. I've seen gravel percolate around the timbers that same way, spillin' over into any open space there is. If that gravel starts movin' your shorings, well . . . what I'm tryin' to say is that I'm willin' to shore up that dam and give the pump a shot—if we're all agreed that we have to accept what it gives back, good or bad."

Shedd grinned. "You know I'm in."

"Me, too," said Pete.

It was decided that Gordy and Shedd would make the repairs while Pete, the most skilled at hunting small game, would search for food. Thus the three prospectors set to work as a team, showing a camaraderie not evident in the past. When Gordy and Shedd returned to camp each evening, Pete had enough rabbit or squirrel frying to feed Deadwood on a Saturday night. Though the men ate their fill, they were too weary to enjoy it.

When repairs were almost finished, rains once again came upon the Black Hills. Spent from their labor and discouraged by the downpour, the men retired early.

The torrent brought with it high winds that chanted an eerie song through the towering pines and whipped and twisted virtually everything not tied down.

It was at first light that Gordy and Shedd discovered their pump half buried at the edge of the swollen creek.

"She ain't gonna fix herself, Shedd, so I reckon we'd better get at it."

They had been two hours trying to set the pump right when Pete walked up with a squirrel, cleaned and ready for the skillet.

"This here's tighter'n a Sunday mornin' corset," Gordy said, breathless from trying to wedge a log under a section of the pump. "Soon as we get her loose, Pete, we'll join you for breakfast."

"You oughta hear the talk downstream." Pete's eyes were round and shiny as a gambler's pocket watch. "The men say there's been one strike after another in them Bear Lodge Mountains over in Wyoming Territory. Some of them fellas has got people comin' in to buy up their claims, then the whole bunch of 'em is goin' to head over there and make their fortunes." Shedd and Gordy ignored Pete, continued working. "Listen to me," Pete demanded, "I think we should do the same thing."

Gordy swung to look at Pete and lost his footing. He slid down the embankment and it took only a few seconds for the gravel to swallow his legs, burying him to the hips and trapping him chin-deep in the flooded stream.

Shedd grabbed a rope, secured it around the nearest tree, and hurled the free end to Gordy. "Dammit, Pete," he yelled, "don't just stand there like you're watching a medicine show. Get me some help."

Pete dropped the squirrel carcass and ran back downstream.

"Hang on, old man. I'm coming in to help you keep your nose above water."

"Don't do it, Shedd. The gravel ain't stable and you could bury the both of us."

"You can't hang on like that much longer. The current's too swift."

Shedd removed his jacket and boots, started into the water.

"Wait." Gordy paused. "Hear that? Sounds like Pete's bringin' the whole damned cavalry with him."

The miners, led by Pete, were carrying everything from flanges to firewood. In short order they had Gordy safely on the bank.

A miner whose smile revealed two gold teeth wrapped a couple of worn blankets around Gordy's shoulders. "You are powerful lucky, yes, you are." The teeth glimmered when the man spoke, making his mouth the only facial feature worth describing. "I seen more than my share of sourdoughs get drowned that way, yes, I have."

Someone handed Gordy a steaming cup of black coffee. After a few gulps, Gordy said, "Shedd, draw up a For Sale announcement and send Pete down to tack it on our claim notice. We're gettin' out of this hellhole."

★

That night, the three prospectors brought small pouches of gold to the campfire and Shedd set to work loading goldshot.

"Is there enough gold to do the job?"

"Barely, old man, but I think it will make for a convincing show." Shedd carefully tamped the case end onto a cartridge half full of gold.

"Let's hope you do better shootin' a cave's insides than you do scarin' up a meal." Pete laughed.

"Don't worry, nothing's going to go wrong. I've checked the timber props and shored them up as an extra precaution." He stood ceremoniously and reached for his Whitney. "It's time."

Gordy seized a lantern and the trio picked its way to the mine and through the brambly undergrowth around its entrance.

Squeezing the triggerlike latch, Shedd swung the barrel breeches upward, cradled the cartridges in the chambers, and gingerly clicked the barrels back in place. "She's old, but my father said she would probably outlive most women—even the ornery ones." He chuckled, then turned serious. "Wait here."

Suspending the lantern in front of him, Shedd moved along

the corridor of the tunnel until he reached the large opening where he had performed the timber work. "You don't look like much now," he told the drab rock walls, "but that's about to change." Shedd backed up, set the lantern beside his left leg, and pressed the Whitney's stock firmly in the hollow of his right shoulder.

★

"It's done?" Gordy asked when Shedd stumbled outside.

"Hell's fire, old man, are you deaf?"

"When can we see the gold?" Pete asked. "When can we leave for Bear Lodge? When can we eat in a restaurant?"

Shedd started toward camp. "Those investors should be here day after tomorrow. I say we take what we can get out of this damned claim and head out with the others."

It was late the next morning when they slipped to the mine to admire their work.

"Hell's bells, boy," Gordy said, "if I didn't know any better, I'd start minin' here."

"That's the idea. Let's get our gear rounded up and then we can go into Deadwood for a few supplies."

After packing their belongings, the prospectors were relaxing around the campfire when a trio of men on lathered horses rode into camp.

"Seem to be taking life easy for prospectors," said the lead rider. "Always heard it was a backbreaking proposition."

The other agreed with their companion, then all three laughed.

Shedd glanced sideways at the group. "When you've got a good claim, you don't have to work your ass off."

"I reckon not." Then: "Mind if we join you for some refreshment?"

"We were just headin' to town for possibles," said Gordy, "but we got coffee from the boys next door, so help yourselves."

"Name's Brady," said the leader as he poured a cup of coffee. "Saw a sale notice posted downcreek. Yours?"

"You interested?" Shedd stepped closer to the stranger.

"Been hearing about a rush in the Bear Lodge Mountains, but we find the Black Hills more appealing."

Pete spoke up. "We're goin' to Bear Lodge as soon as—"

"Pete gets a little excited over things."

"Is that right?" Brady asked, never looking away from Shedd.

"If the boy is serious and you can prove there's a fair glitter on this claim, I think we can make a straight deal for both sides. *You* interested?"

"What kind of deal you got in mind?"

"We'll need a little prospecting gear. You'll need horses and pocket money. Can't get much simpler than that."

"Help yourself to more coffee."

Gordy and Pete followed Shedd as he put the strangers out of earshot. "It's exactly what we wanted and with a day to boot."

"I wonder about them," Gordy said.

"Who the hell cares about *them*," said Shedd. "Don't you see the advantage this gives us? We can get a head start on the crew downstream. Don't question it, man. Let's square a deal before they get wise and change their minds."

Pete was nodding anxiously.

"It seems too easy, Shedd. That ringleader fella didn't bat an eye when he offered us their horses."

"They won't need horses. We will."

"That don't matter. I've got a rotten feelin' in my gut about this."

"Gordy, we're in no position to pick and choose who we swindle." Shedd took another look at the strangers in camp. "We'll be long gone before they figure it out."

Gordy hesitated, then nodded once with a jerk. "Let's get it over with."

Shedd took Brady to the hidden mine while the rest stayed behind. When they returned, each was smiling as if he had struck the more profitable deal.

Within minutes the three prospectors had replaced the strangers' saddlebags and bedrolls with their own possessions.

*

"Boys," Shedd said as they made camp at dusk alongside the trail, "we should be horse traders instead of prospectors, what with how well we did today." He removed the saddle from his roan and gave the animal an appreciative slap on the rump. "Let's get those beefsteaks in the skillet, Pete. Nothing works up my appetite like the feeling of success."

Night sounds of katydids and bullfrogs filled the air as the prospectors finished their meal, curtaining all noise save for the occasional whinny of one of the horses.

Shedd rubbed his belly. "Best meal I've had in ages."

"Weren't bad at that," said Gordy. "I'd plumb near forgot what a good cut of beef tasted like."

A voice intruded from the darkness. "Hope you enjoyed it, because it's going to be your last."

The trio swung around and faced a battery of pistols and rifles.

Nervously, Gordy said, "We ain't botherin' nobody."

"You won't bother anyone again."

One of the men behind the leader said, "Tell 'em, Drake."

Shedd stood carefully. "What's this all about?"

Drake inched forward, followed by a couple of men who were expertly transforming ropes into nooses. "You don't kill my boss and his wife and get away with it."

"Kill?" Gordy turned white. "God, man, we never killed nobody. What gave you that idea?"

"Oh, nobody actually saw you do it, but they didn't have to, you see, because you took one of our prize stallions when one of your horses pulled up lame. You've got it tethered over there with the others." Drake nodded toward the brush, but didn't take his eyes off the trio.

Gordy glared at Shedd. "Now what do you think of those horse-tradin' skills of yours?"

Shedd tried reason. "We're prospectors, plain and simple. Three men came to our claim on Deadwood Creek today and we made a trade so we could check out the gold strike in the Bear Lodge Mountains. I swear on my father's grave that we don't know about any killings."

"It's the truth," Pete cried. "We didn't kill nobody. You gotta believe us." He dropped to his knees. Drake backhanded him, sending him sprawling.

Gordy helped Pete to his feet. "Take us back to Deadwood and we'll prove our story."

"The proof I want is a bill of sale for that horse, but you can't show me that, can you?"

When he received no answer, Drake shouted orders. "Culbertson, tie them up. You others get the horses that these desperadoes think they own." He turned to the trio. "One last ride, boys . . . to hell."

Culbertson lumbered forward through the group. After binding the miners' hands behind their backs, he shoved them toward a nearby box elder where three nooses had been snaked over a serviceable limb.

The three prospectors were placed on horseback, nooses secured about their necks.

"You're making one hell of a mistake," Shedd said.

"Shut up," Culbertson replied, pulling Shedd's Whitney from its scabbard.

"Don't mess with that shotgun. My father gave it to me and it's not real stable. It ain't worthy anything to you."

"I said shut up." Culbertson released the barrel breeches and fished two cartridges from Shedd's saddlebag.

Shedd started to protest again when Culbertson slammed the barrels in place with a jolt, accidentally activating the firing pins.

The roar of the blast echoed long after the three horses had stopped running.

Michael Stotter

McKINNEY'S REVENGE

Michael Stotter is a Brit who has worked at various jobs in publishing, one of which was helping George Gilman (whose violent books about the mythic West became best-sellers in the 1970s) produce a fanzine that kept his readers abreast of the author's forthcoming new books.

Stotter is now involved in the British crime scene, in particular with the fine magazine A Shot in the Dark, *and has turned to writing his own Westerns.*

This is a stand-alone excerpt from his first novel.

Bob Hunder was worked up into such a state that he was just about fit to bust. He'd woken up just before dawn, feeling cold and miserable, only to find that Missouri Clay had deserted them and that Shadow was nowhere to be found. Kicking the fire back into life and setting a pot of java to brew, he set about searching for either Clay or Shadow. Hunder immediately went to the horses and cursed when he found that both Clay's pony and the Appaloosa were gone, along with Clay's gear.

He stormed back to the campfire and poured himself a cup of coffee. Hunder dropped to his haunches and stared into the flames, feeling a black cloud of anger rising up inside of him. He pulled out a cheroot and lit up. Running a hand over his face, he knew that there had always been something in the back of his mind warning him about Clay. This only proved the fact to him. But what worried him now was the why of the matter.

There had been no hesitation for Clay to join them in the

manhunt, and even though the two men had rubbed each other up the wrong way much of the time, he had found Clay a hard and conscientious worker. So what had made the man disappear into the night? And where was the Indian? Never a man to like conundrums, Hunder pushed himself upright.

"Nelson! Jake! Get yoreselves up!" he bellowed. Both youths stirred under their blankets. "C'mon." He moved between them and used his boot to shake them awake.

Jake yawned loudly and rose. "What's up?"

"Yeah. It ain't our turn yet," Nelson added.

"Stop yore whingein' an' I'll tell you." He handed them both mugs of coffee. "Clay's disappeared an' Shadow ain't shown up yet. Clay's taken his and the Indian's horse, so the only way I can read it is that Clay's lit out with an extra horse."

"Why?" asked Nelson, scratching at the growing stubble adorning his lower face.

Hunder snorted, "Hell, boy! If'n I knew that I wouldn't be standin' here jawin' with you!"

Nelson Billings shrugged.

"So we'd best find out what we can, *while* we can," Hunder continued. "Nels, you follow what tracks you can find out by the horses. Jake, you take the path upward an' I'll scout around here awhile."

The Billings twins nodded.

The trio went their own ways. In the gray of the dawn the snow-clad mountain slopes appeared less formidable than they had by night. Nelson Billings found the tracks left by Clay quite easily and began to follow them northward.

Slowly Nelson moved upward, mist billowing in front of his face as he labored on. Wind-driven snow poured down from the unrelenting clouds above him, clouds that held back the sun from giving its warmth to the earth. And what he wouldn't have given right then to be warm! From off to his left he could hear the muffled progress of his brother and the ramrod.

It took under five minutes for Hunder to call out that he had found something.

Hunder waited for the twins to arrive, continuing to stare down at the snow mound next to the large pine tree. The two youths arrived, breathless.

"What've you found, Bob?" asked Jake, reholstering his Remington when he knew that there was no danger involved.

Without taking his eyes off of the mound, Hunder said, "It's Shadow."

Jake looked open-mouthed at his brother, then at the snow mound—the spot where Clay had hastily buried the Ute. If he had taken a minute's more care, Clay would have completely buried Shadow. As it was, he'd missed out covering his left foot, and Shadow's moccasin was distinctive even though a fall of snow partially covered it.

Still without looking up. Hunder spoke softly, keeping his temper under tight control. "Jake, you gather our gear together. Nels, saddle the mounts."

The twins moved off without saying a word. They could sense their ramrod's rising anger and were smart enough to let it be. It was cold standing on the mountain slope. Even though much of the wind was buffeted by the pines and spruce, it was still cutting. Hunder threw the half-smoked cheroot to the ground and stomped on it.

He moved off down the slope, hands pushed deep into his coat pockets, wondering where Clay had gone, but he didn't let that distract him from his main objective—to find McKinney. While searching for Shadow he had also managed to find the Indian's tracks that led up the mountain, and he figured that Shadow must have been on his way back to camp when death claimed him.

Bob Hunder had decided that it would be more Christian to leave the Indian where he lay, instead of digging him up just to find out how he died. He knew for sure that he hadn't died of natural causes. Whether McKinney had crept up on him and Green Rivered him wasn't at the top of his list. No, if Shadow had been on his way back, then it stood to reason that McKinney was holed up somewhere nearby.

With this part of the puzzle solved, Hunder's gloom lifted slightly. He reached the campsite as Jake finished untying their shelter and retrieved their slickers. His face betrayed his concern.

"Now what?" the twin asked as he spotted Hunder from the corner of his eye.

Hunder glanced at his riding companion. Jake was rolling the slickers up.

"We get on after McKinney," he said.

"McKinney?"

"McKinney. You remember him? He's the sonofabitch who shot yore boss, stole a horse, and dragged our asses a hundred miles through Texas into New Mexico—to *this* godforsaken land!"

Just then, Nelson brought the saddled horses into the camp. He stood still as Hunder finished his tirade. He didn't take to the ramrod chewing his brother out all the time but, given the circumstances, he let it go.

*

Hunder, Jake, and Nelson Billings rode northeast when they left the camp. The climb was steadily upward, with Hunder riding point, following all the signs left by Shadow-That-Covers-the-Sun. After about half an hour, the signs grew confusing. Not being an expert tracker but having learned enough to know the difference between human footprints and those of a horse or horses. Hunder brought his mount to a halt and hipped around in the saddle.

"Looks as if we've found out where Clay's headed."

Jake nodded and said, "Sure looks like it. But what the hell is he up to?"

Nelson shrugged. "Damned if *I* know."

Hunder allowed himself a small smile. "D'you figure that Clay might be in cahoots with McKinney?" he asked of Nelson.

Nelson frowned. "How d'you figger that one, Bob?"

"Let's take it one step at a time." He put his spurs to his mount's flanks, kicking it into motion. The Billings had no choice but to follow if they were to learn Hunder's answer.

"First," he continued, "Clay was eager to join us on this manhunt, but he's been bitchin' ever since we started. You remember our little set-to yesterday? well, that's a start." Hunder was in full flow now that the cobwebs in his mind had been blown away.

The twins digested the information in silence as they rode behind their ramrod.

"The only thing that bothers me," Hunder went on, "is the why of the matter. Jest can't figger that one out. *Yet.*"

They held their horses to a slow walk, allowing them to pick their own way over the precarious mountain slopes. The silence was broken only by the muffled sound of hooves and the occasional snort or whinny. The men appeared to be lost in a world of their own making, fighting to keep the cold at bay and using their brains in a way that had never really occurred to them prior to this uproar.

As they climbed higher into the hills there seemed to be a lull in the bad weather and it actually stopped snowing. The riders headed northwest now, and in less than an hour they sighted the cabin.

They reined their horses to a halt and Hunder said in a low voice, "So *this* is where they're holed up."

The twins nodded and smiled. They remained in their saddles as they surveyed the area. The cabin was well sheltered by thick stands of trees but the smoke rising from the chimney gave away its position easily. The two horses were staked out on the blind side of the cabin. Hunder strained his ears to catch sounds from the structure, but there was hardly a noise to be heard.

"We go on afoot," Hunder whispered.

The riders slipped out of their saddles, removed their spurs, and withdrew rifles from saddle scabbards.

"From here on there'll be no talkin'," Hunder said. "I'll lead an' you two cover me. Remember, don't start shootin' 'til I do. We want McKinney alive, if possible."

"What about Clay?" asked Nelson.

Hunder shook his head. "If he steps in front of a bullet, that's *his* hard luck." And as if to underline his statement he drew his Colt .44 out from beneath his coat.

He took the lead, and the others followed him single file. They neared the cabin and shortly Hunder could make out the glow of lamplight through the cracks of the shutters. With a wave of his pistol Hunder indicated that he wanted Jake and Nelson to spread out. He waited until they were in position; then, bent low and trying to make no sound, he moved forward.

When he was within maybe twenty-five feet of the cabin, he heard the voices of two men inside. Easing back the Colt's hammer, he continued to move cautiously forward, eyes darting from the window to the door. He glanced to his left and saw that Jake had kept up with him. To his right, Nelson had taken a slightly forward position.

The first shot took the three men completely by surprise— more so for Nelson than either of the others.

For the bullet from the Winchester slammed into his chest, lifted him off his feet, and threw him against the trunk of a spruce tree.

Nelson grunted in surprise and let go his Henry rifle. As he looked down at the entry hole, a second bullet drilled into his head, killing him outright.

Hunder flattened on the ground, snapping off a shot that went wide.

Jake stayed on his feet. He saw his brother's head jerk back and called out to him. Only when a bullet ricocheted off the tree next to him, showering torn bark and snow over his face, did he instinctively drop to the ground. He looked over at Hunder for help, but the ramrod was busy taking care of himself.

After firing a covering shot, Hunder had hauled his frame behind the relative safety of a pine tree. From there he fired off a couple of rounds that smacked harmlessly into the cabin's solid wooden structure.

As far as he could tell, the shooting was only coming from a carbine. There were no higher reports being made, from a handgun, and he knew that all Clay carried was an old Colt Navy .36 with a seven-and-a-half-inch barrel. If there was only one man in the cabin, then where was the other? He let Jake draw another shot, then stepped out from behind the tree and triggered off two shots in quick succession. Then his pistol was empty. There were more cartridges made up in his saddlebags but to go back and retrieve them would be a dangerous move. Still, there was nothing else for it.

"Jake!" he yelled, ducking back into cover. The youth looked over at him. Hunder mimed that he was moving off to get the fallen Henry repeater and that he wanted covering fire. Jake understood and worked the lever—fired. Levered—fired.

The .44 slugs ripped into the shutters, gouging great splinters out of the wood, and forcing the man with the carbine to take cover farther inside the cabin. Hunder waited until the barrel of the carbine disappeared and made his move. Keeping on all fours, he crawled at a jerking pace to the spot where Nelson Billings lay slumped against the tree. He wasn't a pretty sight. Red and gray mingled together on the white ground in a sticky mulch. But having seen such sights in his life before, Hunder's stomach wasn't turned unduly by it. Jake was still laying down a curtain of lead, and this allowed Hunder to reach the Henry and claim it without any trouble. He jacked a cartridge into the chamber and sighted the window slits. Gently squeezing the trigger, he sent a bullet through the slit and smiled when he heard a shout of surprise. He fired twice more but wasn't so lucky.

Jake's rifle fell silent and Hunder held his own fire. He called out, "What's up?"

"Nothin'. Just reloadin'."

"Got any spare shells?"

"Only what I got in my pockets. The rest are in the saddlebags."

" 'Spose Nels kept his there, too?"

"Yeah, he . . . he did."

Hunder cursed. Still, hopefully they could resolve the matter before he had to reload.

"Hey! That you in there, McKinney?" he called out.

"Yeah!"

"Seems like we got us a Mexican standoff here!"

McKinney laughed. "What makes you think that?"

"Well, we can't get in—but *you* can't get *out!*"

"Really?"

"Yeah, *really.*"

Inside the cabin, McKinney had used the lull to reload the Winchester and to unwrap the LeMat he kept from his old cavalry days. Now both were ready. As was he. Obviously they didn't know whether Clay was in or outside the cabin. Good. He liked the plan they had worked out together. So far it seemed to be working well. And any moment now the next phase would come into operation.

"Let's see if they like what we got in store for 'em next," he said to himself. He poked the carbine through the slit and fired off several rounds at both Billings and Hunder.

Both men ducked behind their shelter and drew breath. The time for talking was over. Hunder didn't want to have to end it this way, preferring to take McKinney alive if he could so he could see the bastard dangle at the end of a rope in Dumas. But there was little choice left to him.

"Hey, Jake!"

"What?"

"Try an' get nearer to the cabin. I'll cover you!"

Billings was shocked. "Say what?"

"You deaf or somethin'?"

"I ain't deaf an' I ain't stupid. *You* get nearer and *I'll* cover *you!*"

Hunder muttered, "You sonofagun." Then louder, "Okay. Jest make sure you don't shoot *me!*"

Hunder pumped a round in the chamber, fired, then moved from one tree to the next. Jake fired at the cabin, directing his lead at the window. From the cabin, McKinney returned fire at alternating targets in an attempt to keep them pinned down, but it was unsuccessful, as Hunder was managing to creep a little closer with each passing shot.

From where he stood, Missouri Clay was higher up the slopes and to the left of the cabin. He and McKinney knew they would be hemmed in if they both remained inside the cabin, so it was a better tactic if one of them went outside. Clay agreed to go because Hunder expected McKinney to be in the cabin, and if they could fool him long enough, Clay could creep up on their blind side and have them trapped.

Clay had got a hundred yards or so away from the cabin when the first shots were fired. Now he was working his way around the cowhands in a wide arc, slowly getting behind them. He listened to the regular boom of the long guns and hoped that McKinney had the sense to keep a check on his ammunition.

Holding the Colt Navy at the ready, Clay crept up to the hobbled horses and pacified them with a low, tuneless whistle. Bending low, he used the cover of the trees as he moved forward. From the sound of rifle reports, the shooting was coming from two different places, both of which were close to him. He elected to move off to the nearest, which was to his left.

Ten feet away from Jake Billings, Clay stepped into a clearing and said, "Drop the rifle, Jake."

Jake turned in surprise and turned his head. His mouth was agape and he looked at Clay and the Colt pointed steadily at his head.

"Don't even think about it," Clay said in a low voice. "Jest let go that Henry an' turn around. We ain't got no quarrel with you."

"How 'bout Nels?"

"What about him?"

"He's dead."

Clay didn't know this and was shocked, but didn't allow the fact to register on his face. He continued to point the pistol at the remaining Billings twin.

"Life's tough, Jake. You both made yore choices an' got a bad roll of the dice. Leave it be, eh?"

Jake still held on to the rifle, his mind racing ahead to what action he should take.

Clay urged him, "C'mon, boy, drop it."

Jake resigned himself to the fact that he would never beat Clay off of the mark, and let the rifle slip from his hands. Clay smiled and moved closer, bent down, and picked the rifle up without taking his eyes or gun off Jake.

"Turn around and put yore hands behind yore back," Clay ordered. Jake complied readily. Using two bandannas, Clay tied Jake's hands together with one of them and used the other as a gag.

"If'n I were you, I'd sit the rest of this out. Okay?"

Jake nodded.

"Good. Now for Hunder." And he moved off through the snow.

From where Bob Hunder had now positioned himself he could get a clear shot through the window but was unable to see Jake Billings and therefore was blissfully unaware that the youth had been effectively taken out of the action. It registered in the back of his mind that Jake was no longer firing, but he had taken that to mean that the boy was reloading. The ramrod figured that he had all but five shots left in the rifle and so had to be frugal with the remaining cartridges.

Meanwhile, Thadius McKinney had watched Clay creep up on Billings and smiled as his newfound partner forced the twin to drop his weapon. Now there was only Hunder to contend with. He hadn't meant to kill Nels, but it was a hastily aimed shot that he had intended as a warning. Still, he had intended his second shot to kill Nelson. He'd seen too many men die from body wounds on the battlefields of war, watched as life slipped away like the blood oozing from the wounds, listened as their pain and anguish made them call to their mothers for help—help that never came.

He couldn't let Billings die like that.

Silence crept over the cabin as the gunfire came to a halt, and the echoes of their bitter fighting echoed over the mountainside. McKinney had thirty more rounds left in the box and a full load in the LeMat. He couldn't hazard a guess as to how many Hunder had, but it stood to reason that he couldn't have many.

In the quietness of the trees Hunder had the strange feeling that something had gone wrong. He voiced his fear.

"Jake!"

No reply.

"Jake, you out there?" His voice echoed over the rocks.

McKinney fired, levered, and fired again—a quick salvo that shattered the silence, hitting the pine tree and ground near to where Hunder had gone down.

Two shots fired from Hunder's rifle forced McKinney to step away from the window and seek shelter farther inside the

cabin, and as he turned away he momentarily caught a movement out in the pines, far back and almost in the darkness.
He raised his Winchester, readying to fire again, when Hunder
broke cover, darting from tree to tree, running at a low crouch.

McKinney fired at him but it was too late; Hunder made it
to the cover of a crop of fallen boulders. Now it would be a
waiting game. Both Clay and himself had agreed that it would
be ideal if they could fool Hunder into believing that Thad was
on his own in the cabin, and in the event of a stalemate, Clay
would play his hand.

Hunder lay on his stomach and used his elbows to raise himself above the rocks and look down the barrel of the Henry
toward the cabin. He knew that unless he showed himself,
McKinney wouldn't know where he was, and so he settled down
to wait.

*

Clay was beginning to feel impatient as well as cold. It had
been three hours since the last shots had been exchanged and
there had been no talking from either man, though he'd expected that much. And now Hunder had taken good cover in
the bowl of the rocks. Clay couldn't get a clear shot at the
ramrod without first exposing himself.

Time was creeping on. Almost noon. Clay realized that he
hadn't had a smoke since dawn. Resting against a tree trunk
with the Colt lying in his lap, he took to building several
smokes, lighted one, and put the others away. He was thankful
for the respite in the weather, but one glance at the skies told
him that it wouldn't last forever. Winter had come early this
year, and it would be a hard one. The cold had long since
penetrated his cheap woolen pants and longjohns, getting into
his bones so that they actually burned with the coldness. Still,
both he and McKinney were lucky enough to be able to move
around, where Hunder was not. One false move on his part,
and his head would be ventilated.

An hour later the snow began falling again, filtering down
out of a slate-gray sky with a vengeance. Within minutes, visi-
bility had been cut down to twenty feet and Clay decided to
make his move toward Hunder's position, assuming that if
Hunder couldn't see the cabin, then McKinney wouldn't be able
to see Hunder. The A Bar A man could take advantage by
either creeping up on the cabin or making his escape. Clay

plumped for the latter and, either way, the ramrod hadn't figured on his presence.

Clay froze at Hunder's voice.

"McKinney, I want to make you a deal."

There was a pause, then: "What kind of deal?"

"Where's Clay?"

Clay tensed, his grip tightening around the butt of the Colt. "Haven't seen him since Dumas. Why?"

"You're *lyin'*! That's his horse tied up there."

McKinney tried to sound surprised. "There's a horse . . ."

"Quit it, will you," Hunder said gruffly.

"Well, what's this deal?" McKinney hollered.

"The way I see it is that you killed Clay for the horses an' was about to leave when we surprised you. You killed both Jake and Nels, so that only leaves me to deal with. Am I right so far?"

Silence.

"Come on out of the cabin an' talk it over, man to man."

Silence again.

"Listen—it's one to one now. You won't get a better chance."

Won't I?

"Answer me, you gutless bastard!"

That's it, work yourself up. Make a mistake.

"McKinney! You yellow sonofabitch! I bet you didn't give Aaron a fair shake when you shot him, did you?"

Keep talking, Hunder.

"I bet you never faced him head-on. Didn't have the guts for it, I guess. No wonder yore woman wanted a *man* and not some back-shootin' swish."

Clay prayed: *Keep your head, Thad. Don't fall for it.*

There wasn't a sound from the cabin. The Winchester barrel stayed in sight, poking out through the bullet-scarred window. Clay had used the exchange to move closer to Hunder and was now in position some fifteen feet behind him.

Ten minutes of silence crept past.

"McKinney!" It was Hunder again. "I'll give you one last chance."

Nothing

"You've got ten minutes, then I'm comin' after you!"

That's a trick I'd like to see.

"McKinney, you hear me?"

Only echoes replied.

"Goddamn it! Answer me!" Hunder had worked himself into a funk. And out of anger he fired, levered, and fired again. McKinney noted the muzzle flashes and replied with his own shots. Hunder's face broke in a wolfish grin; he levered the Henry and fired, levered, and . . . nothing. The hammer hit on an empty chamber and now all fifteen rounds were spent. He didn't have a chance in hell without a weapon, and the pistols were in the saddlebags on the horses some ways back.

If I could use this snow, Hunder thought, *I'd have a chance to get to the spare shells and come at McKinney from another spot. He wouldn't expect it.*

With great care and a speed that belied his size, Hunder withdrew from the safety of the rocks and backtracked to his horse. He thanked God that they had stayed put and busied himself in reloading, wolfing down a few hard biscuits as he did so. Stuffing spare shells into one pocket and chunks of beef jerky into the other, he let his concentration slip.

Clay had waited in the shadows of trees until Hunder started away from the horses, moving away from his original position. Then, using the cover of the trees and snow, he followed him. Over the past couple of days, when he knew what was happening, he'd tried to think of the outcome. How was it going to end?

He had waited two years. . . .

★

Aaron Wyatt worked a lather of yellow soap into the bristles of a week's growth and began to shave. Bob Hunder stood behind him, his back leaning against the cool adobe wall, thumbs tucked into his pants pockets, looking at Wyatt's reflection in the mirror and waiting for a reply to his question.

"You offered him a dollar a head?"

"Yep."

"And he turned you down flat?"

"Yep."

"I see." Wyatt looked at Hunder's reflection in the dirty, cracked mirror. He had seen that look many a time and knew that his ramrod had set his mind on one course of action, but he was still uncertain. "Tell me, Bob, is this the only way?"

Hunder grinned. "I think so. He won't sell out an' he won't sell any head of cattle to us."

"No chance?"

"None."

Wyatt shook his head slowly, wiped the excess soap from his face, and threw the towel down on the dresser. He had resigned himself to the inevitable and said, "How many men do you want?"

Hunder smiled. "Five ought to do it." He pushed himself away from the wall. "I'll pick 'em, if you've no objections. Then there'll . . ."

"I'm coming with you."

"No way, Aaron," Hunder protested.

Wyatt regarded him narrowly. "No dickering. I'm going." He reached for a rig that was hanging on the back of a chair next to the dresser and began to buckle it on.

"Now hold up, Aaron," Hunder said, standing up to his boss. "It's taken you a while to get a respectable business goin' here. An' you'll throw it all away if there's any trouble at Kerr's place."

"Don't hand me that. We'll just have to get Kerr to hand over his land peacefullike."

"Then he'll be off to the sheriff first chance he gets and indict you! No, it's too risky to have you along."

Wyatt demanded, "So; you can do it better without me taggin' along, is that it?"

Hunder hesitated. "It is an' it isn't. Look . . ." He was flustered and didn't like it. "Just leave it to me—like always. There's been no comebacks in the past an' me an' the boys, well, we can handle it *our* way."

Wyatt looked at Hunder, his eyes unblinking, passively letting the other man's cold stare wash over him. He was glad that Hunder was for him and not agin him. The rancher backed down, unbuckled his gunbelt, and dropped into the chair.

"Bob. No trouble if possible, eh?"

"No, sir, Mr. Wyatt!"

Wyatt walked Hunder out of the ranch house and came to a halt at the main door, looking off into the distance with a cloud of doubt covering his face.

"Before you make any decisions, Bob, offer Kerr a deal," he instructed thoughtfully.

"A deal? What d'you mean?"

"Offer him grazing rights on our land. Tell him he can lease some acreage from me to do with as he wants."

Hunder nodded. "What if he still says no?"

Wyatt spread his hands and shrugged, then turned his back on the ramrod and went into the house. Hunder smiled and walked over to the bunkhouse, already having told the men he'd chosen to prepare to ride out.

The six riders came to a halt as they topped the ridge and looked down on the Kerr spread. The man had chosen his land well enough. Pasture spread as far as the eye could see, with a flowing stream providing water all year 'round. There were three buildings in all: a low adobe for the family, a raw-boarded barn, and a weatherbeaten shack that passed for a storage shed. There was a corral off to the right that held a handful of horses walking around, lazily switching their tails at flies. It was a peaceful scene, and the riders remained silent as they looked down into the valley—one or two of them with pangs of jealousy.

The ranch-house door swung open and a man stepped out, stretching his arms. He was followed by a young boy carrying a leather water bucket. They spoke briefly, and the boy ambled over to the stream and filled the bucket.

"That's Kerr down yonder, takin' a stretch," Hunder said. "An' that's his son." He squinted at their surroundings. "Looks like they're the only ones around."

"Seems easy enough," said a rider dressed in a brown jacket with red cord embroidery on its cuffs.

"Sure, Miller. I just hope it stays that way," Hunder replied. "Come on."

They spurred their mounts down the slope and raced toward the ranch. The boy looked up as he heard the thunder of hooves. There were six riders coming at a gallop, scattering grazing cows before them. It was a frightening sight to an eight-year-old, and he dropped the bucket and ran back to the adobe.

"Pa! Pa!" he shouted. "Riders a-coming."

His father turned and caught the boy up in his arms and held him to his chest.

"It's okay, son. Go into the house and stay with your ma." He put the boy down, but the lad wouldn't move from his side. "Do as I say, Davey." Reluctantly, the boy went into the house. Kerr watched the riders ford the stream and bring their mounts to a stop some twelve feet away from him. He swallowed nervously as he recognized Bob Hunder and one or two others from the A Bar A.

"Hunder." He nodded at the man. "What can I do for you?"

Kerr was around forty, with a pocked face and a twitch in his right eye. But for all his nervousness he stood his ground solidly before the six mounted riders.

"I got a message from Mr. Wyatt," Hunder began.

"Have your say, mister," Kerr replied gruffly.

"A Bar A is willing to offer you a deal."

"What sort of deal?"

Hunder eased himself in the saddle. "Well, as you know, you already turned down a dollar a head. . . ."

"Damn right I did!"

Hunder held up his left hand. "Let me have my say, Kerr." He paused. "Now you already turned down one good offer, but Mr. Wyatt is still willin' to lease you land and let you have grazin' rights. . . ."

"*What?*" Kerr exploded. "This is *my* land! *My* cattle. I ain't about to give in to some goddamn claim jumper!"

Hunder's tone turned nasty. "Now, hold on jest a minute."

"No; *you* hold on." The voice came from the adobe building. All heads turned to the young man standing in the doorway. He was dressed in just his red flannel combinations, but the riders took more notice of the big Sharps that he pointed in their direction.

"You fellers 'pear like you got somethin' wrong with your ears. My pa said no."

Hunder stiffened in the saddle and his right hand came off his saddlehorn to brush open his jacket, revealing a Colt Navy .36 snug against his stomach.

"Be careful where you point that carbine, sonny," he warned.

"I am. Now, you fellers want to be ridin' on?"

Hunder looked from the son to the father and leaned forward across his horse's neck. "The deal stands till sundown, Kerr. You want to find me, I'll be at the saloon in Steens."

"And if I *don't* want to find you?"

"Then I'll know you don't want to settle without bloodshed," Hunder replied. "An' we'll run you out. Even burn you out if we have to. But jest remember: All you got to do to avoid such grief is put your mark on an itty bit of paper."

Kerr spat. "Figured you'd have something like that to say." He considered. "I'll take my chances come sundown. You got anything to add, Hunder?"

"Guess not. Except . . ."

"Yeah?"

"See you tonight." He touched the brim of his hat mockingly at Kerr, wheeled his horse around, and rode back across the stream and up the hill, the five ranch hands following him.

Kerr never took his eyes from them—not until they rode to the crest of the ridge and disappeared over the other side. He turned to his eldest son.

"Richard, I want you to take my mount, ride into Dumas, and tell the deputy sheriff what's happened."

"What about you an' Ma an' little Davey?"

"Don't you worry about us. Just do like I say. Ride clear of the main route and away from Steens." He placed both hands on his son's shoulders. "Make sure you get back 'fore sundown."

Richard Kerr frowned. "Sure, Pa."

Kerr smiled at his son and hoped he didn't betray his fear in his voice. "We'll be fine, boy."

"I sure wish Clayton was here."

His father sighed, wishing that, too.

★

By midmorning the six A Bar A riders were seated in a small watering hole in Steens. Steens couldn't rightly be called a town, for it boasted only an unnamed saloon, a blacksmith's, and a hardware store with eight residential buildings scattered haphazardly around. The inhabitants had always hoped for passing trade from cowboys on cattle drives, but the hopes of most of the residents had soon disappeared. The residents, too—eventually.

The men drank lukewarm beer and Taos Lightning, cutting the dust out of their mouths. Someone suggested a game of poker, but this was met with a round of noncommittal grunts. So they concentrated on drinking in silence. Miller broke the silence as he turned to Hunder and said, "Hey, Bob. We jes' gonna set around waitin' for sundown an' get us drunk, or what?"

"Guess not."

"Then what we gonna do?"

Hunder sipped at his beer thoughtfully. His companions now looked at him.

"Listen," he said. "If Kerr's got any sense he'll've sent for help. Maybe the deputy in Dumas. So we won't wait till sundown."

"Good idea," someone said. The man was Gus Homer.

"Sure. An' when we get back to Kerr's there'll be a whole crowd waiting for us." This was Haig, a bald-headed giant of a man. The other men were Goldschmidt, Hallisey, and a Mexican half-breed named Laslo. None of them said a word, willing to be led by the nose like prize bulls.

"That's why—" Hunder stopped, burped aloud, and tried again. "That's why we're leavin' *now!*"

The men followed Hunder out of the saloon and mounted up. Homer leaned across to his ramrod and said. "Listen: What about the woman and child?"

Hunder looked at him coldly. "We give them the chance to leave."

"An' if'n they don't?"

Hunder rubbed at his chin and let the question go unanswered as he spurred his mount into a canter. He didn't hear Homer call him one crazysonofabitch.

*

John Kerr watched the lone rider coming down the slope with a piece of white rag fluttering at the end of the rifle resting on his thigh. Kerr cocked the Sharps rifle and began to walk toward him. He stood on his side of the stream and watched the man ride closer. When he was about fifty feet away, Kerr called out.

"That's as far as you go, mister!"

Miller reined in and eyed the rancher with a steady glare.

"Say what you gotta say, then go."

"Mr. Hunder has had a change of mind."

"Is that so?" The Sharps was pointed at Miller now.

"Yeah. He's giving you and your family *ten* minutes to clear out."

Kerr's face flushed red and he ground his teeth together in an attempt to put a rein on his rising temper. Miller continued:

"Ten minutes to pack what you can—then we'll be ridin' in."

Kerr muttered, "Over my dead body."

Miller smiled. "Either way, mister. Don't bother me none."

"You'd best get out of here before I blast you out of your saddle," Kerr rasped.

"This here's a flag of truce, mister," Miller said, waving the rag around. "You can't—"

Kerr brought the Sharps up to his shoulder and took aim. "You got until I count to three."

Miller sat in the saddle.

"One."

Miller didn't move.

"Two."

Miller fidgeted now, taking up the slack in the reins.

"Three!"

On the count, Miller jerked hard on the reins, rearing up his mount, and turning it at the same instant. He slapped the animal's rump with the rifle barrel and kicked up tufts of grass as he sped back up the slope.

John Kerr knew that there was only a short time left and the odds were stacked against him six to one. He ran back to his house and told his wife to pack only the essentials, load them onto the wagon, and not ask any questions. He swapped the Sharps in favor of his Springfield and pushed a loaded Colt Walker into the waistband of his denims.

As he prepared himself for the upcoming fight, Kerr hoped that his son had gotten word to the deputy sheriff in Dumas and that help was on its way. It was a sixty-mile round trip to town, but Richard was a good enough rider and should be able to make it with time to spare if only Hunder had stuck to his original deadline. But now he had to fend for himself and pray to the Lord.

He knew he could expect no mercy from Wyatt's men now that they were riled up. All he could hope for was that Alice and little Davey would be unharmed. He worked it over in his mind as he fought the horses into their traces. All this was due to greed. Aaron Wyatt's insatiable greed for more land, more cattle, and with it—more power. All little men like the John Kerrs of this world were not meant to buck the way of things. But *this* John Kerr had fought long and hard to get what was rightly his, and his papers lay with Judge William Brace in his Dumas office safe.

An eerie quietness lay over the Kerr spread. Too quiet for John. He quickly scanned the valley. All was seemingly well. The cattle munched contentedly on the lush grass, and the mounts in the corral were happy enough just to mill around. Even the ranch house was quiet.

That was it!

Alice and Davey should have been making some sort of noises, Kerr realized. Without hesitation he ran into his home, the Springfield rifle held out in front of him. It was cool and dark inside the building and he blinked rapidly at the sudden change. A gun barrel cracked down on his wrist and he yelped with surprise, involuntarily dropping the rifle. A large, sweaty hand clamped over his mouth and a sharp rabbit punch to his kidney dropped him to his knees.

Kerr fought for breath as the bald-headed Haig grabbed a handful of his hair and dragged him backward through the house and dropped him on the kitchen floor. Tears made his eyes smart and the infected right orb twitched continuously.

"*John!*" His wife's voice sliced through him.

He gasped and looked up. "*Alice!*"

Goldschmidt and Hallisey held Alice between them, each holding on to an arm, while Laslo held little Davey by the throat. The boy gave vent to his pent-up fear and began to cry. Alice made to go to her son, but the men held her back. Davey looked at his ma with eyes big as overspill buckets and cried even harder.

"Shut the kid up, Laslo," ordered Hunder.

"*Sí, señor.*" He put his hand over Davey's mouth and the child did the only natural thing: He bit down with all his might. The half-breed swore and snatched his hand away, shaking it in the air. Swearing in Spanish, Laslo made to strike the boy but Hallisey caught his wrist in a viselike grip and warned him with his eyes not to do it.

"You harm my boy and so help me God I'll kill you," Kerr said through clenched teeth.

"I don't think that you're in any position to make threats, mister," Hunder said. He sat on the edge of the kitchen table and began to pick at a plate of leftovers. Between mouthfuls of cold ham he continued, "Now, we tried reasonin' with you, but you jest wouldn't listen. So we had to resort to this." He waved his hand around, spraying everyone with bread crumbs. "Mr. Wyatt offered you a good deal. I suggest you sign this bit of paper an' have done with it."

Hunder spread the land deed out on the table, produced a pencil, and offered it to Kerr.

Kerr eyed him suspiciously. "What assurance have I got that once I sign this paper you'll leave us alone?"

Hunder laughed. "Why, *none*! Y'see once you sign over your land to A Bar A then you'll have to leave. Mr. Wyatt don't take kindly to squatters."

Kerr's mouth dropped open. "Why, you gutless, no-good . . ."

Miller lashed out with a left jab at Kerr's mouth and followed it quickly with a right cross. Blood spilled from Kerr's mouth as he fought against Haig, who still held him fast. Miller kicked him in the guts and doubled him over. Alice screamed and pleaded for the man to stop. Davey began wailing afresh.

Miller stepped in close to finish him off but Hunder held him back.

"Look what you're doin' to yore family! Jest sign the contract, man. This little piece of land can't be worth all this pain and sufferin', can it? *Sign it!*"

Kerr lifted his head to look at Hunder, and the ramrod smiled at the sight. Kerr's jaw was broken and hung to one side. Blood trickled down his chin. Alice screamed in alarm, trying to reach her husband, but Goldschmidt and Hallisey held her fast. Hunder nodded for them to let her go, and she rushed to her husband.

Using her apron to dab at the blood, she bent to Kerr's ear. "Sign it, John. For God's sake, sign it." Tears rolled down her cheeks.

"Alice . . ." he muttered.

"No, John. Sign it, please."

Hunder came off the table and stood over him.

"It's for the best, John," he said softly.

Kerr nodded and Haig lifted him to his feet as easily as he would have handled a child. With shaking hands Kerr made his signature on the contract and Hunder countersigned as the witness. The evil task completed, Kerr slumped into a chair, buried his head in his hands, and wept. Alice put her arms around him and pulled him close to her. Laslo let go of the crying child, and Davey joined his parents.

"Like I said before, you've got until sundown to leave the property, Kerr. If you're still here, then we'll have an eviction order brought against you. Judge Brace is a pretty good friend of Mr. Wyatt's, so I'm sure he'll oblige," Hunder said. He slipped the contract into his jacket pocket and laughed.

★

All of that had happened in the fall of '69. Missouri Clay, or Clayton Kerr, to give him his baptized name, received a letter from his Aunt Alice while serving a year in jail for attempted robbery by deception. She explained everything that had happened, including the fact that John had taken his own life in a fit of drunken depression the spring following his signing of the deed and that Richard had been hung as a cattle thief (allegedly stealing from the A Bar A) on the same day that Kerr signed the spread over. Now she only had Davey to look after, and the pair of them were living off other folks' generosity. She could not face her own family and all the inevitable questions.

The law had denied all knowledge of Richard's visit to Dumas, and even their land claim had disappeared from the judge's safe. It was as though they had never existed. Alice felt that only Clayton could be of any help to her now. To avenge her husband and child and the good of the family name.

After being released from the Wyoming County jail, Clayton rode the four hundred miles to his aunt. He found her alone and on her death bed, her body riddled with consumption. Davey had been packed off to her parents somewhere back East, but she had waited for Clayton, knowing that he would come. She confirmed all that she had written him and filled him in on what had happened since. It turned out that theirs was not an isolated case.

Alice suggested that Clayton ride to Dumas in a month's time, when Hunder and Wyatt would be taking on hands for the first cattle drive that year. Clayton agreed and stayed with his aunt until she passed away some three weeks later. There was no legal way in which Wyatt or Hunder could be indicted; the pair of them were too damn canny for that. So Clayton had to take the law into his own hands. He had to be careful, for Wyatt had grown into a powerful man. That meant his vengeance had to be taken at the right time and in the right way.

*

Hunder made slow but careful progress over the deepening snow, deciding to attack the cabin from the west this time. He was past caring what had happened to Jake and even Clay, but knew better than to underestimate Thadius McKinney.

So it came as a great surprise when he saw the seated figure of Jake Billings, covered in snow, gagged and bound, against the base of a pine tree, shivering like a mangy dog.

He crept nearer to Billings, expecting all the time that it was a trap. But there was no shooting. In fact, the mountainside was silent except for the gentle hiss of falling snow.

Bob Hunder stood a couple of feet in front of Jake and called his name softly. Billings didn't stir. His chin remained slumped on his chest. Hunder crouched down and reached out to touch Billings on the shoulder. The exhausted ranch hand jerked his head up, eyes wide with fear; then, recognizing Hunder, he relaxed. The ramrod removed the gag and Billings gasped for fresh air and worked his jaw gently from side to side.

"Here, let me help you," Hunder said. "Turn around an' I'll untie you."

"I wouldn't if I was you."

Hunder froze.

"*Clay!*" he hissed.

"That's right," Missouri Clay replied. "An' I got a Colt pointed at yore fat head."

Hunder looked at Billings for confirmation and saw the answer in his slight return nod.

"What d'you plan on doin'?" Hunder asked. "Shootin' me in the back?"

Clay snorted. "What d'you take me for?"

"Well . . ."

"I ain't no back-shooter. No claim-jumper, either."

Hunder was puzzled. "What the hell you talkin' about, boy?" He looked at Billings, who simply shrugged and made to straighten up.

"Hold it right there, mister." Clay stepped a little closer. "Drop the rifle."

Billings remained seated and Hunder dropped the rifle without hesitation because he was nobody's fool, and stood erect. He turned slowly around to face Clay and found himself looking down the black barrel of the Colt Navy.

"You callin' me a claim-jumper, Clay? What the hell's that supposed to mean?"

"You've got a short memory, Hunder," Clay said. "Try castin' yore mind back 'bout two years."

"Two years?" Hunder said absently.

"Yeah; the spring of '69."

Hunder's mind whirled—two years ago; it seemed more like twenty what with the rapid expansion of the A Bar A. Then he thought he understood what Clay was getting at.

"You're kin to John Kerr, is that it?" he said rather than asked.

"He was my uncle," Clay replied. "*Was.*"

"So," Hunder said thoughtfully. "You're his avengin' angel?"

"That's about it."

Hunder laughed out aloud. "An' you used McKinney to get yore revenge on me, is that it?"

Clay nodded. "That's about the shape of it."

"You figger on finishin' me off here? Where there ain't no witnesses 'ceptin' yore pal in the cabin, an' Jake here? Or are you goin' to do for him as well?"

"Not unless he takes exception," Clay replied, keeping both the pistol and his eyes on Hunder. "Still, we can sort that out after I've dealt with you."

As he looked into Clay's piercing eyes Hunder realized that these few moments might be his last in this world. But being the man he was, he knew that death had to come to everyone sooner or later. He had a gut feeling about this confrontation, and it was not a good one. He breathed deeply as he spoke.

"Are you goin' to give me a fightin' chance?"

"Did you give my uncle one?" retorted Clay.

"We didn't *shoot* him!"

"No, it was worse than that. What you might call a lingerin' death. You took his home and land away from him. Took away his self-respect right in front of his wife and child. You killed him, all right. Not with a bullet, I'll grant you. But you killed him, anyway."

The ramrod never took his eyes from Clay as he weighed the situation.

"I'm goin' to give you a chance, though," Clay said. "There's yore rifle on the ground. I'll holster my Colt an' we let Jake count to three. On three, you go fer the rifle and I'll slap leather."

"You call that fair?" snapped Hunder.

"It's about as fair as you're gonna get." Clay pushed the Colt into the tied-down holster. "Start countin', Jake."

Jake looked up to Hunder. "Bob?"

Hunder sighed. "Do like he says, Jake. Count."

"One . . ."

Clay held his coat flap away from the butt of the revolver.

". . . two . . ."

Hunder flexed his fingers, preparing to drop earthward.

". . . *three!*"

The word was no sooner said than Clay's Colt seemed to jump into his hand. He brought the gun up, easing back the hammer at the same time, and squeezed the trigger.

The bullet entered the top of Hunder's skull as the man was bending down, reaching for the rifle. The ramrod fell backward and lay trembling, but already dead, in the snow.

Clay stood looking at the man, cordite stinging his eyes as he watched the bright red blood spurt from the wound, then subside to a trickle as the heart stopped pumping.

"Nice shooting, Clay," McKinney said as he stepped into view, the Winchester cradled in the nook of his left arm, his finger resting gently on the trigger. Clay turned to face him, surprised.

"How long you been there?"

"Long enough." McKinney jerked his head at Billings. "What about him?"

Billings looked from one man to the other, fear creeping back into his eyes.

"How 'bout it, Jake?" asked Clay. "What d'you figger on doin'?"

"Me? Ah . . . well . . ."

McKinney brought out his wicked-looking knife and approached him.

"No! Wait! I ain't gonna . . ."

"Okay, Jake," McKinney said, cutting through the bandanna tying Billings' hands together. "Quit frettin'. We need you alive to tell whoever comes after us what happened here."

Rubbing his hands together to get the blood circulating in his fingertips, Jake looked up at McKinney.

"You know Wyatt won't let it rest here, Thad."

The man looked off into the distance, eyes glazed. "That's all right," he replied easily. "I ain't finished with *him* yet."

Jeremiah Healy

TO TALLY THE DEAD

*Jeremiah Healy is one of the best private-eye writers
on the scene today.*

*He writes gracefully and well about the upscale lives
of boomers and Yuppies.*

*Healy is also a solid craftsman. He's always wanted
to write a Western story, and so when the Louis
L'Amour magazine appeared, he decided to try a Western story of his own. He ended up writing three or
four, all of which sold.*

Kel McKyer looked down at the dead Apache and thought, Now
you've done it.

To get his breathing back under control, he sat back on his
haunches against the big boulder, rounded smooth by ten thousand years of Arizona Territory wind and sand. McKyer had
lived his life so far—and managed to stay alive doing it—by
studying on things before he acted. When he had time to study,
that is.

Which the Indian hadn't given him. McKyer was just riding
up this slope, which looked more hospitable to his mount and
packhorse than the cactus-filled gully to the side of it. The
animals, along with some gold in the packs, had come courtesy
of a German couple in no further need of them. The sun wasn't
yet broiling high, but it took enough out of your eyes that
McKyer kept the old cavalry hat down low over them. He'd
gotten only halfway up the slope when the packhorse reared
some behind him, which made McKyer rein up and turn in
his saddle. Good thing, too, because that caused the Apache—
jumping down silently from the top of the big boulder—to miss

263

his neck with the knife and land athwart his saddlehorn. The momentum of the Indian carried both men over and onto the ground. Maybe the Apache'd had the wind knocked out of him by the horn, or maybe tumbling down the hill twisted him funny, because he didn't put up much resistance as McKyer reflexively pinned the knife hand to the hot sand with one forearm and pressed his other, hard and final, against the Indian's throat. The light left the Apache's eyes, and it didn't take much studying for McKyer to know he had a problem.

First off, the Apache was only eighteen or so, wearing the dark leggings and white, homespun tunic of what McKyer had come to think of as the Mescalero branch of the family. However, stuck in a sash that served as a belt was an 1874, walnut-handled Colt Peacemaker, like the one resting in McKyer's own holster.

He pulled out the Indian's weapon and checked its loads. The cylinder held five live cartridges, and a pouch inside the sash fourteen more. That was plenty enough ammunition to spend one killing McKyer safely, especially given the extra cartridges the Apache would have seen McKyer wearing on his gun belt. When traveling in a raiding party, Mescaleros would take whites alive and torture them for hours. This Indian must have been alone, though, because he was clearly trying to cut McKyer's throat on the jump, and other braves in his party would have killed McKyer by now. So why use the knife?

It made sense only if the Mescalero didn't want to cause any noise. McKyer thought back a few minutes. No sound from the Apache as he dropped from the boulder, not even a peep as they rolled down the slope. McKyer hadn't a lot of experience fighting Apaches, but every time he'd come upon them angry, they raised war cries, kind of like a coyote pup, once your blood calmed down enough to let you review it. Which made the question in his head, Why wouldn't the Mescalero want to make noise killing me? The answer seemed to lie with whatever was farther up or over the rise. And without the answer, McKyer would be proceeding blind no matter what he tried to do.

Sticking the Apache's revolver in his own belt, McKyer dragged the body behind some rocks, hoping to buy a little time before the buzzards began circling overhead and locating the body for anyone within five miles. Then he moved back up the slope to his mount, a roan, and his pack animal, a chestnut. From one of the saddlebags McKyer took some padded leather thongs the German couple had used to hobble their horses. On first sight, he'd picked the roan for the better mount and put the extra gear—and gold—onto the chestnut. But the roan hadn't picked up the Apache's presence, and the chestnut had. Tomorrow morning, if there was such a thing for him, McKyer would rotate the horses and see how he liked riding the chestnut.

After finishing with the thongs, Kel McKyer drew the Winchester from its scabbard on the right flank of the roan and began working his way slowly up the slope.

★

"Preacher, it'd be best to breathe these mounts some."

Slowing his stallion to a walk, the tall, gaunt man in the black, broad-brimmed hat and black frock coat waited for the one who'd spoken up to catch up. The preacher's name was Sutcliff, and though he'd enjoyed no formal education in the calling, he'd found that most God-fearing men would wither before his practiced glare.

"Mr. Bevins, our way is clear." Sutcliff gestured toward the tracks in front of them. "Even I can see the Apache sign."

"That's partly what worries me, truth be told." Bevins, short and missing two fingers but stolid in his views, pulled away from the three drovers and drew even with the man in black. Just the day before, the preacher and his two children had arrived at the livery station Bevins ran. The son was sixteen years old and named Matthew, the daughter fourteen and named Matilda, but telling Bevins with a smile and a dip of her pretty blond head that she liked to be called just Tildy. She'd complained of a woman's ailment that made travel by horse difficult for her, and so Bevins had agreed to put them up for a while, giving the girl a room all her own. That same afternoon, the three drovers had galloped hell-bent into the station, saying they had an Apache war party trailing after them.

Still walking his horse, Sutcliff said, "Mr. Bevins, my way is speeded by the thoughts of what that big Apache buck may be forcing upon my Tildy."

Bevins nodded, thinking back to his standing watch on the shallow porch of the adobe station and seeing the Mescaleros, under a white flag, ride in slowly. "Majestically," he'd have said, if the drovers hadn't been so edgy Bevins was afraid to say anything, maybe set them off. Running a livery station, he had to live with the Apaches, who long ago had learned that it was far better to raid the travelers the station brought to them than to raid the station itself. Bevins also had learned that you had to honor that white flag or be burned out and run off. Or worse, much worse.

Now Bevins stood up in his stirrups, aiming an index finger toward the rise maybe three miles ahead of them. "Preacher, you see that high ground yonder to the north?"

"There is nothing wrong with my eyes, Mr. Bevins."

Another nod. "Well, I'm no betting man, but if I was, I'd put money on these here tracks we been following all morning leading us there."

Sutcliff shrugged. "Your point?"

Bevins lowered his voice so the trailing drovers wouldn't hear him. "My point, Preacher, is that there ain't near enough of us to weather an ambush, and there're rocks up there Sherman could of hid his whole army behind."

"I myself fought for the Confederacy, sir, before the Lord showed me His way. But I came to know that other way well," Sutcliff said, tapping the rolling block carbine under his right leg, "and I intend on teaching it to the heathen who killed my son and stole my daughter."

Bevins shook his head this time, recollecting the scene at the livery station when the four Apaches drew their pinto ponies up in a line, the leader a warrior with chiseled features and skin so sunburned it looked like oiled leather over his white tunic. Chulio was the name he used, gesturing with a pair of cavalry field glasses, asking if he could water his ponies at the trough. The Mescalero was using the glasses to make a point, that he'd taken these off some pretty good troopers, and he could take what he wanted now, too.

Bevins was standing under the porch's roof, rifle cradled casually in the crook of his arm. The drovers stood around him, their hands fidgety near holstered weapons, ready to fight if necessary now that they were back on what felt like civilized ground. Add in the preacher with his carbine and the boy Matthew with an old shotgun, and Bevins knew he was showing enough force to discourage any trouble.

Until Tildy came out the door of the station.

There was an appreciative murmur from the braves until Chulio held up his hand, and they became silent. The preacher roared at his daughter, she refusing to take the scold, dipping her head so the blond hair swayed and saying, "All's I want to do is just *see* them, Pa." As Sutcliff pushed her back inside the building, Bevins could predict what would come next and braced for it.

"You father to girl?" Chulio said after Sutcliff had slammed the door to the station.

"That's no business of yours, Indian," the preacher said sternly.

Chulio's expression remained unchanged. "How much to buy?"

Sutcliff's face took on a high color. "I won't hear such talk about my daughter."

"How much?"

Sutcliff's son Matthew shouted, "Shut your dirty mouth, you hear," but his voice cracked halfway through it, and the other Apaches, whether appreciating English or not, understood the cracking and laughed among themselves.

Bevins could see the shotgun quivering in the boy's grip. "Steady now, son." Then, to Chulio, "Water your men and your stock. After that, you go."

Chulio neither nodded nor spoke, just wheeled his pony toward the trough, his men doing likewise. It reminded Bevins of the drill team he'd seen at a general's parade near Appomattox Courthouse, what seemed a long time before.

When the Apaches had slid off their mounts and began taking water with them, Sutcliff whispered, "Should we let them live?"

Bevins said, "Yes," in a tone that brooked no argument.

But late that night, Bevins was awakened by a howl of pain, a mannish voice screaming out in agony. He'd gotten to the girl's room about the same time as her father, only to find the son mortally stabbed, gut and throat, thrashing on the floor like a fish on a dock. There were even scratches on his face, from the fight he'd put up. The shuttered window was open, the boards flapping against the adobe wall in the strong desert breeze. The girl was gone, and though the wind might have fooled him, Bevins thought he heard her voice among the thumping of pony hooves fading in the distance.

"Mr. Bevins?"

The livery man still had to lift his head to look at the preacher, though being in the saddle somewhat evened out their difference in height.

Sutcliff said, "I had to shame the three men behind us into joining this mission, and now I fear I'm losing you."

"Well, that's pretty near right, Preacher. What I fear is losing me, too," but he dug his heels once into the flanks of his mount, lurching forward to the pace Sutcliff had been setting when Bevins first suggested they breathe the horses.

*

Kel McKyer moved slowly and quietly, but he didn't have to go very far before hearing the shuffling of feet on the shale and sand just upslope of the big boulder. Had it been his first time hearing the sound, he'd have said a dozen or more men were moving around, trying to stay warm. Which, of course, would make no sense in the desert heat. Then he came upon the little arroyo.

Four pinto ponies behind a makeshift corral of deadwood and bushes, their hooves bound by leather patches tied with rawhide strips, dark bandannas covering their muzzles and eyes so they couldn't see or smell to spook. Or, more important, to make any real noise. Despite the precautions, one of the ponies neighed, McKyer using a hand to soothe the horse by stroking its mane.

Then he sat for a minute, though there wasn't much to study on, just a decision to reach. The Mescalero who had jumped him was guarding the horses and the "back door," so to speak, with instructions to keep things just as quiet as possible. Which meant the rest of the raiding party lay up ahead, probably over the rise and below the ridge on the downslope facing south. What his sergeant from the army called the "military crest of the hill," where a unit could wait, even stand up, without silhouetting themselves as targets against the sky as background. Only one reason for that, and for the lone Indian to be keeping the horses out of sight and hearing. At the moment, the raiding party wasn't raiding, exactly. It was setting an ambush, and the Apaches would be between McKyer and the prey they were waiting on.

The decision involved two choices. One would be to go back down the way he'd come and scatter the ponies, which would delay the Mescaleros some but not stop them. And they'd never stop, not after he'd killed one of their own. Even without the gold, he couldn't outrun them, and he wasn't about to abandon the things his head told him the heavy nuggets could buy.

The second choice was to keep climbing the hill, hoping to come up on the Apaches by surprise and use whatever they were hunting to help hunt them. And kill them, down to the last man or boy.

Realizing he had a headache, McKyer dug the pads of his thumb and forefinger deeply into the places where his eyes met the bridge of his nose. The headache came from too much thinking, he knew. What he'd already been shown wasn't going to get any better without his prodding it along.

Taking a deep breath, Del McKyer continued, slowly and quietly, up the slope.

*

Chulio lowered the long glass he used to see the whites moving toward him. They are abusing their horses, he thought. The one called Bevins had seemed smarter than that, but with whites, Chulio had learned, stupidity often took some time to show itself.

Behind him, from the other side of the hill, he heard one of the ponies neigh briefly, then stop. The brave he'd left with the horses was the youngest, but he had dealt with the pony quickly. It was important to learn what would quiet the ponies before the whites got close enough to hear for themselves. Chulio did not like to divide his raiding party, particularly such a small one, but to spring the trap properly, he'd need only the two warriors with him on this side of the hill. Five whites, three Mescalero rifles. Three shots and there would be only two whites, and with luck, one of those might be captured alive. It had been a while since Chulio and his men had enjoyed what would follow, using blades grown red from a slow fire, and the spines of a cactus to—

"I'm hot," said the white girl from ten feet behind him.

Her voice, so interesting when he'd first heard it the afternoon before, was becoming an irritant, like a sharp stone under soft bedding. In his mind, Chulio had tried to see her performing the puberty ceremony, clad in the traditional white buckskin dress with long fronds and a necklace of red and blue beads. But the vision would not come to him. And that night, at the livery station, he'd learned why.

She put an edge into her next word. "Well?"

Chulio's other two braves were flanked in the rocks and in front of him, wide left and right, to improve the angles of fire on the approaching whites. The girl's voice would not have carried to them, which spared him the need to discipline her. This time.

"I said, I'm *hot*."

Chulio spoke low, meaningfully. "It is desert. Desert is hot."

"Why?"

Why. "Hot is what make desert desert."

"Well, can I at least have some *wa*-ter?"

Knowing the white girl could not see his face, Chulio smiled. She is making fun of the way I speak her language, he thought. Good. Let her have her fun now. I will have mine, later and often.

Then the Mescalero leader remembered what she'd told him riding from the livery station, and he stopped smiling. Raising the long glass again, he kept it on the tall white in black clothing. The girl had said her father was some kind of holy man to his people. Chulio found himself wanting the man in black to be the one they would take alive.

Then he heard the girl move behind him.

★

It didn't take a genius to figure out what would happen next, McKyer knew. From the top of the rise, he could look down on the backs of the Mescaleros, who were facing south. McKyer could count three, which allowed him to relax just a little. Four ponies in the arroyo, and four Apaches, counting the one he'd killed. It was possible that there were more, without mounts, but this far away from anywhere, that was unlikely.

Two of the Mescaleros were close on to the foot of the rise, hiding behind boulders that gave good fields of fire to the front. The third was the closest to McKyer, partway up the slope and in a circle of rocks. From that position the others could look to him for hand signals. The leader, then, and the one to be shot first, all other things being equal.

McKyer didn't have binoculars, but he could see a dust trail to the south. Two miles away, maybe, if the elevation didn't throw off his judgment too much. The prey.

The more he studied on the situation, the more McKyer knew he'd have to wait until the Apaches opened fire on the people approaching before he began shooting. Otherwise the riders would stop or shy off, well out of helping range, and the ambush would turn on him.

Then McKyer saw something that was hard to figure. Another person rose up behind the closest Apache. Only this other person was a woman, blond hair in some kind of print dress, reaching out a hand to the leader in a way that said she wasn't trussed up like a hostage.

★

"If you drink *first,* can I drink, too?"

Chulio turned back to the long glass. "Put canteen away. We cannot drink yet."

"Why not?" said the white girl.

This one, she would need strong discipline. Maybe only once or twice, but clear signs, so she would insult his judgment no further. He could hear her moving closer.

"I said, why *not?*"

At that point Chulio turned swiftly and backhanded the girl across the cheek, knocking her down and nearly out.

★

"Preacher?"

"What?"

"We've no more than a half mile to the base of that rise."

"And therefore?" said Sutcliff, reining in just a bit to allow the livery man to draw even with him once again.

"And therefore," said Bevins in the low voice, "we'd best do some talking about what we'll do when we get there."

"If the heathen are there, we shall vanquish them."

"Or vicey-versy."

"Your point now?"

"Same as it was before. These three boys behind us are skittish now. We run into an ambush, I'm not sure how much good they'll be."

"The Lord has provided them to us as avenging angels. They will discharge their duty in His light."

At which point Sutcliff spurred his stallion onward, Bevins shaking his head as he did the same, waving at the drovers to close up behind him.

★

McKyer didn't like mistreatment of women by anybody, and he was sorely tempted to shoot the leader right after the Apache slapped the woman down. But biding his time still seemed the best course, especially now that a woman was involved. And it underlined for McKyer the importance of taking out the closest Mescalero first.

The riders were getting close enough to distinguish, the waves of heat coming off the desert causing the figures to shimmer, like they were floating in air. Five men, one tall in the saddle, the next short, the other three neither but better riders than the first two. If he had to guess, McKyer thought at least some of them might be kin to the woman, coming in a too-small posse to go against four Apaches. Probably the tall one was the woman's husband, him being out front and riding his mount kind of hard for the conditions.

McKyer didn't think he knew any of the men, because he'd seen most of the people he ever knew riding at some point, and once you've seen a man in the saddle, you can identify him as such from some distance. At least he hoped he didn't know any of them, given that he was pretty sure three of them would be hit by the Mescaleros before he could safely—huh, *safe*-ly—join the battle.

Shifting his stance and leaning down a bit, McKyer swiped the forearm of his shirt across his sweating, throbbing forehead. Damned desert.

★

"You didn't have to *hit* me."

Chulio did not turn toward her voice, coming up from the ground behind him like the whine of a cowardly camp dog. He found himself questioning the wisdom of his decision the prior night. I could have left the whites to themselves as I saw them from the window of the room at the livery station. But the girl intrigued him, as she refused and fought, using her fingernails as a wildcat would its claws. He had not been sorry to catch her attention, throw her his knife.

"I *said,* you didn't—"

"Quiet. No more until it is over, or you die now."

Chulio was uncomfortable speaking so many words together in English. His tone silenced the girl, but he found himself feeling more and more certain that he had made the wrong decision the night before. Pushing that thought from his mind, the Mescalero leader resolved to only wound the father, so he and his braves could take their fun with him.

It would not surprise Chulio if the girl asked to join them.

*

From his superior position, McKyer began to count the seconds until the riders would be within the killing field of the Mescaleros. He wasn't sure if the leader would fire as the signal to his warriors, but once he did and they did, the report of their rifles would deafen them enough to slow them in locating McKyer. By then at least two of the Apaches should be down from his Winchester, leaving one caught between the riders and him. Still dangerous after that, but manageable.

The tall man, dressed in black with a hat like a preacher, was still riding hardish out front, McKyer saw, but the short man now drew his rifle from its scabbard, the three behind him taking their cue from him, two drawing rifles and the third his pistol. The two flanking Mescaleros were watching the riders, not turning at all back toward the leader. Then they lifted their rifles to the serious level and began sighting down on targets, and McKyer knew the leader's shot would in fact be the signal to start things off.

McKyer brought the stock of the Winchester up into his right shoulder, seating it, and rested the elbow of his left arm on the flattest part of the boulder in front of him. His front sight mimicked a black stain on the spine of the Mescalero halfway down the slope beneath him. Then the leader lifted his rifle as well.

*

Scanning the rocks, Bevins found he couldn't move his eyes fast enough. "Preacher, I'm really getting a bad feeling here."

"You must have faith, Mr. Bevins, faith in—"

*

The volley was near perfect, McKyer thought, as the crumping noise of three shots sounded below him. He was aware of the tall man being punched out of his saddle, the leader's bullet striking him high on the torso. The flanking Apaches must have had different instructions, as the one on the left fired into the short man, rocking him but not knocking him off his mount. The Mescalero on the right felled the last rider, who dropped to the ground like he had a sudden urge to kiss it.

As McKyer's ears rang from his own squeezing of the trigger, he saw a red flower bloom on the white tunic of the Apache leader, squarely between the shoulder blades. Satisfied when the Indian slumped down hard, McKyer turned his attention to the Mescalero on the right, who was leveling on the other two riders, wheeling and running instead of helping their comrades. McKyer fired as the ambusher did, each man's bullet finding its target. The rider toppled from his saddle, catching a boot in his stirrup, and getting dragged a ways before being kicked free by his panicking horse. The Apache on the right fell sideways and rolled a bit, his rifle probably making a clattering noise against the rock, had he been alive to hear it.

Turning to the third Mescalero, McKyer was surprised to see the short man charging on his mount. He'd dropped his rifle and drawn a revolver, bearing down on the Indian while firing. The Apache stood his ground, shooting back and then falling before McKyer brought his own weapon to bear. The Indian struggled to rise, and now McKyer fired into him, the Mescalero letting go of his rifle and struggling no more as the short man slid in slow motion from his horse, striking the ground with no attempt to break his fall.

Taking deep breaths to calm the rushing feeling he had inside his head and chest, McKyer watched the dust trail of the sole escaping rider move toward the south, the perspective seeming to slow the man down. Then he was aware of yelling from the foot of the rise, suddenly realizing, too, that he could no longer see the body of the Mescalero leader he'd shot first.

*

"Tildy? . . . Tildy?"

Sutcliff moved forward awkwardly, his right ankle giving him more pain from the fall than his left shoulder from the bullet. He noticed that his hat was gone and that there was numbness all along his left side, the arm swinging loosely. But there wasn't much blood soaking through his frock, and he was confident in a dazed way that when he reached his daughter, the wound could be dressed and he would live.

Sutcliff moved slowly around the body of the livery man—what was his name?—the ants already moving toward the pool of blood collecting in a rock depression bordering the body. Sutcliff raised his head from that image, preferring salvation to the inevitable decomposition of the earthly husk, even if it meant making his legs carry him uphill. If his daughter could just hear him calling for her, she'd meet him halfway. He knew she would.

"Tildy? . . ."

*

McKyer moved fifty or sixty feet to the right of his original
firing position before slowing working down the slope. He
wanted to come at the Mescalero leader's circle of rocks from
an unexpected direction. McKyer didn't think the Apache
would be able to move far, given the placement of the wound
he'd inflicted. He also hoped the Indian was beyond hurting
the girl, but he couldn't be sure the Indian was beyond hurting him. And the yelling of the tall man climbing like a crazy
drunk up the hill might not be enough of a distraction.

Just before reaching the Apache's position, McKyer stopped
behind a low boulder as the tall man's voice said the same
word he'd been yelling, only now in a kind of surprised way.
What McKyer heard was:

"Tildy? Tildy, what are you doing?"

"I can't stop his bleeding, Pa."

That surprised McKyer. The "woman's" voice was that of a
young girl, and she'd addressed the tall man as her father.

"Stop his . . . Why?"

"He saved me, Pa, saved me from what you taught Matthew
to do."

None of this made any sense to McKyer, so he made no move
to interrupt until it would.

The tall man's voice said, "Tildy, Tildy, I've always done for
you. Always. What are you saying, girl?"

"I'm saying that this Indian *did* for me, tossed me his knife
through the window when Matthew came to bother me that
way, bother me the way you taught him. Only it was my
monthly time and I was all cramped up and I just couldn't
stand it anymore. Afterward, I climbed out the window."

"After . . . ? Tildy, Tildy you . . . killed my son? My Matthew?"

"What should I do?"

McKyer thought that sounded wrong, that her words would
have been "What could I do?"

But then a wheezy voice seemed to answer her, a dark voice
that sounded like it was drowning in a fouled well.

"Send him . . . to his . . . God."

As the tall man shouted "No!" there was the report of a rifle,
and McKyer heard a body fall. He rose up then, ninety degrees
off the girl's line of sight. She was still leveling a rifle what
would have been chest-high on the tall man, now lying ten feet
from her, legs splayed, eyes unnaturally open to the searing
sun.

The Mescalero leader reclined against a large, curved stone in a way that said somebody had to have propped him there. The Indian had an exit wound in his chest the size of a Georgia peach, blood dribbling from the lower corner of his mouth, every stitch of cloth below the wound drenched red.

McKyer spoke softly. "Put the gun down, miss."

The girl froze, then let the muzzle of the rifle fall to the ground, the stock following as she let go of the trigger area. The Apache groaned, and McKyer heard the death rattle rise from his throat.

"What was that?" asked the girl, turning toward the body.

"His last breath, you might say."

The girl sighed, then dipped her head and turned toward McKyer. "Well, Pa and Matthew had their way with me, and I know that was on the Indian's mind, too." She brushed back a hank of her blond hair. "I guess it must be your turn."

Trying to tally the dead so far, Kel McKyer knew he'd have to study on the girl's words for quite some time.

William F. Nolan

SHADOW QUEST

Name it, he's done it. TV, movies, books, anthologies, comic books, biography, William F. Nolan has been there.

Recently he's taken to writing a fine, nostalgic series about the days of "Black Mask," noir novels that brilliantly recall the thirties and forties of their genesis. He's also written two very fine action Westerns.

Here Bill Nolan demonstrates that he has the same sure, fine hand for the Western tale that made his hero Max Brand so popular.

His name was striking: John Shadow. Otherwise he was a very ordinary fellow. No wife. No family. A drifter, making his way through life as best he could. No goals. No ambitions. He gambled some, losing more than he won. He boxed for pocket money in Dodge City, cut timber in Canada, punched cows along the Cimarron, rode the rods west as a road tramp, served as a bouncer in Santa Fe, and played piano at a fancy house in El Paso. That job ended abruptly when Shadow ran off with one of the house ladies (her name was Margie). But they didn't stay together. Margie left him for a buffalo hunter two weeks later.

He was at loose ends. He owned the clothes on his back, a lump-headed mustang, and a New Winchester he'd won in a Kansas poker game. And not much else.

That was when John Shadow decided to ride into the Sierra Madres after Diablo.

He heard about him in the border town of Los Lobos along

the American side of the Rio Grande. A wild stallion. El Diablo Blanco—the White Devil. Fast, smart . . . and mean. Two trappers at the bar were talking about the stallion.

"Has he been hunted?" Shadow asked.

"By the best," said the bartender, a beefy man in a stained apron. "With relays of horses. Sometimes they've run him a hundred miles in one day, but he always outsmarts 'em. Disappears like smoke in the wind. Lemme tell ya, if a horse can laugh, he's laughing."

"I'm good with horses," Shadow said quietly.

The barman's smile was cynical. "Got a real *way* with 'em, eh?"

"I'd say so," nodded Shadow.

"Well, then, here's your chance." And he exchanged grins with the two trappers. "Just take yourself a little jaunt up into the Sierras an' fetch out the white."

"I need to think on it," Shadow told him.

He returned to the bar later that same afternoon.

"I'm going after him," he said.

*

It was a full day's ride into the upper foothills of the Sierra Madres. Shadow was following a crude, hand-drawn map provided by the barman after he'd convinced him he was serious in his quest for the white. The barman had indicated the area where the horse had been most often seen—but Shadow had no guarantee that Diablo had remained in this section of the mountains.

He was well aware of the various methods used in the capture of wild horses. Often, a sizable group of riders pursued the target animals, attempting to force them into a circular run, gradually tightening the circle. Sometimes hunters used relays of horses, constantly maintaining fresh mounts in the hope of running down the winded herd.

There was the story of a legendary hunt by a young Cheyenne warrior in which the Indian had traveled on foot for many hundreds of miles over a period of several months in pursuit of a single horse. The natural speed of a wild horse is reduced by its need to graze each day. Whenever the animal stopped to eat, the Indian's tireless, loping stride would close the distance between them. The Cheyenne lived on water and parched corn, eating as he ran, thus constantly forcing the pursuit.

Eventually, so the story went, both hunter and hunted became gaunt and weakened. The long trail ended on the naked slope of a snowcapped peak high above the timberline when the Indian managed to lasso his totally exhausted quarry.

Of course, even if this fanciful tale were true, Shadow had no patience for such an arduous pursuit.

When he was within range of the horse, Shadow intended to bring down the animal with a bullet from his Winchester. The shot would require extreme accuracy, since his bullet must crease the nape of the neck at a spot that would jar the animal's spinal column. This would stun the horse, allowing its capture.

Diablo was unusual in that he ran alone. Most wild horses run with others of their kind, in herds numbering up to fifty or more, but the white stallion had always been a loner, staying well clear of the herds ranging the Sierra Madres. He wanted no young colts or laboring mares to slow his swift progress.

Many attempts had been made to capture him. One group of hunters, led by Colonel Matthew Sutton, had plans for Diablo as an eastern show horse, and ran the stallion for six weeks without letup. Eleven horses had galloped themselves to death during that brutal pursuit, while the proud white drifted ahead of them, beyond their reach, defiant and strong.

One frustrated hunter claimed that the stallion had never truly existed—that he was nothing more than an apparition, a white ghost who galloped like a cloud across the sky.

When John Shadow repeated this last claim to a trapper he'd met in the high mountains, a one-armed veteran named Hatcher, the old man declared: "Oh, he's real enough all right, Diablo is. I've seen him by sun and by moon, in good weather and bad. There was one time I come up on him close enough to near touch that smooth silk hide of his, but then he took off like a streak of white lightning."

The old man cackled at the memory. "A pure wonder, he is. Ain't no horse like him nowhere in these mountains or out of 'em, and that's a fact."

"Then you don't think I can catch him?" asked John Shadow.

"Sure ya can—as easy as you can reach out and catch the wind." And Hatcher cackled again.

*

There was a great difference between the arid, sterile mountains around El Paso and this lush terrain of the Sierra Madres. Here Shadow found water in abundance, and rich grass, and thickly wooded hills—a veritable paradise that provided Diablo with everything he needed to sustain his wild existence.

Despite the old trapper's firm conviction that the great horse could never be captured, Hatcher had nonetheless provided solid hope. The trapper had agreed that Diablo did indeed frequent this particular section of mountain wilderness.

Luck and a keen eye might well reward him here.

Just a day later, as he was riding out of a shallow draw onto the level of a grassed plateau, John Shadow had his first look at the legendary stallion.

Diablo had been nibbling the green, tender sprouts that tipped a thick stand of juniper and now he raised his head to scent the wind. He nickered softly. Nostrils flaring, he suddenly wheeled about to face the rider at the far end of the plateau.

Shadow had slipped the new Winchester from its scabbard, since the range permitted him to fire, but he slowly lowered the weapon, awed by the animal's size and beauty. Easily seventeen hands tall, deep-chested, sheathed with rippling muscle, and as white as a drift of newly fallen snow, Diablo was truly magnificent.

The horse stood immobile for a long moment, studying his enemy. Then, with a toss of his thick mane and a ringing neigh of defiance, he trotted away, breaking into a smooth-flowing gallop that carried him swiftly out of sight.

Dammit! I could have fired, Shadow told himself; I could have ended it here and now with a single shot.

The light had been ideal and he was certain he could have creased the animal's neck. And there had been ample time for the shot. But the sheer power and majesty of the horse had kept him from firing. What if his bullet had missed its mark and struck a vital area? What if he had killed this king of stallions? Many wild horses have been fatally shot by hunters attempting to stun them.

No, he decided, I need to be closer, a lot closer, to make absolutely *certain* of the shot. And now that he's aware of me, it's not going to be easy.

That night, after a meal of mountain grouse roasted over his campfire, Shadow spread his blanket across a bed of fragrant pine needles on the forest floor. Lying on his back, hands laced behind his head, under a mass of tall pines that crowded the stars, he considered the meaning of freedom.

He had always thought of himself as a free man, yet through much of his life he'd been bound by the commands of others— when he had served in the war, when he was working in bars and brothels, when he'd been a cowpuncher and lumberman. In Diablo, John Shadow had witnessed true freedom. The great horse owed allegiance to no one. The whole wide world of the mountain wilderness served as his personal playground. He ran at no man's bidding, served no master but himself.

And now I'm trying to take that freedom away from him, thought Shadow. I'm trying to saddle and bridle him, bend his will to mine, feed him oats instead of his wild sweet grass, make him gallop at my command.

Did he have the right? Did *anyone* really have the right to own such a glorious animal?

With these melancholy thoughts drifting through his consciousness, Shadow closed his eyes, breathing deeply of the clean mountain air. The faint whisper of wind, rustling the trees, lulled him to sleep.

*

He awakened abruptly, shocked and wide-eyed, to an earth-shaking roar.

The morning sun was slanting down in dusty yellow bars through the pine branches, painting the forest floor in shades of brilliant orange. At the edge of the clearing, not twenty-five feet from where John Shadow had been sleeping, a huge, brown-black grizzly had reared up to a full-battle position, its clawed forepaws extended like a boxer's hands. The monstrous jaws gaped wide in anger, yellow fangs gleaming like swords in the wide red cave of its mouth.

The mighty bruin, a full thousand pounds of bone and muscle, was not facing directly toward Shadow, but was angled away from him, in the direction of another enemy.

Diablo!

Incredible as it seemed, the tall white stallion was trotting around the grizzly in a wary half circle, ears flattened, eyes glaring, prehensile upper lip pulled back from its exposed teeth.

The horse was plainly preparing to attack.

Shadow was amazed. He had never known a horse to challenge a grizzly. Even the scent of an approaching bear was enough to send the fiercest stallion into a gallop for safety—yet here was Diablo, boldly facing this forest mammoth with no trace of fear.

Then an even greater shock struck the hunter: Diablo was defending *him*! The bear had apparently been making his forest rounds, overturning rocks for insects, ripping apart dead logs for grubs and worms, when he'd encountered the sleeping figure of John Shadow. He was about to descend on the hunter when the stallion intervened.

It made no logical sense. Yet, somehow, the white horse had felt protective of the man who had been hunting him. That Diablo had come to his rescue was a fact John Shadow accepted, although he was truly stunned by such an act. The scene seemed to be part of a dream, yet Shadow knew he was fully awake. What was happening, *was* happening.

Now Diablo reared up, with a ringing neigh, to strike at the brute's head with his stone-sharpened forehooves. A hoof connected with the bruin's skull like a dropped hammer, and the bear staggered back, roaring horribly, its eyes like glowing sparks of fire.

Then the grizzly counterattacked, lunging ponderously forward to take one of its great paws across the stallion's neck. This blow, powerful enough to take a man's head off at the shoulders, buckled Diablo's legs, and the stunned animal toppled backward and down, blood running from an open neck wound.

The bear lumbered forward to finish his opponent, but by now Shadow had his Winchester in hand, and he began firing at the dark-shagged beast.

The giant grizzly seemed impervious to bullets. With a frightful bellow of rage, he charged wildly at the hated man-thing.

Shadow stopped firing to roll sideways—barely avoiding the razored claws, which scored the log next to his head. With the huge bruin looming above him like a brown-black mountain, Shadow pumped three more rounds into the beast at heart level.

They did the job.

Like a chopped tree, the monster crashed to the forest floor, expiring with a final, defiant death-growl. It had taken five rifle bullets to kill him.

Diablo lay on his side, only half conscious, breathing heavily, as Shadow tended the stallion's injured shoulder. Using fresh water from his canteen, he cleansed the wound, then treated it with an old Indian remedy: He carefully packed a mix of forest herbs and mud over the wound, and tied it in place with a shirt from his saddle roll.

Amazingly, the animal did not resist these efforts. Diablo seemed to understand that Shadow was trying to help him.

If those claws had gone a half inch deeper, Shadow knew, the shoulder muscle would have been ruined, crippling the great horse.

He ran his hand soothingly along the stallion's quivering flank, murmuring in a soft voice, "Easy, boy, easy now. You're going to be all right . . . you're going to be fine. . . ."

And Diablo rolled an anxious eye toward John Shadow.

*

It took more than a week before the white stallion was willing to follow a lead rope. During this entire period Shadow worked night and day to win the gallant animal's trust, talking, stroking, picking lush seed grass for the horse to eat.

The shoulder wound healed rapidly.

On the ninth day after the bear attack, Shadow began his ride back to Los Lobos, with Diablo trotting behind him on the lead rope.

Shadow was smiling as he rode. Now, suddenly, his life held purpose and meaning. Soon he would teach Diablo to accept him as a rider; he would be the first to guide this glorious beast over valley and plain—and riding him, Shadow knew, would be like riding the wind itself. There would be a mutual trust between them. A deep understanding. A bonding of spirits.

Before he had made this trip into the Sierra Madres, John Shadow had never believed in miracles.

Now, looking back at the splendor of Diablo, he knew he had been wrong.

Ed Gorman

PARDS

Publishers Weekly *noted that "Gorman writes Westerns for grown-ups."*

This story, though set in contemporary America, speaks to the way that seven generations have now attached themselves to the mythic West as depicted on the movie screen.

In all, Gorman has authored seven Western novels, including the Spur-nominated Wolf Moon. *Two years ago his short story "The Face" won the Spur.*

1

Bromley always liked it when people asked him what he did for a living because then he could tell them he was a writer. He didn't mention his day job, which was being the only forty-nine-year-old bag "boy" at DeSoto's Supermarket; no, he just told them about his writing, and then showed them a copy of the one and only paperback novel he'd ever sold, a Western called *Gun Fury*, which had been published by a company called Triton. He never mentioned that Triton had declared bankruptcy right after *Gun Fury* appeared, nor did he mention that Triton had been one of the worst publishers in history. Bromley's listeners didn't need to know that.

2

"Never seen anything like these before," the new mailman said on one of Bromley's days off (he usually worked weekends, which most of the teenagers refused to do, and so Sam DeSoto gave him two days off in the middle of the week). Bromley was

284

sitting on the front porch of the aged Victorian apartment house where he lived, reading William Nolan's biography of Max Brand and sipping on a Diet Pepsi. In addition to losing his hair, Bromley had lately started to gain weight, one of the Chicano kids at the store even calling him "Fat Ass" one day, the little bastard, and so now it was Diet Pepsi instead of the regular stuff.

So Bromley was in the shade of the sunny porch, Mrs. Hanrahan's soap opera blaring through the lacy curtains, when the mailman said, "What exactly are they, anyway?"

"Fanzines."

"Fanzines?"

"Yeah, magazines that Western fans publish themselves. There're fanzines for people who like the old pulp magazines and fanzines for people who liked the old Saturday serials and fanzines for people who like the old Western stars."

The mailman, who was just old enough to remember, said, "Like Gene and Roy?"

"Exactly. Like Gene and Roy."

"So do you put one out yourself, I mean being a writer and all?"

"No; but I write for a lot of them."

"Yeah? Which ones?"

"The ones about the old cowboy stars." Bromley wanted to tell him about his dream he had sometimes; standing in this movie lobby in 1948 with all these great lobby cards showing Wild Bill Elliott and The Durango Kid (God, there was no getting around it; guys who wore masks were just great) and Gabby Hayes and Jane Frazee and Tim Holt and the 3 Mesquiteers, and how down on one end there was this table overflowing with pulp magazines, *The Pecos Kid Western* and *Frontier Stories* and *Thrilling Eastern Stories;* and then another table with an old 1946 table model radio with the sounds of "Bobby Benson and The B Bar B Riders" coming out of it; and yet another table with nothing but Big Little Books; and there was a churchlike holiness in the air and Bromley was caught up in it, tears nearly streaming down his face; WAS NOT THIS HEAVEN? And he had this crazy urge to eat Cheerios, just the way Tonto did; or Ralston Purina, just like Tom Mix; or maybe even Pep, the way Superman was always telling him to.

"Those'd be the ones I'd be interested in, the cowboys, I mean," the mailman said. Then he shrugged and handed Bromley his mail. "You're really an interesting guy, Ken, you know that?"

3

He'd been married once, Bromley had, in the early sixties, already working at DeSoto's, to a pretty but dumb woman whom his mother did not like at all ("I don't see why you have to move out when you've got so much room here, especially since your father died, and anyway twenty-two is too young to get married, she's just looking for an easy ride if you ask me"), a waitress who seemed to know what all her customers made per hour at this or that factory, at this or that delivery service. "Four bucks an hour, Ken, you really should look into that." But somehow he never got around to it. Just down the block from DeSoto's was the city's largest used bookstore and he spent most of his lunch hours in there. The air was holy, the dusty air of Ace Doubles and Gold Medal books, of *All-Story Weekly* and *Star Western* and *Adventure,* the cocoon of paperbacks and magazines in which he'd spent his boyhood, never much caring that he didn't have many friends, that he was virtually invisible at school, or that the violent arguments of his parents caused him to shake uncontrollably for long periods of time behind his too-thin bedroom door. No, there were always the Saturday afternoon movies, or his books and magazines to escape into.

One night—this was a year or so into their marriage, the night one of those perfect late spring evenings shot through with fireflies and the scent of apple blossoms—right there in the same wedding bed Bromley would sleep in the rest of his life, right there in Mrs. Hanrahan's apartment house where he would live the rest of his life, his wife said, "I need to be honest with you."

"Huh?"

"I—did something."

"Did something?"

He was smoking a Lucky with the sheet just half on him and listening to the night birds at the window screen, and she was lying next to him in just her underwear.

"You know that Jimmy I told you about?"

"Uh, I guess so." She was always telling him about somebody.

"You know. He makes six-thirty-two an hour out at Rockwell."

"I guess."

"He has the red Olds convertible, remember, with the white leather interior?"

"Oh. Yeah. Jimmy."

"Well, the other day he wanted to know if I wanted a ride home after the dinner rush."

"Oh."

God, now he knew what was coming.

"I knew I shouldn't have said yes but he kept pushing the subject. You know how guys get."

"Yeah, I guess I do."

"Well, anyway, I let him give me a ride home."

"Was this Thursday?"

"Yeah. Thursday."

"When you were late?"

She hesitated. "Yeah, when I was late."

"I see."

Neither of them said anything for a long time. He finished his cigarette and then just lay with his hands on his chest, in his boxer shorts that she was always asking him not to wear ("You're a young man, Ken, you shouldn't wear things like that").

Then she said, "But he didn't take me straight home."

"I see."

"I mean I told him to. But he didn't. He wouldn't listen to anything I said. He just kept driving out along the river road. He just kept saying isn't it pretty at dusk like this, with the sunlight real coppery on the river like this? I had to admit that it was."

"Did you let him do anything to you?"

"I let him French kiss me."

"Oh."

"And I let him feel my breasts."

"I see."

"But I didn't let him put his hand inside my bra."

He said nothing. He wondered if his heart would stop beating. Just *boom* like that and he would no longer be alive.

"And I didn't let him touch me down there."

He said nothing.

"He tried, Ken, but I wouldn't let him."

The tears came abruptly and without warning. There in the

darkness he shook so hard—just the way he used to shake when his parents screamed at each other—that the whole bed shook. His wedding bed.

She leaned over and kissed him then, and it was a tender and pure kiss, and he recognized it as such, and she said, "You're more like my brother or something, Ken. I didn't want it to turn out this way but it did anyway. I mean you never want to go dancing or take me out to dinner or make love or . . ." She smiled there in the darkness. "You're more interested in your book collection than you are me, Ken. And you know that's the truth."

Later on after a long time of not talking, just lying there, her sometimes taking drags from his cigarette, sometimes not, she leaned over and kissed him and put her hand down there and got him hard, and then they made love with a purity and tenderness that broke his heart because he knew this would be the last time, the very last time, and when it was over and they were just lying there again, she started crying too, soft girl tears there in the darkness, her a girl as he was still a boy, and then just before she fell asleep she said—her only bitter comment during the whole night—"Well, your mother will be relieved anyway. Just don't move back in with her. I care about you too much to see that happen. OK?"

The next day she was packed and gone. Three months later he got proceeding papers from a lawyer in Milwaukee and six months after that he was divorced. Throughout the first year, she wrote him postcards fairly frequently. She mentioned different restaurants she worked at and she mentioned how hot Milwaukee was in the summer and then how cold it was in the winter and then one card she said she was getting married to a guy with a real good job (she didn't mention his name nor did she mention how much he made an hour) and then abruptly the cards stopped except, inexplicably, two Christmases later when she sent him a Christmas card with the snapshot of an infant girl inside. Her first child.

He stayed on at DeSoto's, of course, spending his lunch hours at the used bookstore, and he did not move back in with his mother.

4

The odd thing was, Bromley learned about Rex Stone's moving not through one of the fanzines but when somebody at DeSoto's (Laughlin, the smirky guy in the meat department) mentioned that Stone was moving to Center City, a mere eighty miles from the city here: "That fuckin' cowboy guy, you know, the one when we were kids, the one who could make his horse dance up on his hind legs?"

Bromley could scarcely believe it. Sure, he'd known that Rex Stone (a.k.a. Walter Sipkins) had been born in this area but who could have guessed that after fifteen years of being a star at Republic (he'd starred in the studio's very last B Western, despite the fact that most film books mistakenly attributed this distinction to Allan "Rocky" Lane)—after fifteen years in movies and ten more in TV (usually in supporting roles but meaty ones), who could have guessed Stone would move back to where he'd come from?

About a month after Laughlin gave Bromley the word, the local paper ran a big photo of Stone in full singing-cowboy getup holding up a sweet little crippled girl in his arms. The caption read: "Cowboy Star spends sunset years helping others" and the story went on to detail how active Stone had become with Center City civic events. Retired now, he "planned to devote his life to helping all the little 'buckaroos and buckarettes' who need him."

Bromley couldn't believe it. Rex Stone. Only eighty miles from here. Rex Stone. The man he'd always measured himself against. Sure, Bromley liked Hoppy and Roy and Gene and Monte and Lash and Sunset but none of them had compared to Rex because, despite the fact that Rex sang a lot of sappy songs and could make his horse Stormy dance along at the same time, Rex was a *man*. The jaw and the eyes and the big hands and the deep voice told you that. He was a man not in the way of a Saturday afternoon hero but rather in the rough and somewhat mysterious way of, say, Robert Mitchum. That was why, back in the forties and fifties, Rex Stone had not only had a huge kids' following, he's also managed to snag a major following of young women. (TV people had later tried to cast him as a he-man in a short-lived adventure series called *Bush Pilot* but the series had been on ZIV, and when ZIV went down—the other networks inevitably pushing it out—so did Rex's series.)

And now, admittedly paunchier, gray-haired, and jowly, Rex Stone lived only eighty miles away.

5

"Is Mr. Stone there, please?"

"Who the hell is this?" The voice was female and old and accusatory.

Bromley did the only thing he could. He gulped. "Uh, my name is Bromley."

"Who?"

"Bromley."

"Spell it."

"Huh?"

"You deaf? I said spell it."

"B-r-o-m-l-e-y."

"Bromley."

"Yes."

"So just what the hell do you want?"

"I, uh, I'd like to speak to Mr. Stone."

"He's busy."

And with that, she hung up.

6

Six days later:

Dear Rex Stone,

I know that you're probably too busy to answer all your fan mail so let me assure you that while I'm a long time admirer of yours, this letter has to do with a professional matter.

As a published Western author (GUN FURY, Triton Books, 1967 and hundreds of articles in Western and popular culture magazines), I'd like to interview you for a forthcoming book about Western stars of the forties and fifties called: INTO THE SUNSET (Leisure Books).

You may have noticed by my return address that I don't live very far from you. I'd very much like to come up for a day soon, bring my tape recorder, and spend several hours with you discussing your career.

I phoned several days ago but a woman answered and we seemed to have been disconnected or something.

I'd very much like to meet you and help bring your millions of fans up to date on your life. I know that you never attend any of the "Golden Oldie" shows that Gene and Roy and Lash and the others sometimes go to so this would be a particular treat for everybody who has followed your career.

Please let me know your answer at your earliest convenience.

Sincerely yours,

Ken Bromley

7

"Who?"

"Rex Stone."

"Who?"

"Rex Stone. Don't you remember? I used to see all his movies."

"Movies. Hah. Complete waste of time as far as I'm concerned."

And in fact, that had been his mother's opinion all the time Bromley had been growing up, and it was her opinion even now that she was eighty-seven years old and living in a nursing home thanks to the insurance her husband had left her.

But even in a nursing home, she had control of him. She was sort of like the Scarab in one of the old Republic chapter plays. All-knowing. All-seeing. Plus, she had him trained. He always checked with her on anything major, and certainly buying a Trailways ticket was major, even if it was only for eighty miles, even if it was only for a day. She was convinced that she was about to die of a heart attack at any moment and so she wanted him on call twenty-four hours a day. If he wasn't at DeSoto's then he'd better by God be in his apartment. And she certainly didn't like the idea of a trip to Center City.

"Why would you waste your money on him? He doesn't even make movies anymore."

"I want to write an article about him."

"Phoo. Article. They don't even pay you for those things. They only paid you $500 for a whole book. Talk about getting cheated. Why, I read that there Stephen King makes twenty million a year. It was right in *People*."

"It'll only be for a day, Mom. That's all."

"A day? You know how long it takes you to die of a heart attack?" She very impressively snapped her fingers. The sound was of twigs snapping.

They were on the veranda, late afternoon. She had a cigarette going and she was sipping a glass of beer. She'd raised
enough hell with the nursing home people that they gave into
her once every day. One cigarette. One glass of beer.

"I really want to go, Mom. It's real important to me."

How he hated his voice. His groveling. His begging, really.
He was fifty, and nearly bald, and two or three of the clubs he
belonged to gave him "senior rates."

And here he was pleading with this shriveled-up little
woman wound inside a black shawl despite the eighty-eight
degrees.

"He have a phone?"

"Yes."

"You make sure you leave me that number."

"All right, Mom."

"It's all a waste of time if you ask me."

He leaned over and kissed her cheek. "I love you, Mom."

She snorted smoke through her nostrils and said, "You're
more like your father every day."

He knew she didn't mean that as a compliment.

8

"Who?"

"Rex Stone."

"Guess I must be a little young to remember him or
something."

"He was really popular."

"Yeah, I imagine."

Bromley caught the kid's sarcasm, of course. Twerp was
maybe sixteen or seventeen and had an arm's length of blue
tattoos (Bromley's mother had always insisted that a tattoo
was a sure sign of the lower classes) and one tiny silver earring
(which marked him as a lot less than manly, even if a lot of
young men did wear them).

Bromley would've sat with somebody else but this was the
8:30 A.M. Trailways that went to the state capital and so it was
packed with lots of old ladies in big summery hats and so there
was no place else to sit. This was the last empty seat and the
kid had come with it.

"He set an attendance record at the Denver rodeo," Bromley said.

"Oh."

"And in 1949 he came in right behind Roy Rogers as the biggest box office draw."

"Nineteen forty-nine, huh?" The kid shrugged and looked out the bus window.

Bromley put his head back and closed his eyes. The bus engine made the whole bus tremble. The smell of diesel fuel reminded Bromley of boyhood summers, walking down to the Templar Theater to see all the new Saturday matinee movies. It was easy to recall the smell of theater popcorn, too, and the way the sunlight blinded you when you emerged onto the sidewalk six hours later, and the way summer dusk fell, the birds somehow sad in the summer trees, and the girls you saw sometimes, always a little older than you and always blond in a showgirl sort of way, and how they made you ache and how vivid and perfect they remained in your daydreams the whole hot school vacation. Not even after Dr. Fitzsimmons had convinced his mother it was just muscle cramps and not polio at all would she let Bromley go to the movies again. Not until the following summer.

After twenty miles, Bromley opened his eyes again.

Next to him, the kid had this earplug in and his whole body was kind of sit-dancing to the music snaking from the transistor in his lap to the plug in his ear.

The way the kid moved around there—moving and grooving, he thought it was called—struck Bromley as downright obscene.

Bromley closed his eyes again, and thought of the summer he got those funny aches in his legs and his mother went crazy and said he had polio for sure and lit candles to the Blessed Mother all summer and wouldn't let Bromley go to any movie theaters. She said that this was the number-one place for catching polio germs and then she showed him a newspaper photo of a poor little kid inside an iron lung, a photo she always seemed to have handy.

The kid got off way before Center City, and Bromley had the rest of the trip to enjoy by himself. He'd been holding in gas for a long time and it was a pure pleasure to let it go.

9

"Here you go."

"You sure this is the right address?"

"Center Grove, right here."

"But it's a trailer park."

"That's right. Center Grove Trailer Park. See that sign over there?"

Bromley looked and there it was sure enough: green letters on white background, CENTER GROVE TRAILER PARK.

"Huh," Bromley said, "I'll be damned. A trailer park."

Somehow he couldn't imagine Rex Stone living in a trailer. He had an odd thought: Did his horse Stormy live with him in there, too?

He paid the cabbie six bucks, six sweaty ones that had been deep in his summer pocket, and got out, lugging his big old Webcor recorder along with him.

The place was dusty, hot, and midwestern, a high, sloping hill covered with long, modern trailers of the sort that put on the airs of a real house. Lying east and west, bracketing all the metal homes gleaming in the sunlight, were pastures, black and white dairy cows grazing, and distantly a farmer on a green John Deere raising plumes of dust as he did some tilling. A red Piper Cub circled lazily overhead, like a papier-mâché bird.

Each trailer had an address. Just like a house. He supposed he was being a snob, he after all lived in an apartment house, he after all lived in a three-room apartment, but he couldn't help it. People who lived in trailers . . .

And then he remembered: His mother, of course. "People who live in trailers are hillbillies." She'd never offered any proof of this. That was not her way. She'd simply stated it so many times growing up that he'd come to believe it. At least a part of him had.

Hillbillies.

He found the trailer he was looking for. It was an Airstream, one of those silver jobs, and it looked to be a block long and it looked to be almost sinfully tidy as to shell and surrounding lawn. Indeed, bright chipper summer flowers had been planted all along the perimeter of the place. He wondered what his mother would make of that.

He went up and knocked and then there *he* was.

It was a strange feeling.

Here you'd spent all your life with an image of somebody fixed in your mind and then when you meet him—

Well, for him, Rex Stone would always be this tall, hand-

some, slender cuss in the literal white hat astride Stormy. His
Western clothes would have a discreet number of spangles, his
hips would ride a pair of six-guns always ready to impose justice on the lawless, and he'd just generally be—well, heroic.
There was no other word for it. Heroic.

What he would not be was (a) this old guy with a beer belly,
wearing a T-shirt that said I'M AN OLD FART AND PROUD
OF IT, (b) this bald guy wearing a pair of lime green golf pants,
or (c) this fat guy with a beer gut that looked a lot worse than
Bromley's own.

"You Bromley?"

"Uh, yes."

"I'm Stone."

At least he had a strong grip. In fact, Bromley even winced
a little.

Stone hadn't quite shut the door behind him. He said, "Be
right back."

Not even inviting Bromley in or anything.

Bromley stood there listening to the noises of the trailer
park: an obstinate lawn mower somewhere distant; a baby crying; a couple arguing and slamming more doors than you'd
think a trailer could possibly hold; and a radio playing an aching country and western ballad about heartbreak.

Bromley came back out. He carried two folded-up lawn chairs
and a six-pack of Hamms beer.

He didn't say anything, just nodded for Bromley to follow.

On the opposite end of the trailer was an overhang. Some
tiles had been laid down to make a small patio. Here Stone
flicked the chairs into proper position—his motions were young
and powerful, belying his old fart appearance—and then he sat
himself down and nodded for Bromley to do likewise.

"Beer?"

"Thanks," Bromley said. Actually, he didn't care much for
alcohol but he wanted to be polite.

"That's an old one, isn't it?"

Bromley looked at his tape recorder. Indeed it was. A
Webcor, a big heavy box with heads for reel-to-reel tape up
top. Twenty-five years ago a friend of his had desperately
needed money for some now forgotten reason. Bromley had
paid him fifty dollars.

"It still works well, though. Just because it's old doesn't
mean it can't do the job."

Stone laughed a slick Hollywood laugh and winked with great dramatic luridness. "That's what I tell the ladies about myself." Then he leaned forward and with a big powerful hand slapped the arm of Bromley's lawn chair. "Just because I'm old doesn't mean I can't do the job."

Bromley laughed, knowing he was expected to.

Stone seemed to relax some then, sitting back and sipping his beer. He studied Bromley for a while and said, "Sorry, my friend."

"Sorry?"

"Sure. For being this old fart. You know, the way my T-shirt says."

"Well, heck, I—"

"Sure you did."

"I did?"

"Of course. You grew up seeing my movies and you've got this picture of me fixed in your head—this strong, handsome young man—and then you see me—" He shrugged. "I'm an old fart."

"No, you're not. You're—"

Stone waved a hand. "It doesn't bother me, son. It really doesn't. I mean, everybody gets old. Gene did and Roy did and Lash did—and now it's my turn."

Bromley wasn't sure why but he sort of liked it how Stone had called him "son." Made Bromley feel young somehow; as if most of his life (that great golden potential of youth) were still ahead of him and not mostly behind him.

"So you want to wind that puppy up?"

"That puppy?"

"The recorder. That big ole B-52 Webcor."

"Oh. Right. The recorder."

"And I'll tell you how it all started. And how it all ended."

"Yeah. Sure. Great."

So he wound that puppy up and Rex Stone started talking.

10

See, he'd never had any intention of being a movie star. He'd just been visiting in Los Angeles that day in 1934 when he was drinking a malt and having a ham sandwich in this drugstore when he happened to notice that, out on the sunny street, a group of people were standing there watching some kind of accident. Being naturally curious, and being from the Midwest and wanting to bring back all the great stories he could, he went outside to see what was going on, only it wasn't an accident, it was a movie, a bank robbery getaway was being staged, complete with a heart-stoppingly beautiful actress holding a tommy gun and dangling an extra-long cigarette from her creamy red lips, and a fat bald little director who not only wore honest-to-God jodhpurs but also carried a bullhorn and wore, if you could believe it, a monocle over his right eye.

That's how it started, how Presnell, that was the director, saw him standing there on the edge of the crowd, and between shots came over and started talking to him, and then had this very fetching young girl come over and take down his name and the address where he was staying, and four days—literally four days later—he was playing a six-line role in a Western and singing as part of the cowboy singers who backed up the tone-deaf star.

Not that the rest of it came easy. It wasn't overnight or anything. By Stone's estimate he appeared in forty-seven movies (at least twenty of which came from Monogram, for God's sake) before it finally happened. One day Herbert Yates of Republic looked at sagging box office receipts for his Westerns and then decided to give the singing cowboy movies one last try. Yates had been under the impression that singing cowboys had bit the dust about the time television started imposing itself on the American scene. Well, as usual, Herb's gut proved savvy: The Rex Stone pictures, eighteen of them in all, were the biggest-grossing Republic pictures of the era, and came in right behind Roy and Gene in overall grosses. Rex Stone was a star, at least in those small American burgs where the Fourth of July was still a big deal and where men, at least on occasion, still held doors for ladies.

As for Rex personally, he was not only a favorite with the kids, he was also a favorite with the starlets, as Louella Parsons, then the country's premiere gossip columnist, noted with great delight. Rex was a big, handsome lug and don't think he didn't take advantage of it. In one year he was hit with three fists (from jealous husbands), one champagne bottle (from a jealous fiancé), and two paternity suits. It was about then that he started marrying, a practice he kept up until the Rex Stone pictures started losing money and old Herb finally quit turning out Westerns. Some movie historians had him marrying seven times; Rex himself claimed a mere five brides, though he did admit that there was one quickie Mexican marriage that might/might not have been legal. Anyway, the marriages didn't exactly help his popularity. Roy and Gene scrupulously kept their private parts in their pants; Rex seemed to be flaunting his, and in those areas of the country where the Fourth of July still meant something, and where men still opened doors for ladies, his rambunctious behavior with starlets hurt him, and hurt him badly.

Then came the fifties and all those failed TV pilots and TV series. He started looking heavier and older, and then he started flying to Italy, where Westerns were being turned out faster than pizzas, and where Rex Stone, even with something of a gut and something of a balding head, was still a big deal. Meanwhile, he kept on marrying, two brides between 1955 and 1959.

By now the marriages were no longer scandals, they were jokes, the stuff of talk show repartee, and Rex Stone was pretty much finished.

Nobody heard from or about him. Various organizations such as The Cowboy Hall of Fame, which tried to keep members up on news of all the old film stars, did their best to track him down but even when he got the letters, he just tossed them away. He didn't want to go on the rodeo circuit and be this sad old chunky guy on this big golden palomino waving his white Stetson to a crowd of kids who had no idea who he was. He did not want to cut ribbons at supermarket grand openings, he did not want to be surrounded by dozens of sad grotesque aging fans (no offense, Mr. Bromley) at "nostalgia" conventions, he did not want to be featured in every other fanzine about old Western stars, and brag in print about how good movies had been back then and what shit (relatively speaking) they were today.

So for the past twenty obscure years, what he'd been doing was just moving around the country in his Airstream and living in all the places he'd always wanted to live (North Carolina for the beauty and the fishing; Arizona for the climate; New Hampshire for the beautiful autumns and New England sense of tradition and heritage).

11

"Do you ever miss any of them?"

"Any of who?"

"You know, your wives."

"Oh."

"I mean, now that you're older and settled, isn't there one of them it would be nice to have along?"

At this point, Stone started glancing over his shoulder at the rear window.

Bromley hadn't noticed before, but despite the machine noise the air-conditioning unit made, the back window was open about halfway. Bromley wondered why.

"Not really, I guess."

"You ever hear from any of them?"

"Uh, not really."

Then, unable to stop himself from asking this gushy question, Bromley said, "Wanda Mallory, was she as beautiful in person as she was on the screen?"

"She was a bitch and a gold-digger."

The thing was, Rex Stone hadn't said this. He'd just been sitting there holding his beer, with his mouth closed, and then out came the words.

Except the voice wasn't anything like Rex's at all. It was a crone's voice, a harsh cranky old lady's voice, and it had come wafting from the open back window.

Seeing how baffled Bromley looked, Stone said, "Why don't you try and get some sleep, Mother?" He was addressing the partially open rear window.

"You tell him what a little conniver she was. What a little conniver they all were."

"Did you take your medication this morning, Mother?"

"Don't try to change the subject. You tell him the truth about those little harlots."

"Yes, Mother."

"And I mean it."

"Yes, Mother."

"All that money you wasted on them."

"Yes, Mother."

"And I always had the smallest room. The very smallest room."

"Yes, Mother."

And then there was silence and Rex Stone just sat there sort of slumped over in his chair, whipped, beaten, this old man who looked as if some young guy had just delivered a killer blow to his solar plexus. He looked sad and embarrassed, and he even looked a little dazed and confused.

Bromley had no idea what to say.

The voice had reminded him a little of the mother's voice in *Psycho* whenever she got mad at Norman. Or actually (God forgive him) of his own mother's voice.

After a while, still not looking Bromley straight in the eyes, Rex Stone said, "Why don't we hike on up to the rec room? It's a real nice place." One thing: He was whispering his words.

Then he looked nervously up at the open rear window and then he started making these big pantomime gestures that said Follow Me.

Obviously Rex Stone, cowboy star, singer of lush romantic jukebox ballads, wooer and winner of untold gorgeous starlets, was scared shitless of his mom.

12

Ping.

"Every one of them?"

Pong.

"Every single goddamn one of them."

Ping.

"But how?"

Pong.

"Because she got me by the throat the day I was born, and she hasn't let go since."

Ping.

They had been in the recreation hall for twenty minutes. It was a big and presently empty room shady and cool on this hot day, with two billiard tables, a jukebox, a candy machine, a Coke machine, a sign that said I'M A SQUARE DANCER AND PROUD OF IT, and the Ping-Pong table on which Bromley and Rex Stone had been playing for the past ten minutes. Stone was good at it; Bromley not.

"Hell, they even started whispering I was queer," Stone said. "Just married all these women to make things look good, you know, the way some of the actors did but hell, I like girls, not boys."

"So you loved every one?"

"Every single one."

"And your mother broke up each marriage?"

"Every single goddamn one."

"You couldn't get rid of her?"

"Hell, I tried, don't think I didn't, but about the time my

bride and I would move into our new place, my mother would come up with some new ailment and force me to let her move in."

"Is that what she meant by always having the smallest room?"

"Yup."

"So she's pretty much lived with you all your life?"

"All my life, ever since my father died anyway, when I was eighteen."

"And your wives—"

"They'd just get fed up with how she controlled me and then they'd—"

"—leave. They'd leave you. Right?" Bromley said, thinking of his own wife, and how much she'd resented his mother.

"That's exactly what they'd do. Leave."

Ping.

Pong.

The game went on.

And then Rex Stone said it, "You aren't going to put all this stuff about my mom in your article are you, son?"

There was a definite pleading tone in his voice and eyes now.

"No, I'd never do that, Mr. Stone."

"When the hell you going to start calling me Rex?" said the old man at the other end of the pool table.

Bromley smiled self-consciously. "All right—Rex."

"You think you got enough?"

"Yes; yes, I do," Bromley said, and he did, more than enough for a good article about Rex Stone. The fanzine readers would love it.

"You play pool?" Stone said.

"Better than I play Ping-Pong."

"Good. Then let's try a game."

They were each chalking their cues when the black phone on the west wall rang.

Rex glanced at it with genuine alarm.

He shook his head and walked over to it.

"Yes?"

He looked back at Bromley and shook his head. "All right, Mother, so you found me. Now what?"

Now he turned to the wall and muffled his voice, as if he didn't want Bromley to hear a word of it.

"You know how embarrassing this is?"

Pause.

"I'll go to the drugstore tonight. Not right now, Mother."

Pause.

"I get pretty sick of you telling me that I don't take good care of you, Mother."

Pause.

"All right." And then a huge, sad sigh.

Rex Stone hung up and turned back to the phone.

"Maybe I'd better go check on her," he said. "Maybe she really is sick this time. You mind?"

"No, Rex, that's fine."

So they left the recreation hall and went back to the trailer. Nobody, not the little kids, not the mothers pushing strollers, seemed to pay any attention to Rex at all.

Bromley wanted to say: Hey, this is *Rex Stone,* for shit's sake! Rex Stone!

On the way back, Rex told him a couple of stories about Lash Larue and Tim Holt but Bromley could tell that Rex was still embarrassed about his mother's phone call.

Bromley said, "I'll have to be leaving in twenty minutes. There's only one more bus back to town today."

"I've really enjoyed this, son."

"So have I." And then Bromley decided to ask him. Rex would probably just say no, that it was a dumb idea. But what could it hurt to ask?

"Rex?"

"Yup."

"How would you feel about getting dressed up in your cowboy duds and having me take your photo?"

"Ah, hell, son, I don't know about that."

"It'd really go great with this article. Your fans would really appreciate it."

"You think they would?"

"I know they would. They'd love it."

So Rex Stone chewed it over for a while and then shrugged and said, "How about just standing next to the Airstream?"

"That'd be great."

When they got back to the trailer, Rex started whispering again. "Why don't you wait out here, son. I'll go inside and change my clothes and then come back out. All right?"

"Fine."

So while Rex went inside, Bromley went over and got his Polaroid all ready.

Rex didn't come out in five minutes. Rex didn't come out in ten minutes. Rex didn't come out in fifteen minutes.

Bromley could hear it all, oh, not all the words exactly, but certainly he heard the tone of voice. She was chewing on him in a steady stream of rancor that managed to stun and depress even Bromley, who wasn't even directly involved.

Every few minutes, he'd hear Rex say, "All right, Mother," in this really sad, resigned way.

And then it ended all of a sudden and the trailer door opened and there stood Rex Stone in his cowboy costume, the big white hat, the fancy cowboy clothes with spangles and fringes, the big six-guns slung low on his hips, and his trustworthy guitar dangling from his right hand.

Bromley hadn't realized till this moment just how old Rex Stone was.

How the whole face sagged into jowls.

How the whole gut swelled over the gunbelt.

How the hands were liver-spotted and trembling.

"I sure feel silly in this getup, son," Rex said.

"But you look great."

"You sure about that?"

"I'm sure about that, Rex." Bromley waved his hand a little and said, "How about a step or two to the right, just to the side of the door."

And it was at that exact moment that the trailer door opened and out stepped a little Kewpie doll of a woman, no more than four-eight, four-nine, no more than eighty pounds, no more than two or three hundred years old, buried inside of some kind of gaudy pink K mart wrapper, her feet swathed in matching pink fluffy slippers that went *thwap, thwap, thwap* as she came down the stairs and took her place next to her son.

"I forgot to tell you," Rex Stone said. "Mom asked if she could be in the picture, too."

13

He tried for the next six weeks to write the article. Every few days, Rex would call and say, "Just wanted to see how it was going, son," and would then say, "You, uh, haven't mentioned my mom or anything in it, have you?" and Bromley would say, "Uh, no, Rex, I, uh, haven't."

But for some reason he couldn't write the piece.

Every time he started it, it was just too bleak. Here was a

guy who'd been in a very real prison all his life (not unlike
Bromley). Here was a guy who kept trying to break away and
break away but couldn't (not unlike Bromley). Here was a guy
who had obviously wanted to spend his life with beautiful
women but whose mother just didn't like the idea (not unlike
Bromley).

So how could you write a piece about a guy who'd been a
hero to Bromley's whole generation . . . and tell the glum truth?

Because it was a pretty pathetic story.

14

Rex called two days after Bromley mailed him the article.

"Son," he said.

"Yes?"

"I—"

And then he made a familiar sound. "You know what that
is, son?"

"You're blowing your nose?"

"Right. And you know why?"

"Why?"

"Because your article made me cry. And not cry for sad, son.
Cry for happy."

"I'm glad you like it, Rex."

"I don't like it, son. I love it."

"I wasn't sure how you'd feel about it. I mean, I took certain
liberties and I—"

"Son, you done good. You done real, real good."

15

The day the fanzine arrived, Bromley sat down in his recliner
and started reading it, the way he did with all his own articles.

He turned back the cover and flipped through the pages till
he saw the picture of Rex.

He'd stuck to the older photos. He certainly hadn't used the
one with Rex's mother in it.

And then he read the caption under the photo of a young
Rex as the cowboy star: "Here's a heartwarming article about
cowboy film giant Rex Stone and how he's spent his life living
on a horse ranch in Montana, sharing his bountiful life with
his beautiful wife and three children."

Just the kind of life Bromley had always wished for himself. A wife and three children.

Just the kind of life his generation would have expected Rex Stone to live.

16

"You haven't called me for a long time."

"I called you the night before last, Mother," Bromley said.

"I could be dead for all you care."

"Yes, Mother."

And then he thought of Rex Stone's ranch in Montana, Rex and his beautiful starlet wife and their three perfectly behaved children.

He'd go visit Rex there someday soon.

Very soon.

That's just what he'd do.

"Are you listening to me?"

"Yes," Bromley said. "Yes, Mother, I always listen to you."

Someday very soon now.

Morris Hershman

A PRIVATE VENGEANCE

Morris Hershman has written virtually if not literally every type of popular fiction imaginable.

Among many other awards, he's won the Edgar and written a handful of crime stories that are considered classics.

Here Hershman shows that his skills apply equally well to the Western, a form he wrote at some length back in the seventies when, as Sam Victor, he penned an action Western series that proved to be extremely popular.

The angry-looking youth was pitched forward into the dim cool bunkhouse, losing his balance just as the door was decisively shut and held that way from the other side. As he was putting both palms down to the scarred boards to help him rise he felt part of a fiber riata circle a wrist, then the other just before being drawn tight enough.

He must have thought it was some kind of a prank. "Come on, hombres, what in hell's backyard is this?"

On his feet he expected to see friends who would congratulate him on his recent luck and at least a dozen sporting ladies or other range calico for him to choose from after a long drought of female company. But there was no one in the bunkhouse except an older man standing with strong fists clenched and knuckles whitened. No, wait. A woman, too, standing with legs apart and between the males as if to keep both in place.

"No joke." Stuart Weston's words were neutral, but his usually flat voice throbbed with anger.

"What do you want, duffer?" The young one turned shrill

as he recognized Weston, but he was angry instead of being frightened. "If you want to hustle hard money or soft, I can set that up right quick soon as I'm let go."

"What I want is to see you dead. What I really want."

The woman moved calmingly in response. It wasn't easy to recognize Verna Weston, the rancher's longtime wife. She looked different from that quietly dressed female in the court-room at Billings. Three years had surely changed the woman who had suffered under her skin, and changed her rancher husband, too.

"Look, I'm sorry for what happened. I said so in court to the judge and everybody else. It was printed in the papers."

"And you bein' sorry is enough to fix this, huh? Enough to bring my Bonnie back to life, sure—but I tell you this: I don't see my Bonnie anywhere."

"Don't you think I'd bring your daughter back to life if I could?" He wasn't so worried, now. Peter Coffey, wearing mint-fresh rigging for a party, took it for granted that everything would be fixed up after a while, just as 'most always for him. "I never meant to do that. It—happened is how it was."

"Bad things only happen to other people, only to a young girl who is disgustingly murdered. And to her folks, who are in mourning while they watch a gang of high-priced rustlers—I mean lawyers—come into court and steal you from justice by insistin' it was Bonnie's fault anything bad took place, pouring filth over the reputation of an innocent God-fearin' youngster who their client killed in cold blood."

Peter Coffey had been going to say something and stand up for himself. One look at the couple's eyes, the man's agleam with hate and the old gal's probably as dead as their daugh-ter's, and he clamped his lips drum-tight.

"Nothin' goes really wrong for a murderer, not if he's the son of rich people." A deep, jagged breath was drawn up from the tortured man's throat. "Sure he's found guilty even up in Bill-ings where the trial was transferred to, but he's only sentenced to fifteen to thirty years, less time off if'n he behaves in prison. My Bonnie received a death sentence from you, you carried it out, and she's still dead . . . . Dry up! One word and you die . . . . The parents have got friends in politics and they pull the right drawstring, so the walkin' buffalo chip as killed my Bon-nie, he's free in three years. Those parents in Billings—they still have a child, God damn 'em to hell!"

Peter Coffey had been brought here by men who called themselves friends and who he was too elated to recognize, men who swore it'd serve old Weston right to have a celebration on the Box W grounds. Instead of range calico and fine food helping him swing a wide loop again, he was swallowing air and cooled spittle.

"Three years and you're free 'a justice, free 'a obligations, while my Bonnie is still dead."

"I told you I'm sorry. What else can I say?"

Weston paid no attention. "The law didn't carry out your sentence, but I've always been law-abidin', an' I want the law to abide by me. Where the law has been hog-tied, me an' my wife are gonna step in."

"What will you people"—the sound that escaped Peter Coffey's lips was an angry hiss—"you won't do nothin' to me. You won't do nothin'."

Coffey started the fight with a bruising punch to Stuart Weston's kidney and a hammer blow to the older man's strong right arm, but the prison years had cost him some part of his physical condition. Weston, calculating because he had to use his left hand alone, took two blows to drop Peter Coffey out of consciousness.

He could have killed his girl's murderer in half a dozen different ways and wanted to use every one of them, but it wasn't what he and Verna had arranged to get done. They followed the plan that the two of them had originally agreed on.

*

One of Doc Quinn's hoss pills, as Weston called them, eased the pain in his left arm and kidney after the recent uproar, and he managed a full night's sleep. After breakfast with Verna, he reheated coffee and put the mug on a tin tray with eggs. He stepped into the spring sunshine that hugged the stone ranch house his father had built when he combined two ranches into the sprawling Box W, the house cradled by twin hills. One of the hands heard his steps in the dirt and looked down at him from a gray gelding. Recognizing one of the helpers in last night's mission, Weston circled his thumb and forefinger in the timeworn OK symbol.

During the last year he had built a wooden shack behind the house at a grove of rambling cottonwoods. The sight of his own successful work ought to have pleased him, but nothing had pleased him in the past three years and five months. And nine days.

He opened the door. Inside, past a stove for which there was no need at this time of year, was another room that looked almost like a horse stall. A faraway window behind him poured a thimbleful of spring Montana sunshine slantwise down on the black-painted stall. Black for perpetual mourning.

Peter Coffey had ignored the bunk put down for his use, nor was he using the wooden chair or wooden table. He sat on the floor, unmoving.

Weston pushed the food tray into the space taken from the bars for that purpose. "You're going to serve out your sentence, getting two months off for good behavior every year over the next twelve, or two months tacked on for bad behavior. You'll be here for twelve years only; you've already served three years of your sentence of fifteen to thirty, and I intend to see the law carried through."

Coffey half opened his mouth in protest, but it was clear he didn't know any use for it and he had no intention of talking to Weston.

"My daughter will be dead in every minute you spend here, which is your fault and nobody else's." The words came out of a bottomless well of anger. "If'n I didn't b'lieve in the law— God's and man's law, both—I'd have busted your neck last night."

*

Weston went out to get a horse and look at how the longhorns were shaping for the fall roundup. He gave instructions to Hawk Galen, his hardworking foreman, about the care and treatment of some steers who looked a little peaked. He was careful in that matter, and for once left very little to Galen's judgment.

Except for the living animals, he hadn't shown much interest in keeping up with Box W, not since the disaster. He left most of the paperwork to Verna and some chores that most hands hated because each one thought of himself as less than a man if he didn't have sturdy horseflesh between his legs.

What remained left of the afternoon was spent cutting string for new hands, not picking the best horses for each and certainly not the worst. His father had taught him to be fair in dealing with workers, and Weston's memory was long.

In dealing with the prisoner, his judgment wasn't always as good. Over the next months he was unintentionally late in closing the hut window after rain was well under way. He delayed lighting the hut's oil stove, and made a point later of lighting it before time. He collected spare clothes from hands, nothing that was a prime fit. To his disgust, though, he had to send away for boots. To make him more angry, he sent away a second time because something was wrong with the pair he ordered for Coffey. He ended up ordering six pairs so he wouldn't have to do it again.

He had wanted to be the only one who dealt with Coffey, but ranch business sometimes kept him away. He happened to be cross-fencing and helping to dig postholes the first time Verna brought a meal to him. She said that Coffey was becoming fat, which wasn't healthy. She wanted him spending one hour in the morning and one in the afternoon under guard in such fresh air that might drift into a fenced-off area around the hut.

The devil became sick first, resulting in the discreet Dr. Seamus Quinn being called. The doctor turned a deaf ear to Coffey's attempts at talking about his imprisonment. A dentist did some work under Weston's sharp eye, making it clear he was being paid too well to care about some young fool's senseless story.

Coffey's mind had to be preserved, too. Weston would bring a copy of the *Hungry Horse Weekly Chronicle* after he and Verna got through reading it. Verna, who brought it in every so often, didn't think it was ever touched by the sullen prisoner.

*

Coffey managed a short escape from the fenced-off yard while Weston was signing to his deaf Chinese houseman only a dozen yards off. He was found less than a hundred feet away, hurrying as best he could past a stand of winter-ravaged spruce. The scruffy, bearded, once-active prisoner couldn't move quick enough, and Weston needed no help to bring him back, monkey-tying his hands behind him. Weston knew better than to touch the prisoner needlessly. It would have been too easy to finish this agony once and for all by a murder.

*

"Two extra months." Verna always sounded and looked tired these days. "He couldn't have got away, Stuart. What difference could it make if we let him go two months later or earlier?"

"It lets him know he can't get away with anything."

"He must'a learned that by now."

Weston stared at his wife's recently lined forehead, at the crow's nests under both eyes, the tension lines from nostril ends to lips.

"All right, we'll let him out as if this had never took place."

Thank you. The words hung between man and wife.

"I won't tell him, though," Weston said doggedly. "Let that murdering filth sweat it."

★

Verna brought a hot dinner of johnnycake, coffee, and what she called lamb leggings to the prisoner on a chill winter evening. She was deep in thought when she came back.

"He's not even like his usual recent self, and his face looks red whenever I see him."

Weston had just got done arguing with his foreman, insisting that the only branding done at Box W from now on would take place in the corral because his own tests with a few helpers had proved how much easier it could be on the hands. Hawk Galen, the foreman, had been discreetly against making things too easy for them, so Weston wasn't in the best mood for listening to reason.

"I just saw him yesterday," he said, holding his temper, "and I think you're wrong."

The strain of standing up for her daughter's killer was plain in Verna's suddenly higher voice. "We swore to behave as much as possible just like he was in a real prison, and that means we have to keep him in good health."

"Well, if you want, I'll call Quinn to have a look."

"Yes." *Didn't we promise to take care of the jackal?*

★

"All I give him was one of my all-purpose pills, what you call my hoss pills," Dr. Seamus Quinn reported on the following afternoon. He was a middle-aged local man whose wife had been set upon and beaten in the course of a stagecoach robbery not long back, so he was ready to help keep the Westons' secret. "He hasn't talked to me after the first time I saw him, but I think something might be wrong with his teeth. He could be having a dental problem."

"Thanks, Seamus. I'll send for Dr. Erroll and have Verna write you a check first."

"No need, hombre. If you can make a contribution to lowering the crime rate, so can I." Just before Weston took him out to his spanking-new carriage, the grizzled veteran physician glanced wonderingly at husband and wife. "All these years in Montana, and people still surprise me."

*

The dentist came out while Weston was talking about cattle prices to the rep—he hadn't gone on a roundup since Bonnie's tragedy, so he gave sensible suggestions instead. He got back to the ranch house after the dentist was packing up the portable equipment he had brought along.

"Didn't you notice that the patient is having trouble opening his mouth?" Rufus Erroll sounded annoyed by the Westons' lack of knowledge. "He must've complained how his jaw hurts nearly all the time."

Dr. Erroll was in the forties, a man who had lost three of five children, with only a slow girl and a lazy son left to him. He never took a fee as such from the Westons, but asked instead for what he called a financial favor to help keep the daughter after he was gone, "borrowing" twenty dollars in the wake of every inspection.

"The patient prob'ly grinds his teeth a lot while he sleeps," Erroll mused. "Very painful, they tell me."

Too bad. "Can you do anything for him?"

"I'll drop in once a month and check him out. Maybe I can fit him for a steel block he could wear in his mouth at night. Sometimes that cuts down on the problem."

The dentist must have been distracted because this was the first time Verna paid him without having been asked for "a very small—um, financial favor."

*

This particular domestic argument got under way on an exceptionally beautiful evening in early spring. Verna had gone to church in town and run into some lady friend with whom she spent a few very pleasant hours.

"Why don't we let him go?" she asked, the words coming unbidden over not-too-stringy bison haunch at supper.

Stuart Weston was glad that his wife had spent a fine day pleasantly, but wouldn't let himself be swerved from a set course. "We both agreed to hold him for as long as his prison sentence would've lasted, and it's only been seven years so far. October will be eight years."

"If there's any trouble with the law over what we've done, Stuart, we'd be—separated."

"Sheriff Gober won't kick up over it, as public feeling will be strong for us as having done what was right. Besides, half the town knows what we're doing in so-called secret, and is on our string, too, not to mention our hands. If the jackal talks afterward, why, who is there to back up whatever he might say?"

For once she withdrew from the comfort of his outstretched hand. "But what about us, dear?"

"We're doing what we swore to do."

"People can change their minds. We could eventually take another short trip East to Cincinnati. It's bad to keep doing this, to ruin our feelings for each other in arguing all the time 'stead of helping each other in such time as is left to us."

"I know it's hard, yes, but there isn't any institution willing to serve justice and carry out his sentence. What else can we do for Bonnie's eternal rest?"

★

Verna's own teeth were gritted at the prospect of seeing her daughter's murderer again, but Stuart was busy preparing screw-worm medicine for each of the hands, and she didn't want him going near anybody's supper at this time. Less than half an hour after Dr. Erroll left, she went to the hut earlier than usual. It was still possible to see vagrant traces of sunlight risen from the timberline.

Not till she was close enough to speak clearly and be heard did she suddenly draw back, alerted to his manner without knowing why. It was already too late. Coffey had taken his right hand from behind his back and was firmly holding a shiny .44 Colt, a model that the military man's daughter fearfully recognized.

He gestured to the wall at his left, where the cell key was held in a ring on a nail for use in emergencies.

Verna shook her head, refusing to talk in turn.

He deftly eased a bullet out of the cylinder so she could be sure that the gun might kill. He returned the bullet to its place, his finger tightening on the trigger as he raised it to point at her.

If he had to shoot the lock off he'd waste one bullet at least, but there was no way of being sure that his bitter anger might not make him shoot her first no matter what the consequences might be.

Taking the key ring off the wall, she hurled it at the wall of his cell. As it struck a steel bar and dropped to the dirty floor, she was turning to run.

She knew she had to go back to the house and warn Stuart, hoping she would be too far away for Coffey's gunfire to reach her by the time he freed himself.

She suddenly heard the shot.

Her back was on fire now, but she hardly felt herself falling. The smells of warm earth, leaves, and minty grass meant nothing to her. The sound of that bullet to her back must have acted as a warning to Stuart, who had expected her to come back almost immediately.

She tried raising herself to hands and knees. Moving despite pain, she couldn't tell how much time had passed. She didn't know why Coffey chose not to come up behind her and use the gun butt to destroy her.

But she heard his hurrying footsteps and knew he was running to the house to confront Stuart immediately now that her husband had been warned. She hoped it was possible for her to get to the house. Whatever happened, she wanted to be near her husband.

Dizzy with pain and hardly able to think, she was moving in lizard fashion when she heard another shot from the direction of the ranch house.

Appalled because she knew her husband certainly wouldn't have been carrying a revolver in his own home, she was almost grateful when a curtain descended across her eyes and the very surroundings meant nothing to her any longer.

*

Stuart was two rooms away from the kitchen when he heard a shot outdoors. He had been hard at work with a gallon bottle and a tin funnel over its mouth. A gigantic jar of perisylic ointment, intended to heal in the aftereffects of screw-worm medicine to be used on calves, lay open at one side. At the other side was a jar of axle grease to keep calves from blistering on account of the third ingredient, which lay in a six-ounce bottle directly in front of him. Weston made up the screw-worm medicine two times a year because he didn't trust his hands to put up their own. Each hand kept a bottle, according to Stuart's rigid instructions, on his saddle in case of need.

When he heard that shot, the medium-sized bottle containing the third ingredient shook slightly on the table. Though aware of imminent danger, Weston had to take time to cork that bottle securely. He was about to lower the cork in the bottle mouth when he heard the outside door opening swiftly, heard booted steps surge into his home.

Coffey was there and now running into the room. A revolver was in his right hand. Even in that split moment Weston found himself thinking that it was the money-hungry dentist, Rufus Erroll, who had smuggled it in to him. Weston hoped he would live long enough to make his feelings known to that man.

At this time, though, he wouldn't run. He bent down so he was out of sight and upended the table. There was another shot, and a bottle crashed as the bullet dug into that sturdy table, its contents spilling to the floor and onto Peter Coffey's boots and clothes and skin. Peter Coffey screamed once, and his second scream was cut off in the middle . . . .

"Carbolic acid," Stuart told his wife when Verna was almost ready to get out of bed. Dr. Quinn had pulled the bullet out of her and called her the luckiest woman in Montana and on the Idaho border as well. Verna didn't doubt it.

"I suppose carbolic acid *is* strong enough to kill if it lands in certain places on the body," she said, having considered the answer to her question.

"Quinn thinks that the jackal swallowed some of it, too, after the shot scattered that liquid," Weston said.

Quietly she asked, "Has there been any trouble over what happened?"

Briefly, wanting to change the subject, he told her that for once he had asked two hands to make a pine coffin, and Peter Coffey had been buried on a rectangle of sod bounded by brush near the southern border of Box W. There had been no ceremony, there would be no marker—and, of course, no one raised questions. Who wasn't on his and Verna's side in regard to that hellish ordeal?

"What I've wanted most over the seven years was for that jackal to be dead," Weston remarked, pensive. "I suppose it's shameful that I keep telling myself how grateful I am that he's gone where he belonged, but I can't help myself."

Sympathetically, she took his hand and squeezed it.

On the next Sunday, for the first time in almost seven years, the Westons left their ranch together. In town, they went to church and prayed for Bonnie's eternal repose. Leaving, they encountered friends they hadn't noticed in a long time. Responding to a hesitant greeting, Verna smiled warmly. Stuart paused, then felt his lips thinning contentedly in the beginnings of a genuine smile. The sun was climbing higher in a cloudless sky as the two couples walked together, and the Westons felt themselves touched by a breeze that they found pleasant, even invigorating.

Gary Lovisi

ENOUGH ROPE

Gary Lovisi is involved in crime fiction in a number of ways. He's publisher of the excellent Paperback Parade. His Gryphon Press books are among the best example of small-press art.

Over the past few years he's also found time to begin his own writing career, with a number of sales to mystery anthologies and magazines.

Here is Gary Lovisi's first Western story.

I

Hangings were always such festive occasions. The country folk would trek in from the outlaying farms and ranches for miles around—especially when it was a real important hanging. You know the kind, when a real "bad one" was gonna get his due. A first-class neck-stretching, "just deserts" everyone would say as they proceeded to watch the entertainment. And the good people of Pleasantville could always be counted on to be sure to have enough rope to do the job properly.

Today was a particularly interesting day for me—for I was the guest of honor, so to speak—I was the one gonna get my neck stretched 'til I was deader than dead. I had been a bad boy!

The name's Jack Ransom. Entrepreneur. Salesman of sorts and a jack-of-all-trades by the accounts of some of the gentler spirits in the town. Sharp-ass rogue and crook was what some others would say. They wouldn't be all that incorrect either. I was a bank robber, and I had the gumption to make a substantial withdrawl in Pleasantville. Not once, but twice.

So it is perhaps understandable that on this particular occasion the good folk of Pleasantville were in an angry mood. They all wanted me hung real bad, but you see an unexpected problem had cropped up—they'd run out of rope. Why, there wasn't more than a few feet of thick-gauge, prime-hanging, neck-stretching rope in the entire town. And believe me, they turned that town upside down looking for it—but there just wasn't any to be found. Anywhere. Even Old Man Furley's general store was plum out of good, quality hanging rope. More's the pity, they all said to themselves, with all kinds of disappointment and such on their long farmer's faces.

"Have to send away for it. Out to Carson City," Furley said, slightly dejected. "Could end up being a week or more before I get another shipment."

"That's terrible," Sheriff Hodges said. He was a right-proper upholder of the law—the kind of fella that in this case, at least, believed wholeheartedly in the axiom "Justice delayed is justice denied." I wasn't as eager as everyone else for "justice" under the circumstances. You can understand why.

But Sheriff Hodges pursued his duty with a dogged determination. "We just gotta do something. Furely. That no-good Jack Ransom gotta hang—or at least be executed in a properly approved and lawful manner. He's got an appointment with death and it's my duty to see that he keeps it."

I never did like that sheriff very much, and now I think I now why, for he came up with all kinds of fanciful suggestions for my imminent demise. Thereby ending a life, which by the way, I had gotten overly fond of and attached to.

"What about shooting?" Judge Creedy suggested with the aplomb of a drunken circut judge, of which he had much actual experience. "One bullet in the head ought to do it."

"Yeah," Sheriff Hodges replied. "A firing squad would be fine. Put on a nice show and be all legal to boot."

"And we ain't had one of them in nigh on twenty years in this here state. Hangin' bein' the natural way to exterminate varmints." I heard Old Man Furley reminisce with a twinkle in his eye. The old coot would probably be the one to sell the bullets, and turn a dandy profit. Then he continued. "I'd like to see you cut him down, sheriff, after the things that wise-acre thought he could get away with in your town."

The sheriff reddened, barely repressing his anger over my banking deeds. Then, as if doing a double take, he added, "Now wait a minute, Sid, I'm the sheriff here, not an executioner. I'm not the one to carry out any death sentence."

"Well, I sure as hell ain't!" Sid Furley said. "I can barely aim a gun as it is. I just sell them, don't use them."

"And I'm a judge" came forth the venerable voice of His Honor as he took another draught of the stout Mexican ale. "It wouldn't be proper for me to shoot him—though I'd kinda like to try it—I fear it might be construed as some kinda conflict of interest, seeing as it was I who pronounced the said sentence on him in the first place."

"So who's gonna shoot him!" Sheriff Hodges said with growing impatience. And though they asked for volunteers, no one came forward. These were simple people after all, farmers and shopkeepers, not executioners. No one wanted the blood of another on their hands—all they wanted to see was the entertainment promised them by the town leaders.

*

"The guy is sentenced to die in a couple of hours," Judge Creedy elaborated. "And we're not even agreed on the method, much less on who will carry out the execution. This is turning into a fiasco."

There was a momentary silence around the table as each man furiously thought of a way out of their precarious predicament. It didn't look very good at all. With the crowd growing ever larger outside the jail with every passing minute, with public expectations running so high, and the atmosphere so full of festivity and anticipation at the impending show, something had to be done and done soon. Otherwise the sheriff, the judge, and the entire town elders of Pleasantville would be shown to be a bunch of fools. The sheriff might lose his job, the judge might be disbarred or never see another reelection, and all the people of Pleasantville would soon be the laughing-stock of the West. Why, a town that couldn't even find enough rope to hang one of their most wanted desperadoes was hardly deserving of any respect at all!

The men around the table thought up scheme after scheme, only to discard each of them one by one, and found themselves in an ever deepening quandary with time running out by the minute.

"Bring out the varmint!" shouted an angry voice from outside as a bottle was thrown at the jail window, to smash upon the iron bars and spray the room with tiny shards of dark green particles. "We know how to deal with bank robbers!"

"Come on, Judge," Sheriff Hodges said as he watched the crowd growing ever larger outside. "You're the brainpower, here. Think up something!"

Judge Creedy took another swig of his favorite inner lubricant, belched a foul whiff of breath that almost caused Old Man Furley to gag, and then said, "I think I got an idea."

"Well, come on, Judge, don't let it grow cobwebs. What is it?" Furley grumbled.

"Well, we get young Jebialiah Jones, put him on Harry Winslow's, Lightnin' . . ."

"Yeah?"

". . . and send him after the Dark Man."

There was a long pause around the table.

"You mean that guy . . . ?" Furley stuttered.

"The state executioner—the traveling killer?" Sheriff Hodges added with evident distaste. "I don't really cotton to that fella, too damn spooky for my blood, and he seems to like his job a little too much."

"Well, he's in the vicinity, and he's willing. He works fast and cheap," the judge replied. "And besides that, the townsfolk enjoy a Dark Man hanging. People say he's one man that knows just how to stretch a neck to get the most out of a lynching."

Well, you can imagine that didn't go over too good from where I was sitting—which was alone in my jail cell with the nervous twitches. I'd heard rumors about the Dark Man, of course. Why, Dirty Ted Grundy, a varmint desperado what rode with the James Gang once, even quit the damn trade over it. He found out that the Dark Man would be a-hanging him once he was caught. Said he'd rather get a day job and work honestlike.

I guess Sheriff Hodges said it all when he said, "No one wants to see Ransom swing as much as I do, Judge. But the Dark Man . . . ? I mean, hangings all well and good, but this man ain't . . . really . . . human."

"Yeah, yourn Honor, sir," Old Man Furley spoke respectfully. "This Dark Man fella scares the squat right outta me."

"Well, we have to do something, and calling in the Dark Man seems our only alternative."

"Yeah, I agree but . . ." Furley muttered and then was silent.

"Have we got a choice?" Judge Creedy added. He was almost disappointed to see that the other men around the table all agreed with him. He sighed and said, "Okay then, Sid, call in Jebialiah Jones, and then hustle over to Harry Winslow and have him saddle up Lightnin'."

II

The plains were long and dry, with a hot wind and searing sun. The grasses were burned brown and the earth a choked mass of gray dust and parched plants straining brittle leaves vainly skyward.

Jebialiah Jones was a good horseman, and a young lad who listened to his elders, but he wasn't no friend to the Dark Man. He'd seen the fella once and he had damn near spooked young Jones, but his duty was made plain by Sheriff Hodges, and the mission did give him an opportunity to ride Harry Winslow's beloved Lightnin'—probably the swiftest little mare in the entire state.

So he rode the rugged terrain and finally saw the outline of the wagon and oxen way ahead on the horizon. A silhouette of deathly blackness against the fire-burning red of the sun. He spurred the little mare onward, drawing in closer and closer, as the sun beat one wave of dry heat after the other down upon his head.

It was an eerie landscape, made more eerie as he approached the wagon of the Dark Man.

It was an all-black wagon. And that wasn't good to see. It was entirely covered by wood and colored in dusky nightshade. There were strange signs and devices painted on the sides in gold and silver script and fearful drawings of skulls and hanging figures that worked as effective advertisements proclaiming the Dark Man's chosen trade—Death Merchant!

Jones rode up warily, approaching the dark figure seated upon the motionless wagon, and had the prickly feeling the man had somehow known of his mission and had been waiting for him all along.

"Jebialiah Jones, one of the young men of Pleasantville, no doubt," said the mysterious cowled figure in a rasping tone. Jones, shocked at how the Dark Man had known his name, shivered appreciably. For a moment Jones had completely lost his voice as his eyes widened at the strange apparition of the man that sat looking down at him with piercing orbs of red fire.

The figure of the Dark Man was entirely draped in obscuring black cloth and cowl, much like one of the Spanish monks young Jones had seen in the desert churches—but there was nothing of a religious nature about this fellow. His hands were long, boney, white-fingered things, encrusted with all manner of strange baubles and rings. His face was hidden under the cowl, but Jones got the strong feeling that he would not have wanted to view that grim visage even had he the opportunity to do so. Better that it was obscured from his view, he thought with a thankful sigh.

The Dark Man sat quiet and still, evidently a patient fellow, and just as evidently waiting for Jones to continue with his words.

Jones gulped loudly, summoned his courage, and quickly said, "Sheriff Hodges sent me. They planned to hang the outlaw Jack Ransom today. The sheriff and Judge Creedy want to know if you'll take the job."

"Well, well, I see employment staggers to my door, so to speak," the hidden voice issued forth in a sharp rasp, much like a knife being sharpened on a dull stone. "And what of the fee for my services?"

"Well?" Jones muttered, trying to think up the exact words Judge Creedy had told him to tell the Dark Man before he'd drunk himself into oblivion. "Ah, the judge said for me to tell you, sir, that your usual fee would be acceptable."

For a moment there was intense quiet. Then the wind howled up off the ridge and blew the dried earth into Jones's face, causing him to shield his eyes for a moment. When he looked up again, it was to see the dim form of the Dark Man's wagon racing across the prairie at a furious pace—racing with mad abandon toward the small town of Pleasantville.

III

Man, oh, man, oh, man, was I in deep and desperate trouble! Jack Ransom, rogue and robber, petty scoundrel and fornicator, sitting in a stinking four-by-four cell in Pleasantville, a helpless prisoner who was gonna get his neck stretched with proper crudation, as they sometimes say up North—by the Dark Man.

What had begun as an all-around bad day now appeared to be able to go no worse at all. I'd really hit the skids.

"You can't do it!" I cried to Sheriff Hodges, Judge Creedy, even to old man Furley, or to anyone else who would listen— "Hanging's one thing, but a Dark Man hanging is . . ." And I rubbed my throat and then felt at my fluttering heart, ". . . a Dark Man hanging takes the soul right outta a man. He ain't human, sheriff, and I don't wanna die that way! See, it ain't so much the dying I mind, hell, sheriff, my life's been pointed that way since I left home maybe, but I'm scared, scared of what will come . . . after."

Judge Creedy raised his head to my pleas, burped loudly, and then fell back into his drunken stupor once again. Old Man Furley just shook his head and muttered, "Well, I gotta be gettin' back to my store now." And then he was gone faster than a pack rat after a drawerful of shiny silver spoons.

"Sorry, son," Sheriff Hodges said with some sort of feeling. "What's gotta be, just gotta be."

And then I heard the rumble of the mob outside, the tumultous sound of racing hooves entering the street, and the frantic clack of wagon wheels. Finally a whip cracked, accompanied by a loud screech as I heard a wagon come to a sharp halt right outside the front of the jail.

The Dark Man had arrived.

For a long moment there was silence outside in the street, and silence inside the jail as well. Then as though an ill wind had suddenly gusted, the door to the jail flew open with a resounding crack, and framed within the doorway, his blackness surrounded by the fire-red rays of the setting sun, stood the dreaded Dark Man himself.

I shuddered and the grim and terrible visage leered down at me and then slowly approached the sheriff.

"I take it this is the prisoner?" the Dark Man said with such hunger and calm deliberation that Sheriff Hodges barely knew what to say.

He finally nodded and mumbled a lame remark. "We had to call you in. . . ."

"I hear that you ran out of rope" was the Dark Man's response as his head moved to scan the jail, much like a great mantis would stalk its helpless prey.

"Ah, well, yes. . . ." Hodges replied slowly.

"That is one problem that I can assure you will never happen where I am concerned." The Dark Man added in a chilling whisper, "I am always sure to carry enough rope."

Well, my throat muscles sort of tightened involuntarily at that point. I could almost feel those long, white, boney fingers of fleshless death as they placed the noose around my neck. It certainly wasn't a pleasant thought, and it was one that I was somehow determined should not come to pass.

And then the Dark Man moved closer to the bars of my cell

and peered at me with such a malevolent gaze that I found myself involuntarily shrinking back a few paces.

"It is quite useless," he said to me in a dreadful whisper. "You are thinking, rogue that you are, of beating me and winning your freedom. But I am the master of this little game, and the game here is death—of which I am always the winner."

Well, I hardly knew what to make of this at first, but I wasn't going to let him get away with those kinda statements without me getting in a few choice words as well.

"Pretty talk from a killer for hire who ain't got the balls to fight like a real man," I said, practically running off at the mouth with panic and dread and damned near desperation. "You don't scare me a bit and you're gonna find I'm a lot tougher than you ever considered."

"I am intrigued," he hissed a moment later, though his stark form and hidden face showed no sign whatsoever of any emotion. I could imagine his smile as he added, "I can feel your fear of me, and yet I sense a certain power and bravery within you that is most unusual." Then the damned fellow turned to Sheriff Hodges and said, "A most interesting case, sheriff, most interesting. I believe I will forgo my usual fee, in lieu of another recompense."

Sheriff Hodges blinked a couple of times trying to look the Dark Man in the eye, but then only lowered his gaze and stammered. "What do you mean? What is it you want?"

The Dark Man turned a death-head glance toward me and then back to the sheriff. "I believe this man a danger, he should be hung immediately. I desire, as payment for my work, sole possession of his earthly remains."

The sheriff gulped. "But all he's got this side of hell is his life and soul."

"Then those will be sufficient."

"You can't do that!" I shouted. But the sheriff, as though in some kind of a terrible trance responded with a slow and very lackluster nod—as he quietly walked out of the jail.

The Dark Man and I were alone now.

I felt the shiver of his gaze upon me but fought off the feeling and gave him what for, by looking back at him with a hardness I never thought I'd possessed. My eyes sought his face and for a moment seemed to pierce through the obstructing cowl—and what I saw there—what I *thought* I saw there—was nothing even remotely human.

And then I knew that the Dark Man was death itself, the Grim Reaper loose upon the prairie, in a forever insatiable quest to seek the dead—and in places where there was an absence of death—to create it to nurture it, to see that death reigned supreme through the land.

Well, I was in pretty bad trouble, all right. As my old granny used to say, merely waking up from this here nightmare wasn't going to make this bogeyman go away at all. But Granny Ransom always had a lot to say on a lot of topics, fiesty old coot that she was—and she'd fought off death, nigh on a dozen times—and won! What's more, old Granny Ransom had told me how she did it—it was an ace up my sleeve that I was gonna use to my advantage come hell or high water against this here Dark Man.

Actually Granny said it was all really quite simple—when death come alooking for you— just tell him you ain't home! You ain't interested! You ain't going nowhere! He's wasting his time! Eventually, if you can ignore him, don't let him scare you, and be sensible about it and realize that death'll claim you sooner or later—why not make it as *later* as possible! Just tell him thanks, but no thanks. You ain't home, you ain't interested, you ain't going nowhere right now—and that's that! Chances are he'll get disgusted and go somewhere else. Yeah, I know it sounds ridiculous, but so does the idea of a grown man in cowl and robe roaming the West in a black wagon, speaking in a sibilant whisper, and collecting corpses. Eventually he'll just go somewhere else to have his fun!

So that's the way it works, though not exactly in so many words, and I put it to the Dark Man. Forcefully.

"I know who you are," I said with a smile of renewed confidence. "And I know you know. So cut the crap!"

"You are mistaken in your delusions" came the voice from behind the cowl, but it was a bit hesitant and I could almost feel a growing doubt in the timbre of his words.

"No, you're mistaken, fella! If you think you're gonna pull one over on this here boy—one of Granny Ransom's brood— then you're in for the surprise of all surprises."

"I was right about you being a danger," the Dark Man whispered.

"You better believe it, Dark Man," I said. "You see, when you play the game 'nothing is actually as it appears to be,' you run the risk of all sorts of problems creeping into the mix." I smiled. "See, on the outside of it, I'm just another tinhorn rogue, bum sidewinder of a cowpoke, lately turned to robbing banks—and you're just a traveling death merchant out to earn a meal and some bloody coin from doing the dirty work the clean folk don't like to do themselves. Of course, you're a bit more than that, Dark Man, and you might be surprised to hear that I'm a bit more than I appear to be as well."

"I don't believe you" came the voice, almost defensive in its tone this time.

"Believe what you will. My old grandma told me all about you, and how to beat you, and you know that ain't no jive. So, better go on your way, take a hike, I don't want you around here. The people in Pleasantville don't need you around here either. Just leave. Get the hell out! Get the hell out of here now!"

And then from outside I heard a raucous chant building up— it was almost indistinguishable at first but damned if it wasn't the mob of townfolk, yelling and chanting and screaming and shouting—and all they were saying over and over again was— "Get out! Leave! We don't want you here! Get the hell out of Pleasantville and never come back!"

And I looked out the tiny barred window and saw Judge Creedy revving up the crowd, and I saw Old Man Furley throwing rocks at the Dark Man's wagon, and young Jebialiah Jones riding upon his beloved Lightnin'—riding up close to the Dark Man's wagon and spooking his mounts—and finally there was Sheriff Hodges framed in the doorway of the jail—his gun was drawn and his face was a blood-red mask of stone.

"I think you better get out of this town. We don't like the kind of thing you represent. Not at all." Sheriff Hodges said with careful words, "I think you'd best leave immediately."

"And what of the prisoner?" the Dark Man asked contemptuously. "A bank robber. It's a hanging offense. Justice should be served."

"We'll worry about that. Not you!" the sheriff said, and then, so help me, Judge Creedy came in behind him, and so did Old Man Furley, and both of them held handguns—though I'm sure as hell neither of them knew how to use them properly—and they stood there proud and defiant and shocked me right terrible by saying, "See, your kind always has got enough rope. You were right about that. And you're just as right about the fact that our kind don't—and we're right glad of that fact now, Mr. Dark Man."

The Dark Man stood motionless.

"Seems to me we got a bad one on our hands," Judge Creedy explained with a smile. "This Jack Ransom—Black Jack Ransom—is a bank robber, a rogue and a fornicator, and a no-good varmint, but he ain't hurt no one, and we got all the bank money back, and it appears to me that Susie at the saloon is powerfully taken with him. So he can't be all bad after all. And that's why I hereby order a stay of execution and parole Jack Ransom into the care of the good people of Pleasantville—and the damned hell with you, Mr. Dark Man!"

*

Well, it was just like Granny Ransom used to say to me when I was a youngster: if you put up enough of a fight, and are lucky enough to have a few good people stick up for you when you're needing help, you can beat the Dark Man and send him on his way.

And that's just what happened, or so help me may I never rob another bank—or at least another bank in a town whose people are always sure to have enough rope.

Bill Crider

THE HANGING OF CHICK DUPREE

Bill Crider is one of the best-kept secrets in American publishing. He has written exemplary novels in so many categories—mystery, suspense, horror, and Western—that his publishers don't quite know what to do with him.

But with a recent Anthony nomination, and a "breakout" book definitely on the horizon, Bill Crider is bound to become a major star very soon now.

Yes, hell, yes. They hung Chick Dupree a week or so back. Well, it was nine days, if you want to be precise about it. Why're you—say, the way you're dressed, I bet you're one of them reporter fellas from back East. There was two or three reporters out here that day. How come you wasn't with 'em?

Missed your train, huh? Well, that can happen. Too bad, though. I bet your editor would of really liked to have old Chick's story. It has all that kind of thing about the wild frontier they like to hear about back in the big cities.

'Course, I could tell you the story myself if you was interested, 'cept my throat's a little dry. I'd buy a drink myself, but I don't have much money these days, and I been drinkin' quite a bit since old Chick passed away. Don't know why.

Anyway, I—well, that's right nice of you. I been standin' here for near 'bout an hour holdin' on to this glass and hopin' a kindly soul'd come along and see fit to help me out.

Well now, Chick's real name wasn't Chick at all, of course. We just called him that on account . . . Thank you, barkeep. That'll do me nicely, for now. I might be wantin' another later.

My, my, that tastes fine. You know, I could tell you was a

reporter right off, 'cause of your clothes. We don't see many hats like that out here, and that watch chain? It beats all I've ever seen.

Now, where was I?

Oh, yeah. See, Chick's real name was Alfred, or Albert, or something like that. We all called him Chick for so long, I forget his real name. I guess the undertaker could tell you if you really wanted to know. It don't make much difference now.

Anyway, we called him Chick because of his pet chicken. That's right. He had a lot of chickens at his house, raised 'em for the eggs and to eat. Fried up, they ain't so bad, and I like an egg now and again, but I don't much cotton to havin' chickens around the place.

You ever walked in a chicken yard? I didn't think so, lookin' at how shiny your shoes are. Let me tell you, you get chicken mess on shoes like that and it's just pure-dee hell to get off. And smell?

'Course, you can shovel all that stuff into your garden for fertilizer, but it don't do much good. I seen Chick's corn one year, it was as high as a house, I swear to God, but there weren't hardly any ears on it, and what there was, well, it was only about as big as my thumb.

So I don't see much use in chickens, myself, but Chick, he liked them a whole lot. And he had this one old hen, a big fat white one, that took to followin' him around almost like she was a dog.

It's the truth. I see you shakin' your head, but that old hen dearly loved Chick. Followed him all around the yard when he'd check for eggs, and even when he did the feedin'. She wouldn't stop and peck around like all the chickens did; she'd just follow him around, and he'd have to stop walkin' before she'd ever eat.

You're laughin', but it's the truth. You can ask anybody. It all come out at the trial. You locate the judge or the lawyers, why, they'd all tell you the same.

And it got worse. That chicken got to where she just pined for Chick all the time. Wouldn't eat, wouldn't lay, wouldn't do anything without havin' Chick around. It got so bad that he let her follow him all around ever'where he went. Right into town and ever'where.

Why, many's the time Clarice—that's what he called her, Clarice—many's the time Clarice has been right here in this saloon.

It's the truth. Why, I've seen Chick set her right up here on this bar and let her drink water out of a glass. It's a funny sight, the way a chicken drinks. You ever watch one?

No, I guess not. Anyway, it's a funny sight, all right, but nobody much ever laughed at Clarice. It was kinda like she was a friend of Chick's or somethin', and we all got to sort of bein' used to havin' her around.

Even me, and like I said, I don't like chickens all that much, myself.

And he'd talk to that chicken like it was a real person, just like he was talkin' to you or me. "Clarice," he'd say, "don't you think you'd like a drink o' water?"

And she'd peck on the bar. Answerin' him, if you get my drift.

"Here you are, Clarice," he'd say, and he'd put a glass of water, a little short one, like this one I'm drinkin' out of right here—say, it looks like I've done drained this one. How about—why, thanks. I do appreciate that. Set it up, barkeep.

Just as good as the last one. "Have a drink, Clarice, darlin'," he'd say, and she'd dip her beak right in like she knew what he was tellin' her, and then she'd tilt back and, well, you know how chickens drink.

No, that's right, you don't know, but it's a sight, I'm tellin' you.

Well, she'd have her drink and then he'd pick her up and set her on the floor. I guess she coulda hopped down, or flew down, but chickens can't fly worth a damn, even if they do have wings. They can fly up in a tree to roost, and they can fly down out of the tree in the mornin', but that's about all. Clarice coulda flew down off the bar, too, but Chick, he spoiled her a little bit.

Then they'd go on home. "Come along now, Clarice," Chick would say, and he'd start out the door. That big old chicken would waddle right along behind him, shakin' her tail like she had on a bustle.

Say, you ever see any of those bustles on women back East? I seen a picture in the paper once, but you don't ever see things like that out here much. That's what that chicken looked like to me, though.

Where was I?

Oh, that's right. About when they'd leave. You shoulda seen it. When he'd get to the door, he'd say, "After you, Clarice," just like she was some high-tone lady, and then he'd step aside. Clarice'd waddle right under that batwing door, and Chick would go through behind her. Once they was outside, she'd fall in behind him, and off they'd go, headin' back home.

Chick and I was pretty good pals, so I hate to have to say the next part, but two things happened to him.

One was that he fell in with a bad crowd. I'd appreciate it if you didn't put that part into your story, seein' as how people out here don't much like to mention it. They like to think we're just like you folks back East now, all civilized, and that all that business about ridin' the hoot-owl trail is just somethin' you read about in dime novels.

In fact, this whole hangin' business has embarrassed ever'-body a good bit, and they'd just as soon forget it ever happened. But it's true that Chick did fall in with a bad bunch of old boys.

I tried to tell him. "Chick," I said, "you go out ridin' with those Brandon boys, you could get in real trouble."

This was one day down at the livery stables, as I recall, and we were sittin' under a big old cottonwood tree that's down there. Clarice was off to one side, peckin' in the dirt and in the horse apples. Chick liked to take her down there; he said she was always real happy in a place like that, where there was plenty to eat and she could keep an eye on him. He wasn't kiddin' about that last part. I watched her. Ever' now and again, she'd look up and cut them beady eyes over at us under that tree, just to make sure we hadn't gone off anywhere.

Chickens got funny eyes, too. You ever notice how they—no, I guess you didn't. It don't matter.

I was sayin' how I warned Chick about them Brandon boys, but it didn't do much good.

"Those old boys are all right," Chick said.

"All right?" I said. "Chick, ever'body knows they robbed that bank in Cleberg."

Chick was chewin' on a straw, and it wiggled in his mouth when he talked. "Ever'body's wrong," he said. "Those boys never robbed no banks."

"I know they ain't got no proof," I said. "But still . . ."

"They're just good old boys," he said, takin' out the straw and havin' a look at it. He stuck it back in his mouth.

"If they're such good old boys, I wish you'd tell me one thing," I said. "I wish you'd tell me how they get by. I never seen them do a lick of work at that place of theirs. Whole thing's run over in weeds and cockleburs. They don't farm, they don't have no cows, they don't even have no chickens."

'Bout that time, Clarice came over and started peckin' in the vicinity of Chick's boot. He reached down and rubbed her back.

You're gettin' that look in your eye again, but it's true, just like I'm tellin' it. He rubbed that thing's back like it was a cat or a dog.

And it liked it, too.

"You ever done any farmin'?" he said.

I had to admit that I hadn't. I'm a town man by inclination. I do a little of this and a little of that. Carpenter, cook, hell, I've swamped out this bar more'n once or twice. Whatever comes to hand. I haven't been up to much lately, though, not since they hung Chick.

"Well, I have," Chick said. "And it don't suit me. My hand just don't fit a plow somehow. I've tried it, but I don't like it. If those Brandon boys got a better way of makin' a livin', well, I just might like to give that one a try for a while."

There was three of the Brandon boys, all of 'em sons of Old Man Brandon. He died a few years back, but he was the worst of the lot. He killed a man right in that street out there when I was a kid. I saw it myself. Shot him three times.

'Course, two of the times he just grazed him. But the third one went right in the breast. The other man was shootin' back, but he never got a hit.

Like I said, I saw it. They stood right there in the street and blasted away at each other. When Old Man Brandon hit him in the breast, the fella looked like he jumped backward, and then he keeled over in the middle of the street.

Yeah, sure, you can put that in your story. But be sure you say it happened a long time ago. I musta been eight or nine years old, so it was fifteen years ago at least. Be sure you mention that.

Nothin' like that would ever happen now. Not around here it wouldn't.

Anyway, those boys took after their daddy and raised hell all around these parts for years. And I tried to warn Chick about 'em, but it didn't do one bit of good. Before long they was hangin' out together and drinkin' and whatever else it was that they did. Maybe they didn't rob no banks, I don't know. But that's what people said.

The other thing that happened was that Chick met Ellen Anson.

"Met" might be the wrong word, since ever'body in town

knew her, and I guess ever'body in town felt about her the way
he did.

She worked right here in this saloon. You see that little stage
over there? That's the very place where she danced.

I guess back East you have lots of women that can sing and
dance, and I guess there's a lot of 'em as pretty as Ellen Anson
was. But for us out here, well, there wasn't many like her. In
fact, she was the only one.

The only one I ever saw, anyway.

What did she look like? That's hard to say. At the trial, I
heard some people say she had brown hair, but I always
thought it was a sort of a gold color. Maybe you'd have to see
it in the sun to know what I mean, and maybe a lot of the
people who tried to describe her hadn't ever seen her when she
wasn't up there on that stage. But you get her out in the sun,
and that hair would purely shine. I'd say it was gold.

Her face? Sweet, that's the word I always think of. Sweet.
She had that little red mouth, kinda like a bow, but it was her
eyes that made her look sweet. They had a kinda sad look in
them, but it was a look that didn't make *you* feel sad, if you
know what I mean. It's kinda hard to say exactly what I mean.
I wish you coulda seen her. Then you'd know.

And her figure? That's not the kind of thing a man talks
about much, if he's any kind of a man, but I got to admit that
when she got up there on that stage and shashayed around,
swingin' those petticoats—you ever see the kinda petticoats
those dancers wear? You have? Then you know what I mean,
and you know how those things show off your legs, if you got
the kinda legs to show off. If you don't, well, they make you
look like a elephant—you ever see a elephant in the circus?
Well, then, you know what I mean.

Anyway, the long and the short of it is, she was the prettiest
thing that this town's ever seen or is likely to see again. And
could she sing? She could sing a sad song that would bring a
tear to the eye of Old Man Brandon if he was alive to hear it,
which he ain't. And she could sing a happy song that would
make a Indian smile. And you know a Indian don't never smile
so a white man can see it.

I wish you coulda heard her.

I guess ever' man in town was halfway in love with her, and
with some it was a lot more'n that.

Not that it ever did any one of 'em a bit of good.

I know what you're thinkin'. You're thinkin' she was some kinda cheap floozie that looked good to us because we're way out here and don't know no better than to fall for the first woman to come along.

Well, that's not true. There's some mighty nice women here in town. Nice-lookin', too. 'Course, most of 'em are married. Oh, there's a workin' girl or two, the kind you can take upstairs if you got the money and the inclination, but Ellen wasn't one of 'em. Not one bit.

We never did know why she came here, or why she stayed, but it wasn't anything like that. She was a nice girl, and if you so much as made any of what she called "improper advances," she'd have you throwed right out that batwing door before you could blink your eyes.

So don't go gettin' the wrong idea.

The way it started up between Chick and her was right in here. Right about this time of day, I think, middle of the mornin' or thereabouts. Not many other folks around, most of 'em out workin', or in the case of the kinda girls you were thinkin' about, still sleepin'.

I was between jobs, myself, just havin' done a bit of carpenter work down to the Baptist church. Worked there about two weeks. And I had to promise not to take a drink the whole time I was on the job.

I didn't like that part of it, but I needed the work. I can do just as good a job, whether I have me a drink that day or not, but those Baptists wouldn't have it. Said they'd heard about me and how I did good work, but they wouldn't have a man on the job with liquor on his breath.

I can take it or leave it—say, look at that, now. Glass is plumb empty. Could you—fine, fine. Set 'em up, barkeep.

So, like I was sayin', I'd finished that job, and believe me I needed a drink in the worst way. I mean, you stay around a bunch like that, dry as bones, ever' one of 'em, for two weeks, and you'd need a drink, too. There's just no way around it.

Chick, he was hangin' around the Brandon boys, though I'd warned him, and so he didn't do much work durin' the daylight hours anymore. His yard was growin' up in weeds, and he didn't seem to give much of a damn. I'd'a offered to cut 'em, but I didn't know if I'd'a wanted the kinda money he would of paid me with.

Both of us havin' a little time on our hands, we came in for a drink. I needed one, what with bein' around those Baptists and all for so long, and he just wanted one.

He'd come into town on his horse, but that didn't make a damn as far as that chicken was concerned. He'd got to where he let her ride with him, perched up on the saddle horn. It got to be quite a sight in town when he'd come in like that. He didn't ever walk anymore, not now that he was hellin' around with those Brandons. He was too good for walkin'.

So we were in here, havin' a drink like I said. And that damn Clarice was up on the bar, havin' a drink, too, but hers was just water, like always.

That was when Ellen Anson come down the stairs. Sure, she lived up there, just like the workin' girls, but that didn't mean anything. It was just the place where she lived, not the place where she did business, and I'd whip the man who says different.

She had this kind of a thing wrapped around her. I don't know what you'd call it, but it wasn't a dress, not exactly, though it covered up things just as well. And she looked different, too. You'd have to of been there to know what I mean. It was like she was fresher or something. I don't know how to say it, but she didn't look like she did when she was dancing up on the stage. And that hair of hers was just shinin', liked she'd brushed it and brushed it just a few minutes before. And she was lookin' at us with those sad eyes of hers . . . well, I don't know how to put it any better than that, but bein' as how you're a writer you might just make up somethin' or other about how pretty she was. You'd do a lot better job of it than I can, even though what I'm tryin' to tell you is the truth.

She came over to the bar, which I guess is somethin' she never hardly did, but she wanted to see that damn chicken. She thought it was funny.

"I never seen a chicken do that before," she said.

"Do what?" Chick said.

"Drink water like that, out of a glass," she said.

Chick gave her a smile. I don't know if I mentioned it, but Chick was a good-lookin' fella, 'bout as tall as I am, and with those broad shoulders that women kinda like. Broad as mine, almost.

He took off his hat, too, which was something you hardly ever seen him do, even if he was inside somewhere, much less a saloon. He had kinda curly hair, and dimples. Women seemed to like him a lot, and I got to say it, he could of set many a heart to flutterin' around here if he'd had a mind to. Just as many as I could of, but neither one of us was much inclined that way, considerin' the looks of most of the females you see in this place.

Ellen Anson was different, though. When she smiled back at Chick, it was like somebody opened the door and let the sunshine in here.

I asked her if we could buy her a drink, just to be polite, and sure enough, she had one. I hadn't ever seen her take a drink before, much less with a customer.

It was Clarice that done it, I guess. She went on and on about that damn hen.

"I guess you trained her to do that," she told Chick.

"No, ma'am," he said. "It just come natural to her."

Ellen Anson laughed at that like he'd cracked a joke. If he did, I didn't get it, myself.

There was a few other folks in here that day, the bartender—not this one, but another one; don't know what happened to him—and a couple of others. They was all watchin' us pretty close and wishin' they *was* us, I guess, but Ellen didn't have eyes for none of them.

You couldn't blame her much. One of 'em was Donnie Adams, as I recall, and he's about seventy years old and has a glass eye that he can't ever remember to put in, and the old socket is always kinda red and gummy, and besides, he don't have any teeth left.

So she wasn't interested in him.

She talked to me and Chick for a long time, laughin' when we'd say somethin' that was funny or even when we didn't. She had a way of throwin' back her head to laugh, which kinda showed her throat and made that hair shake loose and hang down in back.

"That hen surely does have a red comb," she said one time.

"I feed her good," Chick said. "I take real good care of her."

"I bet you take care of ever'body," she said.

"He sure does," I said. "And I do, too."

She gave us both a look, then, that nearly singed my eyebrows. I don't know how Chick felt about it, but it seemed like he sure came around here a lot after that. Ever'time I came by, he was here, and he always had that chicken right along with him.

The thing was, he could never stay a real long time when Clarice was around, though. You say you don't know much about chickens, but I guess you could figure out that they ain't the brightest or most sensible animal in the world. It's hard for them to concentrate on one thing for very long, and they get real restless. Clarice would come in and have her drink, and she might set up on the bar for a while, but pretty soon she'd get to lookin' around and peckin' here and there, and Chick'd have to set her on the floor.

She might be happy there for a minute or two, dependin' on what she could find, but naturally she wouldn't stray too far from Chick. So sooner or later she'd get to fussin' and cluckin' and bein' a general pest, and Chick'd have to haul her on back home.

The worst of it, though, was that the hen got jealous of Ellen Anson. You'd of thought Clarice was another woman, the way she acted. She'd cluck around real madlike whenever Ellen was around, and then she took to peckin' her on the toe.

I guess you've never been pecked by a mad chicken like that, but let me tell you, they can make it pretty rough. You'd think to look at 'em they're just kinda harmless, but they can make a bruise on you like you wouldn't believe if you give 'em the chance.

And she did, a time or two, till Ellen got fed up with the whole thing and quit comin' around.

'Course, by then, Chick had took to comin' in a lot at night, when Clarice was up on a roost, and lots of folks say he and Ellen would meet after the saloon'd close down. I don't know anything about that myself, though.

It was around that time that the Brandon boys stuck up the bank in Agua Dulce. There just wasn't denyin' who was in on it this time, since Clete, that was the oldest of the Brandon boys, got hisself shot all to hell in the midst of things.

What happened was, Clete's horse stepped in some kinda hole in the street when they was all makin' their getaway. They'd cleaned the bank out slick as a gut, but somehow somebody alerted the town marshal, and he got a couple of men together and got over there.

He was almost too late, since the gang was haulin' it out of town, but then Clete's horse stepped in that hole, like I said, and old Clete went flyin' off, tallywhacker over teakettle, and the horse went down with a broken leg.

Clete come up with his gun blazin', or so they say, but the rest of the boys was done long gone and there was nobody there to help him out. He was just outnumbered and outgunned.

Lord, they shot that boy up.

After it was all over, they took his shirt off and propped him up against a board at the undertaker's parlors and took a picture of him. It was in a lot of the newspapers. You didn't see it, did you?

Too bad. It woulda made a nice thing to put with your article.

Anyway, I saw one of them pictures in a paper somebody brought to town. People around here, the mayor and all, want to think we're gettin' civilized, like I might of told you, but we still don't have much of a paper yet. Oh, we got one, all right, but it don't come out but ever' week, if the editor ain't drunk, and it don't ever have no pictures in it.

Where was I? I could remember better, maybe, if I had another drink.

Thank you kindly, barkeep. Yes, sir, that's mighty fine.

Well, old Clete, he didn't look so good in that picture. I tried to count the holes in him, and it looked like fourteen to me, but some said it was more and some said it was less.

It was a lot, anyhow.

You know, those holes don't look so bad in a picture like that. They look sorta like a bruise, maybe, where a chicken might peck you. Just little black spots like that. They was in his chest, mostly, but there was one or two on his head and a few in his belly. Plenty enough to do him in, no doubt about that.

Now, the thing is, they had Clete, but they didn't have anybody else, and they didn't have any of the money back. Clete wasn't carryin' a single bit of it, which made 'em all mad, but there wasn't much they could do about it.

Naturally, they set out after the rest of the gang, but they never caught up with 'em. By the time they ever located the rest of the Brandon boys, they was all at home with their wives and kids and sayin' that they hardly ever left the house except, off course, on Sundays, when they always made it a point to go to worship services, and that they didn't know nothin' about no bank robberies, and my it surely was a surprise that any brother of theirs would be mixed up in anything like that, since he'd always seemed like one of the quietest members of the family, but you never could tell about the quiet ones, sometimes they were the ones that fooled you.

'Course, the Brandon boys wasn't foolin' nobody, but on the other hand, there wasn't nothin' anybody could do, what with there not bein' any proof of anythin'.

Now, I didn't ever talk to Chick about him and the Brandon boys, not after I warned him off. What he did was up to him. He wasn't a member of my family or anything.

After the Agua Dulce robbery, though, he come in for a drink and we had a little talk. The reason we did was that he looked pretty bad. Not that he'd been shot or anything, but he looked tired and sorta draggled.

"Haven't seen a lot of you lately," I said.

"I don't come around much," he said, which was true, because by that time Ellen Anson had got her a room in old Miz Ellis's place. It was a back room that had its own door and ever'thing, so she could come and go as she pleased. There was some folks that wouldn't of rented to a saloon girl, but old Miz Ellis didn't care what you did, long as you could pay up when the time came.

"How's Clarice?" I said.

"I don't hardly know," he said. "I don't have much time to mess with her anymore."

Well, right there you can see what sorta shape he was in. Not have time for that chicken? That was like him sayin' he didn't have time for eatin' and sleepin'.

"Been anybody comin' around, uh . . . botherin' you?" I said. That was as close as I could get to askin' him if the marshal of Agua Dulce was on his tail or anything like that. 'Course, you know it wasn't for any bank robbin' that he got hung, but at the time I thought it might be that they had found out about him and the Brandon boys.

"You been restin' all right?" I said. His eyes was red, and he'd missed a day or two at shavin'.

"Not exactly," he said. "You know how it is."

I didn't know how it was, not really. 'Course, what I thought he meant was that he'd been on the hoot-owl trail with that gang of his and didn't get much rest while they was robbin' and stealin' and what all.

Then he said, "I been thinkin' about gettin' married and settlin' down."

You could of knocked me over with a apron string when he said that. "Who to?" I said.

"You know who to," he said.

That come as a surprise to me, too. "I hear she's got another fella," I told him.

He looked at me with them red eyes. "She better not have," he said.

"That's the talk," I said.

He turned and looked at hisself in the mirror over the bar, the very one that we're lookin' in right now. "Who's doin' the talk?" he said.

"Folks."

"What folks?"

"Just folks. It's somethin' you hear. That's all."

"It better not be right," he said, turnin' his drink in his hand.

I would never have thought to hear such as that from him. I would of said that he didn't have a jealous bone in his body, if anybody's asked me, but it sure looked like he did.

He was always a big, smilin' fella, a good word for ever'body, and here he was, talkin' like that. It was a disappointment to me, though I didn't tell him so. I didn't think he'd want to hear it.

Some folks, it wouldn't surprise me like that. I mean, I know what they feel like. They think somebody's cuttin' 'em out with a woman like that, and they get all churned up, like their insides was on a boil, those hot bubbles stirrin' around in their bellies, and poppin' in there. They get all twisted up 'til they don't hardly know what they're doin' most of the time.

But Chick? I would of never thought of him that way, and here he was, practically makin' threats.

Maybe I should of let it lay, but I said, "What would you do if it was right, what I heard?"

He tossed down the rest of his drink. "Somebody'd sure as hell be sorry," he said. "That's what."

I didn't see him for a while after that, but then one day he was down at the livery stable gettin' a shoe put on his horse. We got a pretty good farrier down there, old Richard Thomas, if you ever need a horse shoed, but I guess you wouldn't be needin' anythin' like that.

Anyhow, we was there, and I asked him why he was gettin' the horse took care of, not that it was any of my business, of course.

"May be needin' him," he said.

Since I knew he wasn't doin' any farmin' or ranchin' or anythin' like that, I had a pretty good idea what he'd be needin' the horse for. It was a nice horse, a little pinto, could run all day if you'd let it.

I didn't say what I was thinkin', though. I said, "You still got those marryin' plans?"

"I might," he said.

"What about that other fella?"

"Hell, there ain't no other fella. You know how folks will talk in a town like this."

"There ain't no other fella?"

"Hell, no. Never was. It was all just talk. You can tell whoever you heard it from that it's a downright lie."

"Well," I said, "if you're sure." I didn't want to see him get hurt by any woman, you see.

He laughed. " 'Course I'm sure. Don't you worry about that."

"Well, that's good to hear," I said.

"Sure enough. You might not see me much around here after about next Thursday."

I didn't ask him about that, either, since I was pretty sure it might be somethin' I didn't want to know about, and he might of told me. It was pretty easy to figure out, anyhow. See, if he was plannin' on leavin' town the next Thursday, it probably meant that him and the Brandon boys was goin' to pull some kinda job on Wednesday, and then he'd be pullin' out.

The froofraw from that bank job had just about died down, and there was even some talk that maybe the Brandon boys hadn't been in on it after all, that maybe Clete had got himself involved with some other bunch and gone in with them for a job or two. I heard that folks had been slippin' around all over the Brandon boys' land and hadn't found a sniff of that money from Agua Dulce, so maybe it was true.

I told him good-bye and said I hoped I'd be seein' him.

He reached out his hand. "I wouldn' count on that," he said. "But you been a good pal."

I shook with him. "You never know," I said.

And that was the last I seen of him until the trial. Well, I went to the jail to see him, but they said he didn't want to see me. I guess he was too ashamed or somethin'. I don't know.

I would never of thought he would of killed her. It was just like when I warned him about the Brandon boys, and he didn't listen to me. I tried to tell him there was some other fella, but he wouldn't listen then, either. I guess he must of found out for sure, though, and that was all it took.

It was on a Wednesday that somebody stuck up the train over to Wild Horse. Not in the town, of course, but right outside. There's a big hill there, and they greased the rails so the train couldn't get up it. Climbed on and robbed all the passengers, not to mention gettin' whatever was in the mail car and the strongbox.

It was the next mornin' that they found Ellen Anson. She'd been strangled in her room, and she was laid out on the bed so peaceful that she didn't even look like she was dead. But when they moved the scarf off her neck, they could see that she was, all right.

It was a pretty bad time for Chick, I imagine.

It wasn't just the murder, though that was bad enough. See, somehow the word had got around town that he might be in with the Brandon boys and that he could of been a part of the gang that robbed the train.

Folks knew about him bein' sweet on Ellen, too, though I don't think they ever did find out who the other fella was. She didn't show up for work that Wednesday night, and there was some that thought she was dead even then, but there was no way to know.

If she was, that might of saved Chick, but he couldn't very well say that he couldn't of killed her on Wednesday because he was out robbin' a train with the Brandon boys, so could they please excuse him on the murder charge.

They would of hung him for the train robbery just the same.

So he had to set there in the jail and wait for them to get the judge to town and listen to them build that gallows outside. It's too bad you missed the hangin'. That was just about the biggest thing ever to come to this town. We'd never had one before.

The gallows was a big attraction for days, and I went by to look at it myself. Just seein' it there was the kinda thing could make your egg sac get tighter, and when you thought about what they were gonna use it for, well, it just made it that much worse. I had to go to the privy right after.

I guess it was right about then that I started in to drink. I drink a lot too much, I can't say I don't, but thinkin' about that gallows and about Chick is what got me started.

Did they have any evidence? Well, I guess you could call it that. It was enough to convince anybody in *this* town, anyhow.

There was chicken feathers all around, you see, and they found Clarice in there, too.

What was left of her.

The way they figured it was this: Chick heard about the other fella and went over to have it out with Ellen. He took Clarice with him, 'cause as ever'body in town knew, she was crazy about that old hen.

When he found out that the rumors was true, well, he was so jealous that he tore into Ellen, and when he saw what he'd done to her he killed his hen out of grief. Wrung her neck and scattered those feathers all over the room.

She must of been a pitiful sight. The chicken, I mean, but Ellen, too.

I naturally went to the trial, but they wouldn't ever let me get close enough to talk to Chick, or hardly even to see him. It was a big thing for a little town like this, that trial was, so the courtroom was crowded ever' single day.

'Course, we don't really have a courtroom, not bein' a county seat or anythin' like that. We lost out to Wild Horse on that one, but there's some folks say that one of these days we'll be even bigger than them and when that happens, watch out. There's already been talk around town about sneakin' over there some night and stealin' the county records and settin' up here.

But I don't know anythin' about that.

The trial didn't take long, as maybe you heard. There wasn't much of a defense, and Chick never did say that he could of been elsewhere when Ellen was killed. Hangin' for one thing ain't no worse than hangin' for another, I guess is what he thought. Besides, if he'd of said anythin' about the train robbery, them Brandons would of killed him if the hangman didn't.

Mostly he just sat there in the courtroom looking gloomy.

I forgot to tell you about the courtroom, didn't I. Well, you're standin' in it.

That's right. They held the trial right here. It's about the biggest room in town, 'less you count the Baptist church, and they weren't about to let us have no trial there. It wouldn't seem right, nohow, what with ever'body havin' to set in pews and all.

Like I said, Chick mostly looked gloomy through the whole thing, but there wasn't much other way he could look. We all knew what was goin' to happen to him, and he did, too.

It made all of us sad to see him that way and in such a situation, 'cause he'd always been such a cheerful fella up till then. And naturally a lot of us remembered that chicken, and how much fun he had with her.

'Course, he'd sorta lost interest in his chickens by then, and the old chicken yard hadn't been cleaned out in a good while. Most of them chickens didn't even sleep in the roost he'd built for 'em anymore. They took off and flew up in trees and things. I doubt he ever even looked for the eggs.

But he had a touch with 'em when he tried. There wasn't nobody could handle that Clarice like he could. She'd peck the blood outta anybody that tried it. I told you about that.

What? Oh, that's just a place on my hand where I must of hit it with a hammer. Anyway, he set up there lookin' mopey and makin' all the rest of us feel sad, not that we blamed him.

I was thinkin' I might get called to the stand, but I never did. Bein' his best friend and all, I could of said a few words for him. Maybe I could of even told them about how he was plannin' to marry Ellen Anson and go off somewhere with her, but that might just of made things worse for him. Folks would of said that was why he killed her. Because she wouldn't go, I mean.

So I was just as glad they didn't call me. I never would of told them about how I thought Chick was in with the Brandon boys. After all, he never come right out and said that he was. That was all just guessin' on my part, and they don't like to have you guessin' on the witness stand.

I still remember what Chick said when it come time for him to speak his piece. "Your Honor," he said, lookin' right at that judge, "I want you to know I never killed Ellen Anson."

Then he turned right around and looked at the jury. Some of those old boys had known him for years. "Gentlemen of the jury," he said, "I never killed nobody. And I sure never killed my chicken."

Well, I thought that might do it. He sure sounded like he was tellin' the truth to me.

Then he stood down, and the jury went out. It didn't take 'em long, and when they come back in you could see in their faces what they was gonna do. You could tell they didn't like it, but they didn't see any way out of it. If it hadn't been for them chicken feathers all over the place, and of course for Clarice layin' there in the floor, they might of done different, but they didn't.

Chick didn't say a word when they found him guilty. Just kinda sighed, like he was real tired.

They took him back to the jail, and the bar opened up. I had myself more than a few that day, let me tell you.

The hangin' was really a sight. You should of been here for that. I never saw anythin' to beat it, and likely never will.

I told you that our town was gettin' "civilized." Well, there's even a few of the citizens got themselves a brass band. I don't guess it'd sound like much to you, bein' from back East and all, but it sounds pretty good to us out here. So the brass band was there. They started in to playin' early, to get the crowd in a good mood.

And there surely was a crowd. They come in from ever'where. Men, women, and children. I guess it was an education for the little 'uns, and you could tell their mamas and daddies wanted 'em to have a good time. 'Course, it ain't easy to have a good time when you're about four years old and dressed up in your Sunday best on a hot day like we've been havin'.

And a lot of the tiny ones were squallin', too, so not ever'body was havin' a good time. Some of the kids got into fights and got to rollin' around in the dirt, and their mammas would get to screamin' at 'em, and their daddies, too, if the daddies had had enough to drink, which most of 'em had, since there was many a bottle gettin' passed back and forth that day. And it was prob'ly the bottles that caused most of the fights among the grown-ups in the crowd. Some people just don't know how to behave at a solemn occasion like that one, so there was some full-growed men rollin' around in the dust along with the kids, and lots of women yellin' and that brass band playin', and it was just about like the Fourth of July around here, let me tell you.

Ever'body calmed right down when it come time for the hangin' itself, though. Nobody even had to ask 'em, either. They brought Chick out of the jail and started leadin' him over to the gallows, and I swear it got so quiet you'd of thought there wasn't a single soul even breathin' out there. It was so quiet it was almost scary.

Chick marched along like he didn't have a worry in the world. All I can say is, I hope when my time comes to go, I can go as easy as he did. I swear, they'd of had to carry me up there kickin' and yellin' like a hog gettin' its throat cut if it'd been me.

He walked right up the steps, and the Baptist preacher went right along with him. Folks said that Chick had got religion in the jail, but I don't know if that was right. I think he just wanted somebody to talk to, and that preacher was the only one could get in.

But they went up the steps together and the preacher said a little prayer when they got to the top. Then he read that part out of the Bible about walkin' through the valley of the shadow of death.

It always gives me a kind of a chill to hear that.

The preacher went down then, and the sheriff turned Chick over to the hangman, who they'd brought in from somewhere. He wasn't from around here.

As he was puttin' the rope on, Chick looked out over the crowd, and he saw me. I was way out on the edge, but I knew he was lookin' me right in the eyes. It was the saddest look I ever saw, and I'll never forget it. He was the best friend I ever had, and that's a fact. I hated to see him go like that.

But he went. They dropped that trap, and Chick fell straight down and that was all of it.

I went off and had a drink, I felt so bad. I doubt I'll ever feel any worse'n I did then.

I'd drink more if I could afford it, but I ain't got the money.

Say, now that you got the true story, the one the other papers don't have, about Clarice and all, could you stand me one more? I don't have a dollar to my name. Look at this. Nothin' but dust in my pockets.

What?

Oh, them look like they might be feathers of some kind. I told you I was a town boy, and I sleep ever' night on a feather pillow. Can't sleep without it. It's tied on the end with a string, but the string seems to come undone ever' night, nearly. Just lately, seems I been wakin' up with a head fulla feathers, like I been snowed on.

That's where they come from, I guess.

Say, where're you goin'? I thought you'd stand me another drink!

Hey! Don't run off!

Hey!

Robert J. Randisi

THE GHOST WITH BLUE EYES

*Robert J. Randisi is best known to Western readers as
the author of "The Gunsmith" series.*

*In addition, however, he has written a number of
other Western series.*

His best work in the field is The Ham Reporter, *a
beautifully structured and executed look at Bat Mas-
terson's last years in New York City as a sportswriter.*

Bob Randisi's suspense novel Alone with the Dead
*was judged one of the best of the season a few years
back, and his forthcoming one is even better.*

1

When Targett stepped off the train onto the platform in Big
Bend, Oklahoma, he looked both ways and saw no one else
exiting the train. Farther down he could see his horse being
offloaded from the stock car. Apparently he was the only one
with business in Big Bend that day.

"Mr. Targett?"

He turned in the direction of the voice and saw a well-
dressed man of about forty-five or so approaching him. The
man was very slender, not tall, and had a look of apprehension
on his face that was not at all hidden by a heavy mustache.

"I'm Targett."

Targett wore a long duster over a heavy shirt and Levi's,
and a flat-crowned black hat. It was cold and the other man
came close enough for their frosted breath to mingle.

"Are you Kane?" Targett asked.

"Uh, no," the man said, "Mr. Kane sent me to meet you."

Targett once again looked down toward the stock car. A man was holding the reins of his horse.

"He works for Mr. Kane," the man said. "If it's all right with you I'll signal him to take your horse to town."

"Sure," Targett said. "Go ahead."

The well-dressed man waved his arm, and the man holding the reins started away from the train. Targett heard the train start up and it moved away behind him.

"Where do we go?" he asked the other man.

"Uh, to town, also. Mr. Kane has arranged a room for you at the hotel."

"Who are you?"

"Oh, yes, I'm Mr. Kane's assistant. My name is Lyle."

"Lyle something," Targett asked, "or something Lyle?"

"Lyle is my last name," the man said. "My first name is Henry."

"Well," Targett said, "lead on, Mr. Lyle. I'm anxious to hear what it is Mr. Kane wants to hire me to do."

"Yes, well," Lyle said, nervously, "this way, then."

They walked to the end of the platform where the ticket office was and stepped off. Targett followed Lyle into the town of Big Bend, which did not quite live up to its name. It appeared to be a collection of ramshackle wooden structures, unevenly spaced and in the need of repair.

"It's not much now," Lyle said, as if reading Targett's mind, "but Mr. Kane intends to build it up."

"That'll take a lot of money, from the looks of things."

"Mr. Kane has a lot of money."

"Well," Targett said, "I'm glad to hear that."

Lyle put his hand to his mouth, as if he realized that he had said more than was necessary.

There were a few people on the street, and they tossed curious looks at Targett as he continued to follow Lyle to—he assumed—the hotel.

"There's the hotel," Lyle said, indicating a two-story building that was obviously a recent addition to the town. It was new, and solidly built. Above the door was a sign that said simply: HOTEL.

"We haven't thought of a suitable name for it, yet," Lyle commented.

"How about Kane House?"

"Mr. Kane is much too modest for that."

Targett had known a few men with lots of money, and none of them had ever been modest. He was interested in meeting Hannibal Kane.

As they crossed the street to the hotel they passed a woman and a little girl of about seven years. Targett touched the brim of his hat and the woman looked away, nervously. The child, however, stared up at him with complete fearlessness. Her eyes were the bluest he had ever seen, a shocking blue that dominated her face. They were filled with curiosity and an innocence that was completely alien to Targett. The woman grabbed the child's hand and pulled her along. Obviously she intended to extinguish the innocence by teaching the child fear.

"Your room is on the—" Lyle started, but there was a shot and the man jerked, and then slumped to the ground.

Targett turned quickly, his hand reaching beneath his duster for his gun. He stopped when he saw the man pointing a gun at him.

The man holding the gun was tall and rangy. He held his pistol in his right hand, and it was pointed directly at Targett.

"You must be Kane's gunman," he said.

"Who are you?"

"Me? I'm your job."

Targett stared at the man.

"Didn't Kane tell you about me?"

"I haven't talked to Kane yet."

"But you're here to take a job, right?"

"I'm here to talk to him about a job."

"Well, I'm it," the man said. "My name's Cray, and you're being hired to kill me."

"Since you know what I'm being hired to do," Targett said, calmly, "maybe you can tell me how much I'm being paid."

Cray smiled, revealing more gaps than teeth, and said, "Not enough, friend. Not nearly enough . . . to die."

Targett looked at the fallen man, unsure whether he was alive or dead. Then he looked at Cray.

"Do you want me to turn around, so you can backshoot me like you did him?"

Cray laughed.

"That was just to get your attention. I don't need to backshoot anyone."

"Then holster it," Targett said, "and let me get on with my job."

Cray studied Targett for a few moments without holstering his weapon.

"What's your name?" he finally asked.

"Targett."

"I never heard of you."

"Then I guess you don't need to fear me, do you."

The man studied Targett for a few more moments, then shook his head and holstered his gun.

"Let's do it, then," Cray said. "I've got things to do."

What transpired next seemed to Targett to happen in slow motion. Cray went for his gun, as did Targett. While Cray strove for speed, Targett was more deliberate. He may not have gotten his gun out as fast as most, but his first shot was usually more accurate.

Cray snapped off a quick shot that punched a hole through Targett's duster but did not strike him. Targett fired, and his bullet struck Cray in the chest. With a shocked look on his face, Cray fell to one knee. He struggled to bring his gun up again and Targett fired a second time . . . and heard a woman's voice scream, "No!"

He didn't see the little girl until it was too late. Cray was on his knee, and Targett was standing on the boardwalk in front of the hotel. Consequently he was firing at a definite downward angle. It was for this reason that the bullet struck the little girl as she ran between the two men.

Just before she was struck, however, she turned and looked at Targett and he saw her blue eyes staring at him—and then the projectile struck her, extinguishing those eyes forever.

Seconds later he felt the hot lead strike him in the upper chest, on the left side, and he was falling over. . . .

2

When Targett woke he stared up at a cracked, yellowing ceiling. It took him a moment to collect his thoughts and recollect everything that had happened.

He heard voices that seemed to be coming from far away, perhaps outside. He turned his head and saw that he was in a room with two men.

"What . . ." he said, but nothing else came out. The one word, however, was sufficient to attract the attention of the two men. He saw that one of them was wearing a badge. The other was wearing a white coat, and Targett assumed he was a doctor.

"How do you feel?" the other man asked.

He felt lousy. His shoulder hurt, and he said so.

"The bullet hit you high up, so there was no damage to the heart. You were lucky."

Targett wet his lips.

"Cray."

"The other man? He's dead. He got one last shot off at you and then died."

Targett wet his lips again and spoke slowly.

"And the little girl?"

"I'm sorry," the doctor said. "She's dead."

Targett turned his head to look at the sheriff, but instead he saw the little girl standing there, staring at him with those startling blue eyes. . . .

★

"Jesus!" he shouted, and sat up.

He looked around him at the darkened room and realized that he'd had the dream once again. It was accurate except for the little girl replacing the sheriff. He *had* awakened in the doctor's office after the doctor had removed the bullet from his shoulder and bandaged him. He *had* looked over at the sheriff, at which time the man had ordered him to leave town. He *had* heard the murmur of voices from outside from the mob that wanted to string him up for what happened to the little girl. It didn't matter to them that it was an accident. If Targett had died and Cray had survived they would have wanted to hang him.

Targett looked around the dingy room and slowly remembered where he was, in a small room behind the saloon in Dunworthy, Texas.

After leaving Big Bend, Oklahoma, he had traveled quite a bit from town to town, but he could not seem to outrun the dreams, during which the girl with the blue eyes visited him. She seemed like a blue-eyed ghost, following him wherever he went, until he finally sought refuge in the bottle—but the whisky just seemed to make her visits more real.

He had gone to sleep fully dressed again, and was covered with sweat. He swung his feet to the floor and stood up from the pallet he used as a bed. He staggered to the back door and opened it, then staggered again as the sunlight struck his face. He leaned against the doorjamb for a moment, holding his hand up to shade his eyes from the sun, and then stepped outside. He made his way to the horse trough, fell to his knees by it, and stuck his head in it. The water was stagnant and warm, but it washed away some of the cobwebs.

He pulled his head out of the trough and used both hands to brush his hair back. That done, he cupped some more water with his hands, rubbing his face and eyes vigorously.

He stood and then sat on the edge of the trough. He looked around at the area behind the saloon, then up at the sky. The sun was high, so he surmised it was nearly three in the afternoon. Had he gotten drunk last night? Probably. The dream had seemed particularly vivid.

He had been in Dunworthy for three months now, working at the saloon as a swamper. The only thing that kept him from being the town drunk was that he did not get drunk every night. That honor belonged to Caleb Janeway. Old Caleb seemed to be drunk all the time, morning, noon, and night.

Targett knew he had sunk low, but he hadn't hit rock bottom yet. Maybe that was why he had chosen to stay in Dunworthy. As long as Caleb Janeway was at the bottom there would be no room for him.

He removed his shirt and bathed his chest and neck with the lukewarm water, then submerged his shirt and wrung it out. He put it on a nearby fence to dry. Did he have another? He didn't remember.

He watched the water as it settled. When it was still and clear he could see his reflection, and then the reflection of something else, something with blue eyes. He turned quickly but he couldn't catch her. He never could . . . not that she was ever really there. He knew that. Still, seeing her like that was better than the times she spoke to him. . . .

He stood up and walked back to the saloon, entering the back room again. He looked around to see if he had another shirt. He opened an old chest that the owner was letting him use in lieu of a dresser. He did indeed have another shirt, and as he took it out he saw his gun and gunbelt underneath it.

It had been six months since the shooting of the little girl. He'd traveled for three months, wearing the gun but not using it again. When he settled in Dunworthy he decided to take the gun off and put it away. It had been in that chest ever since.

He closed the chest on the gun and donned the shirt. It wasn't exactly clean, but at least he hadn't sweated through it during the night.

He left the room and went out into the saloon. Dunworthy was a small town, but a growing one. The saloon was busier at three in the afternoon on this day than it was when he first walked into it. Frank, the owner and bartender, said it would be even busier three months from now.

"Targett," somebody said by way of greeting, and Targett just waved and kept going.

"Poor bastard," the man who'd greeted him said as he went by.

"He's a drunk," another man said.

There were three men sitting at the table, and the third man said, "I heard he was pretty good with a gun once. I wonder what happened?"

"He's a drunk," the second man said again.

"Yeah, but what made him a drunk?"

"Same thing makes anybody a drunk," the third man said. "He fell into a bottle one day and couldn't get out. Still can't."

"Can't be more than what? Thirty?" the first man said. It had been a long time since he'd seen thirty—or since any of the three of them had.

"He looks forty," the second man said. "That's what bein' a drunk does to ya."

"Still," the first man said, shaking his head, "it's a shame. . . ."

*

Targett got to the batwing doors of the saloon and stopped, staring outside.

"Hey, Targett!" Frank Keller yelled from behind the bar. Frank was in his forties and owned the saloon. He had been a handsome man most of his life, but as he got older he got heavier, until he tended bar because he thought it would hide his girth.

Targett turned and looked at him.

"Ya didn't sweep up this mornin'."

"I overslept."

"Yeah, well ya do it again and you're fired, ya hear?" Frank shouted, not caring who heard.

"I hear . . ." Targett said, and stepped outside, wondering how he'd gotten to this point in his life. Six months ago he'd been fine—happy, even—working, doing what he was good at, and then that damned little girl had to run between him and Cray.

It wasn't even that she died. It was that, even dead, she wouldn't go away. It was that he always seemed to see those blue eyes, whether he was asleep or awake.

They were supposed to be closed forever, damn it. Why wouldn't they close?

3

Targett was still standing in front of the saloon when the stage came into town. The stage stop was right next to the saloon, in front of the hotel. The driver reined his team in and applied the brake before dropping to the ground. He ran to open the door and, as Targett watched, a pretty young woman stepped out, wearing a blue dress and a bonnet. She then turned, reached into the stage with both hands, and lifted a little girl out and set her down on the ground. The girl was similarly dressed in a blue dress and bonnet, and appeared to be about six.

Targett felt a chill run through him as he looked at the woman and the child. Suddenly the little girl turned her head and looked directly at Targett, and he saw that she had blue eyes—startling blue eyes.

He closed his eyes and rubbed them with both hands, then looked again, but by then the woman and child had entered the hotel. Was it his imagination that the girl had blue eyes? Was he seeing the wrong little girl?

He walked over to where the stage was sitting, empty now that its only passengers had disembarked. He turned away from it and walked to the front door of the hotel. From there he could see the woman and girl standing at the front desk, their backs to him. He stared at the girl, trying to will her to turn around and look at him again, but she never did. Her mother accepted a key from the desk clerk and they both went up the stairs.

Targett turned and walked slowly back to the saloon, still wondering if his mind was playing tricks on him. He was going to have to keep an eye out for that little girl. He had to get a closer look at her, see if she did, indeed, have blue eyes like the other. . . .

★

Upstairs in their hotel room Alecia Adams turned to her mother, Margaret, and asked, "Did you see that man, Mommy?"

"What man, honey?"

"The man who was looking at us."

Margaret Adams turned to her little girl and smiled.

"Honey, you're a very pretty little girl. You'll find that as you grow up and become a pretty woman men will look at you."

"Like you, Mommy?"

"Yes, honey, like me. The trick is not to let them know that you know they're looking."

"Why not, Mommy?"

Margaret cupped her little girl's chin in her hand and said, "You'll find out, pumpkin."

"When, Mommy?"

"Soon, darling, very soon. Let's get you out of that dirty dress now and into something pretty and clean."

"I'm hungry, Mommy."

"I know, dear. We'll eat as soon as we're changed."

Margaret Adams was very proud of the fact that her daughter looked like her. She knew what a pretty woman she was, because men had told her for years. She also knew that Alecia was going to be just as pretty, if not more so. She only wished that her daughter had inherited her hazel eyes instead of her father's brown ones.

4

For the next week Targett took every opportunity to get a look at the little girl. It soon became evident that she and her mother were settling in Dunworthy. At the end of the week they were still staying in the hotel, and all Targett had to do to get a look at them was sit in front of the saloon.

Sometimes he followed them, usually when they went shopping. A time or two the little girl saw him and waved. He waved back.

On the first day of the second week someone knocked on the door of Targett's room and woke him up.

"Wha—" he called.

"Targett? This is Sheriff Mathis. Get out here!"

"What the—" Targett said, putting his bare feet on the floor.

He walked to the flimsy door and opened it. He was surprised that the sheriff's knocking hadn't torn the door off.

Targett had met Dan Mathis briefly when he first came to town. It was the sheriff's job to check on strangers. Mathis kept an eye on him right up to when he got his job. From that point on Targett was no longer considered a transient, and the lawman stopped paying special attention to him. They had crossed paths only occasionally since then.

Targett opened the door and the sheriff glowered at him. Mathis was a big man and might once have been considered powerfully built, but now he was just . . . well, big. His face was round, and his belly—which hung over his belt—was, too.

"What's the matter, sheriff?"

"Come out here and sit down," Mathis said. "I want to talk to you."

"What time is it?" Targett asked, rubbing his face.

"Never mind that."

"Let me get dressed—"

"You don't have to. Nobody's in the saloon yet."

"What?" Targett asked. "It's that early?"

"Don't make me ask you again."

There was a time no one would have spoken to Targett that way. He, himself, was a big man, once powerfully built, but he had gone the opposite way of the sheriff. Instead of getting fat, Targett had gotten very thin, almost painfully so, and he no longer cut a very imposing figure.

"I'm comin'," Targett said.

He came out of the room, walked to a table, and sat down, wondering what he had done to bring the sheriff around. The saloon was not quite as empty as the sheriff had said. Frank Keller was behind the bar, getting set up for the day, and he glowered at both of them.

"Targett, do you know a woman named Margaret Adams?"

Targett frowned. His mind was fuzzy these days, usually filled with accusing blue eyes, especially when he'd been pulled from a deep sleep.

"I don't think so—"

"She got to town about a week go. 'Sposed to be the new schoolteacher."

Targett shook his head.

"I don't know her."

"Pretty woman with a little girl."

Targett perked up at the mention of a little girl.

"She says you've been watchin' her, followin' her."

Targett didn't reply.

"Well, have you?"

Targett said something the sheriff didn't catch.

"What was that?"

"I said not her."

"Whataya mean, not her?"

"I've been watchin' the little girl."

"The little girl?" the sheriff repeated. "Whatsa matter, grown-up women don't appeal to you?"

Targett didn't answer.

"Come on, Targett, don't make this hard on yourself. Why you been watchin' a little girl?"

"I don't want anything to happen to her."

Sheriff Mathis thought about that and scratched his head.

"You got some reason to think that somethin' is gonna happen to her?"

"No," Targett said, "I just—"

"Never you mind 'I just,'" Sheriff Mathis said, "just stop it, all right? It don't look good havin' a grown man followin' a little girl around town."

"I just . . . want to keep her safe."

"That's my job, Targett," Mathis said, smacking his chest with his fist. "I get to keep the people in this town safe, not you."

"But—"

"No buts," Mathis said, cutting him off. "Look, if you don't stop I'm gonna have to run you out of town. The town council ain't gonna want you scarin' away their new schoolteacher. If it comes down to you or her, Targett, you're gone. You got that?"

Targett nodded.

"Yeah," he said, "I got it."

"Okay, then," Mathis said, "I'm done. Go back to sleep."

"He ain't goin' back ta sleep," Frank Keller said. "Now that he's up he's gonna sweep this place out before we open . . . ain't ya, Targett?"

Targett waved a hand and stood up.

"Just let me get dressed," he said, and started back to his room.

"Remember what I said, Targett," the sheriff said warningly. "No more followin' women or little girls . . . or anybody!"

5

Josiah Alton was a hunter, pure and simple. When you wanted somebody found, you hired Alton, and that's what Robert Black did. Alton was paid a lot of money to find Black's wife and daughter, and the hunter found them in Dunworthy, Texas.

Alton arrived in Dunworthy the day after the sheriff warned Targett away from Margaret Adams and her daughter, Alecia. He'd picked up Margaret 'Adams's' trail in Oklahoma and followed it all the way down here to East Texas.

Alton took a room in the same hotel as Margaret and Alecia Adams and noticed the woman's name in the register.

"Are there any kids in this hotel?" he asked the clerk.

"Well," the man said, "one, but she's very well behaved. I'm sure you won't have any trouble."

"That's okay," Alton said. "I like kids."

He signed in and went up to his room.

★

Alton watched Margaret and Alecia for the next two days, the same two days that Targett was trying *not* to watch them. Before that, though, he went to the telegraph office and sent a telegram back East, to his employer. It said simply: COME TO DUNWORTHY, TEXAS. BRING MY MONEY.

He signed it.

On the third day both men made a move that would affect everyone's future.

★

Targett couldn't take it anymore. He knew that if he tried to follow the woman and the child again the sheriff would put him out of town, but he had to do something. He decided to go to the hotel and talk to the woman, explaining everything. He hoped she would understand.

★

At the same time, Josiah Alton decided to make his move. He left his hotel room, walked down the hall, and knocked on the door.

"Mrs. Black?" he said when she opened the door.

He could see by the look in her eyes that she was startled.

"I—I'm sorry," she stammered, "you must be mistaken. I'm not—"

"There's no mistake," Alton said, and pushed her inside.

"I—I'll scream," she threatened.

He smiled tightly.

"If you do," he said, "I'll hurt the child."

"Y-you wouldn't!"

"I would, Mrs. Black," he said. "Look at my face."

"Yes," Margaret Black said after a moment of doing that. It was the face of a killer, ugly and devoid of expression or even the *potential* for warmth. "I see you would. All right, what do you want?"

"Mommy—" Alecia said in a tiny, frightened voice.

"Hush, honey. It's all right."

"Just to tell you that you've been found," Alton said, answering her question. "Your husband should be here any day now."

"H-he hired you?"

"Yes."

"To do what?"

"To find both of you."

"Not to bring us back?"

"No," Alton said, "he wanted to come and get you. Apparently you've led him a merry chase, Mrs. Black. I'm the fourth man he hired to find you."

"And the best, no doubt."

He smiled, and by doing so made himself even uglier.

"No doubt."

Margaret turned her back to him and walked to the dresser.

"Please don't try anything, Mrs. Black."

She turned to face him.

"Isn't there anything I can say . . ."

"No."

". . . or do to change your mind?"

Alton looked her up and down. There was something she could do, all right. It wouldn't change his mind, but it would make him happy.

"Sure," he said, "you're welcome to try."

She took his meaning immediately, her eyes flicking to Alecia, who was sitting on the bed quietly, watching them both with wide eyes.

"Put her in the closet," Alton said.

"What?" Margaret jerked her eyes from Alecia to Alton.

"Put her in the closet," he said, again. "She won't see anything."

"But, she'll hear—"

"Do it!" Alton said. "Or I will."

"All right," Margaret said, "all right."

She walked to her daughter and looked at her gravely.

"Come with me, honey."

The little girl got off the bed and took her mother's hand. Margaret led her to the closet door, and the girl balked.

"I don't want to go in the closet, Mommy."

"It'll be all right, honey."

"It'll be dark."

"Close your eyes, baby," she said. "Remember how Mommy told you if you close your eyes you can't see the dark?"

"I remember."

Margaret opened the door and Alecia took small, halting steps until she was inside. The child sensed that something out of the ordinary was happening. Normal childhood fears did not apply here.

"Crouch down, baby," Margaret said, "and put your hands over your ears. Don't come out until Mommy opens the door, understand?"

"Yes, Mommy."

"I love you, honey," Margaret said, and closed the door.

She turned to face Josiah Alton, who had already undone his pants. He had done so without taking off his gunbelt.

"Get undressed!" he ordered.

She walked back to stand in front of the dresser. On it was her purse. She started to undo her dress.

"What happens to you if I tell my husband what happened here today?" she asked.

Alton smiled that ugly smile again. The smugness of it made it even more offensive.

"He wouldn't believe you," Alton said. "You left him and took his daughter—"

"My daughter, too!" she said vehemently. He ignored her.

"To tell you the truth," he said, unbuttoning his shirt so she could see his monstrously hairy chest, "he doesn't even want you back. He wants the girl."

She turned away as she peeled her dress down to her waist.

"Don't be shy," he said.

"What will he do to me when he gets here?"

"If you ask me," Alton said, "he's mad enough to kill you."

"Then I guess I have nothing to lose," she said.

"Wha—"

She turned, holding a small two-shot derringer she had taken out of her purse when her back was to him.

"Damn," Alton said, and went for his gun.

6

Targett was approaching the door to Margaret Adams's room when he heard the shots. One was faint, but the other was very clear. They both came from inside the room. Fearing for the safety of the child and empowered by that fear, he slammed his shoulder into the door, forcing it open.

The woman was down and the man in the room was staggering. Targett saw this in an instant and reacted. He threw himself at the man, who turned in time for Targett to hit him waist high with his shoulder. The two of them fell to the floor, the man's gun jarred from his hand by the impact.

Targett wasted no time. He went for the fallen gun and turned quickly.

Josiah Alton, hampered by the derringer bullet that had entered his shoulder, and jarred by the man who had burst into the room, rolled over and saw the man pointing the gun at him.

"Don't—" Targett said, but Alton was beyond heeding the warning.

The fallen man lunged for Targett, who fired once. The bullet entered the man's chest, slamming him back down to the floor for good.

Targett rushed to the woman, who was now on her knees, blood dropping from a chest wound.

"Alecia—" she gasped. "My little girl—"

"Where is she?" Targett asked.

"C-closet," Margaret said.

"What happened here?"

"My . . . husband hired . . . man. . . ."

"Your husband?"

"Bad man . . ." she said, her voice getting weaker, ". . . bad, bad . . . man."

Targett didn't know what to do for her except lower her into a prone position on the floor. She grabbed the front of his shirt in her bloody hand.

"Don't let him . . ."

"Don't let him what?"

"Don't . . . let him . . . get her. . . ." the woman said painfully. "Please. . . ."

"I won't," Targett promised. He took her hand, sticky with her blood, from his shirt, held it, squeezed it. "I won't."

"Prom—" she started, but she died before she could get the word out.

He knew what it was going to be, though.

"I promise," he said, lowering her hand to the ground.

He stared at her for a moment, then became aware of some noise outside. Apparently others had heard the noise, too.

He stood up and strode across the room to the closet door, tucking the dead man's gun into his belt. He opened the door and the little girl was there, crouched down with her eyes tightly shut and her hands pressed to her ears. She sensed the light, though.

"Mommy?" she asked, without opening her eyes. "Is it over?"

7

Robert Black was incensed.

He stood in Sheriff Mathis's office, his body trembling with rage. The sheriff naturally assumed that the man was upset because his wife had been killed. Little did he know that Black cared nothing at all about that. To this successful eastern publishing mogul his wife was dead to him when she left him and took their daughter with her nine months ago. No, what Black was upset about—*enraged* about—was that the sheriff had not been able to find the man who had taken his daughter.

"Do you know for sure that he has her?" Black asked.

"Well," Mathis said, "people who heard the shots and were in the hall saw Targett come out of your wife's hotel room, carrying a little girl."

"And then what happened?"

"Well . . . nothing," the sheriff said again. "No one ever saw either of them again."

Black, a barrel-chested, florid-faced man in his forties, slammed a meaty fist down on the sheriff's desk. The sheriff was willing to let the act go without remark, because of the man's grief. Also, Mathis was intimidated by Black.

"About the, uh, other man, Mr. Black?"

"What about him?"

"Well, he registered in the hotel as Josiah Alton."

"That name means nothing to me," Black lied.

"He's well known as a, well, as a tracker, somebody who finds missing people."

"What's that to me?"

"Well, I thought . . . maybe . . ."

"You thought what, man?" Black bellowed. "Come on, spit it out!"

"Well, I was just wondering if you might have hired him— you know, to find your wife and daughter."

"Why would I have?" Black replied, lying again. "I didn't need anyone to find my wife. I knew where she was. I was on my way here to meet with her."

"I see."

"And now she's dead."

"So is the man who killed her," Mathis said.

"And how did that happen?"

"Near as I can figure," the sheriff said, "Targett must have come to the door just as Alton was killing your wife. The room looks like there was a scuffle, and Alton was shot twice. Once with your wife's derringer, and once with another gun—probably his own, because his weapon is missing."

"And so is my daughter!" Black said. "What are you doing about finding her?"

"Well . . . there ain't much I can do, Mr. Black. I'm just the town sheriff. My advice to you would be to talk to a federal marshal. If Targett kidnapped the girl, then it's their jurisdiction, but—"

"But what?"

Mathis shrugged and said, "It just sounds to me like Targett may have saved your daughter's life."

"That doesn't give him the right to run off with her," Black asked, "does it?"

8

The first things he saw when he opened *his* eyes were those blue eyes. They were staring down at him, wide and innocent, and filled with . . . what? Trust?

"Mister?" Alecia said.

"Wha—"

"Mister, you gotta wake up." She put a hand tentatively, then got brave and shook him.

"Huh?"

"It's time to get up."

"Ohhh . . ." Targett moaned as he rolled over. It had been a while since he'd slept on the ground—not that the pallet he had been sleeping on lately was much better.

"I'm hungry."

He propped himself up on an elbow and looked at her.

"You are, huh?"

She nodded emphatically.

"Well, then," he said, "let's see what we can do about it."

Painfully, he got to his feet and went to the fire. It had gone out during the night, so he started it up again. While he made a pot of coffee for himself, and some bacon for her, he reflected on the occurrences of the day before. . . .

*

He was still kind of groggy, but he remembered that in the moments that followed finding the little girl in the closet he had grabbed her and run out of the room. People saw him, and called out to him, a couple of them by name, so he knew that by now they were aware that he had the little girl.

From the hotel he had gone straight to his room behind the saloon, entering from the back. He left the little girl there with instructions to say and do nothing, and to hide if anyone came to the door.

"Mister?" she had asked. "Is my mommy dead?"

He hadn't noticed it before then, with all the running and what have you, but suddenly he was aware of her blue eyes.

"Yes, I'm afraid she is."

A single tear rolled down the little girl's face, and she brushed it away with the back of one of her chubby little hands.

"That man killed her," she said, "and my daddy sent him."

"Your daddy?"

She nodded.

"And where's your daddy now?"

"He's on his way here."

He filed that away to be talked about later. Reiterating his instructions until she nodded her understanding, he left her there and went to collect some supplies and a horse. All he knew at that moment was that he had to get the little girl away from Dunworthy, Texas.

★

Targett struggled to remember how far they had come before they stopped. He had one horse, and the child rode in front of him, and had fallen asleep in his arms. She had not awakened when he wrapped her in a blanket and set her on the ground by the fire he'd built.

After he'd unsaddled his horse and rubbed him down he sat by the fire and shivered. He wasn't cold; it had simply been a long time since he had held a gun and used it to kill a man. When the shakes finally went away he was able to lie down and fall asleep.

He looked around them, but the place where they had camped really didn't look familiar. As near as he could put it, they must have ridden for four or five hours. They had to be about twenty miles outside of Dunworthy. What he had to find out from the girl was if they had to go back or forward.

When the bacon was done he put it on a plate and handed it to her.

"Be careful, it's hot."

"Aren't you gonna eat?"

"I'm just going to have coffee."

Targett watched the girl eat and thought back to the conversation they'd had the night before.

★

"What's your name?" he'd asked after they made camp and he'd handed her a plate with bacon on it. Bacon and coffee was all he'd been able to grab at the last minute, before leaving town—along with his gun, and some money he'd put away from what Keller paid him. The horse and saddle were his, the ones he had ridden in with. The dead man's gun was in his saddlebag.

"Alecia," she said. "My name is Alecia. What's yours?"

"Targett."

"That's all? Just Targett?"

"That's all."

"Your mommy didn't give you another name?"

"I don't use it."

"What is it?"

"Never mind," he said. "Tell me about your mother and father."

"They don't get along—I mean, didn't get along."

"Why not?"

"My mother told me that my father was a cruel man."

"She told you that?"

She nodded gravely.

"She even said he was evil."

"Did you believe her?"

"Yes," she said. "My mother never lied to me."

"And did your father lie?"

"All the time," she said. "To me, to Mommy, and to other people. Mommy finally said we couldn't live there anymore."

"Why not?"

She looked down at her plate.

"My father used to hit her."

Targett had no respect for a man who beat a woman, no matter what else he had done, good or bad.

"Alecia, the man who . . . shot your mother. Why do you say he was sent by your father?"

"He told her," Alecia said. "I heard it when I was in the closet. "I . . . I was supposed to not be listening, but I did. Is that all right?"

"That's fine."

Targett thought about asking her why she was in the closet, but he remembered that her mother's dress had been down around her waist. He could guess the rest.

"Do you have any other family?"

"No," the child said sadly. Then she brightened and looked up at him. "Do you?"

The question took Targett off guard.

"Uh, well, no, I don't—"

"Then you could be my new family," she said. "You could be my new daddy."

"I don't know, Alecia," he said. "I mean, you need a mother—"

"You could marry somebody," she said, proud that she had the answer, "and she could be my new mommy."

"Alecia," he said, "you can't replace a mother or a father that easily."

Or, he thought, a child. He was thinking about the woman whose child he had killed, the little girl with blue eyes.

"Besides," he added, "you already have a father."

"I don't like him anymore," she said stubbornly. "He hurt my mommy, and he sent that man to kill her. You saved my life. I want *you* for my daddy."

Targett stared down at the little girl and realized that to her, her logic was infallible. Hell, it even sounded right to him, but . . . he couldn't be anyone's father. He wasn't even a whole man, he was all broken inside . . . unless . . .

"How old are you, Alecia?"

"I'm eight years old."

How old was that girl in Big Bend? he wondered. She had to have been about seven. He wondered what her mother was doing now.

Alecia finished her food and set the plate aside.

"I'm sleepy," she said.

"You can go to sleep," he said. "We'll start again in the morning."

"Where will we go?"

He covered her with a blanket and said, "We'll talk about that in the morning. All right?"

"All right," she said. "Goodnight, Targett."

" 'Night, Alecia."

"My mommy always kisses—always used to kiss me good night."

Targett was quite surprised when, without any hesitation, he leaned over and kissed the little girl's warm forehead.

9

They left soon after Alecia finished her breakfast. Targett knew they were going to have to stop someplace else to stock up on more supplies. Of course, he wouldn't know how much to buy until he knew where they were going.

Not ever having been a father, Targett had no concept of what it entailed, what it felt like. He also had no idea about whether a father could harm his own child.

Apparently Alecia's father was able to harm his wife, but what about the little girl? She had the same blood he had. Did that make a difference?

If Alecia's father—and he hadn't yet asked the girl what his name was—if he could have his own wife killed, could Targett—in all good conscience—give the girl back to him?

Who was he to judge? Hadn't he killed a little girl in Big Bend? Accident or not, he'd taken the life of a child just like Alecia.

He thought again about the girl in Big Bend, and the mother. He never did see the mother again after the incident. He only remembered her from passing her in the street. He didn't even know if he would know her if he ever saw her again. What he did remember, however, was the anguished scream when she realized her daughter was dead.

He often heard that scream in his dreams.

What if, he thought, he took Alecia to that mother? He knew he could never replace her own child, but wouldn't it do Alecia some good? It certainly seemed a better option to him than giving her back to her father. Who knew what he would do to her?

Funny, he thought, as he stared down at the top of the little girl's head, he never thought he'd ever go back to Big Bend, Oklahoma. He'd never even *thought* about going back there, but now . . . it really seemed the only course of action. It would help Alecia, it might help the grieving mother, there . . . and maybe it would help him. Maybe it would take away the nightmares, maybe it would enable him to get on with living his life instead of just existing.

He knew his reception in Big Bend would not be a welcome one. Certainly not from the sheriff, or from the mother. But this sleeping child needed help, and for the life of him, Targett could not think of anything else to do with her.

He certainly couldn't keep her himself.

After last night he knew he'd have to keep watch, because they would certainly be coming after him. Hopefully, he could get Alecia to Big Bend, Oklahoma, before anyone—the law, or her father—caught up with them.

Once the child was safe, he didn't care if they found him or not.

10

When the sheriff looked up from his desk and saw Robert Black enter his office with Mayor Collins, he knew he was in trouble.

"Sheriff."

"Mayor."

Black remained silent, but he had a smug look on his face.

Mathis had seen the look before. It was the look of a man who has a politician in his pocket, even if it was a minor one.

"Sheriff, I've assured Mr. Black that you will be forming a posse to go after the man who stole his daughter," Mayor Alfred Collins said.

"That's not for me to do, Mayor."

Collins was the man who had hired him eight years earlier, and since then Mathis has won six terms of reelection—as had Collins. The sheriff knew, however, that Alfred Collins, at fifty-five, still had ambitions of bigger and better things in politics. He also knew that a man like Robert Black, who had money and power, could offer Collins the help he needed.

"Nevertheless," Collins said, "I want you to do it, before Targett gets much farther away."

Mathis frowned at Collins and asked, "Can we talk without him in the room?"

Black answered before the mayor could.

"I'll be happy to wait outside, Alfred."

Mathis waited until Black had left the office before speaking.

"Alfred?" he said. "You're on a first-name basis already?"

"He can do a lot for this town, Dan," Collins argued.

"You mean a lot for you, don't you, Mayor?" Mathis asked. "What's he gonna do, make you a congressman? A senator?"

"Dan," Mayor Collins said, "he can do you some good, too."

"All I want to do is my job, Alfred," Mathis said. "That's all I've ever wanted to do."

"Then do it," Collins said. "What about that little girl?"

"What about her?"

"What do you think Targett will do to her?"

"He won't hurt her, Alfred," Mathis said. "He's not that kind of man."

"How do you know what kind of man he is? He's only been here six months."

"I checked him out," Mathis said. "He used to live by his gun, but something happened in Big Bend, Oklahoma, that changed all that."

"What happened?"

Suddenly Mathis knew he'd said too much.

"He killed a little girl."

"By God, Dan—"

"It was an accident, the way I hear it," Mathis said quickly. "She crossed between him and another man."

"I don't care how it happened," Collins said. "You get a posse together, or I'll get someone who will."

"Are you threatening my job, Mayor?"

"That's what I'm doing, Dan," Collins said. "I'll have your badge, and you know I can do it."

Dan Mathis was very partial to his badge and his job. This town was his home.

He sighed.

"All right, Mayor," he said, reluctantly, "tell your benefactor he'll get his posse."

"Good."

Collins started for the door, then turned and said, "One more thing."

"What's that?"

"He'll be going along."

Mathis stared at the door as it closed behind the mayor, then shook his head and said in disgust, "Great."

*

The next day Sheriff Mathis collected his posse, which included three men from town, Robert Black, and two men he apparently had brought with him. Their names were Fred Bean and Tom Sullivan. Both men were experienced bounty trackers, and were being paid more by Robert Black than they had been paid for their last five bounties combined.

"I thought a posse was made up of townspeople," Eric Gates said. He *was* one of the townspeople.

"Not this time, Eric," Mathis said. "Mr. Black, there, is a special friend of the mayor's. It was his little girl that Targett took."

Gates shook his head.

"I don't know Targett that well, sheriff, but he don't strike me as the kind of man to steal a little girl."

"No," Mathis said, "me neither."

"What do we do when we find him?" Gates asked.

"Bring him back, I guess," Mathis said. "Him and the girl."

Gates looked over at Robert Black and the two men with him. The two men wore their guns like they knew how to use them. They were two of a kind, in their thirties, their eyes hard and their faces stern. The sheriff had never heard of them, but he knew professionals when he saw them.

"Those two don't look like they're plannin' on bringin' him back."

"I noticed that myself," Mathis said, wishing he had more men along. The way it stood now he had three and Black had two, and while his three were fine for a posse, Black's two looked like they had done more gunwork.

It didn't seem all that even.

11

Over the course of the next three days Targett found his progress impeded by two things. One, the little girl was not used to traveling by horseback, and they had to rest periodically for her. The second thing was more personal. It had been months since Targett himself had been on the trail, and he was not in good enough physical shape to make the trip easily. He found that they had to stop for him to rest almost as often as for her.

He had thought that she could sleep in the saddle, but she napped only fitfully. When she was awake she asked questions.

"Where are we going?"

"When will we get there?"

"Are we there yet?"

"Will my daddy catch us?"

The last one was a hard one to answer. Targett was sure that a wealthy, influential man like her father—whose name she said was Robert Black—would not take kindly to having his daughter taken away. He also knew that by doing so he was probably committing some terrible crime. Still, if the little girl was to be believed in the things she said about her father, he felt he had no choice. Also, he had come to think of Alecia's safety as his redemption, of sorts. He couldn't bring back the little girl he had killed, but he could make sure that nothing happened to this one.

So Black and whoever he was able to recruit would be on their trail, and were probably moving faster than they were due to their frequent rest periods. Targett damned the shape his body was in. At night he found his hands shaking, and when he tried to hold them between his knees to stop them he found *them* shaking as well. The long months of abuse he had heaped on his body were coming back to haunt him.

To the question of whether her father would catch up to them he replied, "I don't know, honey. I guess he'll try."

"But will he?"

He stared across the campfire at her.

"We'll just have to wait and see."

"But Targett—"

"It's time for you to go to sleep now, Alecia."

"And you?"

"I'll be going to sleep, too."

She rolled over and wrapped herself in her blanket. He was amazed at how much she had come to trust him—and he felt that he was betraying her trust because he could not remain on watch. It was impossible to stay awake all night and ride all day. He had to take the chance of getting some sleep, or risk falling asleep in the saddle and falling off his damn horse. He could break his neck that way, or hers.

Tonight he was pleased to find that his hands were not shaking as much as they had been the past few nights. Maybe the meager meals they were sharing were doing him some good. Also, he had drank no alcohol since leaving town with her. He was surprised that his body was not craving it more, but maybe he hadn't been so far gone on whisky as he had thought.

It was chilly tonight, and he knew if he felt it, so did she. He took his blanket and put it on her while she slept, so that the chill would not wake her up. He then sat closer to the fire to keep himself as warm as he could.

He sat with his gun in his hand, and soon his head drooped and his eyes closed.

*

"We're gettin' closer," Fred Bean said. He had one knee on the ground and was studying the tracks left behind by Targett.

"He's not doin' anythin' to hide his tracks," Sullivan said.

"I noticed," Bean replied.

"What's that mean?" Black asked.

Bean looked up at his employer.

"It means he probably expects us to catch up to him, sooner or later."

"Then why keep going?" Black asked.

"From what the sheriff tells me," Bean said, "the man is givin' himself no choice. He's going to keep goin' as long as he can."

"What about my daughter?" Black asked. "Is there any sign of her?"

"Some," Bean said. "She's with him."

"Good."

Mathis studied Robert Black. The man might have loved his little girl, but the sheriff thought there was more pride than emotion behind his desperation to find her. He didn't believe for a minute that the woman had come here to meet him. More likely she had come here to get away from him, and he was upset that she had taken their daughter with him. Black was the kind of man who prized possessions above all else, and to him the little girl was a possession.

Sheriff Mathis wished he could prove that the man who killed Margaret Black—the woman he had known as Margaret "Adams"—had been working for Robert Black. He suspected it—hell, he *knew* it—but he couldn't prove it. If he could, he would have thrown the man's ass in jail. What kind of man has his own wife killed?

"How far behind them are we?" Black asked.

Bean mounted up.

"A day, maybe a little more."

"Then this time tomorrow we might be right behind him."

"It's possible," Bean said. "He's heading due north, to Oklahoma. It's my guess that's where he's headed."

"Why do you say that?" Black asked.

"Because if he's not bothering to cover his trail he thinks he's going to get to his destination before we catch up to him."

"You could be wrong," Mathis said.

Black looked at the lawman.

"And why do you say that?" he asked, almost with disdain.

Bean only stared at Mathis, without saying a word in defense of his theory. He let his employer do the talking.

"Because I know Targett," Mathis said. "He's too smart to be leaving this clear a trail."

"Maybe you give him too much credit," Black said. "From what I hear he was almost your town drunk."

"Ask your men about him," Mathis suggested.

Black looked at them now, Bean and Sullivan in turn.

"Do you know this man?"

"We've heard of him," Bean said, answering for both of them. "Up until about six months ago he had a pretty good reputation."

"As what?" Black asked.

"As the kind of man you might hire to get something done, Mr. Black," Bean said.

"And now?"

Bean shrugged.

"We hadn't heard too much about him until you hired us," he said.

"I don't think he has a very good reputation now," Black said. "Not from what I heard around town." He looked at the sheriff. "Let's not make this more difficult than it should be, sheriff."

"I won't . . ." Mathis said.

"Good."

". . . but Targett might."

12

When Targett saw Big Bend, Oklahoma, ahead of them he stopped short.

"What's wrong?" Alecia asked.

"Nothing."

"Are we there yet?"

"We're almost there, honey," he said.

The thing that most surprised Targett about Alecia was how easily he was able to talk with her. He'd never been very comfortable with children, but he felt as if he'd known this little girl for a long time. Every time she craned her neck to look up at him her blue eyes were filled with such trust that it amazed him. Invariably he found himself looking away, because her eyes seemed ghostly to him, as if another little girl were regarding him through them.

"Is that where we're going?" she asked, pointing at Big Bend.

"That's it."

"Then why aren't we moving?"

"Something bad happened the last time I was here."

"Then why did we come here?"

"Because," Targett said, "it's not right to run away from bad things."

"We're running away from my daddy," she said, "and he's bad."

"We're not really running away from him," Targett said. "It's more like we were running to here."

"And will something good happen now?"

"Yes," he said, sounding much surer than he felt, "something good will happen here."

He started his horse walking toward Big Bend, wondering how much time they had before Robert Black caught up to them.

And he wondered what he would do when he did.

★

Big Bend had changed very little since he was last there. As he rode down the main street the memory of what happened there, right in front of the hotel, came rushing back to him, and he shuddered. He would like to have checked into the hotel so he and Alecia could get some rest, but not knowing how close behind them her father was, he dared not risk it. Instead, he rode directly to the sheriff's office and dismounted. In passing the hotel he saw a sign above the door that said KANE HOUSE. He recalled Henry Lyle telling him that his employer was much too modest to name the hotel after himself. Apparently he'd gotten over that.

Amazingly, as he helped Alecia down from the horse, he felt more like himself than he had for six months. Last night neither his hands nor his knees had shook, and he actually felt stronger than he had in a long time. He'd always liked riding the trail. It had always been as if he drew sustenance from riding the land, and he guessed that this time was no different.

"Why are we going in here?" Alecia asked.

"This is the sheriff's office," he explained. "The man inside is going to help us."

They walked to the door of the office and Targett hesitated a moment before entering. Sheriff Kyle Thompson had told him never to come back to Big Bend, and here he was, six months later. He didn't know how the man was going to react. He remembered that even though the sheriff had run him out of town, he had been solicitous toward him because of what had happened.

He hoped the man would still be so.

★

When the door to his office opened, Sheriff Thompson looked up and couldn't believe his eyes.

"Targett."

"Hello, sheriff."

The lawman gaped at him, and then at the little girl with him. "I thought I told you never to come back here."

"I know," Targett said, "but I didn't know where else to go."

"Why come back here?" the lawman asked. "I'm surprised you weren't lynched in the street."

"The street's pretty quiet."

"Why?" Thompson asked again. "Why come back here?"

"This little girl needs help."

Thompson looked at Alecia, who was staring at him with wide brown eyes.

"What kind of help does she need that you had to bring her here?"

"Can we sit and talk, sheriff?" he asked. "It's a little bit of a story."

Still shocked at Targett's appearance, the man simply waved him to a chair. He watched in fascination as Targett sat and lifted the girl up onto his knee. The girl seemed very content to settle there. Six months ago this man had killed a little girl much like this one—albeit accidentally and now here he was back, with another little girl.

"What the hell is this about?" he asked.

Targett told him.

"That's quite a story," Sheriff Kyle Thomspon said when he had all the facts.

"It's all true."

"Yes," Alecia said, "it is." These were the first words she had spoken since they entered his office.

"I don't doubt that it is," Thompson said, speaking to both Targett and the little girl, "but it still doesn't explain why you came here."

"She needs a new home."

"Here?"

Targett nodded.

"With who?"

Targett stared at him. The sheriff seemed to have put on as much weight as Targett had taken off. His face was much fuller than Targett remembered, and it made him look older. Or maybe it was the disbelieving look on his face.

"Oh, no," Thompson said, "you can't be thinking—"

Targett nodded.

"Yes, I am."

"She'll never do it."

"I can ask her."

"She'll never agree to talk to you."

"You could ask her."

"That's what you want from me?" Thompson asked. "To act as a go-between?"

"Yes."

"Targett," the lawman said, "the woman has gone through hell these past six months and is trying to get her life back together."

"I realize that."

"She's even taken to working with some of the kids in town. We never had a school, you know, so she's, uh—"

"Replaced her daughter with other children?"

"Not *replaced*," Thompson said. "She's just trying to . . . fill her days."

"Alecia could help her do that."

The sheriff looked exasperated.

"You could talk to her," Targett said. "She's a good woman."

"Yes, she is," Thompson said, "but this may be too much to ask, even of a good woman."

"But you'll ask her?"

The sheriff remained silent, remembering all the times he'd seen Mary Pickens since the death of her daughter. Her eyes had been haunted things the first three months, seeming to sink into her head, with dark circles beneath them. During the fourth month she seemed to start coming out of it some. By the fifth month her eyes did not always seemed haunted, and the dark shadows were fading. It was at that time that she began to work with some of the younger children in town. At first some of the parents thought she was trying to use their children to replace her own, but they quickly realized that this was not the case. Mary Pickens simply had time on her hands, time that she was trying to put to good use.

"Sheriff?"

"Huh?"

"Will you ask her?"

"I'll talk to her, Targett . . ." Thompson said after a moment.

"Thank you."

". . . but you're gonna have to ask her."

13

"Why should I talk to him?" Mary Pickens demanded.

"To tell you the truth, Miz Pickens," the sheriff said, "I can't think of a reason."

"He's got some nerve—"

"Except for the child," Thompson said.

"What child?"

"He has a child with him," Thompson said, "a little girl."

Mary Pickens hesitated, and then in spite of herself asked, "How old?"

Thompson shrugged.

"Seven, I guess."

Mary bit her lip.

"My daughter's age."

"Yes."

She hesitated again.

"What is *he* doing with a child?"

So Sheriff Thompson told her the story. . . .

*

Robert Black and the rest waited patiently while Fred Bean examined the ground.

"What's wrong?" Black asked when Bean stood up.

"He's doubled back on us," Bean said.

"Does that mean we've lost him?"

"No," the tracker said, "that just means he's not making it so easy as we thought."

He mounted up.

"Can you find his trail again?"

"I can find it," Bean said. "Come on."

*

Targett entered Mary Pickens's house nervously. He had never been so nervous before. This was the first time he would see this woman since he shot her daughter to death.

"This is a big house," Alecia said.

It was a big house, two stories with several rooms on each floor. Six months ago the sheriff had told Targett that Mary Pickens lost her husband a year before. He died leaving her with the house, a lot of money—and their daughter.

"Yes, it is," Targett said.

Sheriff Thompson led them into the living room, where they waited, sitting side by side on the sofa. He went upstairs to get the lady of the house.

Moments later the sheriff came down.

"She'll be along," he said. "I'll, uh, wait outside."

Before Targett could say anything, he was gone.

Targett waited, watching Alecia, who was taking in her surroundings with great interest. He was looking at her eyes and wondered if something was wrong when suddenly they heard someone coming down the steps.

When Targett saw her, his mouth went dry. He only remembered her from seeing her in the street that day, but he recognized her. She was walking stiffly down the stairs, staring at him. He swallowed and tried to keep himself from looking away.

"Miz Pickens—" he started, but she stopped him.

"Don't speak, please!" she said harshly. He subsided and the woman looked at Alecia for several moments before speaking. She walked to a soft-cushioned chair and sat down.

"Come here, child."

Alecia looked at Targett, who nodded. The little girl got down from the sofa and walked over to stand in front of Mary Pickens. The woman looked at her with an entirely different expression.

"What's your name, child?"

"Alecia."

"What's your last name?"

Alecia shrugged.

"You don't know your last name?"

"It was Black," she said, "but my mommy told me that we changed it to Adams."

"Why did she change it?"

"So my father wouldn't find us."

"And why didn't she want your father to find you?"

"She said he was bad," Alecia said.

"In what way?"

"He used to hurt my mommy," she said. Targett was amazed at how level and strong her voice was while she was answering these questions. "He used to hit her."

"Did he ever hit you?"

"No," Alecia said, "but he would have if my mommy didn't take me away."

"Is that what your mother told you?"

Alecia nodded.

"And did you believe her?"

"Yes."

"Why?"

"Because my mommy didn't lie to me."

"Ever?"

"Ever."

"Alecia," Mary Pickens said, "are you afraid of your father?"

"Yes."

"Why?"

"Because he sent a man to kill my mommy."

Targett couldn't see Alecia's face, but it was either something there, or something in what she said, that caused Mary Pickens's face to dissolve into tears.

"Oh, honey," she said, and took the little girl into her arms. When Targett realized that they were both crying, he knew he had made the right decision.

He waited.

Mary and Alecia cried for a while, with the woman stopping first. Targett thought that the little girl had probably needed this for a long time. He also noticed that Mary Pickens never looked at him over the little girl's shoulder. In fact, she had not looked at him since she first came down. That was why he was surprised when she finally did look over at him.

"You want me to keep this child?"

"Yes," he said. "She needs a home."

Mary held Alecia at arm's length as the child's sobs subsided.

"Alecia, would you like to stay here?"

The child snuffled, then answered.

"Can Targett stay, too?"

Mary Pickens looked shocked.

"Why would you want him to stay?"

"He saved my life."

Mary hesitated, then said, "I see."

"I can't stay, honey," Targett said to Alecia. "You know that. We talked about it."

Alecia hung her head and said "I know" in a very small voice.

Mary Pickens looked at Targett again.

"If she wants to stay," she said, "I will keep her."

"Thank you."

"I'm not doing it for you!" she snapped. "This does not absolve you."

"I realize that," Targett said. "I'm thanking you for the child. I know that doesn't change . . . what happened."

"I'll ask you to leave now," Mary said. "Alecia and I still need to get further acquainted. Come back in a few hours and we'll talk again."

"All right."

He stood up, started to say thank you, then caught himself.

"You're a strange man," she said as he started out. "To even think to bring this child to me is—"

"I know," he said, and left.

14

Targett had only thought to double back once, because he wanted to make sure that he had time to talk to Mary Pickens before Black and his party arrived.

When he left the house he had a bad feeling. Sheriff Thompson turned and looked at him.

"Well?"

"I think she's going to keep her."

"You think?"

"She wants to get acquainted. I have to come back in a few hours."

"Maybe you want to freshen up and get something to eat?"

"Maybe . . ."

"What's wrong?"

Targett looked at Thompson.

"You ever feel like somebody just walked on your grave?"

"No," the lawman said, "and I hope I never do. Come on. I better stay with you, in case somebody tries to give you some trouble."

They started back toward the center of town.

★

"That's Big Bend," Fred Bean announced.

"I should have known," Sheriff Mathis said.

"What do you mean?" Black asked.

Mathis looked at the man.

"That's where Targett had all the trouble six months back."

"Why would he come back here?" Black asked.

"Why don't we go and ask him," Bean said, and started his horse forward.

★

"Sheriff," Targett said.

"What?"

Targett jerked his head, pointing with his chin. Thompson looked and saw seven men riding toward them from the other end of town.

"Those the men chasing you?" he asked.

"I don't know."

"One of them's wearing a badge."

"I see that," Targett said. "Yeah, that's Sheriff Mathis from Dunworthy."

"Texas?" Thompson said. "What the hell is he doin' here?"

"Somehow," Targett said, "I don't think he's got much choice."

"Let me go and find out."

"I'll go with you," Targett said, "in case they try to give you some trouble."

★

"Who are they?" Black asked. "Is that Targett?"

"One of them is wearing a badge," Bean said.

"The local law," Mathis said. "He's going to want an explanation."

"Is that Targett?" Black asked again.

"That's him," Mathis said.

"Where the hell is my little girl?"

★

The two men on foot and the seven on horseback stopped within twenty feet of each other.

"I'm Sheriff Thompson."

"Sheriff Mathis, from Dunworthy, Texas," the other lawman replied.

"You're a little far afield, sheriff," Thompson said. "What can I do for you?"

"We're lookin' for this man," Mathis said, nodding at Targett.

"Goddamnit," Robert Black said, "where's my daughter?"

Targett looked at the man.

"She's safe."

"Where?"

"Away from you."

"You think we won't find her?"

"Take it easy—" Mathis started, but Black was not to be denied.

"I want to see her, now."

Targett shook his head.

"She doesn't want to see you."

"What are you talking about?" Black demanded. "She's my daughter. Why wouldn't she want to see me?"

"Because you had her mother killed, and she knows it."

"That's preposterous!"

"How do you know that, Targett?" Mathis asked.

Targett answered while keeping his eyes on the two men to Black's right. If there was going to be trouble it would come from them. The other members of the posse were townspeople. These two were professionals.

"The little girl told me."

"She's . . ." Black started.

"What?" Targett asked. "Crazy?"

"Mistaken."

"I don't think so."

"Her mother turned her against me."

"She heard it," Targett said. "She heard the man say he worked for you, just before he killed her mother . . . your wife. What kind of a man does that, Black?"

Now Black looked to the two lawmen.

"This man's a kidnapper," he said. "Somebody arrest him."

The two sheriffs exchanged a glance.

"Maybe," Mathis said, "we should talk to the little girl."

"There's nothing to talk to her about!" Robert Black said. "Christ, she's only . . . seven."

"She's nine, Black," Targett said. "You don't know how old your own daughter is?"

"Eight, ten, what the hell is the difference?" He looked to the lawmen again. "Aren't you going to do something?"

"I think talking to the little girl would be a good idea," Sheriff Thompson said.

It had never occurred to Robert Black that his own daughter might speak against him, that she might have been present when Josiah Alton killed his wife.

He turned and looked at Bean and Sullivan.

"Take him!" he said.

The two men hesitated.

"Do what I'm paying you to do!"

"You paid us to find him," Fred Bean said, "not to gun him down in front of two lawmen."

"It would be a fair fight," Black said. "Isn't that some kind of code of the West? A fair fight?"

"One man against one man, Mr. Black," Targett said, "that's a fair fight."

Black looked directly at Bean.

"You take him, man to man."

"Take him yourself."

Black looked at Sullivan.

"How about you? I'll double what I paid you."

Sullivan spat before he said, "I ain't working for a man who had his own woman killed."

Black looked at the other men in the posse, but they looked away.

"You do it yourself, Black," Targett said. "You're wearing a gun and I'm not at my best."

The two men stared at each other for a few moments, Robert Black perspiring heavily and biting his lip.

"Ready . . ." Targett said.

"Wait, wait, wait!" Black shouted, putting his hands up. "Don't shoot. Never mind. I don't have to have her."

"She's your daughter," Mathis said.

"I don't want her bad enough to die for her," Black said.

"Too bad for her." Targett put his hands behind him so no one would see they were shaking.

As long as Robert Black was alive, Alecia would have to deal with him at some time in her life. Targett thought it would be easier for the girl growing up if her father were dead.

Apparently Sheriff Mathis was having similar thoughts.

"That's enough," he said, putting himself and his horse between Targett and Black. He reached over and plucked Black's gun from his holster, then looked at the two bounty men.

"You two been paid?" he asked.

"Up to now," Bean said.

"I think that's all you're gonna get," Mathis said. "Sheriff Thompson?"

The sheriff of Big Bend stepped forward and said to Bean and Sullivan, "I suggest you fellas ride out. I wouldn't want you to change your minds about working for this man."

Bean stared at the sheriff, then looked at Targett, nodded, and turned his horse. Sullivan followed. Targett thought it was odd for him to get the bounty men's approval like that.

"Sheriff," Thompson said, "the members of your posse are welcome to get themselves some rooms. You men, Targett and Mr. Black here, can go and talk to the child."

Mathis turned and told his men they were done.

"Head home, or get a room, it's your choice."

The three men decided to get rooms, get some rest, and head back the next day.

Black glared at the two sheriffs and said, "You're siding with a kidnapper."

"Mr. Black," Mathis said, "if I could have proved that Alton worked for you back in Dunworthy you wouldn't have got this far."

"But—"

"I don't hold with men who have women killed," Thompson said, "especially their children's mother."

"You wanna show me where this child is?" Mathis asked Thompson.

"I'd be happy to," the sheriff of Big Bend said. "What about Targett?"

Mathis looked at Targett.

"I don't think I need him anymore," he said. "Targett, you plannin' on comin' back to Dunworthy?"

Targett looked at Mathis and said, "I doubt it."

"You need him?" Mathis asked Thompson.

"I guess not." He looked at Targett. "You're not stayin' in town, are you?"

"Just long enough to finish my . . . business with Miz Pickens."

"Good," Thompson said. "You done this little girl a good turn, Targett, but I don't think I want you in my town."

"I'll be on my way," Targett said, "as soon as I'm sure the girl is safe."

"Oh, I get it," Black said. "Trying to trade my daughter for the girl you killed? Trying to ease your guilt, Targett?"

Targett looked at Black. If Sheriff Mathis hadn't relieved the man of his gun Targett might have killed him then and there.

"Shut up, Black," Mathis said.

"Follow me, sheriff," Thompson said, and the three men moved away, leaving Targett standing in the street alone.

15

The first thing he noticed about Alecia when he saw her again was that she had brown eyes. How odd. Why had he thought she had blue eyes, this whole time?

Was he crazy?

Maybe he had been. Maybe that had been the problem.

"Are you leaving?" Alecia asked.

"Yes, honey."

"I wish you weren't."

"I have to," he said. "It wouldn't be right."

"I know," she said. "You told me."

"Miz Pickens will take good care of you."

"She's nice."

They were standing on the front porch of Mary Pickens's house. Sheriffs Mathis and Thompson had already been there with Robert Black, but they hadn't allowed Black to see his daughter. They had talked with Alecia, and then asked her if she wanted to see her father. She had said no. She'd recounted all of this to Targett.

"I never want to see him again."

Targett had the feeling that would change, when she got older. He wondered what the two lawmen would decide to do with Robert Black. He really didn't care, though, as long as Alecia was safe. He intended to ride right from the Pickens house out of town.

"I don't blame you, honey."

"Targett?"

"Yeah?"

"Can I kiss you good-bye?"

"Sure you can."

He squatted down and she gave him a hug and a kiss on the cheek. He looked into her eyes again, just to make sure. Yep. They were brown.

"What's wrong?" she asked.

"You have beautiful brown eyes."

"Thank you."

"Good-bye, sweetie."

He stood up.

"Good-bye, Targett."

He waited until she went into the house without looking back at him, then walked to his horse and mounted up. He wondered what would happen that night when he camped and went to sleep.

He wondered if he'd seen the last of the ghost with blue eyes.

Brian Garfield

RIVERBOAT FIGHTER

*Brian Garfield got so successful as a suspense writer
that his early Western novels were almost forgotten.*

He wrote three of the best Westerns of the seventies;
Sliphammer, Gun Down, *and the brilliant, sprawling*
Wild Times. *None of these books ever quite got its due.*

*Here you see Garfield at his best—hard-edged, pol-
ished, and in total control of his materials.*

Clay Goddard came aboard the *Mohave* at Yuma an hour before she was due to depart. He walked around B deck to his
regular tiny stateroom on the port side and remained there
only long enough to stow his carpetbag and comb his hair; the
cubicle was stifling hot. Coming out on deck, he tugged his
brocade vest down and placed his gray hat squarely across his
brows. Clay Goddard was a tall man, thin to the point of gaunt-
ness, with the hint of a stoop in his broad shoulders. His lion-
gray eyes were hooded and his lips were guarded by the full
sweep of a tawny mustache.

He was coming around the afterdeck, passing in front of the
wide paddlewheel, when his alert eyes shot toward the gang-
plank. A solid-square man in a dusty blue suit was coming up
the plank; sight of that man arrested Clay Goddard: He stood
bolt still, watching, while the stocky man ascended to the rail
and paused.

A ball-pointed brass star glittered on the newcomer's blue
lapel. The ship's captain, coming toward the gangway, nodded
and touched the brim of his cap. "How do today, Marshal?"

Marshal Emmett Reese nodded and said something Goddard
didn't catch; then the lawman's deliberate voice lifted: "Believe

I'll be going up with you this trip, Jack. How's the current
running?"

"Slow and easy," Captain Jack Mellon said. He was a legend
on the river: He had steamed the Rio Colorado more than fifteen years. It was said he could talk to the river and hear its
reply. He said to the marshal, "Ought to make an easy five
miles an hour going up. I figure to make Aubrey's Landing in
forty-eight hours."

"That's traveling," Marshal Reese observed. Clay Goddard
watched the lawman's profile from his stance under the shad-
owed overhang of the afterdeck. The captain spoke once more
and turned to go up the ladder toward his wheelhouse on the
Texas Deck, and Marshal Emmett Reese's glance came around
idly. His eyes alighted on Clay Goddard and immediately narrowed; the marshal's whole frame stiffened. Goddard's expression remained bleak, unreadable. Across thirty feet of deck
space their glances clashed and held. The revolver butt at Goddard's hip touched the vein of his thin wrist.

Emmett Reese seemed about to advance, about to speak; but
then the sound of an approaching buggy clattered toward the
wharf, and the marshal ripped his eyes away, swinging heavily
around, tramping back down the plank.

Clay Goddard's face revealed no particular relief. He turned
with deliberate paces and walked into the ship's saloon. The
bartender was its only occupant. Goddard took a cup of coffee,
went to a table in the back of the room, and laid out an elaborate game of patience. Brooding over the cards, he sipped the
cooling black coffee and ran his glance once around the room.

It was neither so large nor so elegant as the cardrooms on
the great Mississippi packets; but then, this was Arizona, and
rivers did not run so deep or wide here. It was engineering
marvel enough that the *Mohave,* one hundred fifty feet long
and thirty-three feet abeam, could carry two hundred passengers and a hundred thousand pounds of cargo and still skim
over the Rio Colorado's shallow bottom. The water often ran
fewer than three feet deep; the *Mohave* drew only thirty inches,
fully ballasted.

Steamboats had been plying the river for twenty-seven years
now, but their interloping presence in the desert country never
failed to strike Goddard as an odd phenomenon. The ships of
the Colorado Steam Navigation Company regularly made the
seemingly impossible run up to Callville, Nevada—six hundred

miles above the river's mouth, and desert country all the way, except where the big ships had to winch themselves up over cascades through the knife-cut tall gorges upriver.

The saloon was a plain oblong room, low-ceilinged and plainly furnished—not at all like the velvet-lined rooms of the New Orleans sternwheelers. But the *Mohave* was the pride of the line, and in the Far Southwest she was queen. The barkeep wiped his plain mahogany counter and behind it, between racks of labeled bottles, hung a lithographed calendar with to-day's sailing date circled: August 24, 1879. Regarding that, and recalling the grim, square-hewn face of Marshal Emmett Reese on deck, Clay Goddard thought what a long time it had been, how the years had flowed silently by; and he felt quietly sur-prised. He was thirty-seven this month; his birthday had passed, he suddenly realized, without notice.

His lean hands darted over the wooden table, placing card upon card. Green sleeve garters held the shirt back from his wrists. He pulled out his snap-lid pocket watch—eight-thirty in the morning, and already he was soaked with sweat. It would hit a hundred and ten inside the saloon today.

His gambler's training laid a cool endurance over him; over the years he had developed the ability to stand off from himself and look on, as if from some long distance. Without it, his life would not have been bearable.

The boat swayed gently as heavy freight wagons rolled up the plank onto the cargo decking. Faintly through the door came the hoarse shouts of teamsters, the profane calling of stevedores. Passengers, early arriving, began to drift in and out of the saloon. With a hissing chug and a resigned clatter, the boilers fired up and began to build up their head of steam. Smoke rose from the twin tall stacks at the front of the pilothouse.

His shirt drenched, Clay Goddard unbuttoned his elaborate vest—the uniformed sign of his calling—and bent over his soli-taire board in concentration. He was like that, frowning over the merciless cards, when a great force rammed the edge of the table into his belly, slamming him in his chair back against the wall.

Tautly grinning, a hawk-faced man stood hunched toward Goddard, a tall, powerful man with a stiff brush of straight red hair standing up brightly on his head. Hatless, the grin-ning man held the table jammed against Goddard, pinning

Goddard to his chair. In a quiet, soft tone, the red-haired man said, "Somebody told me you were working this boat."

Goddard said with deceptive mildness, "Take the table out of my gut, Miles."

Miles Williams took his hands away from the table and laughed unpleasantly. "I ain't got my gun on just now. That's a piece of luck for you, Clay."

"Or for you."

Miles Williams' eyes met Goddard's without guile. "Nobody said you weren't tough, Clay, and nobody said you weren't fast. But I can take you."

"You can try," Goddard answered evenly. He pushed the table away from him and straightened his rumpled vest, but he kept his seat. The cards had flown into disarray when Williams had violently rammed the table. Goddard gathered them unhurriedly into a pack, never releasing Williams from his gaze.

Williams said, "I've got a lot to settle with you for, Clay. Too much to let pass. I'm going up to Aubrey on this boat and I don't figure both of us will get there alive."

"That's up to you, Miles."

"We're still in port. You can get off now. Maybe I won't follow you—I got business upriver."

Goddard tilted his head slightly to one side. "You'd offer me a chance to skin out, would you? I'm surprised."

"I ain't an unfair man," said Miles Williams. "And I don't like killing. Go on, Clay—get off the boat. Save us both a lot of grief that way."

Goddard considered him over a stretching interval of time; at the end of it he shook his head. "I guess not, Miles."

"Suit yourself." Abruptly, with a snap of his big shoulders, Miles Williams swung away and stalked out of the saloon.

At the bar, a few men with cigars and coffee had watched with careful interest. What Goddard and Williams had said had been pitched too low to reach their ears, but the scene had been too charged with action and hard stares to escape their attention. Sweeping them with his guarded eyes, Goddard maintained his cool expression and proceeded to lay out a fresh, slow game on the table.

Shortly thereafter, however, he got up and walked slowly out of the saloon. A deck hand was coiling in the stern rope. The ship was crowded with army men—two companies of infantry on their way to Ehrenberg, shipping point for the inland

Apache-fighting garrisons. Goddard threaded his path among the knots of troopers and entered his little stateroom, where he closed the door in spite of the heat building up. Out of his carpetbag he took ramrod, patches, cloth, and oil. After locking the door he dismantled his revolver and gave it a careful, methodical cleaning. Then he put it back together, loaded the cylinder with six .44-40 cartridges, and let the hammer down gently between the rims of two shells. Standing up, he slid the weapon into its oiled holster and adjusted the hang carefully. His expression never changed; the mustache drooped over his wide lips. He packed the cleaning equipment away, unlocked the door, and stepped out on deck just as the captain shouted from two decks above and the boat slowly churned out into the current.

The wharves and shipyard of Yuma slowly drifted past the starboard beam; there was a last glimpse of Fort Yuma, high on the hill with its precious squares of green lawns, and then the massive rolling paddlewheel drove the ship around the outer curve of the first bend, and the only sight to either side was mosquito-buzzing brushy lowlands and, beyond, the flats and dry-rock hills of the vast southwestern desert.

Goddard stepped past a lashed-down freight wagon and halted abruptly.

Coming forward, arms linked, were Marshal Emmett Reese and a slim figure of a woman. Holding the woman's left hand was a girl of six, wide-eyed and with hair the same tawny color as Goddard's own. The woman's mouth opened and, quickly, Emmett Reese stepped out in front of her as though to protect her. Reese said nothing, but it was plain by his stance and attitude that he expected Goddard to go on about his business without stopping to speak.

The woman put her hand on Reese's arm. "No, Emmett. We'll be on this boat for two days and nights. It's a small boat. We can't pretend to each other that we don't exist."

Goddard stepped forward with the briefest of cool smiles. "It's been a long time, Margaret." His glance dropped to lie on the little girl. "Six years," he murmured.

The woman had both hands on the little girl's shoulders now. Emmett Reese said, "Come on, Margaret, we can—"

"No," she said. "I want to talk to him, Emmett."

Reese's eyes bored into Goddard, but it was the woman his words addressed: "I wish you wouldn't."

"Take Cathy with you, will you? I'll meet you in the lounge."
The woman's voice was firm.

Troubled, the marshal reached down to take the little girl's
hand. He said to Goddard, "Miles Williams is on board."

"I know."

"This boat's in my jurisdiction. I don't want trouble."

"I won't be starting any trouble," Goddard said.

The little girl watched with her head tilted on one side, looking up at Goddard and then the marshal, puzzled but silent.
Soldiers milled past in pairs and groups. An officer moved
through the crowd, creating a stir of saluting and mumbled greetings. The woman, tossing her head impatiently, said, "Go on,
Emmett." She bent down. "Go with the marshal, sweetheart.
Mummy will be along soon."

The little girl stared at Goddard. "Who's he?" she demanded accusingly.

The woman looked up and away; her eyes turned moist. Emmett Reese said gently, "Come on, Cathy," and led the little
girl away by the hand, casting one warning glance back
toward Goddard.

Goddard moved toward the rail, pushing a path through for
the woman. She came up and stood beside him, not looking at
him, but watching the muddy flow of the river. Her eyes were
still clouded with tears; there was a catch in her throat when
she spoke: "I'm sorry. I knew this moment would come. I meant
to be strong—I didn't mean it to be this way. But when she
asked *who you were*—"

"She looks a little like me," he said musingly.

"She has your hair, your eyes—every time I look at her
I—" The woman's head turned sharply down against her shoulder, hiding her face. Goddard's hand came out toward her, but
stayed, and he did not touch her. A solemn mask descended
over his face. He murmured, "Well, Meg."

He took a folded handkerchief from his vest and offered it
to her. She pressed it to the corners of her eyes. She was a
blue-eyed woman, slim and pretty but no longer in the smooth-
cheeked paleness of youth: The veins of her hands and the
creases around her eyes revealed that she was near Goddard's
own age.

He said, "You're traveling with Emmett?"

"In separate staterooms," she said dryly, and then shook her
head. "He wants to marry me—marry us, that is. He loves
Cathy."

"Maybe," Goddard said softly, "that's because he's had the chance to love her."

Her eyes lifted dismally to his. Plainly gathering herself, she used both palms to smooth back her brown hair. "I am going to be strong, Clay," she said, measuring out each word for emphasis. "You and I, we had our chance together."

"And I ruined it," he finished for her.

"You," she agreed, "and that." She was looking at the worn-smooth handle of his revolver. "And now Miles Williams is here. He's been looking for you a long time, Emmett said. You killed two of his friends in a card game."

"I caught them cheating together. They drew against me."

"Is that an explanation, Clay?" she asked. "Or just an excuse?" She reached out; her fingertips touched the walnut gun grip. "You love that thing."

"No. I hate it, Meg."

She swung halfway, facing the river again, the marshes drifting past. The huge paddlewheel left a pale yellow wake stretching downstream with the current. "I wish I could believe you," she said. "If it's true, then you've changed."

"I have," he agreed simply.

She threw her head back. Her voice was stronger: "We were married once. It didn't work. I've no reason to believe it would work again."

He nodded; but his eyes were sad—he was looking forward, toward the lounge where the little girl had gone. He said, "What will you tell her about me? She wants to know who I am."

"I don't know," she said, almost whispering. "I wish I did." She turned from him and walked away, moving briskly. He watched the way she walked, head turned over his shoulder, both hands gripping the rail so tightly his knuckles shone white.

A tall, red-topped figure swayed forward, pushing soldiers aside roughly with hands and elbows. Miles Williams reached Goddard's side and grinned around the cigar in his teeth. "Who's the lady, Clay?"

When Goddard made no reply, Williams said, "I saw you talking to Emmett Reese. With him on board, we're going to have a little problem, you and me. Either one of us starts trouble, he's likely to step in. So I've got a little proposition for you. I gave you your chance to get off the ship. You stayed, so I guess that means you want to play the game I called. All right, we'll lay down some ground rules. We wait, you and me. These soldier boys get off at Ehrenberg in the morning and the boat'll be less crowded tomorrow. Tomorrow night the decks ought to be pretty clear. We wait until everybody's asleep. No witnesses that way. We have at each other, and no matter who's standing up afterward, ain't nobody can tell Emmett Reese who started the fight. The winner claims self-defense, and Reese can't dispute it, see? No law trouble, no trouble afterward for the one of us that's still alive."

"You're a cold-blooded buck," Goddard observed without much emphasis.

"I just like to keep things neat," Miles Williams said, and turned aft. A holstered pistol slapped his thigh as he walked through the crowd.

Showing no sign of his feelings, Clay Goddard went into the saloon, picked a table, and set the pack of cards out, advertising his calling. It was not long before five soldiers were gathered around his table, playing low-stake poker.

The day passed that way for Goddard, bar sandwiches and coffee and poker—a steamy hot day that filled the room with the close stink of sweat weighted with tobacco smoke and the smells of stale beer and whisky. He did not leave the saloon until suppertime, when he went forward into the dining salon. He saw Emmett Reese and Margaret and little Cathy at the captain's table. His eyes lingered on the blond little girl. Margaret's eyes found him once but turned away quickly; she swung her head around, tossing her hair, to respond to some light remark of Captain Jack Mellon's.

Miles Williams was not in the room. Goddard took his customary place at the first officer's table, between the deck steward and an army doctor, and ate a silent meal. Afterward he had a cigar on deck, and returned to the saloon for the evening's trade. The crowd was thoroughly penny ante; he made a total of seven dollars for the day's gambling, and went on deck at midnight. He had to pick a path over the heaps of sleeping soldiers.

The heat had dissipated with darkness. He lay down on his bunk, knowing he needed sleep in order to be alert for the following night's encounter; but sleep evaded him and he lay in the dark cabin with his hands laced under the back of his head, staring sightlessly at the ceiling. The engines throbbed soporifically, but he was still awake at three when the boat scraped bottom on a sandbar and the engines reversed to take her off. She lurched forward once again, going around the bar, and finally Goddard drifted into a semiwakeful drowsiness that descended into fitful sleep.

He was awake and dressed at dawn when the *Mohave* berthed at Ehrenberg. The town was a drab oasis at best. Miles Williams came by and said, "You could still get off right here and wait till the boat comes back down. But then maybe you'd rather not wait another three years for me to come after you again."

"Never mind," Goddard told him.

"All right," Williams drawled. The sun picked up glints in his bush of red hair. He grinned and ambled away. Goddard noticed Emmett Reese standing not far away, watching him inscrutably; it was hard to tell whether Reese had heard what had been said.

The soldiers disembarked with their baggage and wagons, and thus lightened, the boat made faster headway upstream. Its decks were lashed with wagonloads of mining machinery for the camps served by Audrey's Landing, but pedestrian traffic was light and there was hardly any trade in the saloon all day.

After supper he was on deck, savoring his cigar, when Margaret came out of the dining room and sought him out. If he was surprised, he did not show it. She said, in a voice that showed how tightly throttled were her emotions, "That may be your last cigar. Have you thought of that?"

"Yes."

"How can you keep such a rein on yourself, Clay? Aren't you frightened?"

He made no answer. He squinted against the cigar smoke and Margaret said, "You're scared to death, aren't you?"

"I guess I am."

"Then that's changed, too."

"Maybe I've learned to care," he said. He turned to look at her. "Sometimes it takes a long time to learn a simple thing like that."

His talk appeared to confuse her. She folded her arms under her breasts. "Cathy still wants to know about you."

"Have you decided what to tell her?"

"I'll tell her the truth. But I'm going to wait until tomorrow."

He said quietly, "You think I'll be dead by then, don't you, Meg?"

"One way or the other," she said. "Dead to us, anyway.

Whether you're still walking and breathing won't matter." She
dropped her arms to her sides; her shoulders fell. "Emmett
told me that Miles Williams gave you the chance to get off
at Ehrenberg."

"I might have taken it," he said, "except for you and Cathy.
I wanted to have another day—this is as close as I've ever been
to her. I couldn't give it up."

She said in a muted voice, "If you'd gotten off the boat," and
did not finish; Goddard finished it for her:

"You'd have come with me?"

"I don't know. How can I say? Maybe—maybe."

Twilight ran red over the river. The great paddles slapped
the water and a lone Indian stood on the western bank, silhouetted against the darkening red sky, watching the boat churn
past into gathering night. A shadow filled the dining room
doorway, blocky and sturdy—Emmett Reese, who wore the
star. Reese stood there, out of earshot, watching but not ad-
vancing. Goddard said, "I guess he loves you."

"Yes."

"And you him?"

She didn't answer right away. There was a sudden break in
Goddard's expression and he seemed about to reach out and
grasp her to him, but he made no motion of any kind and his
face resumed its composure. He said slowly, "I have always
been in love with you. But I have to meet Miles Williams tonight and my love for you can't stop that."

"Nor my love for you?" she cried out.

"I'm sorry," he said dismally.

Her voice subsided in resignation. "I can't give my little girl
a father who fights to kill."

"What about Emmett Reese?" He was looking at Reese, out-
lined in the doorway, still as a mountain.

"It's his job. Not his pleasure." Her lip curled when she
said it.

"It's no pleasure to me either," he said. "God knows there
are a lot of things I regret, Meg."

"But you won't give up your pride."

"Would I be a man without it?"

She had no answer for him. She turned and walked from
him, toward the waiting shadow of the marshal.

The cigar had gone dry and sour. Goddard tossed it overboard and went into the saloon. Lamplight sent rays through

the smoky air; the crowd was thin and for an hour no one came to Goddard's table. He sat with the pack of cards before him; he sat still, his head dipped slightly like a tired man half asleep.

Miles Williams came at ten-thirty and sat down opposite him. Williams had a cheroot uptilted between his white teeth. His face was handsome and brash, the eyes half lidded. "A friend is a close and valuable thing," he said. "I lost two friends one night."

"They forced it on me."

"Then they should have won." Williams picked up the deck of cards and shuffled it. "Blackjack suit you?"

And so they played a macabre game of cards while the hours ran out, while the passengers drifted away one by one and lamps winked out around the ship. The engines thrummed, the paddles hit the water with a steady slap-slap, and when the saloon was empty but for the bartender, Miles Williams said in a suddenly taut voice, "All ready, Clay?"

"Here?"

"On deck. Loser goes overboard. Neat—neat that way."

"All right," said Clay Goddard.

Williams thrust his chair back with his knees and stood. "After you?"

"Right beside you," Goddard answered, and they left shoulder to shoulder.

The decks were deserted; lamps were off, except two decks higher up on the *Mohave,* where the keen-eyed captain swept the river vigilantly for shifting sandbars. Miles Williams said, "Jack Mellon's got eyes in the back of his head. We'll go on down to the afterdeck—he can't see that from up there."

They tramped along the port B deck and Goddard felt moisture on his palms; he wiped them on his vest and heard Williams chuckle. "Got you nervous, ain't I? Get a man nervous, you got the edge." Williams was flexing his fingers. Starlight glittered on the river. Not a single lamp glowed in the after section of the ship. The two men reached the platform behind the cabin structure. Here the smash of the paddles against the water was a loud racket in the night; the paddles lifted overhead and swept down, splashing drops of water against the stern and the aft yard or two of deck planking. The iron railing protected passengers from the cruel, deliberate power of the great paddlewheel.

Miles Williams stopped six feet from the rail and wheeled,

planting his feet wide apart. "You can step back a way," he said calmly, "or do you want it point-blank?"

"Right here will do," Goddard said. "A man wouldn't want to miss his shot for bad light."

A startled brightness gleamed from Williams' eyes. "You steadied down quick, didn't you?" he observed. Then he laughed with raucous brashness. But the laugh fell away and his face grew long. The brush of his hair stood up against the sky and he suddenly cried, *"Now!"*

Williams' hand spilled for his gun butt. Close in to the man, Goddard did not reach for his own gun; instead he lashed out with his boot. The hard toe caught Williams' wrist just as the gun was rising. The gun fell away, bouncing off Goddard's instep; and Williams, rocked by the kick, windmilled back, off balance. His feet slipped on the wet planking; the small of his back rammed the stern rail and Goddard, rushing forward, was not in time to prevent Williams from spilling over backward into the descending paddlewheel.

The paddles caught Williams and dragged him down relentlessly; there was a brief awful cry, and that was all.

Gripping the rail, Goddard looked down into the churning blackness of the descending paddles. His eyes were hollow. Heavy footsteps hurried toward him along the deck and he turned, nerved up to high pitch.

Emmett Reese said, "I couldn't stop it before it started. But I saw it. He wasn't fast at all—you could have outdrawn him with no trouble."

"I knew that."

"You didn't figure on this?"

"No. I expected a good beating might have changed his mind." Goddard smiled bleakly. "I was always pretty good with my fists."

"Better than guns," Reese said quietly, staring at the heavy falling paddles. He added in a murmur that was barely audible over the slapping wheel, "You're a far better man than I gave you credit for, Clay."

Reese's hand reached out and clenched Goddard's arm. Goddard shook his head slowly back and forth, as if to clear it. He pulled away and walked forward along the empty deck.

He was in his cabin, unhooking his gun belt, when light knuckles rapped the door. When he opened it, Margaret stepped inside. The lamp washed her face in warm light.

She said, "Emmett told me what happened. You could have drawn on him. You could have shot him down, but you didn't—you tried to save his life."

"I told you," he said wearily. "A man learns a few things as time goes by, Meg."

She said, "Cathy's asleep now, and I didn't want to wake her. But in the morning, when she asks me who you are, I'll be able to tell her. We'll have breakfast together, the three of us."

"What about Reese?" he said.

She moved into the circle of his arms. "He understands," she said. She turned her face up toward him.

Frederic Brown

BULLET FOR BULLET

Frederic Brown wrote at least three of the best suspense novels ever published: The Fabulous Clipjoint, The Screaming Mimi, *and* The Far Cry.

In addition to this, he wrote at least half a dozen short stories that were seminal in the development of the suspense tale.

He was equally at home with science fiction and fantasy, his novels The Lights in the Sky Are Stars *and* Martians, Go Home *being among the best books published in the second half of the twentieth century.*

His Western output was small—only a handful of stories—but as you'll see here, while not a great master of the form, he certainly could turn out a competent and readable tale.

I pushed through the swinging doors under the big sign that read "The We-Never-Close Saloon" and went inside out of the gathering dusk.

A fat little baldheaded guy was back of the bar. A funny-looking little gray-haired geezer was apparently asleep on his feet at the far end of it. And a four-handed card game was going on at a table in the corner.

I whanged the outer layer of dust off my chaps and started back toward the card game. Then I heard one of the players say "Two-no-trumps" and I changed my mind and stopped in front of the bar instead.

"Baldy," I said to the guy behind it, "how far is it to a town?"

"Don't call me Baldy," he comes back, "and you're in a town

right now. If you don't like it, you can go back to where you came from. What's your poison?"

"Rye, Baldy. Straight. And who told you this blemish on the desert was a town?"

"Son," he says, dropping my money into the till, "mebbe this town ain't big, but it's gosh-blamed famous. This very saloon used to belong to the Burke boys. And the Burkes rated right up close to the Daltons and the Jameses. That is, before we strung 'em up."

"Must've been before my time," I said, picking up my glass.

He shook his head. "Not unless you're a lot younger'n you look, stranger. They got strung up last month."

The rye went down my Sunday throat, and I sputtered for a minute. When I could talk again, I said, "You don't say, Baldy. Then this wart on the badlands must be Fleury, and the Burke boys you speak so highly of must have been what they called the Fleury gang?"

He nodded. "And this here saloon right here was their headquarters. Bob Burke hisself owned it. I sorta inherited it because I was the nearest thing left to a relative after the posse got through. I had a mare that was a cousin of the horse Bob Burke rode, or something."

I looked at him suspiciously. "Baldy," I told him, "I'll overlook that, on account of my horse has got a stone bruise and maybe I better stop in Fleury overnight. Anyway, I'm willing to be talked into doing it."

He smiled and poured me a rye on the house.

"You're talking," he said, "to the Fleury Chamber of Commerce, and don't call it Baldy. Furthermore, this blemish on the desert is *not* a wart on the badlands. It's an up-and-coming town, and the most thriving metropolis this side of nine miles from here. But I'll admit that right now it's kind of deadlike."

"I thought I smelled something," I told him.

He frowned at me. "They's a big dance tonight over at Wiota. Half the town's gone over there already and the rest of it, except me and a couple others, is leaving shortly."

"Baldy, how far's it to Wiota?"

"Nine miles."

I looked around the room again, averting my eyes from the card game, and wondered if it'd hurt Blackie's left fore to go another nine miles. I decided it probably would and sighed.

"Is it possible," I asked, "that for tonight I could rent or

borrow something on four legs that could go nine miles one
way and be able to come nine miles ba—"

I happened to be looking toward the back of the room and
my mouth stayed open right in the middle of that last word.
Because the door that led to the living quarters in the rear
had opened and an angel floated in.

That was my first impression. Then I saw she wasn't really
floating; she was walking. And she wasn't really an angel,
maybe, but she was the most beautiful girl I'd ever seen. Why,
there was more gold in her hair than in the whole Panamint
range, and more life and laughter in her eyes than—well, you
know what I mean. She wasn't dressed fancy; just a plain ging-
ham dress, but what a shape that dress was in—with her inside it!

She smiled at Baldy and said:

"Hello, Dad." That smile wasn't aimed at me, but just a
glancing blow from it—sort of a ricochet—nearly took me off
my feet.

"Hi, Billie," says the little guy behind the bar. "You going
over to the dance?"

She shook her head. "Nope, Dad. I'm staying home tonight."

Baldy turned back to me, which made me realize my mouth
was still open, and I closed it.

"Stranger," he said, "I reckon we can."

For a minute, I thought he was loco.

"Can what?" I wanted to know.

"Rent you a horse."

"What for?" I plumb forgot asking him about one. "Oh, you
mean if I was going to Wiota. Guess I done too much riding
already today to go that far and back tonight. By the way, I
never introduced myself. My name's One-Eye Sloan."

"Glad to know you, One-Eye," he says. "My handle's
Wagner, and this is my daughter Billie. We'll be glad to have
you stick around Fleury as long as you like. Maybe you'll get
to like it."

I looked at Billie Wagner again and decided that if *she* ever
wanted me to stick around Fleury I wouldn't have to be
asked twice.

She was looking at me curiously. "May I ask why you're
called One-Eye, Mr. Sloan? You don't seem to—"

I grinned. "Yeah, my eyes both work. But you see I used to
pal around with a feller who looked like me except that he had

only one eye. In fact, the only way they could tell us apart was by that, and by the fact that I had curly hair and he didn't. So they called me One-Eye, and him Curly."

She looked even more bewildered. "But why, if it was you that—"

"Well," I explained, "you see, it made him mad to be called One-Eye and I didn't mind because it wasn't true in my case. And, being a little sensitive about this hair of mine, I'd pop anybody who called *me* Curly. But the other way around neither of us minded, so—"

And there was that million-dollar smile back again, which was what I'd been trying for. And this time it was aimed right at me.

"All right, One-Eye," she said, "I'll call you that. I wouldn't risk calling you Curly and getting popped. I hope you like Fleury."

And she started back toward the door from which she'd floated out of.

I picked up what was left of my rye and sighed. I guess there gets to be a time in every ranahan's life when he figures maybe he should quit being a maverick and let himself get branded, but I'd never felt that way before.

And yet here, right out of the middle of unexpectedness, I was wondering how big a little ranch the money I had saved up would buy, and whether gold hair would look better with a ranch house painted blue or painted red, and how big a corral I'd build.

I guess I was so happy I was silly. I caught sight of my image in the mirror back of the bar and I lifted my glass to it and said "Yippee" and grinned.

Bang! The shot was so darned unexpected that it sounded like a box of dynamite going off. And there wasn't a glass in my hand anymore.

I whirled around and my six-gun was coming out of my holster as I whirled. I didn't know what or who I was whirling to face, but I knew which direction the shot had come from—the far end of the bar.

But, luckily, I held my trigger finger. It was the little gray-haired geezer, and his gun wasn't pointing at me anymore. It was aimed up at the middle of the ceiling where the lamp hung, and—of all things—his eyes were tightly closed.

I still held my gun ready, but I said, "What in—" Because

out of the corner of my eye, I saw the card game was still going on. The guys playing hadn't even looked up!

I saw Billie coming back. She didn't look worried, either. She touched my arm and said, "Be quiet, One-Eye. Come outside and I'll explain. It's all right."

I shoved my gun back into the holster. But I didn't relax just yet. I said, "But he shot that glass right out of my hand! A guy shouldn't take chances like that!"

She smiled. "Look at the glass."

I did. It was upside down on the bar, but it wasn't broken. And all my fingers were in place, too.

I grinned sheepishlike. "I didn't used to be jumpy like that," I said. "Here I thought—"

She went on out the front door and I followed. Outside, I stepped up alongside and she hooked her hand in my elbow and we strolled along what passed for a sidewalk in Fleury.

"Uncle Ralph," she told me, "didn't shoot at your glass. He shot at the light. He does that every time someone says 'Yippee' and sometimes when no one does. He's—well, he's awfully old and getting a bit childish, and—"

"You mean he's potty? But why do they let anyone like that go around with a loaded gun? Anyway, he's a poor shot. He missed that light."

"Don't fool yourself about him being a poor shot," she told me. "He can hit a dime at a hundred feet. But we keep his gun loaded with blanks. It's safer, and it's easier on lamps. And he always thinks he hits them; he closes his eyes and he shoots and thinks it's gone dark. Then we tell him we've fired the light and he opens them again."

"Oh," I said. Not that it was much of a remark, but it was all I could think of. I felt like a triple-dyed sap. A harmless old codger shoots off a blank cartridge and I'm so jumpy I whirl and pull a gun on him.

She misguessed what I was thinking about. "Don't feel sorry for Uncle Ralph," she told me. "He has a few little peculiarities, but he isn't really potty. Most people his age are pushing up sagebrush, and few of the ones who aren't get as much fun out of life as he does. And if you think he isn't bright, take him on for a checker game sometime, but don't bet money on it."

We'd reached the end of town—a full block from where we'd started—and turned back. It was a beautiful, star-lit night.

By the light streaming out of the front windows of The We-

Never-Close, I noticed a tall man in city clothes turning in there.

Billie Wagner said, "That's Carl Denton. He's a lawyer. He's been trying to buy Dad's place from him."

"A lawyer in a town this size?" I wanted to know, "It isn't even a county seat. How does he get by?"

She shrugged her shoulders. "There are some people who say Carl Denton was tied in with the Burke boys, but nobody can prove it. Maybe now that they're gone, there isn't enough law business. Anyway, he's been trying to buy Dad's saloon, but Dad won't sell. He thinks Fleury's a coming town, now that the criminal element is practically wiped out."

"Good for him," I said. "I hope he's right about Fleury. Maybe it's got one new citizen already. I don't think it even needs a Chamber of Commerce."

Back at The We-Never-Close, she gave me her hand for a moment before she went on back to the living quarters at the back. And the smile she gave me, too, made me hope she knew why I thought Fleury didn't deed a C. of C.

The card game had broken up and the players were gone. Baldy was deep in conversation with the lawyer, Denton, and kept shaking his head.

That left only the company of Uncle Ralph for me. I felt a little foolish for having aimed a gun at him, even if he'd had his eyes shut because he'd just shot out the light and hadn't seen that I'd done it.

"That was nice shooting you just done," I told him, joining him at the bar. "Have a drink with me?"

And I raised a hand to signal the bartender.

I left that hand right where it lifted to, and brought the other one up to join it. Because there were two tough-looking gunnies standing just inside the doorway, each with a six-gun pointed into the saloon. And I could practically see the nose of the bullet through the muzzle of one of those pistols.

I saw Baldy push his hands up, too, slowly and thoughtfully, as though he was wondering, like I was, what went on.

But the lawyer who'd been chinning with him stepped back from the bar and nodded to the two gunnies.

"Bring the ax?" he asked them.

One of them nodded and brought up his left hand and I saw it held a short hand-ax.

Denton took it and started back toward me. I wondered for

a moment if he had any intentions that included the ax, but he took my gun, and then went around back of the bar and took one out of a drawer there.

"How about the old guy, Carl?" said one of the gunmen.

Denton grinned. "Don't let him worry you, Hank. Blanks." He slid my gun and Baldy's up to the front end of the bar, well out of reach. Then he came around again from back of the bar and went to the middle of the floor and looked down like he was picking out the right spot for something or other.

I glanced at Uncle Ralph, wondering how he was taking this. He was fast asleep, his elbows on the bar and his chin in his hands. I could hear a faint snore, which made me sure he wasn't faking; if he'd been faking, he'd have snored louder or not at all.

Denton lifted the ax and brought it down, and one of the floorboards splintered.

I got it then. I mean the idea, not the ax. And I could see from Baldy's face that he'd figured it out, too.

It all added up. Billie'd told me the lawyer had been suspected of a tie-up with the bandit gang and that he'd been trying to buy The We-Never-Close. And the saloon had belonged to the Burke boys, and it wasn't hard to guess there must be some loot buried under the floor.

That would be why Denton would want the place and why, when he couldn't buy it, he'd brought in a couple of gunnies and was going to take the loot anyway. And he'd picked the time when practically all of Fleury was over at the dance in Wiota.

Well, that was no skin off my neck, so I relaxed a bit. I'm on the side of law and order in general, but not so much when I've been disarmed and am facing a couple of mugs with nervous fingers jammed against their triggers. Baldy hadn't known the loot was there or he'd have dug it up and turned it over to the authorities. So all he'd be out would be the cost of fixing a hole in his floor.

Denton's ax kept rising and falling, and one board fell in and another started to give. But the wood was tough and he began to sweat a bit. My arms were getting tired of staying up and I decided I could take a chance and put them down if I moved slow. They'd taken my gun anyway, and wouldn't worry about me. So I put 'em down and hooked my thumbs in my belt. One of the gunnies looked at me hard, but apparently decided to let it go.

Then, in between smashes of the ax. I heard footsteps approaching the door at the back. I saw the look of concern that swept over Baldy's face, and it was probably mirrored in my own. Naturally, Billie would hear all that chopping and come to see what went on.

She came in before she saw what was what, I guess, and then gave a little gasp. She half turned as though to run back, and Denton yelled to her to stay where she was.

Then he lifted the ax again. Before he could swing it, one of the gunnies haw-hawed and said, "Say, boss, we ain't going to leave anything like that behind us, are we?"

Denton glanced at him coldly. "Plenty of dames when we get across the border, Hank. And we're traveling fast. Forget it."

"Yeah. But how about as a hostage? Then if anybody—"

The lawyer turned back toward Billie and looked at her speculatively. "Ummm," he said. "Not a bad idea at that, maybe—"

He went back to chopping the floor again, but Billie's face was pale now.

I felt myself get tense suddenly. I looked back and forth quick from one of the gunnies to the other, estimating whether there was any chance for a break. There wasn't. Not with two of them; if I rushed one, the other'd get me sure. And they were standing ten feet apart at that.

Here I'd thought a minute ago that this affair wasn't any of my business. But that was a minute ago, not now.

But there wasn't a chance in a million. My own gun was twenty feet down the bar, and I saw Baldy glance that way. But he was ten feet from it, and couldn't have made it either.

Then I remembered there was a gun within a foot of my hand—Uncle Ralph's, loaded with blanks. Could I—but no, Denton knew they were blanks. A bluff wouldn't work. But there were cartridges in the loops of my gunbelt. If I could only—

Very carefully, and without looking down, I sneaked my right hand where I could slip out a cartridge. I shuffled as inconspicuously as I could a half step to my right, which put me partly behind the old guy.

I could use only that one hand, but I got the gun out of the holster, and got the cylinder swung out. I wedged it that way, the swung cylinder holding it from sliding back in, and got the blank out of the first chamber and a real bullet in.

The hole in the floor was getting almost big enough for Denton to step down into it now, and the gunnies were mostly watching that hole. I reached back to my belt for another car-

tridge, but then Uncle Ralph moved a little in his sleep, and
the gun slid back into the holster, the cylinder clicking back
in place.

It must have been the click that drew the attention of the
gunnie Denton had called Mike. He must've seen I'd been trying something, but he didn't guess what. He stepped in closer,
his eyes glaring at me, and his gun pointed straight at my
midriff. "Get those hands up, buddy," he said.

For a fraction of an instant I considered reaching for the gun
I'd just got a bullet into, but it would have been suicide. Even
if I could have got Hank with it, and I didn't see how with
him having the drop on me, there was only one bullet and
two gunnies.

I lifted my hands again. Denton glanced over at me and then
laughed. "He must have been going after the old guy's gun,"
he said. "He didn't know it was only blanks."

Hank leered at me. "Whatever it was you were thinking
about trying, buddy," he said, "better think about something
else."

I did. He hadn't meant it that way, but I did think about
something else. I thought about Billie having told me that
Uncle Ralph could hit a dime at a hundred feet, when there
were bullets in his gun. And there was one there now, right in
the first chamber that would turn the hammer!

I took a step to the left, so I'd be farther away from Billie if
any shooting started.

Then, innocentlike, I says to Hank, "Sure, didn't Denton tell
you? He shoots out the light—with a blank—anytime anybody
says 'YIPPEE!' "

And the way I said it would have waked the dead. It even
waked Uncle Ralph.

He was sure quick on the draw, too. I'd hardly got the word
out of my mouth before there was a bang and the light went
out.

My edge on matters was that I'd been expecting that darkness and the others hadn't.

Flame stabbed out of the dark at where I'd been standing,
but I wasn't standing there anymore. I was running in toward
Hank, but I'd taken a quick right shift and was coming from
a different angle than he expected.

My hand touched his sleeve and I guessed where his chin
could be and hung a roundhouse right in that direction. I had

so much steam on it that I'd have probably swung myself right out into the street if I'd missed. But his chin was there. I felt his head go back with the blow and I heard his revolver crash against the floor as he dropped it.

I didn't stop. I fell over a chair but got up and kept going until I found the other end of the bar, where my gun was. I felt another hand groping there, too, but there was a sharp intake of breath that I thought was Baldy's, so I took a chance and whispered, "It's me, One-Eye!" And I was right, because he whispered back.

Then I had the gun in my hand, and its smooth butt had never felt more comforting.

I must have been dimly silhouetted against whatever moonlight showed against the front windows, or else someone fired at the sound I'd made, because flame stabbed at me in the darkness.

I fired back and ducked around the front of the bar. I kept my head around the corner, though, knowing I'd have to shoot at flashes, and shoot straight. Billie and Uncle Ralph were back there, too, although well in the clear from where the shots were coming.

The gun flash came again, and this time when I fired back, I hit. Another gun clattered against the floor and a body thudded right after it.

I didn't think Denton had a gun. I yelled out, "Baldy, strike a light!"

Something whistled past my ear in the darkness—something I guessed was an ax.

Then I heard the striking of a match and a dim flare of light got brighter under the bar as Baldy must have touched the match to the wick of a candle. Then the candle, and Baldy's head, and Baldy's gun all came up together into sight at the top of the bar.

Denton was making a dive for the back door. Neither of the two gunnies was moving.

I yelled to Denton to stop, and then I aimed carefully at his leg and pulled the trigger. His left knee went out from under him and he went down.

I ran back toward where Billie was standing. She gave me that million-dollar smile, even if it was a bit wobbly. "Thanks, One-Eye," she said. "If you hadn't—"

"Forget it," I said. I clapped the old geezer on the shoulder.

"Swell shooting, Pop," I said. "You sure shot it out that time. That's a swell gun you have. May I take a look at it?"

He sort of swelled up with pride and handed it to me. Baldy was running around from back of the bar. He corralled the pistols of the fallen gunnies. He said, "Keep things under control, One-Eye, 'til I get the jail ready and get the doctor."

"Okay, Chamber of Commerce," I said. I closed the cylinder of Uncle Ralph's gun and handed it back to him.

Billie was saying, "Did you really mean what you said about maybe staying in Fleury, One-Eye?"

I looked down at her and said, "Billie—" and then Baldy came busting back in with a deputy he'd found unexpectedly. He said, "The doc's coming." Then he looked at me. "One-Eye, what happened? How come a blank put out that light?"

I grinned. "I managed to get a real bullet into that gun," I told him. "So when I yelled 'Yippee!'—"

While I was talking, I'd moved closer to Billie. Because I knew it would happen again when I said it. Uncle Ralph's gun roared again and the candle Baldy'd stuck on top of the bar splashed wax and darkness. My arms closed around Billie in the dark.

"One-Eye," she whispered, "did you put *another* real bullet in that gun when you looked at it just a minute ago?"

"Sure," I admitted.

I heard her giggle. "Then what are you waiting for?"

So I didn't wait any longer.

Loren D. Estleman

MAGO'S BRIDE

*Loren D. Estleman is the most accomplished West-
ern writer of his generation. Flat out. No argument.*

*He has won the Spur, and been nominated many
times more, for fiction that re-creates American history
with a vividness and relish found only in the very best
Western fiction.*

*His work is, by turns, dramatic, cynical, poetic, hu-
morous, and spellbinding.*

*And all these adjectives can be applied to his crime
writing as well.*

*Loren is the best Chandleresque private-eye writer
of the past few decades. His Amos Walker mystery novels will endure right along with his Westerns.*

In San Hermoso there was always fiesta whenever Mago took
a wife.

He had had two that year. One, a plump Castilian, had died
during the trek across Chihuahua in August. The other, a dark
and glowering *rustica* from one of the anonymous pueblos along
the Bravo, had bored Mago before a month was out and been
packed off to a convent in Mexico City. No one discussed his
first bride, an American girl seized in Las Cruces who flung
herself from the bell tower of the San Hermoso church on their
wedding night years before; but all remembered the three days
of fiesta that had preceded the ceremony.

So it was that when the Magistas learned of the bandit
chief's approach with yet another prospective *señora* in tow,
they hauled three long tables of unplaned pine from the can-
tina into the plaza, loaded them with delicacies liberated from

pilgrims, butchered three fat heifers that Don Alberto would never miss from his herd of twenty thousand, and laid the pits with mesquite. Tequila and *cerveza* were conjured up from hidden stores, and Otto von Streubing, Mago's lieutenant and a disgraced Hapsburg prince (or so he styled himself), went out with a party in search of antelope. These preparations were made with great solemnity; for marriage was serious business among the Christ-loving people of San Hermoso, and there was nothing frivolous about the way those who did *not* love Christ took their pleasure.

When the outriders returned to announce Mago, his men and their women gathered at the edge of the plaza to greet him. He was galloping his favorite mount, a glossy black gelding presented by the American president to an officer of Porfirio Díaz and claimed by Mago from between the dying officer's thighs at Veracruz. Riding behind the cantle, fingers laced tightly across the chief's middle to avoid falling, was an unknown woman with a face as dark as teak inside the sable tent of her hair.

"Yaqui," muttered the watchers; and those young enough to remember their catechisms crossed themselves, for her soiled blouse and dark skirts were certainly of Indian manufacture.

To Mago, of course, they would say nothing. Half Yaqui himself, with the black eyes and volcanic temperament of the breed, he also had the long memory for personal wrongs that came with his mother's Spanish blood. Even now he was coming hard as in wrath.

"The church!" he roared—and plunged, horse and rider, into the crowd without stopping.

Those with their wits about them flung themselves aside. Those without fell with broken bones and flesh torn by the gelding's steel-shod hoofs. Mago did not stop for them, nor even for the heavy-laden tables in his path, but dug in his heels, and the gelding bounded screaming up and over all three, coming down on the other side with a heaving grunt and clawing for traction on the ground before the church.

Behind him, thunder rolled. Someone—the chief himself, perhaps, for he had continued without dismounting through the great, yawning, iron-banded doors of the church—swung the bell in the tower, clanging the alarm. Shouting, the Magistas and their women trailed him inside and managed with belated efficiency to draw the doors shut. Desperate fists hammered the bar into place.

The church had been designed as a fort in a land scarce in Christians. By the time the men took up their armed posts at the windows, the myriad heads of the enemy could be seen topping the eastern horizon like a black dawn. Here and there an ironwood lance swayed against the sky, bearing its inevitable human trophy. The word *Apache* sibilated like a telegraph current from window to window.

Mago, mounted still, was alone in the saddle. Of the woman there was no sign. He swept off his sombrero, allowing his dull black hair to tumble in its two famous locks across his temples, and barked orders in rapid dialect. Otto von Streubing, who comprehended little of it, asked what had happened. Mago smiled down at him.

"How close?" he inquired of the nearest sentry.

"Still outside rifle range, *mi jefe*. They have stopped, I think."

"The bastard thinks too much. It will kill him yet." Swinging down, the bandit chief started up the stone steps to the bell tower, jerking his head for Otto to follow.

At the top of the steep flight, Mago rapped on the low door. The pair were admitted by Juan Griz. Brown-eyed, wavy of hair, and built along the lines of a young cougar, Juan was easily the handsomest of those who followed Mago, as well as the most loyal and doglike. The simplest tasks were his great mission.

On the opposite side of the great iron bell, limned in the open arch by the sun, stood the loveliest woman the German had ever seen. Her hair was as dark as the Black Forest, her figure beneath the travel-stained clothes trim and fragile compared to the thick-waisted squaws he had known during his short time in the New World. Her eyes were wary. She seemed poised to fling herself into space. Otto thought—and immediately discarded it—of the fate of Mago's first wife. Instinctively he knew that this one would not make that same choice.

"Handsome baggage," he said finally. "Your fourth, I think. But what—"

Mago reached out and snatched the fine silver chain that hung around the woman's neck. She flinched, catching herself on the archway. Mago dangled the crucifix before his lieutenant's face.

"I know that piece," said Otto.

"You should, my friend. You have seen it around Nochebueno's neck often enough."

"*Lieber Gott!* What has she to do with that *verdammt* Christian Indian?"

"Cervata is her name. *Fawn* in the English you insist on
using here instead of good Spanish. I found her bathing in
a stream outside Nochebueno's camp. Mind you, had I known
how she scratches, I would not have allowed her to dress
before we left." He put a hand to the place where blood had
dried on his cheek. "It was not until I saw the crucifix that
I knew she had until late been scratching that Apache
bastard."

"I do not imagine it occurred to you to return her."

"My friend, it is foreign to my nature to return things."

The woman spat a stream of mangled Spanish. The gist, if
not the words, reached the German well enough. "How did you
manage to get this far?"

"Fortunately for my eyes, she hates the baptized savage
more than she does me. I, however, am in love."

A Magista with machete scars on both cheeks stormed
through the open doorway, shoving aside Juan Griz. "*Mi jefe!*
The Apaches are attacking!" A crackle of carbines from outside
nearly drowned out the words.

Otto von Streubing was the finest marksman in San Hermoso. Mago stationed him in the tower with his excellent Mauser rifle, ordered Juan Griz to keep Cervata away from the
openings, and accompanied the other Magista downstairs. For
the next quarter hour the bandit chief busied himself with the
fortress's defense, directing the men's fire and satisfying himself that the women were supplying them with loaded weapons
as needed. The sun had begun to set. As shadows enveloped
them, the Apaches withdrew, bearing their dead.

"What are our losses?" demanded Mago of the man with the
machete scars.

"Two dead, *mi jefe;* Paco Mendolo and the boy, Gonzales.
Your cousin, Manuel, has lost an ear."

"Which one?"

"The left, I think."

Otto descended from the tower, where he had managed to
pluck three savages off their mounts from three hundred
yards. "It is not like Nochebueno to give up so easily," he
said.

"A reprieve," said Mago. "It takes more than his Jesus to convince his braves their dead will find their way to the Happy Hunting Ground in the dark. At dawn the sun will be at their backs and in our eyes. Then they will throw everything they have at us."

"Not if we give them the woman tonight."

"I never give."

The bandits were quiet that night. If any of them wondered that their fates were caught up with Mago's marital aspirations, none spoke of it. As for the chief, he had retired to the rectory, which had become his quarters upon the departure of the mission's last padre. Otto entered without knocking and stood an unopened bottle of tequila on the great oak desk behind which his general sat eating rat cheese off the blade of his bowie.

"I confiscated it," the German explained. "I thought you might like some of them sober in the morning."

"*Gracias, amigo.* I shall consider it a wedding gift."

"Who will perform the ceremony this time?"

"That Dominican in Santa Carla has not done me a favor in a year."

"I suppose Manuel will stand up for you as always?"

"Manuel is infirm. I would ask you, but I imagine you are an infidel."

"Lutheran."

"As I said." Mago pulled the cork and tossed it over his shoulder. "Well, they can hardly excommunicate me again. To my best man." He lifted the bottle and drank.

Otto watched a drop trickle down his superior's stubbled chin. "I would take my pleasure now. You may not live to dance at your wedding."

"I do not bed women not my wives."

Someone battered the rectory door. Otto admitted a flat-faced Magista who was more Indian than Mexican and less man than animal, and who handed Mago a short-shafted arrow with the head broken off. The German could follow little of his speech but gathered that the arrow had narrowly missed a bandit dozing at a window and buried itself in the oaken altar. Mago untied a square of hide from the shaft and read the words burned into it.

"Curse an Indian who knows his letters," he said mildly. "He wishes to meet with me outside San Hermoso in an hour."

"Nochebueno?" said Otto. "What can he want to talk about?"
"We will know in an hour."

★

The site chosen was a patch of desert midway between the
stronghold and the place where the Apaches had made camp.
Nochebueno arrived first astride a blaze-faced sorrel, accompanied by two mounted warriors. Nearly as tall as his late, fabled
grandfather, Mangas Coloradas, he was naked save for
breechclout and moccasins and a rosary around his thick neck.
His face was painted in halves of black and vermilion and resembled nothing so much as a particolored skull. Mago, who
had selected a bay mare while his black gelding rested, halted
beyond the light of the torches held by the two braves and
turned to Otto.

"The ring on his finger, amigo. Do you see it?"

The German squinted. A large ring of what appeared to be
polished silver glittered on the Apache chief's right index finger. "A signal ring?"

"They are wizards with mirrors. You will remain here
and fire your wonderful foreign rifle if he raises that
hand."

Otto snaked his Mauser from the saddle scabbard. "Pray the
torches do not flicker."

The bandit leader left him.

"Mago!" Nochebueno bared uncommonly fine teeth for an Indian. His Spanish was purer than the Mexican's. "I have not
seen you these three years. You look well."

The other drew rein inside the torchlight. "Never better,
Noche. I am preparing to marry."

Although the grin remained in place, something very like
malice tautened the flat features beneath the war paint. "Step
down, my friend," said he. "We have business."

"All of us?" Mago's gaze took in the two stony-faced braves
at Nochebueno's elbows.

The Apache said something in his native tongue. The braves
leaned over, jammed the pointed ends of the torches into the
earth, wheeled their mounts, and cantered back the way they
had come. The bandit leader and the Indian chief stepped down
then, and squatted on their heels.

"You have a woman in San Hermoso," Nochebueno began.

"Amigo, I have had many women, in and out of San
Hermoso."

"This one is a personal favorite, purchased at the expense of several very good horses from her father, who manages a coffee plantation near Chiapas. I would have her back."

Mago showed a gold tooth. "You would have her back, and I would have her stay, and that is how it will be all night and all day tomorrow. I waste my time." But he made no move to rise.

"You waste more than time, my friend. You waste the lives of every man, woman, and child in San Hermoso."

"I hear the lion's roar. I do not see his claws."

Nochebueno reached behind him and produced a knife from a sheath at his waist. It was of European manufacture, with a long, slender Sheffield blade and a heavily worked hilt fashioned after a cross.

"A souvenir from my former days of darkness, stolen from a cathedral in Acapulco," he said. "It dates back to the Crusades."

"Your invitation said no weapons, amigo."

"It did, and you may stop fingering that derringer in your pocket. I have not brought it as a weapon."

Mago waited.

"A game!" barked the Indian suddenly, making the torches waver. "You who know me so well know also my passion for sport. I suggest a contest to settle what would otherwise be a long and bloody fight, most un-Christian. My friend, are you feeling strong this night?"

"What are the rules?"

"My question is answered." With a sudden movement Nochebueno sank the knife to its hilt in the hard earth between them. The haft threw a shadow in the shape of a crucifix. "We shall lie upon our stomachs facing each other, each with a hand on the handle of the knife. If you are the first to snap the blade, the woman is yours, and my warriors and I shall ride from this place in peace."

"And if you are first?"

"My friend, that is entirely up to you. Naturally I would prefer if in the spirit of sport you would surrender the woman, in which case we would still ride from this place in peace. Women—they are for pleasure, not war."

"And yet you are prepared to make war if I refuse this contest."

The Indian's grin was diabolical. "You will not refuse. I see in your eyes that you will not. Am I wrong?"

In response the bandit chief stretched out on his stomach and grasped the handle.

"So it is; so it has always been," said Nochebueno, assuming the same position, fingers interlaced with Mago's. *"El Indio y el conquistador.* To the end."

The Mexican was born strong and hardened from the saddle; the Apache, smaller and built along slighter lines, was as a hot wind with meanness and hatred for Mago and all his kind. Their hands quivered and grew slick with sweat. The torches burned low.

There was an earsplitting snap. Roaring triumphantly, Mago sprang to his knees, waving the handle with its broken piece of blade.

"Congratulations, my friend." Nochebueno gathered his legs beneath him. His right hand shot up. It had no index finger.

As he gaped at the bleeding stump, the crack of Otto von Streubing's Mauser rifle reached the place where the two men knelt. The bullet had taken away finger and signal ring in one pass.

With a savage cry the Apache chief was on his feet, followed by Mago, clawing for the derringer in his pocket. Before the watching braves could react, Otto galloped between the pair. He threw the bay mare's reins to Mago, who vaulted into the saddle and swung toward San Hermoso just as the Apaches began firing. The bay mare screamed and fell. Mago landed on his feet, caught hold of the German's outstretched hand, and, riding double, the bandits fled through a hail of fire in the direction of the stronghold. Behind them, Nochebueno shrieked Christian obscenities in Spanish and shook his bloody fist, unwittingly spoiling his braves' aim.

"Fine shooting, amigo!" Mago shouted over the hammering hooves.

"Not so fine," said the other sourly. "I was aiming for his throat."

*

The Magista with the machete scars opened the church door for them. Otto handed him his horse's reins. "Wake the others and tell them to prepare for siege," he said.

Mago said, "Let them sleep. The bastards will not attack before morning, if then. If I know Nochebueno, he is halfway back to his village, squalling for the medicine man to wrap his finger. Whatever bowels his people's god gave him, he surrendered them when he accepted Christ. Close the door, amigo. Why do you stand there?"

The Magista was peering into the darkness of the plaza. "Did not the others return with you, *jefe?*"

"What others?"

"Juan Griz and the Yaqui woman. He said you had left orders to join you with the woman and your black gelding. He sent me for his piebald."

Mago said a thing not properly spoken in church and charged up the stone steps to the bell tower, taking them two at a time. Otto seized the man's collar. "When?"

"Just after you and *el jefe* left, *señor*. Juan said—"

"Juan Griz never said a thing in his life not placed in his mouth by someone smarter. I knew this woman was a witch when I first laid eyes on her."

Mago came down as swiftly as he had gone up. He was buckling on a cartridge belt. "Fresh mounts. Otto, quickly! They cannot have gotten far in this darkness."

"There is no catching that gelding when it is rested. If we capture anyone, it will be Juan."

"Then I will have his testicles! Why do you laugh, amigo?"

Otto was astonished to find that he was indeed laughing. He had not done so since coming to this barbaric place where Christians fought Christians and men stabled their horses in church.

"I laugh because it is funny, Mago. Do you not see how funny it is? While you and Nochebueno were fighting like knights for Cervata's fine brown hand, Juan Griz was absconding with the rest of her. Not to mention your favorite mount. Or do I mix the two?" He was becoming silly in his mirth. It had spread to the scarred Magista, who cast frightened eyes upon his chief at first, then forgot him in his own helplessness.

Mago scowled. Madness had entered his camp. And then he, too, began to laugh. It was either that or slay two of his best men.

"Well," said he when they had begun to master themselves, "of what worth is a bride who chooses pleasing looks over intelligence and courage? Wake the men, Otto! We have won one victory this night, and a woman is a small enough price to pay for Nochebueno's finger."

That night San Hermoso rang with the din of fiesta.